NEW WRITING 14

Lavinia Greenlaw lives in London, where she was born. She has published three books of poems, most recently *Minsk*. Her first novel, *Mary George of Allnorthover,* won France's Prix du Premier Roman, and her second, *An Irresponsible Age,* appeared this year. Her awards include a Forward Prize for best single poem and a NESTA fellowship.

Her work for BBC radio includes programmes about the Arctic and the Baltic, the solstices and equinoxes, and several dramas. She wrote the libretto for Ian Wilson's *Hamelin,* and is working with him on another opera. She lectures at Goldsmiths College.

Helon Habila was born in Nigeria. He has worked both as a lecturer and a journalist in Nigeria. He was the African Writing Fellow at the University of East Anglia from 2002–2004. His first novel, *Waiting for an Angel* (Penguin, 2003), won the Commonwealth Writers Prize for Best First Book (Africa Region). He was also a winner of the Caine Prize, 2001. His second book, *Measuring Time*, is coming out in 2006. He is currently the Chinua Achebe Fellow in Global Africana Studies at Bard College, New York.

NW14

THE ANTHOLOGY OF NEW WRITING
VOLUME 14

Edited by **Lavinia Greenlaw** and **Helon Habila**

Granta Books
London

Granta Publications, 2/3 Hanover Yard, Noel Road, London N1 8BE

First published in Great Britain by Granta Books 2006

A CIP catalogue record for this book is available
from the British Library.

1 3 5 7 9 10 8 6 4 2

ISBN-13: 978-1-86207-850-5
ISBN-10: 1-86207-850-5

Typeset by M Rules

Printed and bound in Great Britain by
Bookmarque Limited, Croydon, Surrey

Contents

ix Introduction

Short Stories

1   **James Lasdun:** Peter Kahn's Third Wife

11   **Anuradha Vijayakrishnan:** Narayani's Journey

17   **M. Pinchuk:** Memories Like Photographs

33   **Romesh Gunesekera:** Independence

38   **Roy Robins:** The Caretaker

49   **Abdulrazak Gurnah:** My Mother Lived on a Farm in Africa

56   **Chris Womersley:** The Shed

62   **Kirsty Gunn:** Now I Can See How It Was, I Think

73   **Desmond Hogan:** Belle

84   **C. D. Rose:** The *Neva Star*

93   **paulo da costa:** Turning the Page

103 **Nick Barlay:** Stu Zsibinsky's Lost Cause

109 **Shereen Pandit:** Dying to See the Sea

119 **Douglas Cowie:** The White of Her Arms

Poems

130 **David Morley:** Whitethroat

131 **Paul Muldoon:** Eggs

133 **Carola Luther:** Possessions, Afterwards

136 **Greta Stoddart:** Pupil, You Drew Breath, Verfremdungseffekt

141 **Eoghan Walls:** Frogness, The Naming of the Rat

145 **Carrie Etter:** Divorce, Drought

147 **Stephen Knight:** The Edge of Sleep

148 **Iain Galbraith:** Best Man Dead, Stellar State

150 **Sean O'Brien:** Praise of a Rainy Country, The Brazier, Symposium at Port Louis

158 **Jamie McKendrick:** Black Gold, Ire

160 **Don Paterson:** Three Versions from Rilke's Sonnets to Orpheus: Being, Anemone, Taste

163 **Blessing Musariri:** Popular Fiction

164 **Chenjerai Hove:** Counting the Nights

166 **Paul Perry:** Wintering

168 **Frances Leviston:** Dragonflies, Lampadrome

Novel Extracts

172 **Jane Feaver:** from *The Art of Losing*

188 **David Nwokedi:** ABC

201 **Charles Fernyhough:** The Thought Show from *A Box of Birds*

212 **David Harsent:** from *The Wormhole*

217 **Esther Freud:** untitled

223 **Jane Rogers:** from *The Experiment*

231 **Maura Dooley:** from *Malachite and Verdigris*

236 **Maik Nwosu:** In the Shadow of His Excellency from *A Gecko's Farewell*

245 **Vicky Grut:** from *The Understudy*

255 **Natasha Soobramanien:** *Another London*

262 **Benjamin Markovits:** Setting Forth from *Imposture*

Non-Fiction

270 **Ogaga Ifowodo:** Word Games in Prison

278 **Hermione Lee:** Manhattan Days

292 **Joan Michelson:** A Piece of Paving, Commuters, Crash (poetry)

297 **Marina Warner:** from the prologue to *Phantasmagoria: Spirit Visions, Metaphors, and Media*

305 **Michel Faber:** Me and Dave and Mount Olympus

312 Biographical Notes

321 Copyright Information

Introduction

What exactly does one look for in good literature? What were we looking for? We could not say when we met, for the first and only time during this process, in the British Council offices back in June. The answer came as soon as we began reading: writing that surprised, provoked and impressed us, pretty much in equal measure.

There were plenty of well made, proficient submissions which demonstrated a knowledge of genre and technique, but nothing about them lingered. They gave the impression of having been made by remote control, and remained remote in the reading. This had nothing to do with the use of the first or third person, or whether or not a piece was based on 'real life'. It concerned authenticity of sensation and the writer's ability to retain their fundamental impulse in the finished work. It didn't matter if they had swapped twenty-first century Glasgow for seventeenth century Spain; all that mattered was that they knew how to deploy their material (actual or invented) rigorously and artfully.

What if we didn't agree on anything? The joy of this experience has been that while we discussed nothing before we swapped initial lists, those lists were similar enough for us to know that we were looking for the same thing and different enough to keep it interesting. The more we read, the more only what we read mattered. We had several lists of hundreds of names and those we recognized blurred into those we'd never seen before; we were soon taking no notice of who the author was or where they came from.

Before we even started reading, we had to contend with the effects of the British Council's reinvigorated publicity. We were told to expect around 300 entries but over 1000 came in. For a while, the subject of our emails was 'Submissions Explosion', as we tried to reconcile our aim to read everything with the fact that we couldn't possibly. (Some people submitted entire novels – and we here make a plea on behalf of next year's editors, for limits to be put in place.) In the end, a sifter came to our rescue and spent a month trawling through the boxes. We are most grateful for Helen Gordon's judgement and care.

We still received seven boxes each, which we needed to whittle down to a list of forty-five. The emphasis of *New Writing* is on the new, and we have done our best to honour that, although it hasn't been hard. There were more than enough good submissions from people who had never published. Otherwise, as our shortlists consolidated, the anthology announced its character and it became clear what would fit it best.

The total submission, from forty-three countries, was a sample slice of contemporary writing in English and revealed certain characteristics. The dominant perspective was that of the child, suggesting a nostalgia in this virtual age for an old-fashioned kind of authenticity – the child's unmediated, uninformed perspective. The more we read, the more we saw how hard it is to do this well and the child-focused pieces we have included were all the more impressive when they rose out of the sea of those which didn't work, or which were no more than freshness for its own sake. There was a lot of tourist fiction, involving jaunts into the exotic and the underworld. Few explored the fantastic, so it was thrilling to come across dark, mysterious worlds that, like the best kind of surrealism, operated as a trapdoor in the real. There was far more bad poetry than good, but what did we expect? All this proved was the obvious: that good writing is easy to imitate but hard to create. On this front, there was a lot of cruise-control lyrical prose – a smooth ride along a perpetual present tense in which the language was so cushioned that one could barely feel the bumps in the road; realism worn down to an 'ism'.

So we still don't know what good writing is, but we know we found it. Perhaps past editors of this anthology might agree that there is a certain *New Writing* spirit that seems to take over, making it clear exactly what kind of piece fits such a book – something one would not expect to find in other anthologies, but which dedicated readers of *New Writing* will recognize: 'Yes, that!'

One of the rewards of editing is of course the privilege of discovery. There are many writers included here who have not published anywhere, and we are honoured to be bringing them to the worldwide audience that *New Writing* commands. If you go to any British Council outpost, you will meet people who read *New Writing*. It is not just a sounding of this year's literature in English, it is a smoke signal, a way of showing the world what's going on inside this language, and so inside our several countries and various lives.

Lavinia Greenlaw and Helon Habila
October 2005

James Lasdun

Peter Kahn's Third Wife

In a jeweller's boutique in Soho, the young sales assistant was modelling a necklace for a customer who had come in to buy a gift for his fiancée.

'Something out of the ordinary,' he had said, and the assistant had shown him a cabinet with a necklace in it made of lemon- and rose-coloured diamonds. The man had admired it, but after asking how much it cost, had laughed. 'Out of my league, I'm afraid.'

'Let me show you some other things.'

The assistant had led him to another cabinet. 'These are more affordable. They're set with semi-precious stones.'

The man had nodded and peered forward into the lit glass case.

'If you have any questions,' the assistant had said, 'I'll be happy to answer them.'

For a while the man had looked in silence at the things inside the case. 'I'll tell you what,' he had said abruptly, 'let's have another look at that first necklace.'

'The diamond?'

'Yes.'

And so now she had taken the expensive necklace from its case, and was modelling it for him while he sat in a chair opposite her, looking at how it lay on the flesh below her throat.

This was a part of her job, but in her seven months at the boutique she still hadn't grown used to it. It made her self conscious to sit and be stared at by a man she didn't know, and it seemed to her that the men themselves were uncomfortable. They either found it hard to look squarely at her in this moment, or else she would feel them peering too intently, as if they felt it their masculine duty to try to make a conquest of any woman who submitted herself so willingly to their gaze.

But this man was neither furtive nor brash. He was at ease in the artificial intimacy of the situation; intent in his scrutiny, but making no attempt to promote himself.

He was in his thirties, she guessed; dark and heavyset. Brown hair curled on his head in thick, tangled clusters.

He nodded slowly. 'All right,' he said in a bemused tone, as though not so much deciding as discovering what he was going to do, 'I'll take it.'

A moment later he was signing his name, Peter Kahn, on the three credit card payments into which he had had to divide the transaction. Then he went out of the store, carrying the flat box with the necklace inside it in his coat pocket.

Over the next couple of years he reappeared in the boutique several more times to buy his wife anniversary and birthday gifts. The assistant, whose name was Clare Keillor, would model the pieces he was interested in, and each time she would experience the same calm under his gaze. It was as though for a moment she had been taken into a realm glazed off from the everyday world, where a form of exchange that was inexpressible in everyday human terms, was permitted to occur between strangers.

She had no idea whether Kahn himself experienced anything resembling this, or whether he even remembered her from one visit to the next, but she found herself revolving the memory of the encounters in her imagination after they had passed, and when several months went by without Kahn coming back into the store, she would begin to wonder if she was ever going to experience their peculiar, almost impersonally soothing effects again.

On one occasion his cell phone rang while she was modelling a pair of earrings for him. He excused himself, saying that this was an important call, and she waited while he spoke. From what she heard him say, it became clear that he was in business as an importer of wines, and that he was trying to persuade a partner to bid on a consignment of rare French bottles that were coming up for auction. Evidently he was encountering resistance, and his tone became increasingly heated.

'Taste it!' he said. He proceeded to describe the wine in the most extravagant terms, which in turn appeared to prompt even more resistance. 'Well then, let's find customers who *do* give a damn!' he shouted. Then he snapped shut the phone.

Apologizing for the interruption, he tried to concentrate again on the earrings, but his mind was clearly on the altercation he had just had. The strong feelings it had aroused were still milling behind his eyes, and for a moment as he looked back at Clare, he appeared to forget why he was looking at her at all. He was just staring at her as though knowing there was some important reason why he was doing this, but not clear what it was. Then, as she looked back into his eyes, he seemed to stop struggling to remember, and simply accepted that this was what he was doing. And now for the first time she did have the impression that he was seeing her as she saw him; that he too was in that lucid atmosphere, and was encountering her there with the same feeling of ease as she herself felt. Then the moment passed and they were each back in the everyday reality of their own lives.

He decided against the earrings, and left without looking at anything else.

Two more years passed. Then, on a hot morning in July, Kahn appeared once again in the store.

He stood in the entrance for a moment, adjusting from the boil and glare of the street to the store's air-conditioned dimness. He looked less youthful – fleshier and redder in the cheeks, but still handsome, and with a more developed air of consequence about him.

'I'm looking for a wedding gift,' he said, 'for my fiancée. Something a little . . . out of the ordinary.'

Clare looked at him for a moment before answering. He gave no sign of recognizing her, and despite knowing there was no reason why he should, she felt dismayed. A few minutes later, however, as she was modelling some new pieces for him, there was a startled motion in his eyes.

'Still here!'

'Yes.'

'I didn't recognize you. I apologize.' He gave an embarrassed grin. 'What you must think of me, already on to my second wife!'

'Oh, I wasn't –'

'Well, it happens.' He laughed, recovering his self possession. 'Anyway, we're very much in love. What can I tell you?'

'That's good. Congratulations.'

He bought a set of earrings and an expensive emerald bracelet: money was apparently no longer a great concern.

'At least we can say I'm faithful when it comes to where I buy my wives their jewellery!' he said in a parting attempt at jollity. Clare gave him a polite, sales girl's smile. His phrase, 'we're very much in love' had grated on her, and as he left the store, she decided it must have been the formula he had used in breaking the news to the wife he had cast off; *we're very much in love . . .* as though he and his new girlfriend just couldn't help themselves. Clare pictured the wife – a blur of disembodied pain, and the girlfriend, younger, fresher, prettier. It struck her that Kahn hadn't recognized her because she too had started to age.

There was that realm, the glassed-in sphere in which these encounters occurred, and then there was the real world, and Clare lived her life in this world also. She married a man named Neil Gehrig, an airline industry analyst, twelve years older than herself.

At a dinner one evening, someone praised the wine, and the host said, 'Yes, it's a Kahn.'

Looking at the bottle, Clare saw his name on the sticker at the neck: *Imported by Peter Kahn,* and an unexpectedly sharp emotion went through her. Three or four years had passed since their last encounter, and she was caught off guard by the force of her own feelings.

'He set up a company to bring over wines from the last small producers in France and Italy,' the host was saying. 'We grab everything we can afford off his list.'

'I know him,' Clare heard herself say.

'You do?'

'He used to come into the store.'

'Really? What was he like?'

She shrugged, aware of her husband looking at her across the table, and regretting that she had spoken. 'He seemed a nice enough guy . . .'

'Did he talk to you about wine?' the host asked.

The husband broke in: 'Why would he talk to her about wine? It's a jewellery store.'

'He's obsessed with it,' the host answered. 'We get this newsletter he writes. The guy's on a mission. He wants to save the wine world from globalization.'

'How incredibly original,' the husband said, leaning back in his chair.

'One time he took a call on his mobile,' Clare went on impetuously. 'I heard him describe this wine he wanted to buy as like having the Rose Window at Chartres dissolving on your tongue.'

'My god, a poet too!'

Clare smiled at her husband. Neil's jealousy had appeared soon after their marriage, and now lived with them like a third person whose volatile behaviour had to be carefully negotiated. Once, after a dinner like this, he had hit her on the mouth with the back of his hand after accusing her of flirting with another guest.

That November Kahn appeared once again in the boutique. He wore a soft-looking felt hat and an alpaca scarf. His eyes had a melancholy cast. There was a woman with him. The second wife, Clare supposed.

He gave a half surprised smile of recognition as he saw Clare. *Still* here? The look seemed to ask.

'We're ah – we're looking for an engagement ring,' he said.

It took a moment for the implication of this to sink in. Doing her best to conceal her surprise, Clare pulled a tray of rings from a cabinet.

The woman removed a pair of kidskin gloves. Her face was smooth and symmetrical. Its features seemed exclusively occupied in compelling the word *beauty* to form itself in the mind of whoever beheld them.

She glanced briefly at the rings. 'I don't think so, darling.'

Kahn turned to Clare with a shrug. 'Sorry.'

'Oh, no problem.'

He gave her a smile.

'Shall we see some other things?' he asked the woman.

'I suppose, since we're here.'

A necklace of rubies and small gold lozenges seemed to interest her.

'Why don't you try it on?' Kahn said. But instead of handing the necklace to his fiancée, he handed it to Clare. The woman gave a breathy laugh, and Kahn, realizing his blunder, put his hand on hers. 'Sorry. I'm used to coming here alone.'

'Apparently.'

'So you try it on,' Kahn said to her.

Ignoring him, the woman turned to Clare. 'What's your name?' she asked.

'Clare.'

'Put on the necklace, Clare,' she said.

Clare put on the necklace. She was aware of Kahn's glance upon her, but she was careful to look only at the woman. After giving the necklace a cursory appraisal, the woman turned to regard Kahn. As the three sat watching each other, Clare felt as though her relation to Kahn had developed into something newly strange. Everything seemed suddenly its own opposite: his physical closeness the precise expression of his untraversable distance from her, the free air between them a barrier impenetrable as glass. It seemed to her that no one on this earth was more remote from her than this man, sitting less than two feet from her with this, his third fiancée.

But even as she was feeling this she allowed herself to glance at him for a moment, and at once, in spite of herself, she felt the old ease, the sensation of effortless compatibility.

She stopped working at the store soon after that. Neil, who earned a good salary, had been making increasingly scornful remarks about the fact that she chose to work at a mindless job when she didn't need to, and she agreed to quit.

She despised her husband, but the very fact that she had no illusions about this was a source of perverse satisfaction to her: in the irremediable absence of love, it appeared she could make do with someone to hate.

With the new leisure imposed on her, she began cultivating the habits of a pampered mistress. She had their living room furniture reupholstered in raw silk. She bought a pair of Selvaggia shoes for seven hundred dollars. Neil was eager to have a child, and she pretended to want one too, even setting a calendar beside the bed with the optimal nights for conception marked on it. In a morbid ecstasy of self torture, she allowed him to make love to her on those nights, while privately taking care not to get pregnant.

Meanwhile she subjected her feelings for Kahn to a deliberate effort of destruction, aiming at them an unceasing barrage of self mockery. They were nothing more than the symptoms of a sickness, she would tell herself; a fixation straight out of some textbook on mental disorders. The relationship between herself and him in that 'other' world was a pathetic, one-sided fiction. As for Kahn himself, he was nothing: a cipher on to which she had projected her own romantic fantasies, themselves as shallow and unoriginal as those of some overwrought schoolgirl. What, from any sane point of view, could she possibly want with such a man? Why would she even dream of being involved in the calamitous opera of his life?

Numb, bored, detached even from her own desolation, she drifted on.

One evening she found herself once again at dinner with the friends who had subscribed to Kahn's catalogue. She had forgotten about this connection until her neighbour at the table, a young Frenchman, commented on the wine and she saw again, with a familiar helpless pang, the familiar name on the bottle.

As it turned out, her neighbour and his partner, seated across the table, were in the restaurant business, and knew Kahn personally. From the look that passed between them, it was apparent that he was a source of amusing gossip in their world.

Clare glanced at her husband: he was lecturing their host on airline statistics.

'Tell me about Peter Kahn,' she said quietly to Jean-Luc, her neighbour.

'Oh! Where to begin?' the young man said with a laugh.

Mark, his American partner, turned to her. 'You know him?'

'A little.'

Both men grinned at her, their expressions mischievously alert.

'You heard about the wedding?' Jean-Luc asked.

'No.'

'Oh my God! Tell her Mark.'

'He was engaged to this model, Diane Wolfe? She was quite famous a few years ago. It was his third marriage and he told everyone he'd finally found the right woman and to prove it he was going to have the most spectacular romantic wedding, in Venice. They rented a palazzo on the Grand Canal, invited a hundred and fifty guests, hired a jet to fly them over, arranged for the best chef in the Veneto to make the dinner, and had a yacht waiting on the Lido to take the two of them off into the Adriatic for their honeymoon. Well guess what?'

Clare said nothing. Her heart had begun beating violently.

'He jilted her?' another guest asked.

'*At* the altar. *At* the altar. Our friends Sabine and George were there. They told us the whole story. All the guests in the church. Diane waiting in the back all dressed up in her veils and gown, specially designed of course, the minutes ticking by, everyone getting steadily more impatient, when this man arrives, a complete stranger – apparently some tourist Peter accosted on the street after his best man refused to do the job – and reads out loud from a piece of paper: *Ladies and Gentlemen, Peter Kahn has asked me to tell you the wedding is cancelled. He deeply regrets the pain this will cause . . .*'

Clare listened in a daze.

'What did he do?' she heard herself ask.

'He got out of Venice pretty damn fast, I can tell you!'

'What's he doing now?' The conversation had caught the interest of the rest of the table and Clare was aware of her husband looking in her direction.

Jean-Luc answered her. 'Apparently he's become a bit of a recluse. He sold his business, cut off all his friends. The last we heard he'd moved up to the Fingerlakes, looking to buy some winery of his own.'

'Where in the Fingerlakes?' She made a vague effort not to sound too interested.

'I don't know. But we can find out if you like.' The young Frenchman's eyes darted mirthfully from Clare to her husband. She could sense, without looking, the way Neil's mouth would be tightening at the corners.

'Can you?'

'Of course.'

'I'll give you my email address.'

In the taxi home Neil remained silent. The interrogation began as soon as they had closed the door of their apartment behind them. 'Why are you so interested in that Kahn guy?'

'No reason.'

'Are you planning to *visit* him or something, up in the Fingerlakes? Is that why you were so eager to get his exact address?'

She shrugged, aware of being infuriating, but unable to stop herself. 'I hadn't thought. I was just curious.'

'But you don't rule it out? Visiting this man who you apparently hardly know?'

'I don't know, Neil. I haven't thought about it.'

Her husband blinked and seemed to reel for a moment. He stood up. She looked away, her eye fixed on a piece of lint on the rug.

'What went on between you and him?'

'What do you mean?'

'You know perfectly well what I mean. He used to come into your store. Right?'

'Yes.'

'What for?'

'To buy jewellery.'

'Were you having an affair with him?'

'No.'

'Look at me when I'm talking, goddammit!'

She felt the sudden crack of his hand on her mouth. She looked up at him.

'All right then,' she said.

'What?'

'All right . . . I was.'

'What? You were what?'

'Having an affair with him.'

Neil's eyes widened. He looked stunned, in spite of himself. She herself was startled by the unexpected potency of her words. It was as though in saying them she had illuminated some astounding truth.

'When? Before we were married or after?'

'Before. And after. He'd come in the store after Ishiro went home.' Ishiro was the designer who owned the store. 'I'd lock the door and we'd go up into Ishiro's office.'

'And fuck?'

'Yes. Every day. On the chair, on the table –'

A blow struck her on the cheek.

'On the floor –'

Another hit her stomach. She doubled up, covering her face with her hands. Neil was yelling at her but his words sounded like a foreign language or the roars of an animal. By the time she heard the front door open and slam shut behind him, she was in that glazed world again, as if she had stepped inside a diamond. In it, as vividly as if the scene were happening right there and then, she saw herself in the calm greenness of a summer afternoon, Kahn's gaze opening on her like the sun itself as she approached, silver-blue water glittering in the distance behind him. She uncovered her face. *The Fingerlakes*, she said to herself. And what remained for her to do seemed suddenly clear as day.

Anuradha Vijayakrishnan

Narayani's Journey

The fifth one was the blue air bag with something in English printed on both sides. That made it five without counting the striped plastic bag that held the tiffin carrier in which Kanakam had packed a last generous curd rice dinner. Five and then her handbag, large and new, bought for five hundred rupees yesterday. The girl at the shop had picked it out for her with a peculiar smile and she, Narayani, hadn't minded. The girl was young and knew what looked good and Narayani liked to remember that she had paid for it in five crisp notes with hardly a crease in them, taken from the old red purse which she even now had tucked into one of the pockets of her new handbag. The blue air bag too was new and was Sundaram's contribution . . . she knew he had bought it for her, though that was not what he told her.

By the time she had gathered her bags around her, counted them and then counted them again, the train had left. They had been together all this while, staying awake together through the whole night of the journey and now it had left while she wasn't looking. In front of her now, the iron tracks and the concrete building they ran through looked a little desolate and dusty. And a little unfamiliar. Of course, she didn't expect it to look the same after twenty years . . . and of course, she had left by bus then, hadn't come much near the railway station in the time before that.

There was more luggage than she could carry, unless she carried some of it on her head and that she didn't plan to do . . . not here, not now. Narayani drew the fluttering edge of her sari around her shoulder and looked around for a porter and felt a faint thrill flit through her as she did that. She, Narayani, had managed to come back, come back with five full bags of luggage and was now about to call a coolie to carry all of it and would pay him in money that would be pulled out nonchalantly from her grand new handbag.

The platform was rather empty, except for three or four sleepy looking beggars, a man sitting on a bench with a big suitcase in front of him and a few stragglers in front of the clutch of shops near the entrance. Most of the pillars and walls were covered with cinema posters . . . the red-haired hero blazing his wrath down on a couple of cowering, yellow-teethed villains while the sequinned woman of his dreams looked up at him adoringly from her slightly awkward position on a big red car. That one she recognized as something she had watched a few months back. That would be something to talk about, casually, wouldn't it? The fact that most of the movies that were showing here now were already a few months old and she had seen most of them in red-cushioned, air-conditioned theatres right on the day they got released, just by paying twenty or thirty rupees more . . .

One of the men standing near the shops was now walking up to her. Narayani stood very still, one hand cupped around the edge of her handbag, the other holding down the edge of her sari; an unshakeable twenty-year-old instinct sizing him up – the cheap blue synthetic shirt that he wore, the bony hunch of his shoulders . . .

'Coolie?'

He was standing in front of her, across the pile of bags and boxes, his eyes quickly running through all of it and then coming to rest on her . . . face. She took a deep breath, had to get it right . . .

'Yes, for all of that. How much?'

'Thirty rupees.' He said it out of the corner of his mouth.

Too much, she knew, far too much . . . 'Okay, but you will have to get me an auto, put it all in.'

'Okay,' he said and began to pick up the things.

Just okay, no Amma, no Madam, and he didn't most likely have a licence . . .

'Careful,' she said, in English. He looked up at her in the midst of hoisting her blue bag on to the top of the pieces placed on his head. 'Careful,' she repeated, feeling she had to.

As she followed him down the platform, Narayani couldn't help thinking about what it all looked like – a woman in a brown cotton sari worn neatly over a middle aged but straight figure, maybe coming home after a long journey, maybe from her daughter's home, maybe the girl had had a baby and had wanted her mother around to help since she herself was working, that would explain the luggage, and the girl had of course sent her back with lots of things for the family, shirts for the father, a new tape recorder for her brother. The new blue bag held it all, didn't it, even the red silk sari that she had bought her mother for the baby's naming ceremony? It was all bought with her own money and she was very proud about it too . . .

The man standing next to the fruit shop was looking at her, wasn't he?

Her coolie had been walking at a brisk pace. She could see the blue bobbing peak of her bag a little ahead, and the thin shoulders somewhere below it of the man who had not turned back to look at her even once. Between them, there was now a semblance of a crowd. She had been walking at a comfortably slow pace, picking thoughts and sights up and giving them time to mean something, like they did when Kanakam and she would watch English films on video. Anyway, her plan was simple. She would get the coolie to put her into an auto, she would also get him to fix the price and maybe pay him five rupees extra for the trouble. And with that, after twenty years and six months she, Narayani, would be truly on her way back home, wouldn't she? Of course, she was not kidding herself that things were going to be easy, that they would be waiting for her by the gate or that they would even be quite sure why she was back after all this while, and after so much had happened to her and to them . . . she had a feeling that they probably didn't even really expect her to turn up, not after what had been written in the last letter.

She had reached the exit, not really watching where she was going but just drifting with the crowd. The coolie was standing just outside, the luggage on the floor. The precious blue bag was right next to his foot, as if he knew it was important to her. He must have got there at least five minutes back; a wisp of beedi smoke curled away from his face that was turned away from her and he was leaning against the paan stained pillar like he could wait there forever. He must be quite young, she thought, could be the son of someone she used to know or know of. After all, this had been then more of a large village than the little big town that it was now, and most people knew most things and most people. She wondered if she should try and talk to him, get something from him that would make the place seem a little more familiar, a little more known. Then she thought, no, I have to be careful, can't let the boy guess anything . . .

Narayani was glad that the three ten-rupee notes she pulled out weren't so crisp and new as some of the others were. The five she would give him as coins. 'Thirty it was, right,' she said in a confident voice. 'Okay, so I will wait here by the luggage and you'll get the auto.'

He looked a little surprised at that. Aha, so did he think the lady was a fool and would forget, as if she was doing all this for the first time? 'Okay,' he said again, no Amma, no Madam and put his hand out for the money.

'You get me the auto,' she said. 'I am not running away without paying you, am I?' That was good, she thought.

Even before she completed her words, he was loping off, with that same funny hunch to his shoulders and the beedi smoke hovering close to his head like some pet bird.

Narayani was feeling a little tired now. It had been a long journey, even not counting the twenty years, she thought wryly, and she was not so young either. It felt good to lean against the same wall the boy had been resting against. A cup of tea would have been good, but she had to get home first . . . Home?

A wind was rising. There was a hot humid feel to it now, as if there was violent rain in its tow. Dust and bits of dry leaves whirled around helplessly, trapped yet dancing, going round and round till they would drop dead and die. Narayani pushed her hair back as it flew out to meet the wind. She was very tired now and vaguely irritated. The wind had no magic in it for her, it only made her cough and feel even thirstier. It was some time now since the coolie had gone looking for an auto. She had watched him as he slowly made his way to the gate and then stood there for a while looking up and down. Then he had thrown his beedi down, looked to the left once more and then turned and walked off to the right. She hadn't seen him since then, and that was at least five minutes ago. Was it so difficult to get an auto here? After all, the station was quite big. Meanwhile, the wind was getting stronger, sweeping by in large gusts that were damp on her cheek . . . and then she saw him. He was walking in her direction, smoking again and chewing at something. There was no sign of an auto anywhere, though. But Narayani was surprised that she actually felt relieved to see him, his face just seemed so familiar.

'No auto,' he was saying. 'There is a strike going on. They won't run at least for one hour.'

Narayani couldn't believe her ears. One hour? What would she do, where would she wait?

'Where do you want to go?'

She thought she was talking to herself and then realized that it was only the boy . . .

Suddenly, out of some strange frantic motivation, she groped in the side pocket of her grand new handbag and brought out the piece of paper on which the address was written. She thrust it out and then a second later realized in a flush of embarrassment that he might have only been asking her where she wanted to go now, now that she didn't have an auto to clamber into. But he had already taken it from her, was regarding it with a deadpan face and then suddenly looked up and said, 'You are going to the postmaster's house?'

She had to nod her head to that.

'You might as well wait here then. You won't even get a bus going that side at this time. They are saying one hour, but it will take at least a couple of hours. Everybody is expecting trouble. There is police out too . . .'

As he said that, the rain broke. Big chubby drops came pelting down, with the smell of dust, heat and the distant skies in them. They fell at a furious angle, meeting and melding with the loose soil and morphing into tiny mighty rivulets and rich dark puddles . . .

'Narayani, don't, don't . . .' That's what Kanakam would say every time she put her head out into the rain from her tiny hemmed-in window and let the coarse freefalling torrents pull and tug at her head.

'Don't, don't . . .' That's what she said too when Narayani first told her about her sudden, inexplicable plans. Kanakam, bound tight in ropes made of unspent fears and earth-simple wishes, would only say that . . .

'Tea,' Narayani said. 'I think I'll have some hot tea.' She was talking to herself as much as to him. She was reaching inside her purse for the five rupees that would let him go.

'I'll get you the tea,' he said as he stuffed the coins carelessly into his shirt pocket. 'Why don't you wait here? There is a small tea shop on the platform, but it will be crowded, with the strike and now the rain.'

As she thought of saying no, he was gone.

Kanakam wouldn't believe it if she ever heard about it, would she?

Narayani going home after twenty years, and stuck at the station because of an auto strike! Stuck even before it began . . . that was a little funny and they both would have laughed over it, Narayani more loudly because the joke was on her. But Narayani cowering under the shabby roof of the entrance to the same station, Narayani thinking about hot tea and return tickets and about forgetting and being forgotten . . . that wouldn't be bought. Sundaram, maybe yes, Kanakam, definitely not.

Around her there was her luggage, and around them there was the pellmell energy of the rain and the endless mud streams with beedi ends and plastic bags riding up and down in journeys forced on them. There also was a sort of a reverberation, of those words last spoken, of sentences left behind to keep her company, as she huddled there and waited. For the next movement.

For a gap in the rain. For whatever.

M. Pinchuk

Memories Like Photographs

A memory: Usually the memories start with Mom's face. The memories are all I have. There aren't any photographs. My memories are my photographs, my family album.

Mom's face. This memory-photograph looks like a stage set. Or a bad dream. The perspective is off and the photo seems to tilt and curve. Lines aren't quite straight. Corners aren't quite square. Whoever took this photo must have used a wide-angle lens, was trying to see everything.

It's just after my father died.

Mom is sitting at the kitchen table, on the side farthest from the door. I see her feet, her bare legs, the edge of the oval Formica table. She's wearing her bathrobe. It's cotton, pale yellow with small green and pink flowers. The sleeves are too long so she's pushed them back to her elbows. Her thin arms are folded, resting on the table. The heavy glass ashtray is near her right hand. She's not smoking, but the ashtray is full. It's amber coloured, round with a raised pattern that's supposed to look like woven wicker. In it there's a tangle of butts and matches and heaps of ash.

Her face doesn't look right though. It is puffy and blotchy. It looks frozen, as if she's wearing a mask. As if it's not really my mom who is sitting there. Her eyes scare me. They are empty holes in her face. I don't want to look.

But I remember.

It's just after my father died. Was killed. I must be three. I'm in the doorway, too afraid to step into the room.

Mom is humming something: it's not a tune, only random notes and pauses. Her heels tap rapidly on the black and white squares of linoleum that radiate towards me like a giant checkerboard. I stand in a black square. The floor feels cold and gritty. Mom's feet

17

can't stop their nervous dance. The thin fabric of her bathrobe ripples over her knees, silent accompaniment to the nonstop dancing of her feet. I watch the dancing, mesmerized. I try to tap my heels, raise myself up and down, up and down. Join the dance. I try to see her. Don't want to see her. Don't want to meet those empty eyes. But then she notices me, and her lips pull back like an angry cat hissing and about to claw. She grabs the overflowing ashtray and hurls it across the room, not towards me exactly. But it hits the wall next to me and crashes to the floor, spraying ashes and cigarette butts over the kitchen like poisonous, dirty rain.

Her face: I don't recognize her.

A memory: It's a close-up of Mom's shoulder with a view of the hills formed by the back of the caramel-coloured sofa and the horizon of the plain white wall. Mom's shoulder, Mom's bathrobe. The pink flowers are roses: buds and fully opened flowers, all set on short stems that each have exactly one leaf. The edge of my favourite blue blanket is there too, on her shoulder. The satin ribbon binding the edges is frayed into a lattice. The blanket is matted and pilled, especially in the corner where I always hold on to it. And the back of the sofa – tufted at regular intervals – is pushed close to a white wall that has been marked by other pieces of furniture, now rearranged, and a child's messy hands.

I know what we're doing there on the sofa, Mom and me. Mom is holding me, wrapping me in her arms, rocking me, whispering in my ear, brushing ash from my face, out of my hair. Rocking and rocking. I'm crying. I'm crying the way kids do when they get into a loop that they can't get out of. When they can't stop: they only slow down, give a little shudder and start again. The crying is making my head hurt. My cheek is pressed against Mom's shoulder. And she smells like cigarettes, fruity shampoo, that cologne she always wears, the one that comes in a tall bottle with a gold plastic top. With my cheek on her shoulder, she's rocking me and whispering words that I don't understand. She kisses me on the top of my head. She holds my hand and kisses that too. My crying is finally fading, melting into hiccups and short uneven breaths that don't make me start crying all over again. And by the time I feel warm and drowsy, Mom is shaking, trying to hold back her own jagged little sobs.

A memory: A funny shade of blue with a small dab of yellow down in the righthand corner. This memory is a Polaroid. There's a wide white border across the bottom and the squishy feeling of something hiding behind the photo itself.

It's a sort of medium, slightly grey, blue. A midday sky before a storm. It's the blue on an imperfect wall, with bumps and dimples beneath the surface. I picked at a loose piece of blue until it flaked off. I saw sad yellow underneath: a sun with no power.

It's the colour of my bedroom in our new apartment.

We moved and things changed. It was a couple of years after my father died. I was about six. It was just before I started school. We moved far. We never went back to the town where I was born. Where my father was killed. In an accident.

When I smell fresh paint I remember that apartment and how I thought everything had changed. There were no more piles of dirty clothes. No more dishes stacked in the sink. There was food in the fridge. Mom stopped smoking. I see that blue and I think: new furniture, new town, new life. Everything in that apartment was new.

But even after all that newness our life felt like it could change at any minute. Mom never sat still. If she wasn't doing the dishes or sorting through piles of laundry, she was drumming her fingers on the counter. If she was flipping through a magazine, her legs were crossed, the top one swinging back and forth.

Our life was like a Polaroid that hadn't finished developing. Some part of the chemical reaction was still going on underneath the surface and I didn't know when it would finish.

A memory: A doorway to a house. A woman stands in it looking out at another woman and a child. The woman in the doorway is smiling. That's the first thing I notice. This is a bigger picture than some. An eight-by-ten, I think, and it's in colour, vivid saturated colour.

The woman in the doorway is young. She wears jeans and a T-shirt. The T-shirt's bright purple, slightly redder than violet. She's got freckles, but most of her small face is hidden by the slightly-curly blonde hair that hangs down past her chin. Her smile is easy to see, even with her hair hanging in her face. She must be wearing long earrings; something glints through her tangly hair. One of her hands rests on the door, the other points inside the house.

I can only see the backs of the two people standing on the doorstep but somehow I know it's Mom and me. I can see the picture but I'm in it too. We're looking into the house. Mom is wearing a short jacket. Dark green. The sleeves are too long, so she's folded them back into wide cuffs. A skirt – lighter green – comes to her knees. Her legs are bare. I'm sure she's wearing those brown leather sandals that she had forever. She hated buying new shoes, said she never could find any that fit. Her shoulders are raised slightly. She looks stiff and uncomfortable in that way people do when they're trying to hide their nervousness.

The kid must be me. I'm wearing a new pair of jeans and blue sneakers. It looks like I'm wearing a navy blue baseball jacket. I hold a gift-wrapped box awkwardly by my side. My arm is just long enough to pin it against my body.

Mom and I are holding hands, not loosely. Mom's hand almost covers mine. It looks like we're making a fist. But the woman in the doorway doesn't notice; she's smiling at Mom.

I know what this is.

It's my friend Mike's birthday party. We're in the same class at school. I've been to Mike's house a few times. He lives in a real house, not an apartment. I lived in a real house once too. Before. Mike has two parents and two sisters. He's the youngest. I'm the only.

I know what happened.

We were late. Mom hurried me up the walk. Before she rang the bell, she rummaged through her bag for lipstick. It was that bright orange one. I hated it. She ran her fingers through her short, light brown hair. It didn't make any difference: her hair still stood high off her forehead and a few pieces twirled out at the back. She touched her hands to her ears to make sure her earrings were still there. She tugged at the hem of her jacket and sighed. Then she rang the bell.

'Look at me,' she said.

Something in her voice. It was more than a command, but slightly less than a threat. What she really meant was, 'Behave yourself. Don't embarrass me.'

'Look at me,' she said again.

I turned. She tilted my chin up with one hand and brushed the hair off my forehead with the other. 'Have a good time.' Another command.

I lifted my chin out of her hand and stared at the door. I clung to Mike's present, concentrating on not dropping it.

Finally the door opened. Mike's mother was already smiling. 'Hello there. How nice to see you both again.' She put her hand on my shoulder and then ruffled my hair. She smiled at me, and I couldn't help smiling back. I could see past her, into the house and through the picture window on the other side. In the garden there were kids in paper hats, some swings, a slide. I took a step towards Mike's mother, towards the house, but Mom was still holding my hand in a fist.

'Sorry we're a little late,' Mom said.

'No problem. The party's just getting started.'

'Well,' Mom said and then stopped for a second. 'Well, thanks so much for inviting him. He's really been looking forward to it.' She managed a weak smile. 'What time should I pick him up?'

'Oh, probably around four or so. You're welcome to stay if you can stand it.' Mike's mother laughed.

Mom squeezed my hand. 'Thanks, but no. If you don't mind.' She sounded apologetic.

'Not at all. I totally understand.' Mike's mother laughed again. 'It's nice to have some time away from them. I hope you're doing something fun.'

Mom looked a little startled. 'Nothing special.' There was a pause. I looked into the house. I wanted to stop standing on the doorstep. I wanted to get inside, run through the house and into the garden, put on a paper hat and laugh with Mike and his sisters and the other kids.

'Thanks again for inviting him. I hope he behaves himself.' Mom tugged at my hand.

Mike's mother smiled. 'I'm sure he'll be fine. He and Mikey get along so well, it'd be nice to have him over more often. You two could come over together some time if you'd like.'

'Yes. That would be nice.' Mom seemed to run out of things to say after that. I looked at her, wanted her to leave so I could get to the party. I pulled my hand away. She didn't notice. I looked at Mike's mother, wanted her to hold my hand, close the door with me on the inside and Mom on the outside.

Mike's mother tapped me on the shoulder. 'Don't you want to say goodbye to your mother, dear?'

I looked at Mom. Her forehead was creased. 'Bye, Mom.'

She looked down at me and tried to smile, but the shape of her lips didn't match the look in her eyes.

'Bye, honey. Have a good time.' She froze for a moment and then bent down and kissed me. 'Have a good time,' she whispered in my ear as she gave me a squeeze.

I stepped over the threshold, next to Mike's mother, put both my feet inside the house. 'Why don't you run along and join the others? I know Mikey will be glad to see you. You know how to get out to the garden, don't you?'

That was all the invitation I needed: I turned and ran through the house, past the living room, through the dining room, the kitchen, out the back door and into the garden. As I passed the living room, I remembered something I found out on one of my first visits to Mike's house. Mike and I had gone into the living room to watch TV, but I'd been too distracted. There were photographs all over the walls. I couldn't stop looking at them: pictures of Mike, his sisters, his parents' wedding, his grandparents, even his dog. At that time, I thought the only photographs people had were the ones taken at school every year. That's what we had. I thought that was all anyone had. But photographs were everywhere in Mike's house: not just on the mantel in the living room but also in the hallway and even on the wall that ran along the stairs. I'd never seen so many photographs in one place.

I found out something at Mike's party too. Being at Mike's house didn't make me feel like there was something going on that I didn't know about. Mike's mom wasn't moving all the time, she was just there: watching us play games, singing 'Happy Birthday', sitting and talking to some of the other mothers, and taking more pictures to fill all those walls in that big house.

A memory: A living room with a cranberry-red carpet and cream-coloured walls. This photo is in colour and the focus is especially sharp. The photographer must have used a tripod or very fast film or a large-format camera.

Sunlight streams into the room from a window to the left and slices across the wall above the fireplace. A group of five photographs hangs there. The sun glints off the glass in the frames. The largest one is in the centre. It's a wedding photo in black and white. The bride and groom are wearing old-fashioned clothes. There's a newer wedding photo too, in colour. And three pictures of children. And there are smaller photos in frames arranged along the mantelpiece.

It's a visit to Mike's house, maybe the second or third time I'd been there.

I was in the living room. I'd left Mike up in his room and sneaked downstairs. I stood in the middle of the room, first looking at the photos over the fireplace and on the mantel, and then facing each wall in turn, looking at all the photographs covering them, trying to understand why there were so many. Some were only snapshots stuck into small plastic frames, but others were bigger and framed more elaborately.

'Is everything OK in here?' Mike's mother caught me. She was standing in the doorway.

I was embarrassed.

She came over, knelt down and took my hand. 'Are you OK?' Mike's mother looked right into my eyes. I didn't know what to say. I tried to see her long earrings through her curly hair.

'Are you looking at the pictures?'

'I like them.'

She turned towards the mantel and then back to me. 'You probably can't see them too well from where you are. Would you like to look at some together?' She pushed her hair away from one side of her face and then the other. She had a funny way of doing it, using her first two fingers like scissors.

'Yes, please.'

Mike's mother chose a photo album from a shelf in the book-case, took my hand and led me over to the couch. 'There you go. Climb on up. I'll get Mikey and we can all look at the pictures together.' She gave me the photo album and I sat with it on my lap, too nervous to open it until she and Mike were sitting with me.

The three of us sat together, with Mike's mother in the middle, and looked at Mike's baby pictures. Page after page: baby Mike and his mother in hospital; baby Mike and his dad; his two sisters peering down at a squinchy-faced muddle of blankets, both of the girls with the same tangled hair as their mother; and even a few pictures of baby Mike with his grandparents. Mike's parents had written the date and time when Mike was born and how much he weighed. There was even a piece of Mike's hair and a tiny-baby footprint. Mike and I laughed at that, and Mike kept trying to put his foot on the page to compare the size. Eventually, Mike's mother decided that we were being too silly and sent us out to play in the garden. But I wanted to look at more pictures, see pictures of Mike's sisters and Mike's vacations. I wondered if there was a book like that for everyone in the family. I had seen pictures of the dog – a huge St Bernard – and I wondered if he had a book too. But I knew there were no books about me in my house.

A memory: The storage room in the basement of the apartment block. This memory is black and white, but it's hand tinted, so the colours may be slightly off. It's printed full frame, nothing's cropped out.

Dusty light filters through a small window in the wall opposite the door. The window is at street level: a heavy wire screen is bolted over it and divides the tyres of a parked car into a grid. A single lightbulb hangs from almost the middle of the ceiling. Soft shadows are scattered over the floor. They are not hiding much. There isn't much there. In the room: a few cardboard boxes stacked in the far right corner; in the far left corner, the tricycle that I outgrew.

To the right of the door there's a small box covered in gold foil, the kind that chocolates come in. The lid is to one side, flipped over on to its back, helpless. And Mom's there too. She's kneeling: the box is in front of her. Her hands are covering her face. She's curved so far over that her head almost touches the floor. She could be praying, but she's not. I step into the room and hear her crying. It sounds like she's being sick, but she's crying.

In a trail across the room, leading from the box almost to the opposite wall, are about four or five small pieces of paper. No, if I look more closely, I know what they are: they're photographs. Actual photographs.

Mom's trying to stop crying, smearing tears across her face with open palms. The photographs. She doesn't notice me. The smell of dust. I don't know what to do. The photographs. Mom.

It's my fault: I asked about the photographs. I can't stand to see her like this. I want to rush in and grab them all. Take them with me. I don't want to give her the chance to throw them away, tell me we don't have any, that there never were any. I can't stop looking at them, looking at her. I shouldn't be here now. She won't stop crying. I shouldn't know about this.

I push myself backwards out of the room, turn and run through the hallway. I sprint up the stairs to the ground floor, using my hands to push off from the pale green walls so I can take the steps two at a time. I trip over a frayed piece of carpet and smash my shin against the top step. I rush out through the back door of the lobby and head into the garden. Stumbling towards the farthest corner, I push through a stand of bamboo. The stalks snap out of my way, and their rough papery skin prickers my hands. But I keep going until I get to the other side and am forced to stop by the brick wall that defines the boundaries of the garden. I lie down on my back between the bamboo and the shady cool of the wall. I am stretched out like a starfish. My eyes won't close so I stare up at the sky: see the bronze-coloured tufts of plants growing out of the chinks between the bricks and watch one slow cloud drift by. The ground is hard-packed, dry. I try to remember, try to see what is in the photographs scattered across the floor. But I can't imagine anything. I don't know where to begin. All I can see are the tall stalks of bamboo, their leaves sawing away at the edge of the sky.

A memory: A grainy photograph, black and white. Someone's tried to take a photo when there wasn't enough light. I have to squint to make out the details. It's the basement, the storage room. In the dimness, the light bulb hanging from the ceiling doesn't have a shape: it's a glow, looks like it was trying to explode but instead fizzled out, like the end of a sparkler that's burned down to your fingers. Weak light spills through the window and spreads outwards, blurring the outline of the frame.

The boxes are stacked under the window in this photo. They've been moved, rearranged like a display in a shop: the largest one on the bottom, smallest on the top and all the sizes in between carefully ordered. My old tricycle is parked in front of them. There's a broom leaning in the corner. There's nothing on the floor but a faint splash of light.

I look at every inch of the photograph again and again, but I can't see the gold-foil box anywhere. I can't see the pictures that were scattered across the floor.

There's no one in the room this time.

My chest squeezes my pounding heart, trying to slow it down, keep it under control. Mom has cleaned the storage space. Maybe I'm too late. It's taken me a week to get back here, to find a time when she wasn't around. Maybe I'm too late. She's got rid of them. I have to find them.

I plunge into the room, wanting to open the boxes all at the same time, dump them on to the floor, root through whatever they are hiding. I have to find the photos. But I have to be careful. Be careful. Mom can't know I've been down here. She doesn't know I've seen her crying, seen the photos scattered across the floor.

I pace around the room, don't know where to start.

I'm lightheaded. I'm watching myself in a dream. I will myself to go over to the boxes, but it feels like I'm walking through quicksand: every step is an effort but I can't let myself panic. Outside, someone walks through a puddle and water splashes against the window. I pull the smallest box towards me. A shoebox. I force myself to work slowly and carefully. Slow down. Slow down. I lift the lid. The box is stuffed full of old jewellery: multicoloured tangles of beads, single earrings and a few rings. I don't remember

Mom ever wearing any of it. I put the lid back on and place the box on the floor.

The photos have to be here. Where is the gold-foil box? My hands tremble. I take the next box off the stack. Knick-knacks and souvenirs. Postcards – of Hawaii, Mt Rushmore, Yellowstone – they'd never been sent. Some buttons. A couple of marbles: one, translucent amber, the other clear with a flutter of steel blue inside.

Not here. I'm too late. She's got rid of the photos. She's thrown them out, cut them up, burned them. One of my legs starts shaking.

I open the third box. It is filled with children's books and cookbooks. I unpack them one at a time and stack them on the floor. *The Gingerbread Man. Chicken Little.* The *Better Homes and Gardens Cookbook* in its red and white checked cover. *The Joy of Cooking. The Little Engine that Could.* And shoved down along one side of the box is a small handful of photographs.

A memory: This one is in colour. It's my hand. My hand holding three photographs, three real photographs splayed out into a fan. As if I was playing a card game. One photo is black and white. The others are in colour.

The photographs

A wedding photo: Mom and Dad. Taken after their wedding, I guess. This one looks professional. It's in one of those cardboard frames, but it's nicer than the ones school photos come in. The cardboard's heavier, and there's a piece at the back that you can bend into place to make the frame stand up. So you can put it on a mantel or a shelf in a bookcase. This photo stood up once: I can feel that the cardboard support has been pushed out of place.

Around the opening of the frame there's a thin line of gold that loops off into small curlicues in the corners.

The photo. It's just the two of them. Standing together. Dad is much taller than Mom. They both have slightly nervous smiles, smiles just beginning to fade, as if the photographer waited a split second too long before pressing the shutter release.

I can tell it's Mom in the photo. Even though she had long hair then, all piled up on top of her head, it's still her: the same brown hair and the same brown eyes. Like mine.

Her dress is simple, with long sleeves. Not too much lace. In the photo it looks creamy white like that ice cream they call French vanilla, the one with extra egg yolks in it. Mom is holding on to her bouquet: white flowers and yellow and a few long shiny ribbons curving in the breeze. She looks younger, beautiful, happy. A little shy. She's facing the camera but not looking at it. She's looking at the man in the photo – Dad – checking to see if he's still there.

Dad. I try to recognize him. Blond hair: collar length, wavy but not curly. A thick blond moustache. Kind of a big nose. A little squashed looking at the end. He's got his arms around Mom, holding on to her. His big hands are clasped together as if the two of them are playing 'London Bridge is Falling Down', just him and Mom, and he's got to the part where the bridge falls down and captures the person standing underneath. He's smiling – not a big smile – but he looks pleased. His eyes are smiling too. Light blue eyes looking straight into the camera and straight from the photo out at me.

Dad. It must be him. But there's a part of me that's not sure. I don't have any of my own memories of his face. When I was younger, I used to close my eyes and cover them with my hands. I thought that if I kept them closed long enough, his face would appear. I'd find it somewhere in the dark.

I had the idea – or I knew – that he was blond. That's all I could ever come up with. I don't know how I knew that, maybe somebody said something. When I couldn't make his face appear out of the dark, I would try to imagine a face like mine but with blond hair. It never worked. It never seemed real to me. In a way, my dad stopped seeming real too. I didn't have any memory-photographs of him.

Now, though, it must be him, staring out of that photograph with Mom. I look at his face, hoping that it will trigger some feeling in me. That I'll recognize him. That I'll remember him. That I'll feel something.

But I don't recognize him. I don't remember.

Three people: Mom and Dad and it must be me. One photo of the three of us. In colour. Glossy printing. No border. Portrait format, not landscape.

The two of them – my parents – are standing in front of the door to a house. They are on a path that's slightly overgrown with grass. Whoever took the photo must have been on the pavement or close to it. You can't really see me. I'm just a bunch of blankets.

The door to the house is open but the screen door is closed. It must be spring. I was born at the end of April.

Mom. Mom's hair is still long like in her wedding pictures. But it's not on top of her head, it hangs straight down past her shoulders. She's wearing jeans and a long-sleeved shirt, but no jacket. Her shoulders are hunched slightly up and over, and she's holding me as if she's afraid I'll break. She's smiling. She's really smiling. She's looking at the camera but she's squinting. It's a sunny day.

And Dad. The man who must be Dad towers over Mom. He has one arm around her shoulders, the other resting on the blankets that she holds. His hands are big. They almost seem too big for the rest of him but maybe it's an illusion – they only seem so large because Mom is much smaller than he is. I'm taller than Mom now but not as tall as he is. As he was. He must have been over six feet. He's not looking at the camera. He's looking at the baby – at me – as if there's no one else there at all, just him and the baby and Mom.

I stare and stare at the photo, searching every detail of it for clues, for something that will make me recognize this man, this stranger. For something that I can remember. I want to feel like I know him, know about him, know what he sounds like when he laughs or gets angry or says to Mom, 'You're great. I love you. It's nice to be home.'

But those memories aren't there. I've looked everywhere for them and there's nothing. Nothing at all.

My grandparents: This photo is in black and white. Glossy paper. A funny small square size with a narrow white border. It's my father's parents. I know who they are because I saw them a couple of times after my father died. Was killed. Before we moved away.

I never thought they liked me very much.

They're standing in front of a dark-coloured car, one of those old ones that's all swooping curves. They're standing side by side. A couple of boxy suitcases sit next to the front wheel of the car.

My grandfather is tall but not thin. Everything about him is neat: the way his hands are folded in front of him, one holding a pipe. The way he stands so straight. The way his shirt and trousers look freshly ironed. Everything is carefully arranged except his hair. It's white and woolly. It reminds me of those pictures of Einstein where he's smiling but his hair makes him look like he's completely mad. My grandfather's hair is like that but his expression is different. It's as if he doesn't want anyone to know what he's thinking. He's looking straight at the camera. He's not smiling, but he's not frowning either. I'm not sure but his nose might be slightly squashed on the end.

My grandmother is tall too. She comes up to my grandfather's shoulders. Her hair is white, pulled back into a bun. She's wearing a dress, a summery dress printed with large flowers. It has short sleeves and a matching belt. One arm is around my grandfather. The other is by her side holding a straw handbag. She's smiling, looks like she might start laughing, as if someone behind the camera is telling her a joke.

My grandfather's pipe. My grandfather smoked a pipe.

The scent of a pipe woke me up. My grandparents were at our house. Our first house. It had something to do with the accident. My father wasn't there. He was in hospital. My grandparents didn't stay with us. Our house was too small. I know that now. They were at the house all the time but they weren't staying with us. When I asked Mom about it once she snapped, 'And where would they have slept?'

We don't talk about my grandparents.

It was night. The smell of a pipe. A nightlight on, plugged in near the floor. A deep sound, smooth and comforting, reached my bedroom. My grandfather's voice. Then Mom's: short bursts of short words. Silence. I got out of bed. I took my blanket and snuck down the unlit hall towards the wedge of yellow light leaking out of the living room through the half-opened door.

More words. Sounds I didn't recognize. I crept closer to the door and peeked in. Mom sat in a chair next to the fireplace. My grandparents were on the beige sofa: my grandfather at one end, my grandmother near the middle. My grandfather was talking but the words made no sense. Mom stood up and found some matches on the mantel. She lit a cigarette and leaned against the fireplace. Her left elbow rested on the mantel; her chin was propped in her hand. She had her back to my grandparents.

My grandfather took the pipe out of his mouth and stood up suddenly. Grandmother reached out but couldn't catch him. He crossed the room to face Mom.

Mom said something to him, quietly, but he started talking before she finished. They went on like that, voices overlapping, voices getting louder, words I didn't know. They kept talking, always louder, each not waiting for the other to finish.

Grandmother's mouth moves; she says something softly, but no one hears. Her quiet pleading is wrapped up in the noise that's reverberating against the walls, beating against the door and pushing out into the hallway. All those words. All those sounds.

Then, something disentangles itself from the pulsating anger of their voices, and I hear it so clearly, it's as if someone whispered in my ear during a pause in a church service. It's so clear that I know the words are meant for me even though no one knows I'm there.

My grandfather says: 'How could this have happened? You'll have to do something.'

Mom says: 'He's just a child.'

A memory: Another photo of my hand. It's in colour. But this version is a little blurry, as if the camera, or my hand, moved slightly. My hand is holding three photographs, three real photographs splayed out into a fan. As if I was playing a card game. But it's the backs of the photographs in this memory.

Part of the cardboard frame on the wedding photo has a slight bulge. I look closer. A scrap of paper sticks out from where the cardboard can be bent back to make a stand.

I pry the cardboard frame back and pull out a small square of folded paper. It's from a newspaper. The paper is brittle and the background is no longer grey-white. It's the colour of a manila envelope. The edges of the square are ragged. It's been torn, not cut.

I unfold it slowly. On the page there is one short paragraph.

> A local mechanic died yesterday. He had been in intensive care since Saturday. He was shot with his own gun. A child is thought to have been involved. Police are not releasing any more details until their investigation is complete.

Romesh Gunesekera

Independence

Rohan mopped his face. The afternoon temperature was ninety degrees and rising; the band on the veranda was in full swing. All of Colombo's jazz enthusiasts were in the garden: tapping their feet, sucking smoke, taking in loads of cold beer and chips. Outside the club, beyond the military grounds, the city's blistering roads were choked with new checkpoints, air-conditioned jeeps and clattering three-wheelers. Rohan gulped his beer and looked around for Sonya. She was up at the bar with a glass of gin. He saw her wiggle a finger, then her hips as the saxophonist went into rhapsody.

Rohan and Sonya were back in Sri Lanka after an absence of several years. They found it an uneasy mix of promise and desperation: chic bars with army sandbags, local elections between rising war cries, and overshadowing everything a surreal plan to celebrate fifty years of independence in a jubilee parade watched by a bemused Prince of Wales.

When the tune ended, Rohan went up to Sonya. 'I'm going now,' he said. 'Are you staying?'

Sonya drew back. 'You don't want to hear any more of Aravinda's new band? Too hot for you?'

'I'll see you at home later?'

'You don't really want to, do you?' She crumpled an empty packet of cigarettes in her small hand.

As the main road had been cordoned off, Rohan decided to walk across Independence Square and catch a taxi down by the radio station.

The Square, despite the military presence, was the main exercise route for Colombo's well-heeled walkers. Every evening they charged through the black gasoline clouds in Nike trainers and CK vests: staunch and determined boomtown joggernauts deflected only by a skipping CD player, an unexpected cricket match or an exploding bomb. Sonya had been scathing the first time she had seen the fat roll. 'All those poor village kids sent to war, and this lot are battling against blubber.' But now, cocooned in her cosy club she seemed, to Rohan, just as oblivious of what was going on as the rest of them.

When he reached his rented apartment, Rohan found a message on the answerphone. A bright young tycoon whom he had met a few days earlier had called. 'Hello. Nara here. Drop in for a drink, Rohan. It would be good to see you again.'

Nara and his friends were sitting out on the veranda. They were giggling over one of Nara's stories about snorting on the beach. 'I thought the Italians wanted to go snorkelling, so I took them down the south coast. How the hell was I to know . . .'

Everybody burst out laughing. But in the open air, among the shadows, their laughter seemed overexcited. The night, emptied of its usual traffic, magnified the darkness around them. Silence was close.

'Did you see CNN?' someone asked. 'That nutter was saying Colombo is getting ready to party. Must be Colombo on another planet. Don't they know everyone is waiting for a bloody bomb?'

'More like showdown than showtime,' Nara added. He pulled Rohan's arm. 'Never mind that. I want you to meet Vijay. He is my general manager. You must talk to him about what we are doing. He knows about real investments. Tell you what, come with me to Kandy. We have a new factory opening. I have a lovely house in the hills. You'd love it.'

'Factory?'

'We do industrial strength detergent,' Nara tittered. 'It's a very dirty war, this. The army needs tons of it.'

'When are you going?'

'Thursday. When they open the roads. You know how it is, as soon as the parade is over, all this security lark will disappear. It's just a game, you see. The dare is whether the buggers will attack while Prince Charles is here and the drums are rolling. Afterwards nobody will give a toss. So, Rohan, what do you say? Will you come with your Sonya? I have a fabulous pool; the view is out of this world. She'd love it. You'll want to stay forever.'

Rohan shrugged. 'I'll ask Sonya.'

'You ask her, Rohan, ask her now. Here, use my cell phone.'

'She's gone to a friend's house to watch a video. I don't have the number.' Rohan didn't know why he made up such a complicated excuse. He was sure she was still at the club, but he didn't care any more. He remembered the conversation they had, in their small Hackney house, back in London, while packing for this trip. She had asked, 'What do you want so much to go back for?'

'I thought we might get ourselves sorted . . .' he had started to explain, remembering a holiday they had by a beach, once when they were happier, but she had not let him finish.

'You want to settle down there?'

'I was thinking of our future,' Rohan had claimed, resolutely folding a pair of sandy chinos into his suitcase.

On the other bed, Sonya had clicked her matching case shut. 'You mean yours?'

Rohan had looked up at her, briefly. Her face had looked tired, as though it had been pulled about by too many conflicting expressions.

She had stared back at him, until he felt his words break between them. She had waited, her light fingers smoothening her hips. He'd have had his with hers once, but all that seemed too far in the past now.

A sudden rattle of what seemed like gunfire, outside Nara's house, shattered the silence around them. Everyone ducked down as though the bullets might still be flying towards them.

'Christ!' Nara spread out his hands to hold his small flock of startled guests together.

Another string of small explosions crackled. A siren wailed.

Nara flipped open his phone and called up a contact in a radio station. 'Is it an attack, or some trigger-happy jackass?'

'Turn off the bloody chandeliers,' someone hissed.

In the darkness Nara listened, closing his other ear with a hand. Then he put down his little silver mobile phone and lit a cigarette. 'Nobody knows a fucking thing. I'm going out on the road to have a look.'

'Be careful,' another voice warned.

'You'll see my cigarette when I come back. Don't anyone shoot me, OK?' He laughed awkwardly.

Every slight sound beyond the trees played on Rohan's nerves like a Kalashnikov opening fire. If this was an attack, Nara's house, for all its fortified elegance, was not the best place to be. Nara would surely be a target, whoever was firing. He had too many fingers in too many places; his allegiances – communal, ideological, economic – were suspect to everyone on every side.

'It's OK. Turn the lights on,' Nara called out from the gate a few minutes later. A cigarette glowed and advanced slowly. 'It's just some morons with firecrackers.'

'Firecrackers?'

'Building up for the big day. The dodos had forgotten about the bloody war.'

At about eleven o'clock the group began to disperse. Nara arranged for his chauffeur to drive Rohan back before the curfew. 'Talk to Sonya, then, about a little trip, Rohan, will you?'

Rohan nodded and got into the dark, sleek car with its burly driver decked out in an absurd white liveried uniform and white cap. He waved goodbye to Nara as the car rolled down the driveway. Out on the roads they seemed to glide almost in silence without seeing another vehicle anywhere. Union Place – usually a frenzy of three-wheeled trishaws and the occasional Boxter Porsche – was long, straight and empty. They drove past ghost-points and shopping malls – piped all day with Back Street Boys, Hindi pop and husky new commercial radio voices – now all dormant in the dark like colossal gravestones.

After he was dropped off, Rohan stood for a while outside watching the car speed away. Even though it was almost time for curfew, he didn't want to go in. The road behind him, which had been teeming with kids playing street cricket earlier in the day, was now empty except for three soldiers with guns and torches searching a ragged flowerbed.

When he got inside, Rohan noticed that Sonya's sandals, usually parked by the front door, were missing. He went into the kitchen and poured himself a large glass of ice-cold water. There was a slice of pizza on a white plate in the fridge. He took it out and ate it over the sink. Then he made his way to the bedroom. The cupboard where they stored their luggage was ajar. He pushed the door back but it swung open again. His suitcase seemed to have got in the way. He looked inside the cupboard. There was plenty of space, more than there had been. He knew what had been removed. He shoved his single case back in and shut the door firmly. He switched on the air conditioner and sat down on the edge of the bed to wait for the room to cool.

Roy Robins

The Caretaker

When I was nine years old, my best friend, Daniel Kessler, had an epileptic fit in my room. He had slept over that night, and we had stayed up listening to the radio (*Family Hour* began at seven, followed by Walter Stuart's *Comedy Round Up*). I had a bunk bed, and he lay on the bottom bunk, in his khaki army sleeping bag, with his glasses on, paging through one of my brother's old *Mad* magazines. We had spent the evening playing War and Snap with a pack of cards that had frayed and worn thin so that I knew which card was which. I envied Daniel, who knew how to play Solitaire and whose short-sightedness gave him a sullen and intelligent air.

We had been discussing our plans to develop a settlement for children on the moon ('But how would we get there?' I remember asking, over and over), when my mother came in to turn off the light. When Daniel protested that his mother let him stay up till half-past nine, my mother had replied, 'Well, I'm not *your* mother.'

I had a nine o'clock bedtime on week nights, although my mother often let me stay up until ten, provided I helped her in the kitchen and promised not to tell my brother who was forever complaining that he had been deprived of these privileges when he was my age. My brother, who was fifteen at the time, stayed in his room all night listening to Pink Floyd LPs, and writing letters to girls in his class. He was, I suppose, unsuccessful in love even then. My brother had braces and was in the process of developing a method of speaking without actually opening his mouth. He was one of those fifteen-year-olds who had taken it upon themselves to act like someone in their early forties, and he referred to Daniel and I collectively as 'the boys'. Daniel and I, in turn, called my brother 'the pain' or, and this was my personal favourite, 'the girl'.

My bedroom had served as my father's office before my parents' divorce. I had Donald Duck curtains, and a Mickey Mouse lamp which turned bright pink when you first switched it on. I had a battalion of plastic soldiers that I strategically positioned around the house: a platoon kept guard on the edge of the bath, and another was stationed behind the bushes in the yard. That winter, my mother found a soldier in the drainpipe, his head knocked crooked in the storm. I had a shelf of Little Golden Books, the complete set of *Encyclopaedia Britannica*, and eleven of the sixty-seven *Hardy Boys* books, each one worn clean at the spine. I had a denim Disney jersey which, when draped across my chair at night, resembled the arms of an owlish man.

Each night before I went to sleep, I read a story out loud in the clean and quavering voice of one of my radio heroes. Mine was the last generation of South African children who listened to hour-long broadcasts with their parents, and who could think of nothing more comforting than the sound of a radio crackling damply in a nearby room. There was Jackson Howard who, every Saturday afternoon in the borrowed voice of Biggles, would recall a story about the finest moments of his country in the First World War. So acrobatic were my imaginary excursions that it was not unusual for one or another of my teachers to exclaim, 'Aidan, have you lost your head!' Somewhere around this time I obtained a nickname – a commodity of sorts in my school – I became 'Fred, the boy with no head'.

That particular night, after my mother left my room, I turned my nightlight back on, and Daniel and I began our ritual conversation: an admission of the names of the girls we *liked*. There was something magical and potentially devastating about that one word *like*. It was, at once, thrilling and fulfilling – as though to *like* was a reward in itself, never mind being *liked*, an almost impossible ambition. At this particular point in my life I was in *like* with Tracy Atlas, who sat behind me in history class. She was a small, dark girl, and she rode the afternoon bus back to Wynberg where her father was the manager of McLean's All Night Pharmacy. She was a ballet dancer, and I loved the sight of her in the mornings with her hair pulled back and her sleeves rolled up, the small blonde hairs on her arms. Whenever I saw her I felt a pang – a pang of *like* but also of regret – and when she smiled at me in the afternoons, on her way home from school, I had to look away. It had taken me three months to say hello to her, although to my credit I said it very slowly. I had dreams about asking for her hand in marriage, although these dreams were always confused with my mother entering my room in her dressing gown and waking me up for school.

Daniel was two and a half months older than me, a difference which was of the utmost importance when we were nine and ten. He lived three blocks from me, down a steep hill packed with dusty pines. We used to walk there after school, or ride our bikes out to the park on Saturday afternoon. He insisted on writing down the licence plates of suspicious vehicles in a small black book which he kept hidden among a heap of comic books and bits of bust balloons in the basket of his bike. He was a conspiracy theorist: he believed in ghosts, refused to talk about girls on the telephone – he rarely phoned me, something which might have had more to do with his parents' financial situation than his own night fears – and was one of the great teacher-haters I have known (the feeling was frequently mutual).

He wrote stories – hundreds of stories – in his rough, dark, clumsy hand. These stories had names like 'The Planet of Mars Returns to Earth', 'The Mystery of the Missing Nostril', 'The Secret of Slime Creek'. He wrote these titles in the stilted letters used for the posters of old movies. It was not unusual to come across a sentence like this in one of these early stories: *On his way to the ship Zorg tripped on the evil eyeball of Commander Zalton.* He was an impatient writer; his characters often died in snowstorms, in outer space. I was jealous of his talent, of the imaginary worlds he created whose inhabitants looked suspiciously like the children in our class, but who spoke fantastic languages and knew the secrets of the universe. Occasionally, I would attempt the illustrations for these stories. Back then I thought I wanted to be an artist ('my little Picasso' was my mother's favourite jibe – as if Picasso wasn't small enough on his own). Daniel's bedroom walls were plastered with old magazine photographs of Neil Armstrong: first young and trim, and then older and fatter and looking rather lonely, as though he could only ever be happy on the moon.

Daniel's father was a failed lawyer, and one of the strictest men I have known. He beat his son routinely, secretly, harshly. He was careful to beat his son where no one could see the marks: across his stomach, on the back of his legs. He beat him for no reason, because he loved him perhaps, because he was overwhelmed by the resourcefulness of his son.

I alone knew of these beatings: I had undressed with Daniel, had seen the hard red welts on his knees, the chafed and gritty skin. Once or twice I saw him wince while playing soccer after class, or watched him cry out in pain when he walked up the steps to school. He tried belatedly and unsuccessfully to turn these cries into a hollow, horsy laughter. Daniel was, among other things, a lousy liar. When I asked him about these marks he said, 'I fell.' Or, 'I wasn't looking where I was going.'

But then one night he told me the truth, as though he expected that all children were beaten, that it was something secretly acknowledged between fathers and their sons.

Daniel resented the fact that there was no father in my house, that I had what he imagined was an open kind of freedom. He swore me to secrecy about the beatings, and I imagined that if I told anyone, his father would beat me too. I did not think of the consequences of Daniel going home, day after day, to an unemployed and abusive father. I thought: this is my life and that is his.

Later I thought about Daniel when a girlfriend told me how her father would beat her every time his rugby team lost a match. 'I memorized the days of the matches,' she said, 'and those were the days that I stayed away from home.' This same girl had to be coaxed into intimations and expressions of love across a telephone line.

When I stayed over at Daniel's house, Mr Kessler – a ruddy, sturdy man – would make conversation with me, would sit at the dinner table with a glass of whisky, his arm around his wife, or play soccer with us kids in the yard. I could not associate this man with the stories his son had told me in secret. The truth is, I liked Mr Kessler – liked the confidential nature of our conversations, the way he would put his hand on my shoulder when he asked me a question, or ask me, teasingly, if I wanted a sip of his Scotch. I even thought, for a time, that I would not mind being his son. Daniel's mother was a stout and quiet woman, who worked in the secretarial college in Milner Road.

I remember the first time I watched Daniel have a fit: his body shaking wildly on the classroom floor. Our teacher held open Daniel's mouth so that he would not swallow his tongue. I was horrified and excited because, in that moment, his body seemed spiritless and only half alive. Daniel was ashamed of his epilepsy; refused to speak of it. There were days when he did not come to school, and when I asked him where he was, he would reply, 'I went out', and I knew that he had been slowed down by another fit.

When we fought – and we fought often – he always knew the most hurtful things to say. 'I feel sorry for your mother,' he would say. Or, 'No wonder your father left you. Look at you!'

The night of Daniel's epileptic fit we ended our discussion earlier than usual, and I lay in bed listening to the sound of my mother typing in the room next door. There was something quiet and comforting about that sound which I missed the nights I spent away from home. If I listened carefully, I could hear my brother's footsteps, as he went out on to the back porch to smoke a cigarette. This was another ritual: first my brother would creep outside, then my mother would switch the porch light on, to show that she knew where he was. It was not unusual for me to wake to the sound of my mother and my brother arguing in low voices outside my room. Their argument would go something like this: 'You think I don't know that you smoke.' 'I don't.' 'You don't think I know, or you don't smoke?' 'Stop accusing me, you're always accusing me. I was next door, they were smoking next door.' 'They don't smoke next door. You smoke next door.' And on and on.

In the bunk below I could hear Daniel, snoring. I put a sheet over my nightlight and switched it on so that I could look through the slats at his mouth moving while he slept. I could see his glasses upended on my bedside table next to my brother's *Mad* magazine and my pitted pack of cards.

I woke again at midnight, or soon after, to the sound of my best friend thrashing about in his bed. In my dreary sleep-state, I confused this sound with heavy breathing and bad dreams, and I soon fell asleep again. When my mother came in to wake us at nine he lay still, downcast with sleep, and I listened as she called out his name.

'Daniel,' she said, 'Daniel, honey, wake up.'

I still have the image of his body below me, pale and still, made beautiful by sleep. I stood beside my mother and watched as she slapped his face (her hand made a hollow, chiming sound as it touched his cheek), lightly and quickly, slapped him as his father had slapped him. I could see his dark head reflected in the glasses on my bedside table.

'He's cold,' my mother said and then, as if she had only realized at that moment, she took his hand in hers. He had no pulse.

In the unspoken moment of his fit he had swallowed the long rope of his tongue.

'Go out of the room,' my mother screamed at me. 'Get out now.'

It was half-past nine. From the passageway I could hear her telephone first an ambulance, and then Daniel's parents. From across the hall I could hear my mother screaming at my brother: 'Hang up the phone, Malcolm, hang up the goddam phone.' And then, 'Come quickly, I think your son's had a fit in his sleep.'

My brother came out, barefoot, wearing tracksuit pants and the Motley Crue shirt he slept in with the holes in the front.

'What's going on?' he said, when he saw me in the hallway.

'Daniel wouldn't wake up,' I said.

My mother came out when she saw Malcolm standing at the door.

'Don't you dare go in there,' she said to him. 'Take your brother outside. The ambulance will be here any second and I don't want Aidan to be here when they come.'

'*You* take him outside,' my brother said. 'I want to stay here.'

I have been writing about this moment, in some form or other, over and over, these last few years. The truth is, I have begun to forget the order of the events; to reshape them, to blame myself for his death. Sometimes, when I have been drinking, I go as far as calling myself a murderer. If only I had woken when I heard him shaking at midnight. Held his mouth open and his body still. Had called my mother – she would have known what to do. She was a caretaker, my mother. She saved lives.

I watched the ambulance arrive: three men in their white nylon jackets, taking turns breathing into Daniel, pumping his heart, shaking his body. From the hallway I watched his body bounce dully against the bed, and I knew then that he was gone. They covered his face with a sheet. The three tall men carried him out on a stretcher, and my brother opened the front door for them as they filed out of the house. One of them even winked at me as he passed – I remember that much.

From the front window I could see Daniel's parents pull up in their old grey Ford. I could see Mr Kessler step out of the driving seat, in running pants and a woollen sweater. I could hear Mrs Kessler scream when my mother approached them. From my brother's window I watched Mr Kessler comfort his wife, holding her towards his chest. I could see that she was screaming at my mother, that they were both screaming at my mother. For a moment I worried that he might hit her in his rage, that he would walk into the house and find me and beat me. I could imagine his rough hands over my chest and throat.

My mother told me later that they blamed her for having him over so much, for closing the door when he slept (I could only sleep with it closed), for not visiting him in the night, for not telephoning them earlier, for killing their son. What they did not say – but what we learned later – was that he had been overmedicated on epilepsy pills.

I was not allowed to attend the funeral, and we never saw the Kesslers again.

What I do remember is our teacher breaking the news to us in class, in a low whisper, and my classmates looking up at me conspiratorially, then gathering around me at break. How did it feel, they wanted to know, to sleep in the same room with a dead body? Did I *touch* him? Did I *kill* him? For the first time in my life I was popular with the other kids in my class, and it was only some months later that I broke down altogether.

I began to miss school for days at a time. My mother moved into my room and I slept on the floor of the lounge. I failed in all my subjects except English and art. Most days I refused to exercise with the other children, refused to undress with them, refused to read out aloud in class. I thought obsessively about death. I had vivid dreams – 'imaginings', my mother called them – in which I felt alien hands stretched clean across my spine, a black cloak draped around my head. So afraid of sleep was I that I often stayed up for nights at a time.

The seat beside me in English class was left empty, ghostly, and it was some weeks later before a new boy, Matthew Shelter, sat beside me. He was a mean-spirited, sullen and beautiful boy, who would copy my English homework over my shoulder, and I let him, because I was in love with him for a time.

For years afterwards I forgot all about Daniel Kessler. Then, last month, I ran into Mr Kessler in a bar off Church Street. I was with my girlfriend at the time, Jacqui Lowenstein. We had gone to the theatre to see a student production of *Murder in the Cathedral* (she had a friend in the cast), and had stopped off on the way home for a drink. Jacqui worked full time for a foreign-language school in Hatfield Street. I met her at a Writer's Circle meeting – we were both 'invited visitors' – and we ended up having coffee in a restaurant across the road. She was tall with curly dark hair and, like Tracy Atlas, she had danced as a child. Her parents were Polish refugees. I would come over to her flat on Sunday afternoons – Sundays always depressed her, she said – and we would lie in bed and listen to Miles Davis and smoke cigarettes. Her last boyfriend was a philosophy major who had named his three cats after his heroes: Wittgenstein, Heidegger and Nietzsche.

'Every night when I got up to pee I would walk into one of his cats,' she told me. 'And Sam was neurotic. His cats were neurotic. Nietzsche was a depressive, a loner. Heidegger was mean-spirited and broody. Wittgenstein – Witty – was in a world of his own.'

'In the end,' she said, 'Sam preferred his cats to me.'

To survive Hitler's Holocaust her father had become an informer to the Nazis. He had had his teeth knocked out with a crooked metal pole in the ghetto in the years before the war.

'My father's parents were religious Jews, and my father forbade religion from his house. He felt his religion had disappointed and destroyed him. God – the idea of God – disgusted him.'

She told me that there were holes in the doors of her house where her father had unscrewed the mezuzahs.

She read Martin Buber at midnight and the stories of Isaac Babel. She chastized me for not knowing enough about my Jewish heritage, for being indifferent to the Talmud.

'I felt neglected without a childhood God,' she said. 'All my friends had one. Instead I was taught that there was no God. It's one thing to be an atheist, but to make a religion out of atheism is another matter altogether.'

As a teenager she used to go to synagogue on Saturday mornings, and tell her father that she had been to a film. 'He would ask me what I saw and I would make something up. And he would say "And it was good?", and I would say, "It was good," and that would be that.'

I would visit her on Tuesday afternoons, walk up from the station, with my book bag, and my *Norton Anthology of Poetry*, and knock on her rough wooden door, and she would answer, in her damp slacks and shirt, with her reading glasses on and her hair pulled back, and we would talk for maybe half an hour and then kiss for some time and then, if I was lucky, we would go to her bed, which looked on to the station.

I told her that I had suffered from depression and she said, 'Everyone does from time to time.' I told her that I had tried to kill myself and she said, 'But you didn't and that's the important thing.' So forgiving was she, so all-encompassing, so understanding, that I confused all this with love. I even considered – though I had no job at the time, no money, no place of my own – asking her to marry me. I was twenty-two. I became defensive, selfish, jealous of her affections for other men.

That particular night I had been drinking steadily all evening and she had informed me, politely, that if I had one more drink she would never speak to me again.

'If you never spoke to me again,' I told her, 'I would have no reason to drink at all.'

I drove her home after the play, and, although I spoke to her occasionally on the telephone, or in the company of mutual friends, it was the last time we would see each other alone.

On my way home I stopped in at the Crow Bar, one of those old-time beerhalls with low lamps and heavy, burgundy drapes. It was half-past ten and the place was full of middle-aged men. There were occasional women – lovers perhaps, or lonely kamikaze drinkers – but they seemed almost accidental. It was then that I saw Mr Kessler, drinking alone at the bar in a denim jacket and grey sweat pants. His hair was grey and thin and his face was hard, the brow and neck broader, plumper, but I recognized him all the same.

I recognized him immediately and hated him suddenly, though I had hardly thought of him these last thirteen years. I watched him down his Scotch with the sullen single-mindedness of a regular drunk. I came up to him and sat beside him and ordered a drink.

'Mr Kessler,' I said.

He turned towards me, darkly.

'Do I know you?' His voice was thick with Scotch. I could see that his face was heavy, jowly, and that there were smoke circles under his eyes. I could see also that he no longer wore a wedding ring, and that his jacket was stained and frayed at the sides.

'No,' I said, and I ordered another drink. 'I used to be friendly with your son, Daniel Kessler.'

I suppose I was waiting for a confession of some kind, but he looked at me sullenly and then turned away.

'That was awful,' he said. 'The whole thing was awful.' He looked to see if I intended to stay at the bar and then, when I did not move, he looked away.

'You were awful,' I said. 'You never cared about your son. You used to beat him. You bastard, you beat your son all the time.'

'You're drunk,' he said. He put down his drink. 'You don't know what you're talking about. I loved my son.'

'He was at my house all the time, because he couldn't stand to be alone with you.'

'You were the faggot who let him die,' he said. 'You lay there while he died you little fuck, you listened to him die.'

I was aware then that the music had slowed, that the other customers were staring at us from across the room. Then the barman leaned over his counter.

'I think you should go,' the barman said to me.

'Fuck off,' I said. 'This is none of your fucking business.'

'I don't know this man,' Kessler said loudly. 'He just sat here and started threatening me.'

I left soon after, or was asked to leave. I walked back to my car, and then drove down to Mackenzie Bridge, and sat in my car in the dark until I made myself throw up. Behind me I could hear the slow churning of the midnight ferry, and the schooners across the shore. I dreamed about Mr Kessler that night. *You think you should be pardoned for your sins*, he said. *But what about me? Shouldn't I be pardoned, too?*

Some weeks ago I telephoned my mother and we spoke about Daniel's death.

'It must be difficult being a caretaker,' I said. 'I mean the responsibility.'

'It isn't the responsibility,' my mother said. 'I mean it is, but it isn't just that.'

Abdulrazak Gurnah

My Mother Lived on a Farm in Africa

'My mother lived on a farm in Africa,' she heard her daughter Khadija say. She preferred to be called Kadi, especially in front of her friends, and Munah tried her best to remember. She and her friends, the usual two, Clare and Amy, had been watching *Out of Africa* on the video that afternoon. They did that most Sunday afternoons, took turns to go to each other's houses to watch videos. It was video in their house anyway, DVD in the others.

Then when the film finished, and in the brief silence that sometimes follows the end of a story, Kadi said that. It was an echo of the film's repeated dirge, *I had a farm in Africa*, spoken like a hoarse lament over the landscape, to make Karen Blixen into a tragedy. Lost love, lost farm, lost paradise, the Fall. Then Kadi said that: *My mother lived on a farm in Africa.*

Munah wanted to rush in there and tell them that it wasn't like that. It was nothing like that. But she heard someone snigger just a second after Kadi spoke, and that made her hesitate and retreat. It was Amy, she thought, giggling with surprise or pleasure. Did your mum really!? Perhaps Kadi's remark was nothing more than a boastful exchange between adolescent friends.

It was one of the stories of her childhood back home. When the children were younger, they loved to hear the stories. They would sometimes prompt her to tell one, as if they had recognized a cue in something she had said. Jamal, her elder, used to remember them in detail, and speak about the people who appeared in them as if he knew them. *Oh, Uncle Abdalla is always like that with money, isn't he? Really mean.* Now Jamal was old enough to answer back and stay out all night, sleeping over at a friend's house but really doing who knows what. His clothes had the slightly nauseating smell of sweat and smoke and cheap food that she associated with the places young people went to, but he shouted and sulked at her if she went into his room to sort through his clothes for the wash. He liked them as they were. He walked in a disjointed shuffle, as if his legs and hips were dissolving slowly under him. In any case, he no longer had any interest in her childhood spectres. Or when he had no choice but to show interest, because she had reminded him of someone he once used to speak about with some familiarity, he nodded his head constantly, eager for her to finish, anxious for her not to allow the story to sprawl as she used to.

Kadi did not remember with the same fidelity, and often had to be reminded. Yes, you *do* know who he is, my Uncle Omar, who owned the farm where I went to live for several weeks when I was fourteen. Then unexpectedly, at times she would remember. Like now, after watching some empire nostalgia and passion, she remembered the farm and told her friends, *My mother lived on a farm in Africa.* Only it was nothing like that, no sweeping drive and horses and crystal glass, no servants, no subject people to save from themselves. She was the subject people, subject to life and to others, sent from here to there and back by those who loved her and owned her. That was what made Kadi's friend snigger. She knew very well it could not have been anything like the beautiful life they had just seen on the television. She would have known without reflection that Kadi's mother could not have lived on a farm in the real Africa of open skies and deep shadows, and avenues of acacia and lamplit verandas. More likely, Kadi's mother's Africa was the other one that you also caught glimpses of on television, streets crowded with people, and dusty fields full of children clinging to their mothers.

Perhaps Kadi's friend did not know she thought like that. Perhaps she did not snigger. It made Munah feel foolish that she had even considered rushing in there to rail at them. She wondered at the bitter taste the feeling left behind. Was it her age? She had heard a plea in what Kadi said. Please pretend that my mother looked like that when she was in Africa, and that I look like you. Perhaps it was not a plea at all, and Kadi could only think of Africa as the pictures she had just seen and could only see her mother living like that.

They were fourteen years old, and she would have embarrassed them, and Kadi most of all, if she had gone in there and told them that the farm she lived in was nothing like that make-believe luxury, that it was small and paltry and human, that it was not in *Africa,* but in a real place with names for everything, from the smell of grass and leaves to the smallest change in the weather.

She had not moved since her daughter spoke, paralysed by the rage she felt. Then slowly the rage receded, and was replaced by regret and spreading guilt. What was there to feel such rage about? They lived in different worlds. Her warmhearted daughter and her kind friends would weep over the fate of a wounded turtle or a stranded seal, but would turn away with indifference from the mean suffering of those they had learned to think of as deserving of it.

Memories troubled her. She could not forget. She did not even know why some things would not leave her. She wondered if that was how it was with all those people she saw in the streets who were far away from their homes. She wondered how distance made remembering different.

The arrangements were made in her earshot, but as if she was a casual listener rather than the person whom they concerned. Her father was absent, away for some months already and not expected in the near future. When she was a child, she never wondered at these long absences of her father. She became so used to them that she did not really notice, or rather only became aware of them when their father was living at home. Things happened when he was living with them, as if their mother waited until he was back before making any decisions or carrying out any big task. Maybe this was how he liked it too, or maybe they had to wait for the money he brought back from his long absences before they could get anything done. In later years, Munah thought her mother slowed down in his absence, and that the life she and her sister lived with her was subdued.

The weight of things became too heavy for her at this one time, and she became unwell. She sat for lengths of time with her head in her hands, complaining of headaches and unable to do the simplest things. Munah and her elder sister Hawa tiptoed round her, sat with her when her slow breathing was the only sound between them, tried to keep their bickering down. They were helpless with her tears. When they started, nothing could stop their mother's tears until, so it seemed, she had shed all of them. Sometimes she cried all day long over a petty offence or a small hurt, until in the end all three of them were paralysed with weeping over their incomprehensible pain.

One day their Aunt Amina came to visit, and it was then that Munah heard the arrangements that would take her to the country. Aunt Amina, who was their mother's elder sister, said that the two of them were too much work, and that she would take Munah away with her until their mother was feeling less tired. 'Hawa can look after her mother and allow her to rest and get her health back. You come to the country and we'll find work for you.'

Later she could not remember if anyone said anything about missing school, but it was one of the first things Munah herself thought. A few days off school. Within the hour Munah had made a bundle of her belongings for a few days' stay and was walking beside her aunt to the bus halt, wearing one of the new silky shawls her father had brought as a gift the last time he came home. She remembered that, because it was the first time she wore it. The farm was only fifteen miles out of town, and she had visited several times as a child, and she saw Uncle Omar four or five times a year because he sometimes called on them when he came to town. She had no idea that she would spend weeks there.

Uncle Omar did not smile much, but you knew it was not because he was annoyed or unhappy. He just did not smile, although he did when he saw Munah walking up the footpath to the house. He was sitting on the covered porch, weaving a basket out of palm leaves. Then he looked up when he heard them walking from the road, and his face turned into a speechless smile.

The house stood on a slope, at the bottom of which ran a small stream. The farm ran behind the house for six acres on both sides of the stream. She always remembered the first night she spent on the farm, and the deep silence of the country. It was not really silence, because there were scratchings and rustlings and an indescribable suspension of the inaudible noises of night. It was a silence that leaped at her with a muted roar when she went out to the outhouse. In her sleep she heard raucous yells that were gone when she opened her eyes, and she heard the thick breathing of the frogs in the stream.

They gave her a room of her own. 'You'll be here for a few weeks,' Aunt Amina said, 'so make yourself comfortable.' The house was small, just two rooms and a store, not a shack but a small farmer's dwelling. At various times in the year, the room she slept in was also used as a store, so there were splash marks and plant juices which had soaked into the whitewashed wall and could not now be removed. The small window was barred and looked away from the stream, up the slope towards a grove of banana trees.

In the day, she was expected to stay close to Aunt Amina, and wait for chores to be given to her. She understood it was really to keep an eye on her because she was fourteen and a girl. She helped with sweeping the yard, with cooking, with washing clothes and with cleaning the fruit and packing it in the baskets for transport to the market in town. It was tiring at first, but she settled into a dull routine that she found surprisingly pleasant. In the afternoons, if she was not too tired and Uncle Omar was in the mood, he showed her the work on the farm, and sometimes took her out to the road where they walked as far as the huge mango tree where people waited for the bus to town. There was also a little shop there, and the shopkeeper made coffee for them while Uncle Omar stopped to exchange greetings and news with the people sitting on the bench. 'Go and greet the people inside,' he said the first time. After that she always went to greet the women in the house and sat with them until Uncle Omar had finished his conversation with the men sitting under the tree.

One day, another man rose from the conversation and walked with them. He was many years younger than Uncle Omar, perhaps in his early thirties, with a smiling face and bright curious eyes. His name was Issa, Uncle Omar told her, and he was their nearest neighbour. She walked behind them and could hear from the tone of their voices that they liked each other. Issa usually called on them often, she found out later, but he had been away accompanying his wife and children on a visit to their relatives in Pemba. When he came, he sat with Uncle Omar in the porch, chatting and laughing and drinking coffee. Sometimes Aunt Amina sat with them, he was such a good friend. She asked after his wife and children and sometimes called him son.

He always asked for Munah to come and greet him. Munah could not help noticing that he glanced at her when no one was looking. She could not help noticing his interest. It went on like that for many days, and as time passed his visits became daily, and her body became heated under his scrutiny and his stolen glances. His looks became less hurried, and one day he gave her a secret smile. She smiled back and looked away, pleased.

It was impossible to mistake what was going on. Uncle Omar looked nervous and uncomfortable when she appeared while Issa was there. Aunt Amina always had something for her to do. Neither of them said anything to her. His smiles and glances thrilled her but also frightened her, but since he said nothing and her uncle and aunt were so vigilant, she felt safe, as if in a game.

One night he appeared at her window. Perhaps it wasn't the first time, perhaps he had done so before. The window was high in the wall, and had two wooden shutters. When she first arrived she was afraid of the country darkness and shut both shutters. Later she took to keeping one open. She woke up with a sense that something had happened, and her eyes went directly to the window. There was enough glow in the night air for her to see a silhouette of a head at the window. She could not prevent a frightened gasp before she put a hand over her mouth. It took only an instant, and then she knew it was Issa. She steadied herself, as if she was still asleep, and after a moment she heard his breathing. She realized that some straining quality in it must have been what woke her up. The head disappeared after a while, but she dared not shut the window, in case he reached in for her when she went to shut it. She lay awake for most of the night, dozing and waking, her face turned towards the window.

The next morning she went to look outside and saw that there was a small mound of hard earth that he would have stood on to look in, although even then he would have had to hang on by the bars on the window. When Issa came to visit that afternoon, she stayed inside the yard and heard a tremor in her voice as she called out a greeting. That night she shut both shutters and lay awake, waiting for him. She heard him when he arrived, and sensed his hand on the shutter, pushing at it. 'Don't hide from me,' he said softly, pleading. She lay in the dark, listening to his breathing. After a moment she heard the soft thud as he let go of the window bars. She could not bear the fear of it, and told Aunt Amina when she saw her in the morning. Aunt Amina said nothing for a moment, just looked sad, as if Munah had given her news of a terrible loss. 'Don't say anything to Omar,' she said.

She told her to get her things ready, and within the hour they were on their way to the bus halt under the mango tree. Uncle Omar could not understand the rush. 'Has something happened?' he asked.

'No,' Aunt Amina told him. 'I just forgot that I'd promised to take her back today. She's been here for weeks, you know.'

Munah heard Kadi calling for her. 'Where are you?' she called out.

She came into the kitchen, fourteen and smiling, safe as houses, and came to where Munah was sitting at the table with her memories. She leaned over her mother from behind, her long hair falling round her mother's head.

'What are you doing?' she asked, kissing the top of her head and then retreating. Without waiting for an answer she said: 'We're going round to Amy's. I'll be back in a couple of hours.'

'It wasn't like that, the farm in Africa,' Munah said.

'Oh, you heard,' Kadi said. 'I was just winding them up, trying to make them jealous.'

Chris Womersley

The Shed

1

I still can't believe how quickly he took over, or how he did it. Incredible how the inevitable is hardly ever obvious. I found him one afternoon in the shed at the bottom of the garden. It was mid-winter, June or July. It was cold and wet. I remember the thick smell of damp earth. The clouds hovered low and it was dark by 4 pm. I don't know how long he had been there – it might have been years. I wasn't really afraid of him, although I probably should have been.

The wife was gone by this time, of course. Packed up some weeks before and wandered into the sunset. Told me I'd had my chances. Told me she was unhappy. Told me it was the end. Just the usual things women will tell you.

2

I confess I was drinking at this stage and the house was falling to pieces bit by bit. The kitchen was in ruins, cluttered with pans and plates and takeaway containers. The lounge room was vanishing beneath mountains of unread newspapers and biscuit wrappers. The brackish air in the bathroom had begun to take on a life of its own. There was a pile of dry shit in the hallway, which was odd because I had never owned a dog and couldn't even remember one being in the house. Some windows were broken and somebody – perhaps even me – had covered the spaces with cardboard that fluttered when it was windy. It was a large two-storey house but it smelled suddenly small, like some mangy cupboard.

The only place to be at times like these was in bed. I retreated from the rubbish and mayhem, room by room, until the bedroom that overlooked the backyard was the only vaguely habitable space. I climbed aboard the large, soft bed and hung on like it was a raft of some sort, floating above the swell of bottles and butts and broken things.

And you can pretty much do everything you need to in bed: eat, sleep, dream, stare at the ceiling and jerk off to your heart's content. The television sat on a milk crate at the foot of the bed and at my right hand was a chair on which was scattered an assortment of reading material and odds and ends. And, of course, in bed one can drink.

And drinking – and I mean real drinking – is pretty much a full-time occupation. It's not just a glass of wine here and there, the odd longneck after lunch. It's true that drinkers are disorganized and irresponsible and unreliable, but that's only concerning things other than drinking. A drinker might forget his daughter's birthday or be incapable of managing laundry, but his mind is crystalline when it comes to locating drink. When he needs to call in a three-year-old debt of twenty dollars, or remember the Monday night opening hours of a bottleshop on the far side of town.

When drinking, there is planning to be done, things to be considered, decisions to be made. Total destruction takes precision and concentration. It's not as haphazard as it looks. You can't buy takeaway alcohol easily at 4 am, for example, so you need to be careful of running out at an inconvenient time such as this. Far better to run dry early in the morning – but not so early as to be caught empty-handed too long before business hours – so all that's required is a short trip to the pub down the road for your morning cask of wine. Drinking is not a social event, it's an interior monologue. God forbid you should ever have to sit with others to get it done. Doing it is only half the work. There's thinking about doing it as well. It all takes time.

3

I can't even remember why I went down to the shed in the first place. Probably looking for something to pawn or scrounging for empty bottles to sell. The only light was that of the late afternoon coming through the open door. Everything looked grey and furry. One wall bore the drawn shapes of garden tools, like the crime-scene outlines of murder victims. Grass was growing through the floor and vines curled between gaps in the walls. A light rain grizzled on the tin roof like an endless army of tiny feet. The shed smelled like all garden sheds, of dirt and oil and the bitter tang of fertilizer.

But there was something else. I was surprised to detect my own sharp smell, perhaps drawn out by the rain I'd staggered through to reach the shed. It was the machinery of my body, working vainly to expel the toxins I was pouring into it. I sniffed my armpits and yanked a handful of wet hair in front of my nose, but I was inured to myself. The smell was of something different, something muddy and fecund.

I stepped further into the gloom. An ancient handmower rested against a wheelbarrow, small packets of seeds were arranged on a wooden rack designed for the purpose. The desiccated remains of failed gardening enterprises. A battered paper kite hung in one corner.

I trailed some fingers across a dusty cardboard box of papers and books and reached out idly to caress a thick, squat roll of brown carpet standing on its end in the middle of the floor. To my surprise it was not just wet, but warm as well. It moaned and turned around heavily. I found myself staring into a pair of dark, apelike eyes, framed by dank hair.

By now the rain had stopped. There were just the sounds and smells of our breathing.

4

He sat in the kitchen, naked and wet. A grey puddle formed on the floor beneath his chair. The long hair covering his entire body was flat and black against his shiny, pink skin. He didn't seem afraid, and made no sound apart from the occasional low groan, which may have been of distress or satisfaction, it was hard to tell.

He sat with his round shoulders hunched and hands clasped loosely upon his lean and hairy knees. Although his bearing changed very little, those large, sooty eyes circled ceaselessly and took in the entire room. It was difficult to know what he knew. He took no interest in the tin of baked beans open on the table in front of him, although his nostrils flared slightly when it was first set down. By now it was night. There was just the two of us. The back door and kitchen windows were all open wide to rid the house of his stench, a thick stench I could feel on my skin.

I was drinking from a bottle of sherry and eating chips from the local fish-and-chip shop, popping them into my mouth one by one. They were barely warm, like the small, narrow corpses of recently murdered things. I sat watching him on the opposite side of the table. Despite his hairy, unwieldy torso and barnyard eyes, he looked like a man. He breathed like a machine, deep and even.

5

He was still there two days later, but no drier. His wetness was apparently something that seeped from his pink skin. The puddle on the floor expanded and trickled away beneath the kitchen door. As far as I could tell, he had barely moved. I waved a hand in front of his eyes, I held up a piece of toast to his dark lips. When I tried to scare him by clapping my hands or banging two old cooking pots together, he just angled his head away and screwed up his round face a little. His body made a sticky sound when he moved.

'What are you, then?' I asked. His unresponsiveness was getting to me. 'What are you? Are you human? You stink like a fucking animal. You know that? You really stink.'

He sort of looked at me with his watery brown eyes and let out a rumbling groan, not of anger or frustration, but something darker and far more terrible. The sound vibrated in the air. I lit a cigarette and watched him. Smoke filled the small space between us. I drank.

6

Some time later, the following day or week, he was gone from the kitchen. I wondered if I had imagined the entire thing, but on the floor was a shallow puddle, and closer inspection revealed several clods of long, black hair. I looked through a grimy window into the garden. It was still raining. The shed door was still open. I imagined him snuffling around in there with his long, articulate fingers and liquid eyes. I would wait until the rain stopped and the place had dried out and then I would close the shed door and set fire to it, with him inside. I could wait. What else was I going to do?

It was only late morning and I was already in ruins. I checked my alcohol supplies and was relieved to discover an unopened cask of wine and half a bottle of port that I had forgotten buying. I made a quick calculation. If today was Friday, then tomorrow was Saturday, which meant I could still buy something locally until late if I needed to. Perfect.

I cut the mouldy corners from some bread to make toast and even managed to find some coffee on the laminated bench under the window. The wife must have bought it before she left. I was suddenly, inexplicably, in good spirits. I ate my breakfast, shaved off several weeks' worth of thick beard and stood in the kitchen doorway to smoke a cigarette. Rainwater fell from the gutters and eaves like a trembling curtain. God knows why, but the world seemed suddenly full of possibility.

There comes a brief moment in every bender when you're able to see things for what they are – not just what you construct in order to be able to keep drinking – and this was that moment. It is always frightening. I saw the tatty garden dotted with empty bottles and cans, the sink full of broken, mouldy dishes. I saw the stains on the walls and the wreckage of furniture, the cold skulking in the sharpest corners of the house. I held a hand in front of my face. It was like a foreign object, the nails ragged and worn, like something you'd use to dig in the dirt.

I flicked my cigarette butt into the garden and went back inside. It was time to clean the place up, to try and get things together again. I walked into the lounge room. It was dim and musty. I opened the curtains and window and there he was, sitting on the low couch with those hands, as always, clasped gently between his knees. He looked up at me with a look of something like embarrassment and it was like the first time, just the sounds of our breathing in that small, enclosed space. We looked at each other. 'What are you doing?' I yelled. '*What are you doing?*'

He didn't answer, of course. Made no sign he'd even understood. And then slowly, very deliberately, I picked up the telephone. I was going to call the police, call someone, the local loony bin or something and get them to come and take this thing away, this thing that had taken up residence in my house. In my house. He watched me with those begging eyes as I did it, as I raised the plastic receiver to my ear. And I watched him watching me, just so he knew exactly what was happening, but when I put the receiver to my ear, there was no tone, no sound of any sort, just the humming silence of an unpaid bill.

The moment, it seemed, had passed.

7

I woke up at some point in the day and waited. The bed smelled grey. Even from behind closed eyes, I could sense something was different but I was reluctant to find out what it could be. Whatever it was could wait. Things had moved beyond the point where I could reasonably expect them to actually get better. I could hear birds outside and the sighing of wind through trees.

When I opened my eyes, it was no surprise really. Just his dark eyes staring down at me. His body was still wet, and dripped slightly, although the terrible smell was gone. Either that, or I had become accustomed to it. We stared at each other for a long time, me lying on my back under a thin duvet, while he stood slack-shouldered at the end of the bed. I'm sure we could have stayed like that forever, trading blinks, waiting for something to happen.

After some time I pushed the duvet aside and swung around to put my feet on the cold, rough carpet. He stayed utterly still while I moved around the dim room and pulled on some clothes, although I knew in the time I staggered down the hall and through the front door on to the street, he had lumbered into my bed and eased himself beneath my covers.

Kirsty Gunn

Now I Can See How It Was, I Think

The McKays came in most weekends, or that's how it seemed anyhow, and always smelling of blood. Everyone knew they killed their animals. Uncle Neil, but the boys too, he taught them how to do it, then they'd all walk in through Gran's kitchen door Saturday morning, smiling the big white smiles like they had knives in them and carrying in their arms their parcels of meat.

'A beast . . .' That's what Uncle Neil called it, the thing that they were bringing in. Not cow, or sheep, or deer, only, 'I've got a beast for you here . . .' like it had never been alive on the farm, a creature with eyelashes and breath, but was altogether different and now it was dead.

'Hey.'

That was Davey. He was the eldest, and kind of like a man. He never used to say hello just 'hey' like that, while he chewed gum. 'Pull in, will you, so I can get past . . .' He'd come in behind me that way, so close, kicking the back of the chair where I was sitting and hoisting the newspaper lump he was carrying up on to his shoulders. 'Move in, I said.'

The second of his talking was gone before I could even think of anything to say. Gran might ask him a question, she might flip up the corner of the newspaper to look inside, 'What you got there, Davey? Forequarter?' but he didn't even answer her sometimes. Or he said, 'side' to Gran, like that, just one word for a reply, or it could be 'haunch' or 'shoulder', who knows? None of them spoke much. Just 'home-kill', that was McKay talk, their own language, like 'beast'. 'You want me to butcher that side further?' 'You want me to take a saw to that leg?' It seemed as though the rest of the world didn't exist when they were around, but everything had to be to do with hammering or saws or knives. As though everything about them in the end rested in those hefty, bloodied parcels that they carried into Gran's kitchen, piece after piece, to unwrap and rebag and label, lay down end-to-end in her freezer and try to kill the smell, the smell of more than skin that always hung around the McKays; a reminder, that odour, of who they were, and the kinds of things they did.

So Davey, sure, but they were all like that, three of them plus Uncle Neil, three boys, I mean, but they all seemed grown through and much older than boys Elisabeth and I knew, though Davey was younger than me and my sister, and William and Christopher just kids, still, who would have guessed it. They were skinny and tall, with long hair straggling down their backs, and burned dark by the sun, from being outside all the time, I guess, and Aunty Clare not bothering to call them in. Going past those mornings, through to the laundry where Gran kept her freezer; a big one like a coffin and, twice as cold, she said. They would sort things out in there, and Elisabeth and I were supposed to just finish our breakfast while they did it, eat the little triangles of toast, put the jam spoon back in the dish.

'You boys okay in there?' Gran called out, but of course they didn't answer and then Uncle Neil would come out and he smiled the big smile again.

'Get the pan on, honey . . .' he said.

That was the routine, the way they'd come in and offload, then Uncle Neil liked to cook up something from the animal they'd just brought in. There was the smell the cooking gave off, in that sunny kitchen of my grandmother's, and she hated it, because of the mess they made, she complained about it, but Uncle Neil would just come up beside her and kiss her, snake his hand a bit up her skirt.

'C'mon . . .' he'd say to her. 'C'mon . . .'

I don't know what was going on there. Our gran showed her teeth like an old wolf at him when he did that, she would turn around and whip him hard with a metal spoon or dishrag, but she was often laughing too. And Uncle Neil, well, nothing would scare him. He'd hold out pieces of the liver or heart he was going to fry for us to look at while they were still raw.

'Not much of him left now, girls, eh, that old beastie? But we'll eat him up, anyhow. What you say?'

He kept his hand there with the red on it and I could smell its blood smell and Uncle Neil's breath.

'What you doing, Dad?' said Christopher, when he came out of the laundry, and the others, Davey and William behind him.

'Just showing our little town girls something from the country . . .'

'Yeah?'

'Yeah.'

Davey kept chewing gum. The others smiled.

For our uncle it was like an act he went through, this kind of talk, as though he had something to flaunt in front of us and we had no way of coming back, no words. There really was nothing my sister and I could do that might make any sense to him. He put on a voice for us, sometimes, when he arrived, like we were supposed to understand it as a joke and find it funny, something about us being the little girls from town, and asking how was our daddy, don't you know, 'the professor'. 'Do give your father my *kindest* regards . . .' He wouldn't have talked that way to anybody else. Our father wasn't there to hear it for himself, once or twice maybe, but mostly he drove us up there to Gran's at the beginning of summer and he might stay one night, but the McKays and my father together is not an image I hold a lot of in my mind. So, it was Uncle Neil saying to me and my sister instead, 'How was it, *gels,* in . . .?' and he pronounced 'town' this way: '*tine*'. It was because of our father, he said, to show respect. 'Don't we boys? Have to show some respect here, though the professor isn't with us?' But the boys just stood around, they weren't even listening to him, Davey grinned maybe, his face dark and bony and strong looking, just chewing that gum.

So it's pretty clear Elisabeth and I were made to be the children there, made to feel we were. Just dumb town girls, our own enlarged hearts with the McKays around the only certain thing about us, like the way we felt the whole world was full of boys when they were there, of men. Of their smell, and the darkness of their skins, that hair they pushed back out of their eyes . . . They were our cousins but something else, because of where they lived; 'farm boys'. Sometimes I used to say those words to myself in my mind, before I went to sleep, saw the boys take shape around the words, those old T-shirts of theirs ripped through, their dark, capable hands, the way they would twist their fingers into their mouths to make the high shrill whistle that would bring back dogs and horses from the hills. *Farm boys . . .*

Hard to believe our mother had been their mother's sister. That's what I thought back then, hard to believe there could be any connections. After all, Aunty Clare had married entirely in, become so farm herself that way, so entirely McKay by now it could have been as though she'd never had any other family. She let Uncle Neil grab her whenever he wanted and kiss her in that hungry, gobbling way – she didn't mind. And she had a new baby and another one growing inside her. She arrived with the rest of them those mornings, but coming later in, her stomach sticking out and the baby balanced on her hip like an extra bag of shopping. The bra strap might be coming down off her shoulder and the skirt of her dress riding up, and she just flopped down on one of Gran's chairs and stretched out her legs before her. 'Make me a cup of tea, will you, Mum, I'm exhausted. Hi girls, want to hold the baby?'

I remember she wore red lipstick though, and I guess that was a bit of her there, in the lipstick that I could see might be like my mother still.

'No, no. They were different,' Gran said, when I asked her about the two of them. 'It suits Clare, but that life never would have been right for Charlotte. You can see that, can't you?' she said. 'You can see it in her room?'

You could see it. My mother's bedroom Gran kept just the same as when she'd been a young girl still living at home with her, and my sister and I spent a lot of time in that place. It had a fragrance to it, a kind of sealed-off reminder, like a chamber in a fairy tale where something had been live once, a princess, but now she was somewhere else and sleeping. Might she come back? There was a little dressing table, glass jars for creams all laid out upon it like our mother might just walk in and sit down before the mirror, start brushing her hair in that long, quiet way. That's how it would have been I can imagine. That she would have kept herself apart that way, in front of her mirror with the creams, preparing herself for the moment when she would step outside again to do whatever it was she was going to do out there. It was the kind of mirror you could turn out or in so you could see the back of your head in it and I bet my mother used to turn it that way, too, when she was a girl; look in the mirror and see from the back how she might appear later, to someone who was standing behind her, who could see for himself how exposed it was, that bare and empty part at the back of her neck . . .

Oh, yeah.

That's what Uncle Neil said.

Your mother was something else, all right.

Until I got that part figured, though, my sister and I only had little bits of detail like the things in our mother's room to go on. These bits of memories, and maybe we were making them up too. The dances and the clever university lectures with our dad . . . Making up all that stuff about her out of the room Gran kept with the hairbrush and face powder compact laid out and the silky underwear in drawers because, really, in the end, who knew who she was? We were kept apart, Elisabeth and I, outside the possibility of knowledge, the way adults hate to think children might be living in the same world as their own. Though we took the baby sometimes, put him down to crawl around on the floor . . . Though we lived whole summers in our grandmother's house . . . We were the girls, 'the two girls'; it's what I could have named this story. And we stayed being 'the two girls' for quite a while, the boys still pushing past us those Saturday mornings, going straight out into the garden after they'd eaten, when they were done with the meat.

But more and more Elisabeth and I wanted to be in the coolness of our mother's room. There was the perfume, powder that we could dust behind our ears . . . It was safe there, with its quiet and shade, a place where my sister and I could believe we had a kind of power, gathering something up in the scent and silken underwear that, like our mother, maybe later we could go out into the world of men and use.

Aunty Clare got worse at not letting us be there though. She'd never liked the idea of our mother's bedroom. Gran said that she wasn't allowed to go in there, not Aunty Clare, not any of the McKays, but still Aunty Clare would come looking for us after we'd put the baby down. 'You girls in here again? Get out, it's not healthy!' Throwing open the door. 'Come on, now! Outside!' Calling through the open window. 'Davey! Be a sport, honey! The little girls want to come outside and play with you!'

No one wanted to play, of course – we were all of us growing up, and for my part it scared me how much I wanted to watch Davey when his mother forced us to be together this way. Watching him from the corner of the garden where Elisabeth and I sat in our little huddle by the roses, this boy who wasn't even twelve yet but he seemed to have all knowledge in him, a thing that reached down to a part of me I hadn't even known was there. Aunty Clare would have shooed Elisabeth and I outside like we were chickens and foolish, with our cotton dresses on, and our knickers underneath, and he'd be just laid out there on the grass in the sun, his long skinny body of a boy, or he'd get up to stretch, reach up to the branch of the apple tree and hang from it: 'What you girls want to play then? Eh? What game?'

It worked for a time then, as his mother wanted: Davey and Christopher coming up with things to do, and though Davey seemed bored with us already, still we went through the motions of children playing. Walking along the tops of the cattle fences over the road from Gran's house, that was one game, and they were high, those fences, and you could fall. Or they'd make us go running across the highway at the end of town, counting five first when you saw a lorry and then out on to the road and you had to cross it before you got killed. Yet, though in those games I tried harder and harder to be first, to be fastest, nothing either Elisabeth or I did made any difference, in the game, or outside it; made the McKays like us, Davey notice me, want to talk to me. He'd just stand there, maybe with the others, with Christopher and William, or on his own, chewing that wad of gum of his and I was the one wanted to be inside his mouth, with his tongue and his white teeth, to be right inside and for him to let me stay.

So . . . like mother, like daughter, I suppose. Leaving the most private place to come outdoors, and, though I was forced to go and my mother may have chosen it for both of us we were closing behind us a door that kept behind it the mirror, the wardrobe and the neatly made bed as though they were contents of a dream. Outside, of course it was so different. Yet the dream knowledge was there, just the same, in us like a memory, and from it I guess came the same things, to want the same things, my mother and I, the same kind of people. It was the scent of my mother's powder, after all, I was wearing, and though the paleness in the bright sunshine of my sister and I next to our cousin's dark is an image from the past, from me, it's also from my mother's life, you see it now, how it rises up again here in my grandmother's garden.

The day Aunty Clare called Elisabeth and me 'the little girls' for the last time was one of these same mornings I've been writing about, Elisabeth and I in our mother's room, at the dressing table, and Aunty Clare came in and made us leave and outside the McKays were over by the fruit trees. Again I felt that brutal thing of the closeness of the boys, after being somewhere separate and protected, the closeness of Davey standing there, but then he said to me that day 'Hello' when he saw me. 'Look what I've got . . .'

It was the first time he'd ever done that, spoken to me that way, not a 'hey' or a kick.

He had something in his hand. 'Come over here,' he said, and then he smiled.

I saw it was alive, the thing he was holding, a little cat, the stray who lived under Gran's house we called Alice, and sometimes Gran let us feed her and let her come inside.

'I want you to help me with something,' Davey said to me then.

The other boys were looking on, grinning. 'Go on . . .' they were saying to him. 'Get on with it. Just get on with it.'

'What?' I said. I took a step towards Davey.

'Don't,' came Elisabeth's voice behind me. The McKays did this, after all, all the time, had these animals that were half tame, like Alice, like pets almost, but then they finished with them just the same.

'I know,' I said to Elisabeth, but still I took another step towards my boy. He was still looking at me, wasn't he? He was still smiling.

'You going to come over here,' he said, 'or what?'

Elisabeth said again, 'Don't, Susan,' but I said to her, 'What? What's wrong?'

I remember the grass, bright green, around us, and this feeling of a thing in my body and my body couldn't contain it. *Bang, bang*. My heart.

'Nothing's wrong,' Davey said. 'Just come over, Susan,' and I did, I walked towards him.

He had a string round Alice's neck, I saw when I got close. He was holding her by the legs and she was scratching him and biting him but he didn't even notice. He closed his other hand over her face, crouched down.

'Listen . . .' he said to me.

I squatted down beside him.

'I want you to help me decide, okay? Because animals like this are no use to anyone, they don't do anything, just get diseases and the mange. So we have to work out, see? What we're going to do. How we're going to do it.'

His face was right next to mine, there was the close tangle of his hair. I didn't know what to say. Sometimes I had patted the cat, in the past when she was inside, or had had something to eat, but she was wild and terrified now and Davey's face was next to mine, his arm was touching my arm.

'I don't know,' I said.

'You scared?' He leaned in, breathed the words into my ear. *You scared?*

'We kill cats like this on the farm, all the time.'

I looked at him and Alice twisting in his hands, this boy made of dark skin and hard bone and muscle. I could feel him right there, his whole body, and the texture of his breath – does that make sense? – was all around me, his presence, those words in my ear, and I put both my hands on his arms then, and I closed my fingers tight as I could around his arms.

'Shit!' he said. 'What are you –' and the little cat went crazy, she struggled, raked him up the leg and drew a thick line of blood. Then Davey went to lick it but I got him first, opened my mouth and found his mouth, I slid myself right in. I pushed my tongue in deeper and deeper, until he opened up wide enough to let me and then it was like I couldn't stop, I couldn't.

I had blood on me, from him, when I was done.

It was the scratch on his leg, smeared everywhere. Maybe I should have licked it clean – but I was finished with him by then. I pushed his hair back from his face, and blood was on his face too, from me, where I'd been on him, it was on his neck, his arms . . . I helped him sit up. The little cat was still there. Davey must have released her but the string around her neck had caught against a bit of the tree and she was caught, half strangled trying to get away. I reached over and unthreaded the piece that was tied up and she shot off, the string still attached, back under the house where she'd come from.

Elisabeth was there beside me then. 'Look,' she said, and pointed.

I turned, and there at the kitchen window was Uncle Neil. 'He's been watching you,' Elisabeth said.

'What have the girls been doing?' Uncle Neil said when we all got inside. His back was to us, at the kitchen bench and his arms were messy with something he'd been chopping, lying along the draining board in pieces.

'Just nothing,' I said.

He put down the knife and turned around. 'I've been watching nothing then?' he said.

I looked at his eyes, blue as ever, blue, blue in that dark face.

'I saw what you did to my poor little boy . . .' he said to me and then he looked at me, up and down, very slowly, and he gave a long, low whistle. 'Whee-ew . . .'

Then Aunty Clare came in. 'What's going on here?' she said.

It was like everything was gone still, like a painting, vivid, the boys there standing at the window, Elisabeth by the bench. My dress was torn from the cat scratching, and there were smears of red from Davey's blood but I felt very still myself, in the painting, like my colours were done very bright.

'Well, I don't know,' Uncle Neil said. 'But you should have seen her, honey. What she did to our little boy.' He was talking to Aunty Clare, but not taking his eyes off me. 'I mean, just look at her, will you?'

'Oh, shut up, Neil!' Aunty Clare turned away.

'But what she did. To Davey, here. It's got me thinking. Maybe, you know, your gorgeous big sister didn't drive herself into that wall after all ...' He touched my shoulder with the tip of his finger. 'Maybe ...' he said. 'Because seeing my girl here ... Why, it's like ...'

'Shut up!'

'But it's like she's still here, sweetheart. Your big sister. Going to come out now from that room where you've been playing –'

Aunty Clare swung around and punched him.

'Oh, yeah,' he said to me then, 'your mother was something else, all right.'

Aunty Clare yelled at him, 'You jerk!' and she punched him again but it made no difference, he didn't even notice. He just kept on talking and it was all about my mother, and I didn't look away, I looked right back at him as he went on and on. The boys were still hunched over by the windows in a little pack, and my sister was standing beside me, Uncle Neil telling me all this stuff about him and my mother and Aunty Clare was starting to cry ... And looking back, at all of this ... Now I can see how it was, I think. It's taken me long enough, but writing it down I understand it, I think so: that they'd needed to keep us at a distance, my sister and me, in order to keep us all safe. Because none of us had any choice in any of this. We were family; despite everything we all did to make each other feel otherwise, Elisabeth and I were connected, related, to these people who swore and showed their teeth and used their hands the way they did ... And it must have been just as strange for them, having us around. In the end, no choice for them either, and all because of our mother. The one who'd left. Left first that scented room, her mother, these people who still lived here now she'd left them behind, then left her husband too, her children ... Left all of us, so in the end, all we had left, somehow, was in each other, of her.

*

'It doesn't matter,' I said to Uncle Neil.

'Doesn't matter?' he said. 'What do you mean it doesn't matter? About your mother, course it matters. Just remember it was you who got me started, sweetheart, why . . . You should have seen her, Clare, this one . . .' But Aunty Clare was only crying, 'Just shut up, shut up.'

'Stop it the pair of you,' Gran said, coming in.

Elisabeth and I had to let them be. It was over with, just repetition now of the same thing, the same old thing they might let for years go round and round. We just walked out of that room where they all were and went off somewhere; Elisabeth's idea, I don't remember where. Hours seemed to pass, a whole long day in itself though it wouldn't have been that long and when we came back to the house they'd all gone; it was quiet. Elisabeth never said anything about what had happened, with me, how I'd been with Davey on the grass, she never said another word. We went and looked under the house to see if we could see Alice and she was there, and we coaxed her to come back out. Carefully I cut the thread from around her neck that was so tight and we brought her inside. We put her on the bed in our room and stroked her and settled her but when we stood up, my sister and I, to go, she ran out the open window and back under the house to that dark place where she'd come from, where she'd been born, I guess, and where she would stay.

Desmond Hogan

Belle

I first made her acquaintance in the cabin the little man who worked on the railway lived in, when I was eleven.

On his wall was an advertisement for Y-fronts based on James Fenimore Cooper's *The Last of the Mohicans* – Hawkeye and Uncas the Mohican with butch cuts, in Y-fronts, marching alongside one another with a turkey in longjohns bearing a mace on front of them; a photograph of Cardinal Tien, Archbishop of Peking and exiled Primate of China; Margaret Mitchell in a black ante-bellum dress with an aigrette of gems at her neck; a photograph of a boy with sideburns in nothing but a peach, waisted coat and brothel creepers; and his sterling possession, a postcard of Belle Brinklow, the London Music Hall artiste who'd married the young Earl of the local manor – red cinnamon hair, heliotrope eyes, mousselaine Gibson Girl dress with scarlet flannel belt, the words *To the Idol of My Heart* underneath.

The manor was now a boys' school and when I started there boys had pudding-bowl Beatles haircuts, wore dun and wine turtleneck jerseys and Australian bush shoes with elasticated sides.

There were three mementoes of the Belle still in the school

A lunette-shaped daguerreotype of her music hall colleague, Maude Branscombe clinging to the cross of Christ.

A Worcester coffee pot with tulip trees and quail on it that she and Bracebridge, the young Earl, used have their hot chocolate from.

A portrait Sarah Purser did of the Belle when she was working on the stained-glass windows of Loughrea Cathedral nearby – for which the Belle donned her music hall apparel: shepherdess hat with a demi-wreath of cornflowers, ostrich feather boa, pearl seed choker, tearose pink dress with double puff sleeves, bouquet of lavender and asters from the autumn garden in her hand.

Belle Brinklow, who was from Bishop's Stortford, used to perform in theatres with names like the Globe, Royal Alfred, Britannia, Surrey, Creswick, Trocadero, Standard, and in singsong halls of pubs like the Black Horse in Piccadilly and the Cider Cellars in Maiden Lane.

An orchestra in front with brass, woodwind, percussion; a bit of Brussels carpet on the stage; a dropscene of Edinburgh Castle or a Tudor village.

In a Gainsborough hat or a Cossack hat, she'd do the cancan – 'La Carmagnole' of the French Revolution, a handkerchief skirt dance, a barefoot Persian dance or a clog dance; in a Robin Hood jacket, knee breeches, silk stockings, in Pierrot costume, in bell-bottom trousers and coatee she'd sing songs like 'They Call Me the Belle of Dollis Hill' or 'Street Arab Song':

'Out at
Dawn, nothing got to do.'

Then a man in a bat cloak and viridian tights might come on and recite a bit of Shakespeare:

'Now for our Irish wars –
We must supplant those rough rugheaded kerns,
Which live like venom . . .'

One Shakespearian actor who followed her died on stage, in a biretta and medieval cardinal red, reciting Cardinal Wolsey's farewell speech from *Henry VIII*.

Occasionally the Belle teamed up with her sister who was another Belle – who otherwise wore woodland hats – for the purpose of doing leg shoes, both of them in winged Mercury hats, tight bodices and gossamer tulle basket skirts with foamy petticoats.

They did matinées at the Gaiety Theatre on the Strand where Ireland's leader, Charles Stewart Parnell and the hoydenish Kitty O'Shea, who wore dresses fastened to the neck with acorn buttons, fell in love in a box during a performance in 1880.

The duettists were known to conclude performances with the singing of 'Shepherd of Souls' from 'The Sign of the Cross'.

Bracebridge was one of the few men who were allowed back-stage. Others were Lord MacDuff, the Marquess of Anglesea, Sir George Wombwell and the notorious Posno brothers, both of whom were fond of turning up in deerstalkers.

In a Chinese red waistcoat from Poole's Gentleman's Outfitters, Limerick gloves in hand, cornucopia of golden cockerel hair, eyes the blue of the woodland bugle flower, Bracebridge came into her dressing room one night and escorted her to Jimmies – the St James's Restaurant in Piccadilly.

Afterwards they'd go to the Adelaide Galleries – the Gatti's Restaurant in the Strand or Evan's Song and Supper Rooms where there was a madrigal choir.

She married him in a dragonfly blue Art Nouveau dress with a music hall corsage of myrtle blossoms in St James's in Piccadilly.

At the end of the nineteenth century and at the beginning of the twentieth there was a craze for music hall girls to marry into the peerage.

In 1884, Kate Vaughan, star of 'Flowers and Words' by Gilbert Hastings McDermott, married Colonel Arthur Frederick Wellesley, son of the Earl of Cowley and nephew of the Duke of Wellington.

Three years after the Belle married Bracebridge, Connie Gilchrist married the Earl of Orkney.

Maud Hobson married a Captain of the IIth Hussars and went to Samoa with him, where she befriended Robert Louis Stevenson and sang 'Pop Me on the Pier' at Brighton to him while he was dying.

In the mid nineties, Rosie Boote, the County Tipperary music hall girl, who was fond of posing in Doges' hats, married the Marquess of Headfort and became the Marchioness of Headfort.

At the beginning of the twentieth century, Lilian Sylvia Storey became the Countess Poulett. Denise Orme, Baroness Churston. Olive 'Meatyard' May, Countess of Drogheda. And Irene Richards married Lord Drumlanrig.

One music hall girl was courted by an Italian count who bought her a silvered leopard skin coat worth three thousand pounds. She ran away with him, he divested her of her coat and she came back to the stage door begging for work, was sent to music halls in the

North where Jennie Hill used to polish pewter in pubs during the day and sing in the song halls at night before being acclaimed on the London music hall stage.

As late as 1925, Beatrice Lillie married Robert Peel, great-grandson of the Prime Minister.

Before the Belle left for Ireland, Bracebridge brought her to a production of *The Colleen Bawn* at Her Majesty's in Haymarket, which was about a young lord in the West of Ireland who married a peasant girl, got tired of her and drowned her. The horses refused to cross the bridge to his place of execution and he got out and walked to his own execution.

In the small and foul-smelling Broadstone Station where they got a train to the West she wore a black riding hat with foxtail feathers and a bear muff, he a Hussar-blue covert coat with brandenbourgs – silk barrel-shaped buttons.

On the terrace of the manor he showed her how the pear and cherry blossom came first, then the apple, then lilac, then the chestnut and laburnum, the oak last. He indicated the kitten caterpillar, the thrush snail, the speckled wood butterfly which were abundant because the garden bordered on the woods, approached by the Long Walk.

A year after she arrived in Ireland, the Irish clown Johnny Patterson, with whom she frequently appeared on the London stage, was killed during a riot at a circus in Castleisland, County Kerry.

Four years after she came to Ireland her friend, the Belle Daisy Hughes, after a performance at the Brighton Empire, threw herself from the balcony of the Grand Hotel, Brighton, to her death.

The Belle gave two performances in Ireland.

One at the Gaiety Theatre where, shortly after its opening in 1871, Emily Soldene rode a horse on stage in Renaissance page boy leggings.

In a beefeater-red chiffon dress, trimmed with petals, against a dropscene of Sleepy Hollow in Wicklow, she sang 'When the Happy Time Shall Come' from H J Byron's 'The Bohemian Girl', 'The Belle of High Society', 'Molly the Marchioness', 'O, I Love Society', 'Tommy Atkins', 'The Butler Kissed the Housemaid, the

Footman Kissed the Cook', 'It Was a Year Ago', 'Love, in the Balmy Summer Time'. She shared the bill with an underwater acrobatic couple in broadly striped bathing costumes who displayed in a tank, and 'Nat Emmett's Performing Goats'.

The other was at the Leinster Hall in Hawkins Street where, shortly after it opened as the New Theatre Royal in 1821, a bottle was thrown at the Lord Lieutenant. In the Old Theatre Royal in Smock Alley, guns were used to clear the audience off the stage.

In a tartan dress and glengarry – a Scottish hat – against a dropscene of Galway Docks with swans, she sang 'The Titsy Bitsy Girl', 'Tip I Addy Ay', 'Louisiana Lou', 'Her Golden Hair', 'I Saw Esau Kissing Kate', 'Our Lodger's Such a Nice Young Man', 'Maisie is a Daisy', and the oldest vaudeville song, 'Lillibulero', sung by the victors after the Battle of the Boyne, and sung in Dublin as part of an all child cast production of *The Beggar's Opera* in 1729.

On the bill with her were dogs ridden by monkeys in jockey caps and Miss Hunt's possum-faced Ladies' Orchestra, all in bicorne hats and Hussar uniforms, who played Thomas Moore's 'Melodies' to a weeping audience.

Captain O'Shea, Kitty O'Shea's husband, whose mother was a papal countess, had been Member of Parliament for Bracebridge's area, Parnell having endorsed him with a speech in Galway in 1886; and the Bishop of Galway alleged it was a prostituted constituency in return for Captain O'Shea's connivance in the Parnell–Kitty O'Shea liason.

When Captain O'Shea finally decided to sue for divorce at the end of 1889, the year the Belle came to Ireland, by all accounts the London music hall stage had a feast, and the hilarity was compounded by a maid's declaration at the divorce trial that Parnell had once escaped out of the window by means of a rope fire escape.

Parnell was represented with a Quaker collar, frock coat, Shetland clown's trousers, hobnail boots. Comediennes wore whalebone corsetting to emphasize Kitty O'Shea's rotundities. Captain O'Shea was usually endowed with an enlarge-curliecue moustachio, like a Dion Boucicault sheriff.

'Notty Charlie Parnell!' Dropscene painters had a Hibernian

spree. One Parnell production featured a Barbary ape in a bowler hat, sealskin waistcoat, trousers embroidered with salad-green shamrocks.

At the end of the 1890s the Belle heard how comedians came on stage in London dressed in prison uniform, and their comedienne partners addressed them as 'Oscar' with a flip of a hand.

Lord Alfred Douglas wore a school straw or a domed, wide-brimmed child's hat, Eton jacket with white carnation, drawers, calf stockings, his cheeks the red of a carousel horse's cheeks.

The Prince of Wales, shortly to be Edward VII, an afficianado of the music halls, was said to have turned his back in his box when Lord Alfred Douglas was presented in black and pink striped drawers. But shocked ladies actually left the theatre when he appeared in Jaeger pyjamas with frogged breast buttons.

In 1900 the Belle was one of the ladies who helped serve bon-bonnieres to 15,000 children in the Phoenix Park on the occasion of the visit by Queen Victoria, a return visit to the city where in 1849 she autographed the *Book of Kells*.

The Guards Band on the terrace of Windsor Castle were one day playing one of the music hall songs the Belle used to sing, 'Come Where the Booze is Cheap', when Queen Victoria, who was taught singing by Mendelssohn, sent Lady Antrim to find out what the wonderful music was.

The Belle's colleague Kate Vaughan's marriage broke up with Colonel Arthur Frederick Wellesley and she went to Johannesburg where, in elbow gloves on bare arms and a corsage of wild garde-nias, she became the Belle of the Gaiety Theatre there. Shortly after she wrote to the Belle about the mauve raintree and the coral tree with cockatoo flowers, she died; on a night when Gertie Millar, who was to marry the Earl of Dudley, was playing in one of her roles in 'Ali Baba' in London. The Belle had a photograph of her disembarking at Capetown in a matinée hat.

The owl-like Catholic landlord in neighbouring Loughrea, renowned for promoting boys' choirs, decided to build a new cathedral, and the Belle and Bracebridge would often take a brougham there and watch the stained-glass windows being put in, most often speedwell-blues, and sometimes at evening the Belle would stand under windows depicting the Ascension and Last

Judgement and recall visits before shows with the French music hall artiste Madame Desclause in her black Second Empire dress, to the Royal Bavarian Church in Piccadilly.

On late autumn afternoons as they returned from Loughrea, the beeches would be old gold and the bushes assaulted to misshape.

A music hall poster which depicted a chorus girl holding up a short dress edged in chinchilla-like material caused clerical outrage in Cork but the clergy were appeased by the King's frequent visits to the music hall, very often in a kilt with cockade on his stockings. A Dublin music hall caused all round offence by featuring Admiral Nelson from Nelson's Pillar in Sackville Street with Lady Hamilton in a negligée. The King visited Galway for the second time in his reign, in gaiters, the Queen in pillarbox red with a Spanish riding hat; a group of Connaught Rangers singing a music hall song, 'Tara-ra-boom-de-ay', as an anthem for them.

Bound in red morocco, the Belle read *Jane Eyre* by Charlotte Brontë, who'd died in childbirth in the neighbourhood, married to a parson, Arthur Bell Nicholls, and was remembered for walking alone in a barège dress by the Shannon.

On the terrace the Belle and Bracebridge would incessantly play on a horn gramophone a Gramophone and Typewriter record of Joseph O'Mara singing 'Friend and Lover', as they had their hot chocolate from a tray with the rose, the thistle, the shamrock. Bracebridge sometimes took an opera hat to Kilkee in the summer where they had listened to the German band on the boardwalk. The gilt and cranberry theatres of Dublin magneted with pantomimes – *Jack and the Beanstalk*, *Puss in Boots*, *Aladdin* and *Princess Badroulboudour*.

There was a brief visit to Belgium where they looked at a Rubens painting. Auburn moustachio. Watermelon-pink cleavage. Plumed hat. Boy with peach slashings on his arms. Cirrus horse. Despite the smiles the sky tells you that war is near.

The Belle was one of the Ladies' Committee who saw the Connaught Rangers off from the North Wall in August 1914, with chocolates and madeleines.

The swallows in the eaves had a second brood that year and didn't leave until October. When the alders were in white, pulpy berry on either side of the Forty Steps at the end of the Long Walk she'd go there, stand on top of the steps, sing her music hall songs lest they be stamped out in her.

Soldiers camped in the desmesne and at night sang 'It's a Long Way to Tipperary' which the Melbourne music hall girl Florrie Forde, who ran away when she was fourteen, used to sing, the words printed an inch high at the footlights so thousands could join in.

A late Indian summer visit to Kilkee – dramatic mare's-tails in the morning sky, a dense fruit of bindweed flowers on the bushes, ladybirds doing trapeze acts on withered fleabane, the late burnet roses becoming clusters of black berries, a dolphin threshing in the horseshoe bay. A coloratura rendition of 'Take, Oh Take Those Lips Away' from *The Bohemian Girl* at an evening get together by a man with a Van Dyke beard, when news came that the mail boat was sunk just after leaving Kingston Harbour, with the loss of five hundred lives.

During the War of Independence, from a window, over bonfires at night or under the ornamental crab apple tree or the weeping pear tree in the garden she could hear the soldiers sing songs from the music halls: 'On Monday I Walked Out with a Soldier', 'The Girl the Soldiers Always Leave Behind Them', 'All Through Sticking to a Soldier', 'Aurelia Was Always Fond of Soldiers', 'Soldiers of the Queen', but especially, 'Soldiers in the Park', which was where they were, burning leaves.

When the Black and Tans raced up and down Sackville Street in vans covered in wire and there was a curfew, she was one of Dublin's few theatregoers, taking the train from a house in Dalkey – which replaced summer bivouacs in Morrison's Hotel in Dawson Street – to Harcourt Street Station, in a taffeta hobble skirt, tied near the ankle with sash lace, so that the Horrible Hobble of British taste made her less likely to be a target.

It was commonplace in those days to see Countess Marcievicz, the Minister for Labour in the Revolutionary Government, cycling around Dublin on a battered bicycle, in a beehive bonnet from which cherries dangled. Her sister, Eva Gore Booth, had devoted part of her life in England to the rights of women music hall artistes.

The need to perform overcame the Belle because she sang 'Goo-Goo' from *The Earl and the Girl* at a concert in the Theatre Royal, Limerick, spring 1922, in aid of those made homeless by the War of Independence. She was photographed on that occasion outside Joseph O'Mara's house, Hartstonge House – Eton crop hair now, pumps with Byzantine, diamanté buckles.

The Belle and Bracebridge were in Saint Nicholas Cathedral in Galway in early summer 1922, to see the Colours of the Connaught Rangers, the Harp and Crown on yellow, which dated back to 1793, being removed, on the first stage of their journey to Windsor Castle.

At the beginning of 1923, during the Civil War, the Belle started out two days early, joining hordes from his native Athlone, defying derailed trains and broken bridges, to hear John McCormack singing 'The Last Rose of Summer' in a black cloak lined with ruby silk, at a home visit concert.

Near the Forty Steps that spring, with its bloody cranesbill and its blue cranesbill, she found an abandoned blackbird's nest, covered in moss.

There were ladybird roundabouts in the Fair Green when she and Bracebridge left, childless, to live in a Queen Anne Revival lodge near the redbrick Victorian Gothic Church of Saint Chad's in Birmingham; but not before she was received into the Roman Catholic Church, under a portrait of Cardinal Wiseman in garnet red, in the local church – joining the faith of a London music hall Belle who claimed to be related to Father Prout the Poet, a Cork priest who penned 'The Shandon Bells', rowed with his native city, was an associate of Charles Dickens and W M Thackeray, mixed his priestly duties with the Bohemian life, travelled as far as Hungary and Asia Minor with his Latin translations of the songs of Thomas Moore, was a leading attraction at Mrs Jameson's Sunday evening parties in Rome, and ended up with his rosary and palmbook in a mezzanine in Paris.

The manor was sold to priests, there were people cycling on the Suck that winter it was so cold, and the priests came and taught Thucydides.

One of the inculabula which survived the transaction, which

instilled fear in the boys, especially at Lent, was one with an illustration of Charlotte of Brunswick in a celestial blue dress, with matching jacket edged in swansdown, and a high-crowned Elizabethan gentleman's hat, banging on the doors of Westminster Cathedral during the Coronation of George IV in 1820, demanding to be allowed in as the Queen of England, the doors barred against her.

It joined the books which the priests favoured, which were books with illustrations by Arthur Rackham so that boys going to the school got a vision of life with boys in bathing costumes and girls in dresses with sailor's trim by the tide's edge; New York streets crowded with pigs in Derby or cloche hats; women in mobcaps cherishing their babies in clapboard New England towns; couples enshrined in fourposter beds with rose motif curtains; barefooted girls carrying bundles wrapped in peacock-eye patterned cloth through fox-coloured forests; Ancient Irish heroes in togas doing marathon runs; small boys in glove-fitting short trousers stomping on plethoric daisies; barebreasted Rhinemaidens in Heimkunst rites.

Just before I left England I visited a man in Bath who'd been a student in the school during the Second World War when a song the Belle sang, 'Maisie is a Daisy', was revived and sung on radio by Maidie Andrews alongside Gracie Fields's 'So I'm Sending a Letter to Santa Claus to Bring Daddy Safely Home to Me'.

A Palladian square of the Adam style, facade breaking into towers . . . A man with a Noah beard in the green, brown and off-white of the Epicurean Graigian sect on it . . . A room with lyres, garlands, acanthus on the walls . . . A man with mud-green eyes, hirsute brows, in a lap robe, reflected in a photograph of a Beau Brummell of the Irish Midlands in a striped beach jacket and cricket shirt.

Christmas 1943, shortly after Churchill, Stalin and Roosevelt met in Teheran, he played Fifi, in Salvation Army fatigues, in *The Belle of New York* at the school, having played Prudence in *The Quaker Girl* the year before, and Countess Angela in *The Count of Luxembourg*.

The production was directed by a priest who'd seen the new

Pope, Eugenio Pacelli, being hailed with the Nazi salute by German boy scouts summer 1939. He'd caught a swim in the shock cerulean Mediterranean in Portovenere, where Byron used to swim, on the day the German-Soviet Non-Aggression Pact was signed.

As Fifi, the man I visited had to to sing 'Teach Me How to Kiss, Dear', a song which became popular in the rugby changing rooms.

The priest-director commented that he was an annual reminder that the Emperor Nero had married a boy.

Each night when Blinky Bill – who had a slight goat's moustache and was fond of quoting, 'Tragedy is true Guise. Comedy lies' from his schoolteacher father in Creggs, County Galway where Parnell made his last rain-soaked speech – sang 'She is the Belle of New York', the ghost of the Belle could be seen in the wings in a harem-scarem skirt – a skirt with cuffed and buttoned ankles like Turkish pantaloons, summer sombrero, music hall droplet earrings under shingled hair.

C. D. Rose

The *Neva Star*

There is a ship moored in the port of Naples that has been there now for three years. In all this time, it has moved no more than a few inches, backwards and forwards, from side to side. This is not an entirely unusual situation, as there are many ships in many ports around the world which have found themselves abandoned by bankrupted owners, impounded by national authorities, deserted by soon to be ex-magnates, orphaned by unpaid bills. In Genoa there is a ship that has been there for five years, and in Venice one for seven. An old ship moored in the port of Naples for three years is not an entirely unusual situation. All over the seafaring world there are ships that are flying the flag of the Bolivian and Mongolian merchant navies.

The *Neva Star* is a large dry cargo and tanker ship, designed for sea and river use, with a reinforced hull so it can break ice from Archangels to Murmansk. It is registered in Odessa and is as rusty as a nail. It is 115 metres long and has three thin decks. It is painted orange and white. The bottom part of the ship is orange, and the upper part of it is white. White and rust, orange and rust. The ship was built in Rumania thirty-five years ago and has since travelled over twenty thousand miles, sailing from Valletta to Leith to Rotterdam, from unlikely capital to unlikely capital, back to Odessa where it began and, now, to Naples.

There used to be a crew of seventy, but sixty-seven of them (mostly Russian, some Ukrainian, many Rumanian, and many others from many other countries) have now all disappeared. There are now three sailors on board. The three sailors have now been there for three years. Three years plus the three months they spent arriving in Naples from Odessa. Nobody knows what happened to the captain. Sergei, the first mate, passes much of his time thinking of his wife Masha. He has lived with Masha since when

St Petersburg was called Leningrad. Once, many years ago, Masha had the chance to leave Russia and go to Israel. She packed her one small black leather bag with everything she had and got on the tram and sat on the tram circling the canals of the Fontanka again and again and again. Late that evening, she turned up back at home. Sergei opened the door of their flat to find her standing on the doorstep crying. He had absolutely no idea why she had arrived home late, crying. This is one of the things he remembers as he passes away the many days lying on the small bunk in the same cabin he has slept in for more than three years. He still doesn't know why Masha arrived home late that evening, her cheeks wet with secrets.

Sergei, one of the other two sailors, occasionally finds himself thinking about the time when, returning from a voyage as far as Cuba, he and his old friend the first mate Sergei both took the trip from Odessa up to St Petersburg to visit that beautiful city where Sergei lived. He stayed for a week with Sergei and Sergei's wife Masha in their small flat on the twelfth floor of an apartment block on Ploshad' Mus estva. Their flat was as small as a ship's cabin, he remembers, although the view from the window was always the same. Now, out of the small porthole in the cabin he has on board the *Neva Star*, the view is always the same.

Sergei hasn't seen his wife for five years. They met at a party when they were eighteen and married soon after that. Tatiana disappeared soon after that. Sergei wasn't worried. He heard that she had gone to Moscow and moved in with a wealthy importer-exporter and decided to leave it at that. Still, he sometimes misses her, even though he now thinks he never really loved her. He thinks about Sergei's wife Masha, and the time when he stayed in their tiny apartment and the time when he kissed her once, very quietly and very quickly, while she was cooking potato soup in the kitchen. He wonders what the Italian girls are like. He has heard that Italian women are all very beautiful. Before he disappeared one of the other sailors, a Rumanian called Sorin, told Sergei about a friend of his who'd been stuck on a ship stuck in Porto Marghera. He'd jumped ship and married the first girl he'd met, a

Venetian. Sergei remembers reading somewhere that Venetian women are supposed to have webbed feet.

The third sailor is called Sergei. Sergei has often been tempted to jump overboard, to chuck it all in and go onshore. If he went onshore, he'd get sent back to the Ukraine immediately and not be eligible for any pay for all the time he has spent on board the *Neva Star*, should it ever get out of the port of Naples. This is why all three sailors stay on board. If they left, they would be summarily repatriated and forfeit any right they had to any money they should have accrued. Sergei has heard that there are other Ukrainians in the city, though, and he is sure that if he could find them he could set himself up here in Italy. Even though the others don't know it, Sergei has found eight hundred American dollars in a small bundle that smells of dried sweat in a worn brown envelope under the bunk in the captain's cabin.

There are three sailors left on board. They are all called Sergei. There is enough canned food on board to last them, they have calculated, for up to five years. They've been there for three years. They still have enough canned food to last them for two years.

Sergei, solid, dependable, practical and realistic, thinks that it's better here than the time when he got stuck in Antwerp for three months. Even though he's been here for three years now and has never set foot on the land that is but a few metres away, he already knows that he likes Naples more than he liked Antwerp.

Here, the sky seems closer, heavier, bluer and thicker, especially when he thinks of the distant, pale, thin and airy Baltic sky. He sometimes wonders why a boat registered in Odessa should be called the *Neva Star* and, despite his solid, realistic practicality, can think of no other reason than some vague intention to make him feel even more homesick.

They've been there for three Augusts, when the bright heat is enough to split paving stones. It creeps on board like an animal and rubs around them and sticks to them like fur coats that they can't take off. They've been there for three New Years, watching the fireworks over the city and listening to the other ships sound their horns at midnight, then celebrating their own muted vigil a week later with one of the few bottles of *sovetskoe champanskae* that they have carefully stored away for New Year, Easter and three birthdays every year. They have already drunk all the vodka that was on board.

Sergei dreams all the time and not only when sleeping. He dreams of the sun sliding down the steps in Odessa, of his family and the house where he grew up. He dreams of being trapped on board the *Neva Star* for three years, of being on board this very ship, a dream which is inseparable from reality, and this dream worries him. It worries him mostly because in this dream there are only two of them, not three. He wonders what has happened to Sergei in his dream, but there's no answer. He has a bad dream where Tatiana's new husband comes looking for him armed with divorce papers which turn into a gun which turns into a dead fish. He dreams of Masha's trapped eyes and women with webbed feet. Waking, he remembers his dreams and remembers that it's supposed to be two travellers who imagine a third. *Who is the third who walks always beside you?* He wonders why he's dreaming the opposite.

Sometimes they are incessantly together, eating, sleeping, breathing and shitting in rhythm, all but holding hands twenty-four hours seven days four weeks in a near hysterical attempt to ward off the vacuum of being alone. They have played more games of chess with each other than they can remember. Sergei always wins.

At other times they have spent months not talking to each other, going about their business (such business as they have) alone, not consciously avoiding each other, spending time lying eyes open on their bunks, looking up, reading slowly so as not to finish the few books they have, speaking little so as not to exhaust topics of conversation, moving slowly as if trying to conserve time, as if trying not to breathe too much for fear they'll use up all the air they have left.

Sergei has taken to disappearing when he thinks the others won't notice him gone. At night, usually, though sometimes during the day when it's quiet, he stretches a plank across the water and walks on to land. The solidity of the stone quay under his feet throws him off balance and makes him feel sick. He steals into the city, crossing the deadly road and scuttling up through the alleys that permeate the tall, ugly buildings. He loses himself, finds himself, then finds himself lost and has to ask a group of Polish people under the main station the way back to the port. He sees plaster peeling off the old buildings in the centre like the skin off his own sunburned lips.

Fearing the thieves he has heard about in Naples, he keeps tight hold of the tight bundle in his pocket, fingers clenched around the clenched notes. He had worried about looking out of place or conspicuous and wonders why nobody takes any notice of him. He feels as though he must have become invisible. Not even the Poles were surprised to see him. He regrets not asking them if they had any Ukrainian friends, and promises himself he will come out again and find them and ask them. He doesn't want to wait too long. He is starting to feel anxious. When he was counting his dollars he had heard the click of the door opening and the click of a throat clearing in embarrassment before seeing Sergei slip out of the room. Since then, he has moved the worn brown envelope to a new place every day. He spends a lot of time thinking where he's going to put it next.

Once a journalist came to visit them and asked them lots of questions about their life on board the ship. He brought greasy cardboard boxes with pizza in them, and bottles of beer. A few days later, there was an article in the local paper about them, complete with photograph showing them sitting in the deserted dining room, all embracing each other and grinning, but they never saw it because the journalist never sent them a copy of the paper, even though he'd promised to.

This also meant that the feverish negotiations that were then going on to sell the ship and release the men that were also described in the article took place completely unknown to them. In oak-lined rooms with green leather chairs and air-conditioned offices with marble floors and desks the size of Wales in London, Lisbon, Athens, Istanbul, Liberia and New York, faxes had tickered back and forth, talking to each other of agents and auctions, terms and conditions, get-out clauses and loopholes, prices in lira, roubles, dollars and sterling.

Sergei has often thought about trying fishing. He looks down at the narrow canal of dark water that surrounds the ship and wonders what may be swimming around down there. The froths of white and brown foam and the sickly rainbows of shiny oil that occasionally slide across the green-black surface aren't encouraging, but he's seen people fish in water much worse in St Petersburg.

He rigs up a rod made from a broom handle and some twine weighed down with the broken bottom of a vodka bottle which he also hopes will act as a fly and perches on the edge of the *Neva Star* and sits there for hours, fishing without catching anything. Once, he sees an enormous grey cod, evidently lost, but it doesn't bite. Every now and then he pulls up the twine to check. There's nothing to use as bait. He thinks that might be why he doesn't catch anything.

He wonders what any fish who might live in the waters of the port of Naples would eat and what he would find in the belly of a fish he caught when he gutted it with his penknife. Bones, little fish, jewels. As he sits there fishing he thinks about the money he saw Sergei counting and wonders where it came from and where he's hidden it now. He sees a girl sitting on the deck of a yacht passing in the distance and she reminds him of the mermaid he saw sitting on a rock in Copenhagen. She reminds him of Masha, and he wonders what his wife is doing now. He wonders why she left him after his friend Sergei had been to visit, and why he never told Sergei she'd left.

When they go out on the deck and look at the city beyond the docks, they see rows of ugly, tall, barrier-like white cement buildings and a wide road on which cars speed past at all hours of the day and night. At night the road is dimly illuminated with fuzzy yellow light, and they can see a few people loitering in the blocked yellow spaces under the shadows of the tall ugly buildings.

After the article in the newspaper, the sailors briefly became a minor tourist attraction in the city of Naples. Small groups of people used to come and look at them and wave to them from the shore. They would wave back, and the two groups would shout things to each other in mutually incomprehensible languages. After a while, though, the novelty faded and people stopped dropping by. Now they've become such a fixture that people don't even see them there any more. In the future people will tell stories of the three Russian sailors who spent three years on a boat in the port of Naples.

Sergei thinks that if anybody should ask him where he lived now, he would still say in that house in Odessa. That's where I live, he'd say, there in that house with its high windows and wooden floor and the old stove we light in the winter to keep warm. That's where I live, with my mother and my little sister. He would get out the picture he keeps with him and show the house with its moulded ceilings and crumbling arches and the dark entrance hall where the old *dezhurnaja* who never speaks to anybody lives. Nobody asks him where he lives.

Sergei knows that this is siren land, that he is stranded in a city founded when the mermaid Parthenope fell in love with one of Odysseus's men who ignored her by blocking his ears and sailing right past her. She was so heartbroken she cried until she died and her body was washed up on a rock here.

Rust wears the bow, salt eats up the paint on the hull. There are no seagulls to make any sound, as there is nothing to scavenge. The only sounds you can hear on the *Neva Star* are the distant roar of traffic from the city, the creak of fatiguing metal, the sea sweating oil in summer, the gnaw of advancing decay.

Sergei squirrels himself out after dark and heads back for the station where he met the Poles. At night, there is no one there but a few drunks. He tries asking them if they know any Ukrainians round here, but nobody answers him apart from a man with a face so red and swollen it looks like it's about to explode. The man with the red face recognizes Sergei's accent and asks him where he's from. The red-faced man is from Moldova and they start speaking in Russian. Sergei tells him he's been stuck on a boat in the port for three years. The man with the red face tells him a story that he's heard in Naples. Once there was a boy called Cola Pesce. Cola Pesce loved diving down and swimming for hours and hours in the waters of the bay of Naples. His mother got fed up with him doing nothing but sploshing around in the water all day and said that if he didn't give up he'd turn into a fish. That's why they called him Cola Pesce. Cola dived deep deep down into the water and let a huge fish swallow him up. Then he travelled all over the world, under the sea, in the belly of the fish, before eventually getting out his knife and cutting himself free. When the king heard about Cola Pesce's talent he demanded to see him. 'Tell me,' he asked the boy, 'what does the bottom of the sea look like?', and Cola Pesce replied that it was filled with gardens of coral, wrecks of ships, pieces of amber, phosphorescent fish and precious stones scattered about among the bones of drowned sailors. The king told him to go down again and bring up some of the treasure for him, but Cola immediately had a bad feeling. 'If I go down again,' he told the king 'I'll never come back up', but the king insisted and Cola went down again. In some versions of the story he takes down a handful of lentils with him, in others a piece of wood, in others a drop of blood, and he says that if this thing rises to the surface before I do, then I shall be dead. The lentils, the piece of wood, the drop of blood float to the surface. They're still waiting for him to come back up.

Sergei gave the red-faced man some of his money, and headed quickly back for the ship, making sure he didn't get lost on the way.

Shipwrecked on board a ship, stranded afloat under a flag of inconvenience, they listen to the distant roar of traffic from the city. Unquiet ghosts, snoring sailors. The fax machines have stopped their ticking now, ink fading on sheets of curling white paper piled up on dusty office floors or chewed up by the long sharp teeth of shredding machines.

Every day Sergei walks out on to the deck of the *Neva Star* and looks out across the bay. He fills himself up with the luminous intensity of the big silver mornings, watching the rigs and funnels of other ships, the hunched cranes and walls of containers on the docks, the wide flat mirror of water in the port basin and the broken-topped triangle of Mount Vesuvius in the distance. He thinks it's one of the most beautiful things he's ever seen, and thinks about how it would be to live here forever and spend every morning looking out at that looming shadow. He thinks about the money that has been stashed away and gets moved every day and where it came from and what will happen to it. He wonders how many Poles and Ukrainians and Rumanians and Russians and Turks and Cubans and Albanians and Portuguese and people from everywhere and nowhere there are in the city, and how they got there and what they do there. He wonders how many other sailors are stuck on other ships on other ports in other parts of the world and how they got there and what they do there. He ponders over what may or may not have happened to the captain. He remembers the brief wife Tatiana, Masha's face after he'd kissed her and Sorin's friend's Venetian wife. He thinks about legends of mermaids and mermen, at home neither in the sea nor on the land. He thinks that being on board a ship is like leaving and leaving and leaving and never arriving anywhere.

paulo da costa

Turning the Page

The man and the woman stood facing each other, blank expressions in their eyes, heads slightly tilted in surprise. They could not imagine what to say, what to do. He cradled a gold ring in his palm, but could not recall a previous memory. The intensity of the stare shifted and they inspected the space they occupied.

White surrounded them. Light bounced freely off the rectangular walls. The writer had neglected to furnish the room. Without a love seat or a chair for them to sit and relax, the man and the woman had no idea how long they would stand there staring at the ring or at one another, waiting for the wind of restlessness to move them. The writer had also neglected to dress them. The man and the woman tilted their heads, curiously. Anatomical differences both attracted and made them anxious. Their limbs swayed nervously, eyes travelled from the blank walls to their own bodies, up and down the opposite body and back to the blank walls.

Both secretly sensed they existed in a computer where everything had started with a flicker of light, a current pulsing across a screen. A simple cut and paste intervention, and a little moving around might salvage them. Perhaps even the relationship. They were glad their lives were not being written in the forties when there was no turning back. Either it worked from the beginning or they would be crumpled up and thrown in the waste basket, albeit together. They lived in the ethereal space of electric impulses and signals. Was life compulsory?

The man and the woman searched the room for clues. They craned their necks, they set their ears against the wall, they listened for the tapping of fingertips against a surface, or the scratching of a pen against paper. Nothing.

They shrugged. They kissed. It was an intuitive, soothing response to silence and emptiness. It also justified being unclothed. But instead of feeling aroused or awakened, a tiredness overcame them and they fell asleep.

The man stirred with the first rays of dawn. Through the slit of his eyelids he focused on the floating specks of dust spiralling up, then slowly down, across the room.

The woman had vanished. A puddle of white, in the shape of her body, had spilled on the floor next to him. The residue of her presence. He tentatively touched the soft and slightly moist white-ness, staining his index finger. A pungent scent that he could not relate to anything he knew. He preened his head. Puzzled, he walked the perimeter of the room. Slippery and shiny, the floor glossy, crinkled. One could easily slip off. He glided his finger over the baseboards. No sign of dust. No one else had walked on the surface. That was important to him, although he did not know why. He stood in the centre of the room and sought clues. Soon he found himself pacing along the edge of the space pressing himself against the border. His elbow pressed a white and paper-thin cover that immediately rolled up the wall to reveal a window and light behind it. Streams of people moved back and forth outside. He leaned on the window, pressing his nose on the glass, watching people walk, holding Styrofoam cups, buying newspapers.

A black liquid spilled from above, splashing against his thigh. The liquid, hot on his skin, exuded a sharp aroma. He spit on his fingertips and rubbed it to a rust-coloured mark. He licked his fingers, enjoying the bitter taste on his tongue. Repeated efforts did not clear away the stain. His skin had absorbed the mark. The mark had become part of him.

His birthmark.

The man leaned against the wall, his fisted hands pressed against his forehead. He let his body slide down to the floor. He went backwards, with the sensation of his body falling unsupported. The wall had folded like an accordion, revealing a closet.

A pair of khaki shorts and a beige T-shirt hung from a peg. Writers were not overly generous with wardrobes, although he admitted counting more pockets in the shorts than he would ever find useful. The colourful ear of a book showed in one pocket. The cover was blank. The sentence, *For you beloved, I will grow a face, become a surface . . .* was printed on each of the one hundred and fifty pages. Snakelike, the sentence slowly and randomly moved across the body of each page.

Flicking open the window, the man leaped through and on to the sidewalk below. He found a kiosk on the corner and asked for a map.

'What type?' the vendor asked, pointing at a vertical rack.

'Arial, preferably. If not, Courier.' Then he added, 'Can you discern character by the type?'

The vendor scratched his beard, puzzled. 'You're a tourist, right? English ain't your first language, is it? All maps are aerial in this part of the world.'

'Is there a difference between them?'

'Some say yes, others say no. You pick.'

'I'll have these four, please.'

'That's eighteen dollars.'

He offered the ring.

'Hey guy, this is worth a lot more than eighteen dollars!'

He shrugged. Smiled.

'Thanks. And thanks for the name too. Guy. I like it.'

He sat on a bench and unfolded the orange map first. His finger followed the contours of the topographic lines, studied the roads, the landmarks. After a time he stared at the bleached sky.

'Who are you to drop me here and disappear? Where do I go? What do I do?' he asked.

Studying the maps he experienced calm. Time passed quickly as he focused on the mountainous surroundings. The highest peak stood at the top of the page. He decided to climb the highest point, up to the pristine white, clear of imprints, and find out what he could see from above – climb to the very edge of his world.

Feeling faint, his legs wavering, Guy sat on a street corner and quietly hummed a tune he did not recognize. He was hungry. A sweet, calming melody. Coins began to fall at his feet, tossed by pedestrians. An apple and a muffin followed. Suspicious, he looked around. Was someone planning this, taking care of him? He gladly bit into the apple.

A strange stirring flooded his being, as if he was doing exactly what he was supposed to be doing. Was it possible that his story had already been told, that he was merely following the clues? What then was the point of proceeding, living a predictable life with nothing original to add? Nothing to separate him from another. No clever turns awaiting. Did he want to distinguish himself?

Hearts, snakes, anchors, initials. The symbols embedded on ankles, arms, shoulders hurrying past him while he sat on the sidewalk. Shades of blue and red. *For you beloved, I will grow a face, become a surface* . . . The rasping of one surface on another. Love. Writing with the body, for the body. A face upon a face. The abstract curved line on the woman reached downwards from the shoulder blade. A blue butterfly alighted on her moving ankle. Effortless steps among the crowd. A willingness to be imprinted, to bleed even, and leave a mark. To be perforated. The impressionable and malleable body of a message.

Maple leaves, loose newspaper, and the smell of fried chicken entwined in the air. A longing, an incompleteness resembling hunger, resonated from a place deeper than his body or his stomach. It was not food he longed for. Guy closed his eyes and saw almond-shaped eyes. The first eyes he had ever encountered. He realized he had been searching for those eyes ever since the first morning in that vacant room. Searching through the crowds that carried him back and forth like the wind. Aquiline nose, smooth skin. Yes, there was also a scent, a milky scent. He wondered if they would ever meet again. Why did she leave the story? A pain stabbed in his chest. He listened to the lonely drumming of his heart. Strange. The vast white sky. Clouds. Mountains. He, infinitely small. A mote, floating in a dust filled universe. Maybe she had been eliminated, whited out. And who decided, who erased her? He could not bring her back. Not in the same way, no. His head spun with whirling thoughts. A sharp rip echoed in his chest, as if his skin had unexpectedly torn. Silence. The road abruptly ended at his toes. He could see nothing beyond. At his feet, green found a way up through the cracks in the sidewalk. He turned back.

*

For you beloved, I will grow a face, become a surface where you may write your life with the sway of your hand, the pressure of your fingertips. And for you, the traveller, who traces with fingernails the contours of a map, who etches impressions, the guiding path, I too will grow a face and become a surface. Time and use will wear it down. The paper will be forgotten. You will see and remember only the words which found a home to be held.

Guy imagined the visible carried on the backs of the invisible. A background against which outlines encounter their borders. Where people encounter themselves and their limits. Skin-thin borders. Paper-thin.

He raised his eyes skywards and saw an extraordinary white radiance on the horizon. A beam of light and the blank pages at the end of the book fell towards him. Was that it? Was this the end? A mosquito landed on his nose. He hummed softly. The heavy darkness of the book cover came crushing down.

Guy remembered a bookstore, browsing through endless sagas, volume after volume, surviving across the generations. A compelling, soothing stirring about matters that lasted. The pyramids in Giza, the travels of Marco Polo, classic tales clasped tightly in the hands of thousands. Walking a thin black thread of words that leaped into the next room as if uninterrupted . . .

He had tired of sitting on a street corner waiting for what might fall into his lap.

There was a sense of familiarity walking the streets, watching people's mannerisms. He was not surprised to hear the word love and at times tried to guess what might transpire next in a conversation – 'I never stopped loving him.' But what they would do – marry someone else? – that was less predictable.

He remembered objects, understood their use. He voiced the appropriate words at the appropriate times. Had he been here before? Was he living the practice of not forgetting?

Tonight he was famished. Guy paced the parallel streets as if moving down a page in search of meaning. A bowl of soup and fried rice filled his mind. A car whispered in the distance. The street he walked was deserted. The wind puffed his shorts. He sang. Wordless sounds. Patches and drones. His own body a canyon wall echoing and echoing without end. The moon rose and disappeared. He continued on. Coins rattled in his pocket. Finally resigned, preparing to stop, he smelled food. The pale sky, drunk with dawn, spat a shooting star. The star dropped in a curve, leaving a trail of fluorescent ink behind it.

He peered inside the establishment but did not walk in. The sign read *Open*. He saw no one. 'Why did it take this long to find food? Why this particular place? Why?'

Would his future change drastically whether he entered or not? . . .

Guy stopped at a window display. Colourful covers adorned the faces of books and stood up at odd angles, some suspended by nearly invisible threads, inert unless touched.

He stepped inside. The smell of coffee soothed him. The pleasure of its taste satiated his subterranean hunger. Thousands of books were lined against the walls, the execution squads of people's fingers pointed at their spines. He reached for a book, opened it. Crowded with words. He opened another and another. Every book full. At random he created a pile of books and walked to a sofa by the fireplace. Flames had been painted on the hearth. The heat was real.

A month later Guy had not finished reading one of the hundreds of rows of books in the store. He lived on half-finished beverages abandoned by the customers, half-eaten muffins and pastries. He noticed that books written in the past tense prevailed. Most people spoke from the past. Abruptly, he stopped. He could be there, sitting, reading, his whole life. His body felt restless. Weak.

He would only survive, live on and prosper if he stood out. If his life was impressive. Impress and sell.

A radio blared in the little cafe. The hum of the drink cooler vibrated Guy's cheeks. The man at the counter lowered his newspaper and greeted him. Guy sat down and ordered a coffee. Plenty of cream.

He unfolded the white map.

Printed everywhere were crosses. Tall intricate buildings. The predominant colours: black and white.

His attention drifted to the radio.

'Why now?' He questioned aloud.

'I can bring it later if you want.' The server standing beside him sounded perplexed.

Guy measured him suspiciously.

'What do you do in your spare time?' He scrutinized the face for clues, the hands for ink.

The server frowned.

'Don't mind me. I'll have the coffee now,' Guy said dismissively, as if his question had become unimportant.

At the end of the news, the radio station broadcast a financial report.

This is Tony Kwiet from Wuld Ghandi Private Investments reporting on the financial markets for Friday the twelfth. Overall, stocks rose in the principal world markets, although analysts warn that any false hopes will crash the market. Buddhist shares climbed half a point after industry experts released a report confirming that meditation lowers cholesterol and slows the cancer of progress.

Guy sipped his coffee. The announcer continued.

'Christian shares oscillated wildly during a tumultuous day of trading following the release of conflicting reports. Shares plummeted when a senior Christian official reported that the number of shareholders did not accurately reflect their loyalty; numbers were overinflated, enormously overrated. Later in the day a report by respected quantum physicists, stating they were on the brink of proving the existence of God, sent shares sky rocketing again and they closed unchanged at seventy-seven point seven-seven dollars. No fluctuations were seen in smaller offshore subsidiaries. The Pope and the Dalai Lama will meet tomorrow. Rumours of merger talks were firmly denied.'

Guy returned to his map.

He unfolded the green map. The most colourful. Drawings of animals, rivers and trees, filled its pages.

He had longed to stand on the highest peak but the careful path he followed had unpredictably led him elsewhere. Instead, he stood at the edge of a canyon where he could not imagine the distance to the bottom. It was late in the day. He had missed the zenith, the moment the sun stared straight down at the earth, when light could touch the bottom of the canyon. He wondered if the bottom dwellers wished for that bright moment to linger, never moving on. Or had they grown accustomed, never expecting more than the fleeting, brilliant shower in their day?

He sat on the edge of the canyon, his legs dangling.

'What do you want me to do?' Guy yelled. He yelled towards the huge space and the sound bounced back. He yelled until his throat burned as if bitten by ants.

He flipped urgently through several books he carried in his pockets. They weighed. At random, he flipped to a book's first page.

On the seventh line, and not unlike his own experience, the author had gone to rest, 'to sleep', he corrected his thought aloud.

'The woman leans over the edge of the pier and scoops a handful of ocean water for her asthma. She coughs. A hundred paces away, her newborn sleeps in grandmother's arms. Her father stands beside her, breathing the salty mist. The punch of a wave knocks her down and drags her into the ocean and away, whirling her among the white caps. She struggles to undress in the freezing water. Her hand, last, disappearing into the depths. A strange farewell wave.'

Guy ripped a handful of grass from the edge of the canyon and tossed it, watching its downward dance. Compassion is what he must have for the Creator, Guy thought. Yes, we are here to teach compassion to this imperfect Creator.

The wind lifted a hawk by its wings.

How did a hawk feel when a bullet entered its flesh, ripping open its chest? A novel form of dying. The hawk's world changed without warning. Its wings folded. It plummeted towards the unexpected, the grave fast approaching.

He held his own body so tightly he drew blood with his nails. The reflection of his face in a rain puddle revealed deep scratches on his face. His skin stung. 'Why am I doing this to myself?' He sucked his thumb, found relief. His body softened.

He tried to read one book, and instead he found himself simultaneously flipping through others. He did not finish sentences, skimming, scanning the texts. Looking for hidden answers. Guy thought he heard a voice. Was it inside or outside his head? Did it matter? He could answer his own questions, discover for himself what was true. Damn it, he must live and walk on. He stared at the walking stick he had found along the way. He could walk with a cane, something to lean on during the steep times when his strength waned. But carrying it required effort, energy. 'Do I have to carry something today so it may carry me one day too?' he wondered aloud. With his walking stick he scratched the letter *y* on the dirt. A fork on the trail. As he contemplated his work, a gust of wind swept through, covering the trail and filling his eyes with dust. Guy wanted to find that beginning page and return to a time without memory, to rest in comfort and security. He craved coffee. His mind was swimming in a dark undulating liquid, the medium of life. A womb. The imprint.

Perhaps memory was illusory. Time refurnished the past and filled in the blanks, recreated experience.

Guy waited at an intersection for the pedestrian light to turn green. As he prepared to step into the crosswalk, a body rushed from behind and pushed him. He lost his balance, falling sideways. He heard the loud screech of tyres. A thump, a crash, an eruption of screams.

An elderly woman, with her hair coiled in a bun and a cigarette hanging from the corner of her mouth, helped him to his feet.

'Luckily the boy hurried just in time so not to miss his end,' she said, nodding towards the street.

A strange statement. Brutal even, Guy thought. But the woman had tears in her eyes.

'We'll suffer for as long as we believe things last.' She offered a quiet smile and walked away.

And why continue on at all if it was going to end? *Continue on because you do not know what is next*, the voice in his head whispered. He could see a boy through a maze of legs. A slanted line of red spilled on either side of him. He was not moving. No one touched the corpse.

The boy had been slashed and edited.

Guy wrote his thoughts on the spacious, untitled book. He wrote around, over, at, along, against, for and with the sentence, 'For you beloved, I will grow a face, become a surface . . .' Sentenced by the sentence? The sentence was there and not there. He was there and not there. The existence of another realm. Between the lines, perhaps. In space. A leap of imagination. The poetry of day to day. He sought clues. The genuine. Maintaining one eye here, another there. What lay beyond the obvious. What was not said.

At the coffee shop or on the street, people peered over his shoulder, read his words. They enquired. Nodded their heads. Adopted his answers. Their numbers grew. There was comfort in numbers, comfort in gathering at that empty place beyond up or brown, left or fight. Comfort in believing they would meet again.

Whistling steam and grinding coffee beans filled his ears. Voices climbed atop of each other, reached higher, perilously balanced on the last octave. He could not hear his own thoughts; he could not hear the woman next to him. People screamed at each other to be half understood. Fictions, assumptions, beliefs, colliding in the air. Dissolving. The space already filled. Without room to meet, for anything new to arise. And be seen. Unmanoeuvrable.

He left the coffee shop and walked on. One step after another. One step indistinguishable from the last, taking him beyond the edge of the horizon into open space.

Nick Barlay

Stu Zsibinsky's Lost Cause

As Radical Activist Stu Zsibinsky wondered about the thirty years of political struggle that had led him to a peeling council flat in a tubeless suburb, he realized he had unwittingly circled an ad in the *Women Seeking Men* section of a reviled Saturday newspaper. His problem was that he had been involved with many causes but unfortunately not with many women.

Looking back, he had campaigned against a range of isms and phobias, against animal experiments, genetically modified food, food additives, foxhunting, hedgehog culling, the extinction of the tadpole shrimp, third world debt, first world complacency, and the second world generally (wherever it was), deforestation, motorways, ringroads, bypasses, banks, nuclear power, nuclear weapons, nuclear families, NATO, US military adventures, the community charge, police brutality, the closure of schools, hospitals, mines, shipyards and his own bank account, drug companies, pesticides, live exports, emissions from cars, trucks and aeroplanes, stockbrokers on horses, bailiffs with chainsaws, vivisectionists in Volvos, and on and on and on. In the same period that he had campaigned so vigorously for such causes, he had known Jane.

In other words, in his life, causes outweighed women by a ratio of 24:1. He knew this because he had worked out that, on average, he had to campaign for twenty-four different issues before he met a woman who liked him. In the old days, calculated over time, he could campaign for a dozen issues a year and get laid every two years, especially if Christmas was a factor.

The trouble was, he was forty-eight. He hadn't seen Jane for over four years and, in any case, the romance had only lasted three convoys of live sheep to France before she'd packed in both him and the sheep. Neither had a future, she'd told him. The struggle is forever, he'd replied. Not in your case, she'd said, pointing out that he'd lost the struggle with his three chins and two guts. He'd insisted that his body had successfully campaigned for freedom and who was he or anyone to stand in the way of the masses?

His physique, she'd said, was the least of his problems. He was also a terrible dresser, and being a Radical Activist didn't mean you had to be either. This was the new millennium, the age of connectivity. Who'd want to connect with him? Radical Activists, she'd pointed out during a bypass protest, needed to be photogenic, telegenic, and have a cyber profile. They needed laptop computers, mobile phones, credit cards and the latest urban warrior fashion accessories, all of which added up to the modern campaign lifestyle, a lifestyle from which Stu was a lifetime away. After a frosty silence, Jane had carefully folded her designer pure wool balaclava, and cadged a lift back to London in a cycle campaigner's Range Rover.

It was the very moment that Radical Activist Stu Zsibinsky stopped liking women (and cycle campaigners). It was not that he didn't support women's rights. *Course he did.* It was not that he didn't listen to women. *Course he did.* It was not that they didn't like him in their own way. *Course they did.*

But his souring looks, and the fact that new millennium single issue supporters generally insisted on total lifelong commitment to looking the part, meant that sex and relationships were not on the cards. They would, he thought, not even be listed in the index of his life. To change this, he couldn't very well take to the streets: *What do I want?* A shag. *When do I want it?* Now . . .

It was clear to him that people would have willingly chained him to a railing and the fire brigade would have left him there. Anyway, it would have been like campaigning for himself, which was contrary to all his beliefs about campaigning for others. Answering an ad, therefore, was the only way left to meet a like-minded woman and, crucially, to improve his cause:women ratio.

The ad was looking for a non-smoking, non-beer drinking, fashionable man with a political conscience. At least he was one of these. A list of campaigns, his phone number, and the line *I'm badly dressed but I can change*, brought a swift reply two days later. The woman's name was Jane, a coincidence that did not escape Stu's notice. She claimed to be an extremely young forty-something. She used to be in fashion but was currently in campaigns. In fact she was launching a new campaign that, she felt, was so 'now'. It was a campaign against badly dressed campaigners.

A week later, they met in a non-smoking independent fair trade café over a soya decaff and a peppermint infusion. Jane was impressed that he had given up active smoking and was now a committed passive smoker. She was less impressed with his old brown Doc Martens, his black denim jacket and black jeans that he never washed in case the anarchist black faded to sit-on-the-fence grey. They say retro is never *passé*, she'd pointed out, but that's one fashion that's never coming back. However, he won her over with the following ingenious argument: I can be both a campaigner for your cause and the reason you undertook it in the first place.

Soon they began to relate on a regular basis. They even had sex. It wasn't exactly the dirty socialist shags Stu had in mind but, with her extreme youthfulness and his faultless logic, they were a team. Enthusiastically, he helped her to campaign against himself. Although it did take some getting used to. You can't take on the police wearing that, she would say. And: If you think you're going out to reclaim the streets in those shoes you've got another thing coming. And: That banner doesn't match your socks.

Little by little, the outmoded garb of a people's revolutionary was modified. His DMs became hi-tech trainers, his black jeans became labelled combat trousers, his checked shirt was replaced with a clubber's T-shirt, his denim jacket became a micro-fleece, zips and buttons became Velcro straps. He was fully accessorized with an underarm mobile phone pouch, personal organizer belt-bag and more pockets than he knew what to do with.

Barely three months into the campaign against badly dressed campaigners and the fashion industry was flocking to Jane and Stu – or 'J-Zee™', as they were known – with sponsorship deals. J told Zee when to speak, when not to speak, what to say and what not to say. After the sponsors came the photoshoots for lifestyle magazines. J-Zee™ spearheaded sponsored rioters dressed in carefully vetted outfits, and fashion photographers were on hand to record the synchronized action.

After five months with J, there was no trace of Stu Zsibinsky, Radical Activist. He was no more. He had been reinvented.

Women, from teenaged animal lovers to reborn grey pound activists, would have given themselves to Zee without a second thought. His cause:women ratio would have been 1:9 if he'd bothered to work it out. But with the money rolling in, Zee had it all: *the* woman; *the* politics; *the* clothes. He even started to like *the* newspaper. Before long, he bought his peeling council flat, and turned it into a minimalist protest nerve centre, courtesy of a globally aware interior design guru. Out went the bookshelves with their dusty anarcho-syndicalist manuals, rare secondhand Marxist contemplations, diaries of obscure proto-socialists, the memoirs of Trotskyite prisoners, situationist ramblings, and the collected maxims of martyred revolutionaries. In came wardrobe space, wooden hangers, high performance 'intelligent' washing powders, and a slim volume entitled *Pilates for Protestors* by one of J's Californian disciples.

J got a book commission of her own: *Riot Gear – a photographic journey*; Zee got a pedicure for a lifestyle magazine photoshoot: 'Treat yourself to a pre-march buff and shine. Top protestor Zee says . . .' But, while his Communist corns and anti-Fascist cuticles were being pumiced, Zee began to feel something he hadn't felt in five months. He began to feel like a complete prick. It was not a feeling he wanted to share with lifestyle journalists, and especially not with J, in case she agreed.

A few weeks later, while having what J called 'third way' sex, part private, part public and a bit metrosexual, Zee experienced a nostalgic wave of proletarian discontent. He used to shag in the spirit of class war; now he was being used to mime lyrics to a pre-recorded pop song. Politics was just the soundtrack to a fashion parade; sex was a twelve-step programme devoid of bump and grind, slip and slide, rock and roll. Out on the streets logotyped mass culture was being positioned by brand consultants, developed by personal fulfilment specialists and satisfied by customer experience directors. 'Nostalgic waves of proletarian discontent' could be bought on CD for £4.99. Free poster included. And the worst of it was, nobody felt insincere. Just the opposite. Words like *honest*, *real*, *committed* and *passionate* were used to describe 'us', and words like *wrong*, *immoral*, *hypocritical* and *corrupt* were used to describe 'them'.

After sex, Zee slapped a Nicorette patch on his arm and imagined smoke rings drifting to the ceiling. Then he turned to J and said: 'I feel like a complete prick.' Her answer, as she dialled her publicist, shocked him: 'It doesn't matter,' she said, then to her publicist: 'Hi darling, just to let you know, the colour for today is saffron . . .'

It didn't take Zee long to realize that this wasn't the beginning of the end but the end itself. He told J he was going to Pilates. But he wandered the streets. Soon he was overwhelmed by an urge to sit in a stinking pub with a pint of bitter, a roll-up and a copy of *Socialist Worker*. But he couldn't find such a pub. Instead, he sat in a glassy piney non-smoky gastro pubby over a goat cheese quiche with leafy salad, a white wine and the latest edition of *Protest*, the magazine for the lifestyle protestor, in which he was featured having a pedicure.

'Top protestor Zee says: "I feel like a complete prick" . . .' Only he wasn't quoted saying that. 'Top protestor Zee says: "If it's gonna make you protest better, just go for it."' Above was a picture of him grinning and pointing at his left foot, a foot whose former address had been a DM boot which, in turn, had stomped on Nazi heads and kicked in scab doors.

I really am a prick, Zee thought. *It's just that it doesn't matter.* Maybe everyone felt that way about themselves but didn't mind. In other words, maybe there were lots of totally self-aware pricks (and cunts) out there who didn't mind being pricks (and cunts). Maybe it was time to protest against self-aware pricks (and cunts). And maybe the final battleground was right here: a fight to the death between a roll-up and a leafy salad.

And that, according to the various eyewitness accounts, is more or less what happened. Zee, screaming, 'Do you know who I am you pricks (and cunts)?', apparently shed his clothes, ripped them off himself, then tried to smoke as many roll-ups as he could from his secret stash before the law arrived. When it did, two-headed and uniformed, he screamed: 'It doesn't matter everybody, it doesn't fucking matter.'

But it did matter. It mattered to the other customers and to the quality of their dining experience; it mattered to their health, which had been damaged by the smoke, and to their emotions, which had been traumatized by the sight of Zee's left-leaning penis. It mattered to the police, to the law in general, to the fashion industry sponsors, to the journalists and, most of all, it mattered to Zee's cause:women ratio, which he thought he had under control.

Some might have concluded that he'd reached the end of his tether. But Zee was not a horse or any other quadruped. He was an anarchist, he explained, and he did not like government in any of its forms. He did not like to be told what to do and when to do it nor what to say and when to say it. Is that so? asked J. Oh no, said Zee, you're not dumping me, are you? In fact, J did not dump Zee although she did email him to point out that his role as a stakeholder in the partnership was terminated.

Shunned, lonely, desolate, and terminated, Stu Zsibinsky became a barely remembered relic of a bygone and best forgotten age. He wasn't to know it then but, one day, while buying back a few of his donated socialist volumes from a charity shop, he would meet a new Jane. They would attract each other instantly with their vacant stares. Both would have protested against so many things that there was nothing left to protest against, including each other. And so they would live, with the occasional, shared, nostalgic wave of proletarian discontent, apathetically ever after.

Shereen Pandit

Dying to See the Sea

Freddie was always dying. When she came home from teaching school, she was 'dying' for a drink. Once ensconced on the thick rug in front of the fireplace if it was winter, or out on the stoep if it was summer, drink in hand, she was 'dying' for a fag. Things never killed her, like her very high-heeled shoes which she managed to teach in all day. Nevertheless, when she got home she kicked them off as soon as she came in the door and padded about barefoot on the highly polished wooden floor, because she was 'dying' to get out of them.

'Oh, god, I was dying for you to come,' she called out when I pulled my battered blue VW on to the equally battered cement of her driveway. 'Come in, come in. Don't worry about your stuff. Pull the car all the way round the back. We can unload it later.'

I had just been offered a job at a nearby college and Freddie, my cousin whom I hadn't seen since we were teenagers, had agreed to put me up till I found my own place. I glanced nervously around the car, into which the sum of my worldly possessions – besides the car itself, that is – were crammed.

'It's OK. Really. Nobody will touch your stuff. It's such a quiet area. And it'll be round the back. Who'll see it? Come on. I'm dying to show you what I've got for you.'

The first of a long line of gins, topped with lime and lemonade, poured into a tall glass over a pile of ice, that were to become our 'Friday afternoon specials'. I moved in on a Friday afternoon, because Freddie's school closed at noon and my weekly timetable at the Tech tapered from a staggering nine to nine on Monday to a mere two periods on Friday.

It was winter then, fifteen years ago (how time flies, how memory lingers) and the dogs were lying by the log fire as I came in. Ears pricked up, tails thumped the floor, then lay still again with the rest of the long, hairy bodies they belonged to, sprawled like two additional rugs over the big one.

'Some watchdogs,' Freddie scolded lovingly. 'You're supposed to bark at strangers, you dumb mutts.' The tweaking of ears and scratching of heads, the tone of voice, belied the criticism. She turned to me: 'Meet Lassy and Laddie. Part of my inheritance from Granny, as in: "I leave my house and all its contents to my grand-daughter, Frederika ..." Granny's imagination was much more limited when it came to naming dogs than when it came to naming me.'

She drained her glass, tipping it so that the ice fell into her mouth and she crunched the remaining ice. 'Wanna come over to the field with me when we've finished our drinks? These two must be just dying for a run.'

'Could take them to the forest or the beach once we've unpacked the car,' I said.

'No. Be too late by then. This lot will be having accidents all over the place. I get enough of that at school.' Freddie taught kindergarten classes. Six-year-olds whose bladders and bowels had not yet become regulated by the school timetable.

'Come on, walkies!' She slammed her glass down on the coffee table and headed for the back door, reappearing to clip leashes on to the collars of the dogs.

'Why bother with those?' I asked, draining my own glass. 'It's only over the road.'

The cheery face fell. 'Stupid cops knocked Laddie down a while back. Chasing kids from that last big march. He was in hospital for ages. Lucky it wasn't a Caspir, I suppose. Bastards didn't even stop let alone apologize.'

I shook my head. Did she really expect people who shot down protesting kids in cold blood, who chased them and ran them down in the armoured tanks the kids called Caspir the Unfriendly Ghost – to stop and apologize for running a dog down? But then again, these Boers were strange people. In the rural areas, they drove with dogs sheltered in the cabins of pickups while labourers braved heat and cold, wind and storms, in the open backs of the pickups. They fed good meat to dogs, washed and sheltered and cared for them, and gave workers scraps from off their tables and sheltered them in hovels. So maybe Freddie wasn't so far off the mark in her expectations of apology and concern for a dog from them.

The house Freddie'd inherited from our grandmother stood on the border between two townships – 'African' and 'Coloured' in terms of mad apartheid racial classification. Freddie and I were 'Coloured' and the house was just inside the 'Coloured' border. Most nights, despite the state of emergency, you could hear the youth who'd been told by the ANC to 'make the townships ungovernable' dancing the toyi-toyi down the roads behind us, accompanied by various urban war cries, followed soon after by the screams of police car sirens – and the cries of the kids changed to fear as they dashed for safety from bullets and batons. Afterwards there would be silence, save for the rumbling of Caspirs patrolling through the night.

It took some getting used to, at first, and I began to think that I'd never get the sleep I needed to teach the next day, to wonder how Freddie managed, but then Freddie's nightcaps began to have their effect and the after-dark noises became as unnoticeable as animal noises on farms.

The field Freddie walked her dogs on was just over the road from the house. As the weather improved and the days got longer, I'd sit on the stoep with a drink, watching them. Spring turned the field into a mass of daisies and they made a pretty picture, something so idyllic it was hard to place alongside the smoke we could see in the distance, rising from burning barricades in the 'African' township. Most days the charming scene was expanded by the addition of some kids from Freddie's school, stopping to romp with the dogs among the daisies, watched by an older sister who stood a little apart.

'Your school's been out a long time ago,' I remarked to her one evening when she ran home breathless with the dogs, waving to the kids as they trudged home. 'How come they're going home so late?'

'Vuvu and Sandile? That big girl with them,' she said, 'that's their sister, Mpandikaze. They have to fetch her from her school.'

'You mean they wait for her to fetch them? She must be at high school.'

'No, I mean they fetch her,' she insisted. 'She's older than the twins, but she's a bit slow – you know? Learning difficulties. She managed OK when they were going to schools near their home. Other kids fetched her and brought her home. But since those schools were shut, some of their kids are coming to our schools. It's hard when the parents are both working. They can't just let the kids wander around all day. And you know how some parents are about not wanting kids to miss their education in spite of the boycotts. Anyway, in their case the small ones are too young to join the boycott and the marches and the older girl would get herself killed if she went with her classmates, so what could they do? Good thing some of our principals are progressive enough to ignore the law.'

It was the first time I'd heard Freddie talk politics. Even with everything happening around us, we never spoke about what was going on. We were just two girls, living on our own without parental restraints, enjoying our first grown-up household, working hard but also relaxing into things. I was looking forward to the summer, planning the parties and the braais in the backyard.

Besides, my college – not exactly the most radical campus around – was in the heart of town, far from the hub of student activity. Her school consisted of infants. We were quiet islands in the midst of the river of protest that had burst its banks and flooded the country. The schools in the 'African' townships were . . . well, they were the river. They, the unions, the community organisations.

'Anyway,' she said, 'That reminds me. You know how you're always saying we should go to the beach with the dogs? I was thinking, the weather's getting nice now. Maybe we could squeeze the kids in too. They're just dying to see the sea.'

Then seeing that I was about to protest that no way would my small car take two big dogs, three children and the two of us: 'Or maybe make two trips? Come, Wendy. You'll never believe this, but those kids have never ever been to the beach.'

I laughed. 'You're joking, right? We live on a peninsula, in case you haven't noticed. There isn't a person in Cape Town who's never been to the beach.'

'Yes, there are,' she insisted. 'For you and me it's just getting in a car and putting in a bit of petrol and off we go. But there are people over there so poor they can't afford the bus and train fare to the beach. Like those kids. They're just three of a big family. It costs a lot of money to take them all by public transport. And to provide food and all that. And for the mother and father to be docked a day's pay on top of that. She's a servant, he's a gardener and you know how much that pays – it's not a lot of money to lose, but it's probably the rent money.'

I listened, open-mouthed. Of course I knew about poverty. Starvation in the homelands on the tiny bit of arid land meant to support too many people. Homeless people begging for food everywhere. All that. But that was different. These kids looked clean and well fed.

'This year,' Freddy went on, 'their parents promised them they could go to the beach as their Christmas present, but that means they would have had to go without all sorts of other things. Now with the schools closed and them having to get new uniforms for new schools ... they probably had to borrow the money. I just don't see Father Christmas bringing the bus and train tickets ... Come on. I'll pay for the petrol. You take me and the dogs first and leave us there and come back for the kids. Or the dogs can go some other time. They've already been to the beach in their life-times. Those kids never have and they're just dying to go. And I'm dying to take them.'

Once she started 'dying' to do something, there was no stopping Freddie. She started making plans for the next hot day – never mind waiting for Christmas. It was hard not to get caught up in the excitement. I began to feel as if it was my first outing to the beach too, instead of my zillionth. I mean, what was the big deal? Get in the car. Drive to the beach. Walk, swim, buy ice cream, drive home. How often hadn't I done that with my parents as a child? With my friends as an adult? Why, we could drive over there right now, if it wasn't for the car stoning going on over there, ask the parents for the kids, take them to the beach and at least do the shell collecting, paddling and ice cream thing.

But no. Tyre burning and stone throwing aside, Freddie wanted it to be a big deal. A special occasion. A big outing on a long hot day. A cold roast chicken and hardboiled eggs and ginger beer gone warm and flat and tea turned blue in flasks kind of day.

The day she gave the children the note she had all prepared for their parents, asking permission to take them and explaining what was involved and how it was to be her treat because the children were so good and worked so hard, blah, it's not a charity case, was the day I first spotted the blue Toyota.

Actually, I might have seen it before; it was just that this time it registered with me, maybe because the daisies had died down and the field was just trampled brown grass now and you could see it so clearly. Maybe because what Freddie had said about the children made me start noticing things more. I don't know. Anyway, there it was again.

It occurred to me that it was an odd place to park. It wasn't as if the occupants got out and walked dogs. It wasn't as if they lived on the other side of the field or came to visit people there. There weren't any houses on that side. It was too exposed for lovers – and too broad daylight for some township mamma not to knock at the window and tell them they should be ashamed of themselves, kids walked to and from school that way.

Anyway, when I got up and walked towards Freddie, pretending that I was going to join her, but really looking at the car, I noticed there was only one person in it. 'Don't look now,' I said to her, 'but looks like you've got yourself a stalker.'

'Yes, I know,' was all she said.

'So? You want me to go over with you and tell him to piss off?'

'That's an offence called "swearing at a policeman",' she said. My jaw dropped. 'You've got a cop for a stalker?'

She shrugged. 'He's not really my stalker, as you put it. He's actually hoping a bloke I used to go out with will stop by here someday. A bloke who's been on the run for the last year or two.' She snorted and threw a ball for the dogs. 'As if! He'd have to be crazy to come back here. Stupid bastards!'

I looked at Freddie in her floral print dress and teacherly sandals. With her hair in that bun, all she needed were square black-rimmed glasses to complete the parody of a schoolmarm. True, she could swear like a trouper and drink like a sailor, but she didn't look like someone who'd be involved with a politico, much less one on the run from the security police. But then she didn't look like someone who made speeches about poverty either. Or like someone who drank long alcoholic drinks after school and heavy nightcaps before bed.

She grinned at the look I gave her. 'Surprise!' she said. The word lacked the light tone of the Freddie I'd lived with these last months. 'It's my disguise,' she whispered, leaning down to pat Laddie who'd brought back the ball, chewed and dripping with saliva. 'Works well, don't you think? The image?' Then straightening up she said more bitterly: 'I'm hoping to convince them,' she raised her eyebrows in the direction of the car, 'just long enough to make my escape and go and find him.'

'You mean you're still in touch? But haven't they pulled you in? Questioned you? All that torture stuff?'

'A bit,' she said, tone light now again. 'But I reckon they think they'll get more by letting me go. See who I can lead them to . . .' The snort again. And again: 'As if!'

'So what about me? What if they think I'm? . . .'

'One of my contacts? Don't worry. They've probably already checked you out by now. You're so clean living – politically speaking, I mean – it couldn't have taken too long to check you out. I mean, even that place you teach at – hardly a hotbed of radicalism, is it? You said yourself, your college stayed open during the boycotts. You've been teaching – or at least in to teach, even when your students stayed away.'

'So why are you telling me this?' I said, half annoyed. She was coming pretty close to calling me a collaborator. 'How do you know I won't go over there and tell them you plan on skipping out to join the boyfriend?'

'You'd have to be a better actress than I am.' She laughed this time. 'And I'm bloody good. The best. You might not be the activist type, but I don't reckon you're a squealer either. Besides, you don't like blood – and there'd be a helluva lot on your hands if you took the walk to that car.'

*

The field burned that night. Probably by accident, the grass being so dry and so many petrol bombs flying between the police and the toyi-toying youths who spilled out of the neighbouring township into ours, coming right down our street in the night, so that not even Freddie's best nightcap could keep me in my bed asleep. We watched the battle from behind our curtains, fleeing youths flinging stones and Molotov cocktails, police firing, bodies falling, screams and shouts. It was mayhem.

Freddie let the dogs out into the yard in the morning instead of taking them over the road. The children weren't in school that day, nor the rest of the week. Freddie reckoned their mother was making them stay home because now it was getting dangerous in our area too. Sunday was to be the day, so by Friday we were wondering whether we shouldn't risk the stone throwing – not much of a risk since my car looked enough of a 'township car' to not be hit by any but the most indiscriminate missiles – and check out what was happening.

The problem for Freddie was her watcher, who might just get ideas about the children's parents if she suddenly took off to the 'African' township which, to the best of my knowledge we technically needed a permit to enter – being black but not black enough, as it were. We decided to postpone. Odds were that any Sunday from now on would be a sunny one. On the other hand, the kids had spoken about the possibility of being sent to their grandmother in the misnamed 'homelands' for safety. Their parents had apparently mentioned it, but just didn't have the money to send them – and then there had been the issue of the disruption to their education.

Monday. The township war the entire country had been involved in, in one way or another, finally reached my college – the students voted to join the boycott and in spite of instructions that we were to stay on campus to fulfil our contractual obligations, most of us left after lunch. I arrived at home before Freddie did. A strange sick-looking woman was sitting on the steps leading to the stoep. Thinking she'd stopped for a drink of water, I hurried towards her and was about to speak to her, when Freddie opened the garden gate.

'Mrs Ndebele!' Freddie exclaimed, rushing towards the woman. 'What is it? You didn't have to come all the way to tell me . . . we assumed the children couldn't come . . . we'll go on another day . . .' The words tumbled from her, as if she was trying to stack them up as some defence against what she knew was bad news. Only bad news would have brought a woman so desperate to keep her job that she usually worked on Christmas Day, to our door on a working day. Mrs Ndebele seemed unable to speak at first. She remained sitting on the step, Freddie sitting next to her, holding her hand, giving her the drink of water I'd brought. She drank, then nearly threw it up. Finally in a flat monotone, she said that she'd only come to see Freddie to explain why the children would not be coming any more, because Freddie had been so kind to them. She knew Freddie gave them her own sandwiches when they came to school without any. She knew about the money Freddie sometimes gave them for food which they said they'd 'found' because they knew their mother wouldn't take charity. Yes, Freddie had been very kind, even offering to take the children to the sea.

It seemed that the oldest girl, Nosizwe, didn't always understand when things were explained to her. That was why the younger ones were always with her – it was not she who looked after them, but they who looked after her. Sometimes, when she had a notion to something, it was hard to deter her.

The mother had explained to the children that it was dangerous for them to go out to school or to see Freddie. She had asked them to remain at home until things settled down a bit and she could arrange for them to go to their grandmother. She'd promised they could go to the beach with Freddie as soon as it was possible. The children were very upset by this, but they obeyed their mother – at least for the first two days. Then, she said, the oldest girl must have become too impatient. She had taken it into her head to go and visit Freddie anyway. Somehow managing to escape her younger siblings, she had wandered too close to the tyre burners, had not been quick enough to run off when the troops opened fire, had died in a hail of bullets.

The other children would be sent to their grandparents as soon as their sister's funeral was over. She did not think it wise for

Freddie to attend the funeral, but she had thought that Freddie should know why the children would no longer be coming.

Freddie listened in numbed silence. Then something seemed to snap in her. Before I could think what she was about, before I could reach out to stop her as the knowledge came to me, sprint after her, hold her back, she was out the gate and haring over the field, unhampered even by the silly teacher sandals.

I didn't see her pick up a brick from among the debris of the last battle in our street, but she must have snatched it up, because as I reached her she hurled it at the windscreen of the blue Toyota. The driver ducked down to avoid the shattering glass as Freddie shrieked at him. 'Bastard!' she shrieked. 'Murdering fucking bastards!'

Or maybe he'd ducked for a gun he had in the car, because the next moment she was falling against me; a new red flower on the gay floral print dress.

Douglas Cowie

The White of Her Arms

Jose Medina stood leaning against the tailgate of his white 1976 Ford pickup truck, watching the cars pass on the dusty highway and hoping that one would stop, and hoping as always that if one did, the people wouldn't recognize him, even though the likelihood was slim; he was safer up here.

It was August, it was hot, and there wasn't any shade. There wasn't even a tree anywhere within Jose's range of vision to give the impression of, the hope of, the broken promise of shade. Six dozen ears of corn were piled in the back of his pickup. He'd stolen them from a field somewhere in Indiana, but the sign he'd written in black magic marker on a piece of cardboard, and clamped underneath his windshield wipers, said: FRESH ILLI-NOIS SWEETCORN 1/2 DOZ. $3. He'd stolen them, like always, at about three in the morning, moving through the tall stalks as fast as he could and breaking off the ears, hoping the ones he was taking were ready, getting the job done and driving off after making sure there were no headlights coming in either direction.

But it wasn't because of the corn that Jose thought he might get recognized. That was a different story. The corn was just the way he tried to earn some money, so he didn't have to bite into too much of the little savings he had, spread out in various denomina-tions under the floormats and in other hiding places in the Ford. He heard the sound of a car engine and looked off into the distant heat shimmers to see if it held promise. But it was still too far away, miles down that straight, hot highway, to tell whether it'd be lucky. Jose took off his straw cowboy-style hat and wiped his arm across his forehead, then spat at the rear right tyre, but missed. He put the hat back on and watched the shimmers, waiting for them to release the car, which he hoped had some vacationing Chicago family in it, on their way home and wanting some sweetcorn for

119

dinner when they got there, that damn three days' drive from Disneyworld finally over.

But the car drove past, and so did the next one, ten minutes later. And the next three after that. Waiting for all these cars to pass, for their tyres to spit pebbles at his Ford, for the speeding metal to send a hot, dusty breeze into his lungs, took almost an hour. Every time the same pattern of sound, look, wait, hope, watch, wait, wait, wait. Jose Medina was out of necessity a patient man.

The sixth car stopped. It was a brown Oldsmobile, something from the late eighties, Jose guessed from the shape of it, when cars were still square, even the Camaros and Trans Ams. There wasn't a family inside, just one man. He left his engine running, and Jose could feel the cold exhale from the air conditioning as the man opened the door and got out. A salesman; Jose didn't even need this guy to tell him. He'd combed what hair was left over the top of his head, the wet, thin strands inadequately covering his sun-burned scalp, like the spread-out fingers of a child pretending to cover its eyes. He was a little overweight, but not much, only a slight sag around the waist, where his white, shortsleeved dress shirt tucked into brown slacks. Jose guessed what the man might sound like before he had said anything, and Jose was right.

'I'll say,' he said, chuckling and rubbing his hands together. 'Illinois sweetcorn, I'll say.' He pronounced the 's' in Illinois, so it sounded like Illinoise.

'You want some? You want a dozen?' Jose almost never both-ered trying to exchange pleasantries with his customers, mainly because he never really knew what pleasantries to relate.

'A dozen? Yeah, sure, why not? A dozen.' The man smoothed his comb-over with his palm. 'How long they gonna keep for, though, pal? I got a couple-two days on the road yet, and it'd sure be great if I could take some home to the family, you know, cook 'em on the grill.'

Jose moved towards the cab end of the bed, where the ears were. 'Oh, they'll keep until then,' he said. 'No problem.'

The man chuckled. 'Hah, that's just great. Haven't had Illinois sweetcorn since I was a kid. Grew up in Illinois, you see, used to get it all the time, eat it raw, just like that, on the way home from the farmers' market, and do the rest on the grill. Illinois sweet-corn.'

Jose had never eaten Illinois sweetcorn, raw, grilled or other-wise. 'You want to pick them out yourself?'

'Naw, you're the professional.' The man chuckled. 'You can take care of it.'

Jose reached in and pretended to be selecting the best ones, picking up a couple and examining them, then putting them back down and taking others. He put twelve ears in a plastic grocery bag and held it up almost to eye level. 'One dozen,' he said.

'So that's, uh –'

Jose watched as the man reached his arm behind him, and hitched a little as he pulled out his wallet. Jose never believed it was a wallet until he saw it, and this time was no different. He pre-pared himself to throw the bag straight in the guy's face, if necessary, and tried to judge the quickest route to the running car. Straight past the guy to the passenger's door was quickest, but then he'd have to slide across to the driver's side, and that assumed the door wasn't locked, which it probably was. Sliding over the hood never seemed like a good idea. Past the guy on his left, then sharp turn to go between the front of the pickup and back of the Oldsmobile, and straight to the driver's door, which was not only guaranteed to be open, but also meant having a barrier between him and the assailant.

'Hey –'

Jose snapped his focus back to the customer, who was waving two bills in the air. 'Oh, yes. Six dollars.'

The guy handed the bills to Jose, and Jose handed over the corn.

'You have a nice day, sir. Drive safely.'

'Thanks, pal. Have a good one.'

The salesman took the bag back to his car and drove off, dis-appearing, after a while, into the shimmers. Jose took off the cowboy hat and wiped his brow again. His paranoia was so famil-iar that he didn't even really notice it any more; the constant situation assessing and escape planning that made up nearly every human interaction. He hadn't always been like that, of course, only for the past three years, since he crossed the river, but he no longer remembered, or didn't much remember his old self.

Jose watched the horizon, listening for the next rumble of distant engine and trying to judge how far away the horizon was. It was hard to tell. A long way. This was the flattest, emptiest place Jose had ever seen, just fields, low soy plants hugging the earth, almost emphasizing how flat it was. In the distance, on the other side of the road, he could see a vague shape that he assumed was a barn, but it was too far away to be able to say for sure.

All that flat land made him think of the contrast with home, and the steep hill, so steep it was almost a cliff, dotted with small wood and corrugated tin shacks that most of the people in Nogales called their houses. Occasionally somebody, trying to climb home drunk, would fall and roll all the way to the bottom, killing themselves, and when it rained, there was always the danger that one of the shacks might slide down into the town below, where during the day the Americans came and bought handblown glass, knitted wool blankets and shawls, and bottles of cheap tequila. When it rained, you'd hope it wasn't your house that slid down the hill, or your house that stood in the path of one that did.

Another motor, and Jose looked up, and waited. But after a minute he threw himself on to the hood of the Ford, his belly flat against it, and stretched out, ignoring the hot metal burning his forearms as he yanked his sign from under the windshield wipers and folded it over a couple of times, in uneven folds, before tossing it through the open window on to the floor of the truck. He opened the door and climbed in, sliding across to the driver's seat, and reached for the key to start the engine, as he glanced in the rearview, but it was too late. The state trooper had already pulled over, and Jose had to watch helplessly in the mirror as he got out and walked slowly towards the Ford, glancing down at the licence plate. Once he was out of the rearview, Jose stared straight forward, left arm resting on the window, right hand on the steering wheel.

'Afternoon, sir. Having trouble?'

'Uh.' Jose tried to think of the best answer. *Yes* seemed least complicated. 'Yes.' He lifted his hand from the steering wheel and gestured towards the hood. 'Engine died. Won't restart. Maybe just needs to cool down, you know, the heat.'

'Uh-huh. You want me to have a look?'

'You can, but I just looked, I don't see nothing.' Jose reached down with his left arm.

'Just freeze right there.'

Jose stopped, and turned to look at the trooper. 'I was just going to pull the hood release.'

'Okay.' The trooper pointed at the steering wheel. 'I want you to put both hands on that steering wheel – slowly.'

Jose did as he was told, looking through the windshield and down the road.

'Now I want you to tell me where your licence and registration are.'

'Licence is in my wallet, in my pocket. Registration in the glove compartment.'

'Okay, I want you to slowly reach into your pocket and take out your wallet and show me your driver's licence.'

Jose took his right hand off the steering wheel and pulled his wallet from his back pocket. The driver's licence was the only card. He handed it over, silently telling himself all the information that was on it. He looked at the trooper.

'Okay, Mr Alvarez. Now I want you to show me the registration. Slowly.'

Jose leaned across to the glove compartment and took out the piece of paper, which said that this pickup truck was registered to Juan Alvarez of 18th Street, Chicago, a street in a city to which Jose had never been. He handed it to the trooper.

'Okay, Mr Alvarez. Just wait right here.'

Jose watched in the rearview mirror the trooper walking back to his car, and hoped that it was as airtight as he'd been told it was. He'd gotten the licence, the truck and the registration from a bareknuckle fight in Detroit several months before. His job was to let a skinny black kid beat him up, and make it look convincing, while a bunch of grey-haired men with moustaches shouted and passed wads of money back and forth. They'd taken his picture before the fight, and when he'd done what he was told, they gave him this licence and took him out a back exit, where the truck was parked. Jose had never had to put the documents to the test before.

The trooper came back, and handed the documents through the

window. 'Thank you for your patience, Mr Alvarez. Can I ask what you're doing out here?'

'Indiana,' said Jose. 'I was visiting my cousin in Indianapolis, and now I'm driving home. To Chicago. I prefer not to drive on the interstates, you know? Too busy.'

'Uh-huh. Well, let's have a look at that engine.'

The trooper walked around to the front of the truck, and slapped his palms on the hood. Jose pulled the release, waited until the trooper had pushed the hood up, then turned the key. The truck started, of course. The trooper let the hood drop and walked back to the driver's side window.

'Must've just needed to cool down,' he said.

'Must have.'

'Well, have a good day. Drive safely, Mr Alvarez.'

Jose waited until the trooper had gotten back in his car, then tooted the horn twice and raised his arm out the window, trying to act as American as possible. The trooper flashed his lights, and Jose drove off, keeping his eyes on the rearview, and crossed himself, whispering, '*Gracias, Maria,*' when the police car made a U-turn and disappeared in the opposite direction. Jose glanced at the speedometer to make sure he wasn't going too fast, and kept driving west, towards the sun, which was now just dipping into the view out the windshield. He had an almost full tank, and didn't stop driving for hours, until he'd passed through Decatur, through Springfield, to someplace called Quincy, where he stopped to fill up, and crossed the Mississippi river into Missouri as the sun dropped below the face of the earth. He kept driving all night, seeing almost nothing, only the occasional car and the asphalt in front of his headlights, insects passing almost like rain in front of them, and splattering on the windshield. Jose didn't even know if they grew corn in Missouri, which meant the corn was wasted now, but he'd have to keep going, keep going, out of Illinois, because he didn't believe, didn't trust that he'd really gotten away. He drove through the night and through Missouri, on unlit rural highways, passing through the occasional town, at some point, although he wasn't really sure when, crossing over the Missouri river and into Kansas, his highbeams ploughing into the black space in front of his truck for several more hours, until in the rearview he saw the sun pushing above the horizon. Still he kept driving, until he had to stop because there was something blocking the road.

He'd come to a railroad crossing. The red and white gates pointed to the sky, the mesh chains hanging like a horse's mane against the upright wooden crossbars. In the middle of the tracks was a carcass, big, and positioned in a way that blocked the entire crossing. He couldn't just drive around it. He got out of the truck to take a closer look, leaving the door open and the engine running. What would happen, he wondered, when a train came along?

Jose stepped on to the tracks, and before looking down, looked both ways up the tracks, just to be sure.

It had been there for a while. Flies crawled around on the intestines, which coiled out from a gash in the belly. Pale pink fungus was growing around the gash itself. The fungus was fluffy, and reminded him of cotton candy. He'd only eaten cotton candy once, several years ago, on the sixteenth of September. Flags had fluttered in front of all the shop fronts in Nogales, as always, and they'd taken the kids to see the fireworks. Twice as many stands as usual lined the streets, selling tacos, antojitos, punch, balloons, plastic flags and other souvenirs. Marco wanted a flag, so he bought him one, the size of a postcard, and watched his son as he ran ahead of the family, shouting and waving it above his head. As he watched he felt a tug and looked down to see Gracia pulling on his little finger. She was pointing at a stand, between one with balloons and another with sombreros, where a man was looping paper cones around a vat of pink fluff. Jose went over and spoke to the man, who he knew vaguely, and bought a cotton candy. He handed it down to Gracia, and then pinched off a little for himself. Jose could still remember the way it felt, the soft spun sugar melting over his tongue, the one time he'd eaten cotton candy. He tried, for a moment, to think what they'd look like now, his kids. They'd left them with enough money for a few months, Gracia was twelve then, and they'd said, that night, not to worry. '*Vamos a regresar muy pronto*,' they'd whispered, and they'd meant it, but of course, it hadn't worked that way. When he imagined them now, it was hard to think of Marco without a dirty face, sitting on the sidewalks of Nogales, selling Chicklets for five cents. Gracia was fifteen now, and it was hard to conjure an image, not difficult, but hard, because he didn't want to see her in the back room of a bar, on her knees, or worse; it was hard.

There was a plastic yellow tag in one ear, with some letters and numbers stamped on it, but the code didn't mean anything to him. The tongue was hanging out of the mouth, resting in the gravel between the ties. Insects crawled on it, too. He could see the yellowish teeth where the lips were drawn back. It looked like it was snarling, an unnatural expression. The eyes were gone, just blank hollows in the sockets.

He kicked one of the hind legs, to see if it would break. It didn't. The carcass shuddered, as though it were waking up, and the flies scattered briefly before resettling on the exposed guts.

He looked back down the road in the direction from which he'd come. Nothing except the fields and the distortions of the heat rising from the asphalt.

He could probably drag it to the side or something, but he didn't feel like touching it. He ran his fingers through his hair, then scratched at his scalp until it hurt. Maybe he could just drive over it. Might fuck up the truck, though, and he needed it. He unbuckled his belt and unzipped his fly, then took out his cock. After a few seconds of rocking from his heels to his toes the piss came, and he soaked the carcass. The flies scattered again. When he finished they all landed back in the same spot. He closed his fly and rebuckled his belt. As he was rethreading the loose end through the belt loops he heard the sound of an engine. He turned and saw another vehicle approaching from the same direction he'd come. It started to slow down and eventually arrived and stopped right behind the Ford. He watched it the whole time, never taking his eyes from it.

The driver got out and shut the door of his van, too loudly. He was a big man, and wore a suede cowboy hat, but he didn't look much like a cowboy. He kept his attention on the Ford as he walked towards Jose, running a finger along the edge of the bed.

'Don't make 'em like that any more,' he said. 'Seventy-eight?'
'Seventy-six.'
The driver whistled a long, low note. 'Had it a long time, eh?'

'You could say that.' Jose watched closely as the driver hooked his thumbs into his waistband and hitched up his pants.

'What's the trouble?'

Jose tilted his head towards the tracks by way of answering.

'Holy shit! What the hell is it?'

'A dead cow.'

'I can see that, buddy, but how the hell did it get there? Where did it come from?'

'I don't know.'

'How long have you been standing here looking at it?'

Jose looked at his watch and shrugged. 'I guess about half an hour.'

'Shit, buddy.' The driver took off his cowboy hat and ran his arm along his forehead, then replaced the hat. 'Should we try moving it?'

'I didn't really want to touch it.'

'Shit, buddy. The thing's dead. Ain't gonna bite you.'

'It probably has bacteria. I don't really want to touch it.'

'Huh.' The driver took off his hat and wiped his forehead again. He was balding. 'What do you think we should do about it, then?'

'I don't know.'

'Huh.'

They both stood looking at it.

'Can't just drive over it, I suppose,' the driver said after a minute.

'Don't think so.'

The driver removed his hat and wiped his forehead again, then walked to the tracks and bent over it, at the hind legs. 'Well,' he said, and grabbed the legs and tried to drag it. The flies scattered as it shuddered with the driver's touch. He grunted and his face showed the strain. He couldn't move it, and only succeeded in shaking loose a few more coils of intestine before letting the legs flop back to the ground.

'You mind giving me a hand here?'

'I told you already. I don't want to touch it.'

'Come on, buddy.' His voice was angry. 'Give me a fucking hand here.'

'No. I already said.'

The driver swore, grabbed the legs again, and yanked, his feet planted against the cross ties, his shoulders trembling with the strain; and the white of the cow's legs reminded Jose of the white of her arms that night, and the way they'd dragged her out. He'd realized, under the Arizona moon, what that shade of white meant, and when they let go he'd walked over to her. They stood, looking at him, not at her, because she was nothing to look at any more, and he'd knelt down, one knee in the dirt, and lifted her head. He'd kissed her lips, just softly, and her lips were cold, and then they'd said, 'Come on, *vamos,*' and he'd had to follow, there was no choice, and they'd left her there, and he'd tried to look back, but he could only see the coyote behind him. And that was that.

'Goddammit,' the driver said, and let go. He looked up at Jose. 'Okay. I got it.'

Jose watched as the driver walked back to his van, then returned with a long rope. Neither of them said anything while he worked, tying the rope around the cow's ankles, then holding the other end as he walked back to the van again, dropping the rope when it was out straight. He made a U-turn and backed the van up to the rope end, got out, and tied the rope to the hitch on the back bumper. When he'd finished tying the rope, he looked up at Jose from his crouching position, then stood and got back behind the wheel. Jose watched the carcass slide over the railroad tracks, and watched some of the intestine unravel and spill into the dirt as the van slowly dragged it past him. Eventually it was sitting just behind his truck, and the driver came back, and untied the rope from the hitch and from the white legs of the cow. When he'd finished coiling the rope, the driver stood straight, took off his hat, wiped his forehead, and looked at Jose. Then he gave the carcass a hard kick. Spores of cotton candy fungus floated into the air. The driver sneezed.

'Not so fucking hard, buddy, see? Not so goddamn hard after all.' The driver wiped his hands on his jeans and looked down at the licence plate on the Ford.

'Shit, buddy, Illinois. You're a long way from home. What the hell are you doing out here?'

Jose hadn't moved since the driver had arrived. 'Driving,' he said.

'Driving where, buddy?'

Jose licked his dry lips. 'Away.'

The driver shook his head and walked back to his van holding the coil of rope, started the engine, pulled around Jose's truck, and drove over the tracks and down the highway. Jose stood watching until the van disappeared into the heat that shimmered from the asphalt, considering whether he might be better off if he just drove all the way back to Nogales, and whether he wanted to know what he'd find there.

David Morley

Whitethroat

Whitesmiths work the tinct tin into leaves.
They could weave, if they chose, a whole whitten of
    it.
It would glitter, that false wayfarer's tree,
as the whitethorn, or the whitethroat calling from its
    false leaves.

Paul Muldoon

Eggs

I was unpacking a dozen eggs
into the fridge when I noticed a hair-line crack
at which I pecked

till at long last I squeezed
into a freshly white-washed
scullery in Cullenramer. It was all hush-hush

where my mother's mother took a potash rag
to a dozen new-laid eggs
and, balancing a basket on her bike,

pushed off for Dungannon. This was much
before the time a priest would touch
down from the Philippines with a clutch

of game bird eggs
and introduce a whole new strain of fighting cocks.
It would be midnight when my mother's mother got
    back

from Dungannon, now completely smashed
on hard liquor bought with hard cash,
fuck you, cash on the barrel. It was all hush-hush

as she was taken from a truck
painted matter-of-factly MILK & EGGS
into which they'd bundled her, along with her bike,

for delivery to Cullenramer. It would be all hush-hush
next morning in the white-washed
scullery where she wrung out the potash

rag and took it to another dozen-or-so new-laid eggs,
from any one of which I might yet poke
my little beak.

Carola Luther

Possessions

I could have fallen after you down the burrow of your breathing
but something kept shivering beyond my thoughts like a saviour,
a vagrant out of sight, making up stories about the jars and shelving
and forgotten boxes of my life, so it was all I could do to keep
my nerve, eyes glued to the morse of a possible star, and ignore
the moon, blowsy and drunk as it was, lurching after clouds
in this strange half-dark, as if a city were approaching
over a hill, or we were that far into summer, that far north
that we mustn't lie still, mustn't rest, any of us, in this leaking
of light from the cracked-open arctic, this melt-coloured sky,
this night half-shut, a sign, like the eye of a man so tired he *must
lie down, must stay awake,* unable to trust we won't steal
his suitcase, any of us that is, except you, so far down in your sleep
the shuffling's nearly stopped on the soft leaf floor of your wood.

Afterwards

get out of town, driving your car fast along the new ring road,
going west for a mile and swerving hard left at the main junction,
following the diversion for a few hundred yards to the crossroads,
turning right, and right again over the bridge, before the sharp
left corner which you take swiftly, changing down a gear
as you twist between pylons and make the quick short cut
through the disused warehouse, heading in the direction
of the old road to the sea, and here you'll pick up
the first lane you come to, which appears to turn inland
but doubles back in fact upon itself, bringing you out
several miles on between a quarry and a vee-shaped spinney
of trees, and just a little further, in unkempt countryside
you can slow right down, looking for where a shadow of a track
meets the lane at a mound, and bear left here, and keep bearing
left, continuing through woods to a clump of the darkest
and most silent pines, and when it feels possible,
and in the distance you begin to think it probable
that the moors will open out on every side,
bring the vehicle to a stop, anywhere where a quiet pool
of sunlight may be found. Turn off the engine
and look at your hands. Look at the sun on your knuckles,
the deep folds and grooves of skin over the joints
of your fingers, the way the veins rise above the fine
hand-bones like tributaries of a dark grey river, how
two grey branches almost meet between the third finger
and the fourth, how the shadows plummet here
into the ravine between them, how going over the edge
in a small canoe would contact the rock-white water
drumming through the rapids of the rolling dark
plunging in and out of the roar of the river and turning

over, and over, and over, and calming right down
in the slow shallow width of the palm,
and beginning to drift between reeds of the delta,
you'll manoeuvre later through tricky marsh islands,
and somewhere here disembark and meander
through dunes to the deepcut valley of the heart,
and falling in a basket made of rushes
you'll bask in the sun, feeling the thrum
of the water beneath you bearing you onward
to the place where the fate line crosses, and allowing
the hollowed-out log that you now lie down in,
clothed in the swathes of your white linen clothes,
you'll follow the inexorable pull of the current
towards the slopes of the mountain of Venus,
and from the summit if you decide to climb it,
you will see the road carved at the wrist,
glimmering and pale beside ancestral bracelets,
and life keeping time like the heartbeat of bird
held in, held together, by a few twig bones
and the very thinnest of skins.

Greta Stoddart

Pupil

I could no more know
myself than this flame
seated in the air
one quarter of an inch
above its burnt root
– so self-contained a form
you'd think it held in ice –

no more know that flame
than one drop of rain
or a single leaf
let alone this draught
slicing in across the sill
nudging the little
corpse-boat of a fly;

no more know you, fly,
than this cat – the cat
perhaps but what about
the way it holds us
in a gaze so void
of an idea of self
our own can only fail.

If we could return
that look we might learn
to take something from
nothing, might begin
to steady and see,
figure who we are
in that slit black flame.

You Drew Breath

as a boy draws something silver from a river,
an angler from the sea a bale of weed;
as a woman draws herself from a bath,
as blood is drawn from a vein.
You drew breath as thread is drawn through
the eye of a needle, wet sheets through a mangle,
as steel is drawn through a die to make wire
and oil draws up through wick its flag of fire.
You drew breath as a reservoir draws from a well
of ink and a mouth and a nose and eyes are drawn,
as a sheet is drawn from under the dying
and over the heads of the dead.
You drew breath as the last wheezing pint is drawn,
as money and a bow and the tide are drawn;
as up over her head a woman draws
a dress and down on to her a man.
You drew breath as a cloud draws its pall
across the moon, across the car park
where a sky-blue line draws the way
all the way to Maternity; as all in blue
they drew a semi-circle round the bed,
a line and then a knife across the skin;
as in another room someone drew
a curtain round its runner, a hand across
a pair of finished eyes. You drew breath
as they drew you – besmeared and blue – out
and sublime was your fury at being drawn
into this air, this theatre; you drew breath
for the first time – for a second I held mine.

Verfremdungseffekt

Our budget was the biggest joke.
We blew half of it on a fat hack in a Chinese
'All You Can Eat for a Tenner!'

We sat and watched as he helped himself to thirds
of Ham Foo Yung – next day we read his piece
on a local midwife's prize ornamental cabbage.

We pulled out all the tricks: natty flip
of a baking sheet for thunder, our hero walking
away to a pair of hand-clopped brogues.

Pulled them out *literally*, you understand.
We'd read our Brecht and were completely sold;
no bourgeois suspension of disbelief for us!

So really the conditions couldn't've been better
that July evening in Speke Youth Club where,
impossible to get a black-out – the sun, the skylights –

we still crept on 'stage', careful not to follow
the shredded pitch-markings nor make eye contact
with the audience we outnumbered five to three

(had we an ounce of common decency
we'd've pulled the show and paid their refund
in the pub but we were young, and all that mattered).

I've forgotten every word of *Kleines Organon für das
    Theater*
but not how it ended that night:
our final dramatic pause filling

with the chittity-chit of swallows, the M6's rivery
    hum,
our faces lifting their faces up
not to some fusty old gods but a heaven

of swing ropes and gym ladders suspended there
like something unbelievable that did once and would,
with faith enough or a full house, happen again.

Eoghan Walls

Frogness

is the taste of oxides through the skin.
Winter as a buried square of oak.
Limbless dreams of bites at wavering algae.
Rare wakeful blinks onto brown films of moisture.
Slow pulse; the weighted world a rootful murmur.
Spring a tingled ooze of warmth in threetoes,
memories. Awareness, nosing earth
to wind electrified with the pull to feed.

Horror as a skyfall feathersweep.
Roar of lights on tarmac. Wellyboots,
sloshing palmfuls of spawn destined to sour.
The squeal of cousins rattled in fingercages.
Traces of opened bodies. Freeze at horror;
stalks make cover, soil is like-my-colour,
leaves my-shape. Sweat when it gets close;
leap is panic, leap is fling-of-flesh.

The wind is tug of moist hooks through our pores.
This journeylife. The need for other places,
ratless waters, bog of nightsongs, marsh
of grabbing skinbirth. Smelling the horizon,
gone to them. Hide under things, and watch.
My tongue is half-my-gaze, the flies are food
gripped. This travel on roughbelly concrete,
groundhug mud. We march, and taste the words.

Crocus, column; break, murder, walk;
church, meagre, brick; walk, squad;
scrotum, squad; root, shrub, stench;
wench, bottom, relish; marriage, chorus;
rummage, wench, wrench; felch, squirt;
breach, retch. Learn the song in belchnotes,
in soft farting. Brood, grass, squad;
murder, blemish. Blood. Chorus. Walk.

Danger and leaves and no two close, and sing.
When she is there, saddle her thrust, her bridge,
and stirrup and buckle. Aware of the comet above
burning skin, bursting to nibble at clouds,
flaring through your frogsoul as you spurt.
Then break, to hold the soil. Winter is soon
and you have memories. The comet will come
and this will be again. But first the winter.

The Naming of the Rat

Foreigner. Coiled on stones, fur thorned and black
on bald skin, like His crown, staring from Antrim's shore
over the Scottish sea-world. Who dared the hobbled swim

once the frozen saltbridges had melted. Or huddled
in the wooden core of longboats, hushed, recoiling
at the seal-clad shins in *brokke*. To parleyed nobles,

you shall be *Francach*, French one; and to their servants,
your name the hiss of boiling water poured in holes;
till monks close you in pages. *Rattus Norwegicus.*

Clutch four pink fingers to the rock. There's eating here.
And not till the eleventh raid, within a burnt church,
nested in a native's ribcage, dense with grasses,

five suckling polyps of youth, blind at your thinning teats,
shall Christ walk to you, past the grey-haired scavengers
collecting bits of metal from the fresher corpses.

His hand inside to touch you, matted organ. *You too
are mine; but every night shall be a night of long knives.
They will train dogs to snap the spines of little ones,*

*make poison, snares of steel. Though you hide in crisp-bags,
run through streams of shit, clutch to corner-rubbish,
they shall hunt you. Whenever their children wail with jaundice,*

wander with eyes like holes, you will be blamed by them.
And crucified, injected, smothered, drawn and quartered.
But still, I ask you, never be more than ten rat-lengths

from each. Eat what they leave, and learn to creep. Stay close.
Red eyes of the white rats, black eyes of the brown
still locked behind the birth-swelling of lids, shall nuzzle

into His skin, lick blood trickling from His palm wounds;
sky gaze turned to the mewling runt. *Even you,*
the littlest of all. I call you Sailor's Warning.

Carrie Etter

Divorce

Forced to apologize
for the dirty sheets, he looks
proud in his shame.
I left that bed years ago
and have returned to collect
a forgotten book, a favourite blanket.
He knew the names of trees better
than makes of cars, but neither well.
He remembers which sister
I like least and asks
how she is doing.

Drought

Three farmers amble into the diner, pulling on the rims of baseball caps blazoned with brands of corn seed. They wait for a waitress's wave before sliding over naugahyde into a booth. At another table, a five-year-old begins to pout. 'I'm hot,' she says. 'It's hot.' Her mother nods and shushes her, tells her to eat her fries. The farmers order sodas and the special, and relax into their seats, raising an arm to rest on top or lowering an elbow onto the Formica's cool slickness. Johnny Cash comes on the radio, and the oldest gives in to a smile, a slight crease in either tanned cheek. 'I'm hot,' the pig-tailed girl repeats, louder now. 'I want some water.' Reflexively the farmers' spines straighten a little, and the men's conversation dies as they listen. The mother reproaches her daughter in an indiscernible undertone, but the intent is clear. The girl, however, is not having it. 'I want some water,' she says again. 'Now!' At which point the skinny, grinning waitress, having heard the first plea, places a sweating glass before her and anticipates a good tip from the sighing mother. The farmers are looking at one another, trying to find their way back into talk, appalled and thrilled by the girl's blunt confidence, and, with it, immediate satisfaction.

Stephen Knight

The Edge of Sleep

(i)
There goes the light,
Leaving Rhossili Bay
Particulate grey –
And that's all right.
Nothing palls like white.
But should we stay
To watch the day
Turn into night
Now, hand in hand,
Waves flow
Across the sand?
Or should we go?
If we can't understand,
At least let us know.

(ii)
Enterprising snow
Builds on all the land.
A few sheep stand
And wait while, yards below,
Black waves flow
Across the sand
Like something planned.
– Time to go?
Yes. Time to walk away.
None too bright,
The sheep will stay
Another night,
Another day:
White on white.

Iain Galbraith

Best Man Dead

A lime-kiln's tumble in the drum of the wind
the dovecot slipping its marches to roll
to a field of crushed clams – accidental
here as the scurrying shadows of clouds
the man who strains with the yellow pail
the turnstone piping beyond the links . . .

and the two knights of solemn vow, small bodies
twisted apart by the mortar-blast of their choice
smile in calamity's face, inviolate now
their closed eyes and lips candescent with return.

Stellar State

If the valley fills with water, if the valley
fills with light, if the stars can trip our gaze
so surely, surely they can stay till May.
Stellata if you leave my bedside
while I watch the water rise, if the air
is damp, if we are sinking, if my sight
sees not a person pass alone
but clouds and blue and window days
a garden, tree, the petals burning
blind then nothing here but white.

Sean O'Brien

Praise of a Rainy Country

in memory of Julia Darling

The popular song that first season, remember,
Was 'Rhythm of the Rain' by The Cascades.
In tower blocks on dripping summer evenings
The impossible girlfriends stood at their sinks
In slips and curlers, rinsing out their blouses
While it pleaded – *Listen* – from the radio.
They mouthed the words and drew the curtains shyly.
It rained on the examination halls
And on parades and wedding photographs,
On funerals and literary episodes, on rich and idle
   hours
When we required no occupation but the noise
As rain, like imperial clockwork, ran down in the
   streets
Or thundered intermittently in vast
Defenestrated Steinways haunted by Debussy.
Rain fell in the hair of all those girls. It fell
In silver columns on the stroke of midnight,
Fell during the rows and the football results
Or while we were sleeping or eating or bathing
Or watching the telephone. Fell in the sea,
In the desert where no rain had fallen for years,
And fell behind the waterfall and on this book
Left out overnight in the garden
To flower illegibly. If there was a dry place
It waited for rain. If there was a damp one
It lay in a state of arousal. And we, my friends,
Were the innumerable heirs to this republic.

– Ours was just a period in the history of rain,
One called by some *The Inundation*
And by others *L'Apres-Moi*, since we were young.
The rain is all digression, touching
Everything and nothing, as peremptory
As the Creation, emptying itself
Afresh into this iron river, pooling
In the hand I offer you, and still it seems
Behind the roar and hush there is a chord
We know but never hear, that rain awakes,
To hang suspended there between
Acceptance and desire, that calls to us
And, for no reason, speaks on our behalf.

The Brazier

Someone was up before dawn
To light the brazier by the path
Between the wood and the allotments.
It adds its slow grey smoke to fog,
As a choked pipe adds
Its trickle to a stagnant pool.

I study the half-closed eyes of the brazier
In downtime. This too will pass,
I have it on authority.

But who comes here to warm themselves?
The dead old men who dug this iron ground
Before we'd even heard of it?
Their sheds retire to the earth
Among white grass, while winter
Holds its siege and trains go past
To somewhere else, the place
Where meanings wait impatiently.

The brazier issues the idea of heat,
Like a twist of clear water
Fed into the murk of the pool.
I try to warm my hands,
But there is too much winter in the field.

The brazier grows a cowl of smoke,
Then doffs it slowly, a magnifico
Assigned to this unfinished hell,
This foggy swamp of burning ice.
What was the sin? Austerity?

This is the world we were promised, it seems,
Grey pastoral, an enclave in the North's
Built-over fields, a grave in all but name,
Among frostbitten beans and cabbage-stalks,
A world with one season, whose nights
Are moonless, starless intervals
Of cold within the cold, whose days
Begin and fade beneath the brazier's
Slow, grey-lidded, parsimonious gaze.

Symposium at Port Louis

Drifting ashore on a salt-cracked book-box
Buoyed up with Byron and Shakespeare,
Once again we ship *Coles' Notes*

To Newcastle. No home these days
For obsolete litterateurs,
Only temporary anchorage

Deep in the southern hemisphere.
Safe for now in the cyclone's eye,
With scribbled notes on a borrowed page

And winging it like Hannay,
It seems our task is to discover whether
Concordia et Progressio can

Ever be more than contraries
Yoked by violence together.
– Someone would know, as your man

Remarked. We have come a long way
To sit in this elegant council chamber
Emblazoned with creole

Chevaux-de-mer; to hear
A grave centenarian entrepreneur
Set down his ledger and appeal

To his gods, to whit: Carlyle
And Chesterton and Masefield's 'Cargoes'.
Here the rolling English drunkard

Looks in secret at his watch and longs
For a sober world of prose,
Where objects are allowed

To be themselves, and stern embargoes
Seal the ports of commerce and of dreams
To grand abstraction and the soul alike:

Let Jesuit and Mameluke
Politely anchor in the roads
Till Mrs Hawoldar decides

To fire the sunset gun and bring
Proceedings to a close.
The names of former mayors

Are allegorical in spades:
Monsieur Charon, Msrs Forget,
Tranquille and Martial. Their shades

Are words alone and yet persist
To haunt the carnival,
To make this page a sheet of surf

Dissolving as it slides
Across the reef, till danger meets
The sea-change into pleasure, when the mind

For all its radical intent gives in
To ocean light and Phoenix beer,
Reef-walking fishermen at dawn

Who glide and strut like Sega's
Dancing girls in skirts of flouncing surf –
And in the steady winter sunshine

Distances so vast and theoretical
That fear and ecstasy are one.
Yet on the *menu touristique*

There are items never mentioned:
Race and class and money
And the iron status quo,

Concerning which guests do not speak:
Out of this place, tradition states,
Desire not to go. Meanwhile

Like peasants in Van Gogh,
Cane-cutters with their cutlasses
Relax at noon beside the road

And over dinner at Grand Baie
Among the careless trove of pearls
And smirks and scallop-sconces

The Chinese minister confers
His poems on three hundred Hindu guests,
As Muslim families in fear secrete

Kalashnikovs between the joists
And Creole says what people mean,
Not what they ought, and all day long

The smell comes up the cracks
In concrete-covered gutters –
Rum and Phoenix, poverty

And wasted time, because
The afterlives of colonies
Are everywhere the same.

Meanwhile at Cascade Chamarel
The rainbow will explode
And Ganesh, god of memory,

Will accommodate it all,
Gazing calmly inwards
Underneath the waterfall.

This stormy chamber in its garden is
A southern cell where Prospero
Might set to right the grievances

Of this extended family –
But this time let the magus drown his book
Before he bids us all adieu.

Let poison run back up the leaf,
The will resume its innocence, and all
Before they go join hands downstage

To take the sea's applause and look
Once more at how the waves come in
As ever, faithful to the shore

And yet asleep,
As soundly as the drowned men in the deeps
Beyond the coral shelf,

To whom the upper world
Is sealed, as firmly
As the mind of God himself.

Jamie McKendrick

Black Gold

Here are the Carthaginian figs, Ciano
grinned as he handed Mussolini
some specimen chunk of shiny
copper ore from the Lezhë mine
in conquered Albania.

And here are the figs of Mesopotamia,
Vice President Cheney
traces on the map the red-marked pipeline
from the fields of Rumaila and Kirkuk
to the Turkish port of Ceyhan.

Ire

Not for a moment was the real wasp fooled
by the fake wasp's black-and-yellow costume:
instead of being flattered or amused,
she seized the hoverfly and stung its face
while her jaws hacksawed through its torso.
In that embrace you could clearly see
how such clever jewelled mimicry,
all jasper and jet, was several shades astray,
too beetle-bright and ultimately pointless.
But so much deadly ire at imitation!
The counterfeiter pulsed its flimsy wings
so the wasp tore them out and let them fall
then flew off with the rest of her disciple
to whisper in its ear one final lesson.

Don Paterson
Three Versions from Rilke's Sonnets to Orpheus

Being

Silent comrade of the distances,
Know that space dilates with your own breath;
ring out, as a bell into the Earth
from the dark rafters of its own high place –

then what feeds on you grows strong again.
Learn the transformations through and through:
what in your life has most tormented you?
If the water's sour, turn it into wine.

Our senses cannot fathom this night, so
be the meaning of their strange encounter,
at their crossing, be the radiant centre.

And should the world itself forget your name
say this to the silent earth: *I flow.*
Say this to the rushing stream: *I am.*

Anemone

In the meadow, the anemone
is creaking open to the dawn.
By noon, the sky's polyphony
will flood her white lap till she drowns.

The tiny muscle in her star
is tensed to open to the All,
yet the daylight's blast so deafens her
she barely heeds the sunset's call

and finds the willpower to refurl
her petal-edges – her, the power
and will of how many worlds!

In our fist of violence, we outlive her.
But which new life will see *us* flower
and face the heavens, true receivers?

Taste

Gooseberry, banana, pear
and apple, all the ripenesses . . .
Read it in the child's face:
the life-and-death the tongue hears

as she eats . . . this comes from far away.
What is happening to your mouth?
Where there were words, discovery
flows, all shocked out of the pith –

What we call *apple* . . . Do you dare
Give it a name? This sweet-sharp fire
rising in the taste, to grow

clarified, awake, twin-sensed,
of the sun and earth, the here and the now –
the sensual joy, the whole Immense!

Blessing Musariri

Popular Fiction

she's looking for love in a CLK
silver like a bullet straight to my heart
she said
that's what i want   she smears her lips
orange flame and pouts   yes
i would be somebody then   a yard
bigger than your fields of maize in
tribal trustlands and walls like those of Jericho
behind which i sleek and spoiled will hide
from these narrow streets   endless acceptance
of mediocrity   she strokes a rough palm
over stretched denim and winds her waist to a silent
      tune
this body has a future you know – two kids no more
she smiles
repairs to follow   yes
would you ask me to sweep your muddy floors then
offer me day-old sadza and sugar bean stew hmm
i would laugh in your face
she draws on some eyebrows in black pencil
lines her eyes   shakes
a mane of sixty thousand dollar hair
from union street flea market   oh yes
baby-girl's got a dream   silver like a bullet
a crown on this pretty head   me – ghetto queen

Chenjerai Hove

Counting the Nights

Another night
spent without you.
Another echo
in the distance,
far away from my dirty fingers.

I let sunlight
filter
through my numb fingers.
For once,
the silent echoes crush my heart.

No,
this is a dream I did not dream.
Was it your birthday today?
And the wind carried away
the cakes littering my mind?
Was it someone's funeral today?
A funeral with more corpses
than mourners?

Oh, this distant place
they call birthday!
Oh, this intimate place
they call deathday!

All places are faded
in these tremors of bleeding hearts,
you, far away,
me, so frighteningly near myself,
but torn
between nearness and far away.

just take your time,
count the leftover trinkets
in your palms.
Count the lone stars
left gazing at you,
Smile along
hum along
like our little honeybird.

Paul Perry

Wintering

That was my last year in Florida,
illegal and thinking of marriage
as one way to stay. Sleepless nights
of argument and indecision. And

to keep us going I worked a cash job
at an orchid farm. Long hours in
the sun, poor in paradise, the heat
on my back, drilling for a living.

I worked with a Mexican man.
My man Victor, the orchid keeper
called him. Friendly and amused
at the affluent couples who came

to purchase the rich, ornate dreams.
We buried a dead owl together.
I remember that. And my body aching
in the sun. Floating home to argue.

What we were doing I was told
was wintering. Getting ready for
the cold, its indiscretion, its disregard.
Nailing sheets of plastic on to a wooden

frame, hammering, drilling, and sweating
to protect the fragile flowers
and their steel interiors, their
engineered hearts and worth.

That is already a long time ago.
Its contradictions apparent.
Wintering in sunshine. The past
still growing towards the light.

I think of them now as some sort
of emblem of that past, ghostly
orchids shedding their gracious
petals, as we winter here ourselves,

batten down the hatches and wait
for whatever storm is coming, whatever
calamity the cold has to offer us
in the same way the orchids do,

I suppose, waiting through winter
to emerge with budding, fantastical
and colourful insistence to wake and
remind us to be nothing less than amazed.

Frances Leviston

Dragonflies

Watching these dragonflies
couple in air, or watching them try,
the slender red wands
of their bodies tapped
end to end like fingertips, then faltering wide
on the currents of what feels to me
a fairly calm day,

I think of delicate clumsinesses
lovers who have not yet mentioned
love aloud enact,
the shy hands they extend
then retract, the luscious fumbled chase
among small matters seeming massive
as rushes are to dragonflies,

and in the accidental
buzz of a dragonfly against bare skin,
how one touch fires
one off again on furious wings
driven towards love and love, in its lightness,
driven the opposite way,

so in fact they hardly meet
but hang in the hum of their own desires.
Still, who would ask
these dragonflies to land on a stone,
and like two stones to consummate?
How can I demand love stop, and speak?

Lampadrome

Lampadedromy n. (Gr. Antiq.) A torch-race ... 1848 Craig has the incorrect form Lampadrome – OED

It's late, but here's the linkboy's light for hire.
He lifts it, dripping, high above his head
and waits his corner, watching textures fade,
till night robs even Corinth's meanest sires

of nerve. Then they approach him first, demand
his guidance, knowing how their silvered palms
are dim – as dull as all the temples' alms –
without the benefaction of his brand,

which, with careless alchemy, transmutes
their proffered coins and greying hair to gold.
The boy, despite his edge, is still compelled
to mark the sought address and pick their route,

falling with awful calm through a dark door
his torch reveals to be the road, unpaved,
between the walls of dwellings so depraved
his passengers, for all they are aware,

have shifted planes. They huddle in his float
of light, afraid of what they see much less
than what their formal consciences can guess –
the thieves and whores, the madman's single note –

must somewhere now be living, since they don't
appear to dirty men's and merchants' air.

Inside the open doorway of a bar
full cups lie smashed, and women creak with want,

and some rough parley's trailing down the street
like smoke. The boy's a marvel! Unafraid,
and honest, too: his fee already paid,
he could – no loss – have left them there for meat,

but now they spill like syrup from a tap
and find they're on a thoroughfare they know,
carrying them around the lampadrome
past fans who throng and crane at every gap.

Our boy is one. The merchants never twig
that every fare he's taken passed this way,
no matter what the risk, what loop awry
to skirt the roaring, monolithic rig

and through those columns' black interstices
to glimpse a distant nimbus – five, or six,
now clumped, now stringing out and out, like tricks
upon the eyes – distending in a breeze

and lapping glory: fickle, minor gods
disguised at play, and each one's brazier hitched
to an athlete lit and lofted from the pitch
of rank obscurity – like Aaron's rod,

its roadside yellow flowers blazing high
to lead the funeral march through any map.
Applause unfolds inside, that honey-trap.
He'd like to run the race before he dies

or die right now, his unsung torch nipped out
and silver gone to get some bastard pissed.
What difference is there – linkboy, lampadist?
The one who burns within, the one without.

Jane Feaver

from *The Art of Losing*

1

We watched her from the bedroom window, striding along the edge of the road, tripping in the ditch, catching her balance, *thump*, *thump*, *thump*, her fist beating time against her side. She was almost skipping to get there, heading for the phone box another twenty paces or so. We could see the dark, muffled shape of someone framed in red, in pieces, with his back to the world, head to one side, phone nestled to his ear by a raised shoulder: Daddy.

She arrived. She was talking to the door of the booth, holding out her hands to it. Daddy was all black until his head, still attached to the receiver, swivelled around showing the pale skin of his face. She began knocking almost politely on the glass, tapping with her knuckles, like Little Red Riding Hood.

Then she gave it a slap with the palm of her hand, and another, and another. 'Let me in! Open the door! Let me in!' She was jumping on the spot, crossing her arms and hugging herself, 'Get out! Just get out of there!'

We squirmed as if we were watching a film. *Mr Spark's going to hear her! They're all going to hear!* The four of us were crammed against the small bedroom window. 'She shouldn't make so much noise!'

The door of the booth was heavy and stiff, opening slowly and unevenly as Daddy pushed out, his elbows ready to lift around his head like a hostage. We saw a curtain blink in the row of cottages. It was too late to go and get her. And she was swearing at him now . . .

*

Bank Top is built against the slope of the valley like it has pitched up at the end of a long walk and refused to go any further, its head resting on the ledge of the road. From the top, the road side, it looks like a tiny bungalow, two shuttered windows either side of a doorway. But over from the opposite side of the valley, from the old school, for instance, its backside is like anyone's picture of how a house should be, four crossed windows around a solid green door. It is a fixture in our treasure maps that include rabbit village, the bank of reservoir on the horizon, and by the crease of the river the chapel with its graveyard, and the jumble of buildings at Mill Farm.

There are four of us: Me, Amelia, Biddy and Jack. In our family, there are rules. We're not allowed to use the words 'cute' or 'toilet', or 'nice', not at home, anyway. We're allowed to say 'bloody' and 'shit', but not in front of granny and grandpa and not at school. The toilet is the bog. But not at school. And at granny's it's the loo.

If we go out at the cottage we have to bring something back, wood for the fire, or gooseberries or mushrooms, otherwise, we get sent out again. 'Lazy bleeders,' Daddy calls us.

The bog is outside at the bottom of the house next to the cellar. The cellar is a black, dank hole with a door that won't shut properly, and a pile of coal inside that needs collecting from. The air in the doorway feels electric and heavy as if someone is hiding in there, waiting. We only go to the bog in broad daylight and even then, Biddy and Jack bang their legs against the wooden seat to frighten the monsters.

Another rule: you're not allowed to pee in the bucket because it fills up too quickly. Someone is always peeing in it because you can clearly see turds floating. There's a particular shade of blue I can't see without the prickle of Sanilav in my nose; sometimes even the sky can make it run.

When the bucket is almost overflowing, there's a stand-off about emptying it. Always, eventually, Mummy gives in and we watch her, staggering out with the weight of it, muttering that Daddy is a selfish sod. She digs a hole in the old strawberry patch and tips the bucket out, battling to hold on to the handle and aim straight, turning her face from it in disgust.

Strictly peeing's supposed to be done in the garden. There's a burnt band of grass and dandelions by the wall, where three of us squat before bed. Every evening, when he thinks of it in time, Jack tries to catch us, arching his wee over the low wall to land at our feet, splashing up our wellies, or worse, on to our bare skin. Each time someone is tangled in their knickers, trying to avoid him, stinging themselves on nettles and shrieking and swearing as if the dusk was a room that contained us.

Another rule: water has to be collected every morning, by everyone, except Daddy. The water comes from a spring, down the lane at the bottom of the hill. Mummy goes with two huge beer-making canisters with taps and we follow in a line behind taking big plastic juice containers. Mummy has the strength of an ox, Daddy says.

Drinking water is rationed. Washing water has to come from the rain butt outside the front door, which we strain with the tea-strainer for mosquito larvae. There's one stinking flannel and a pecking order for it, Mummy first. After a few days, we don't bother. Every now and again Mummy remembers and we have to wash our teeth in a mug of water outside.

At the cottage there is no one else. We have no visitors, no friends. The world is contained by the drawstring of horizons: we explore, we fight, we collect wood on walks, occasionally we collect bunches of flowers to say we're sorry.

From London, it takes seven hours' driving, us wedged together on a back seat that smells of orange peel and the threat of someone being sick, eking out the fruit pastels, occasionally lunged at from the front by Mummy when Daddy says he'll crash the car if we don't belt up.

We had hardly arrived – Biddy, Amelia and Jack not helping, Mummy fraught because there are mice droppings everywhere, waiting for Daddy to tell her that she's bourgeois so that she can ask him why she puts up with it at all; Daddy grim but offering, after he's lit the fire, to make scrambled egg, Biddy making a sound as if she's going to be sick so that he sends her to the bedroom, lifting his hand in the air above her head, and I can see the knob in the middle of his forehead twitching and bulging like it does when he is going to blow – when the noise began.

It sounded like a chainsaw at first and we were all stopped in our tracks, as if the world outside was made of wood and being cut up into the tiniest of pieces; and then, more purposeful, as if someone was engraving the hillside, criss-cross, up and down, a long word, like NORTHUMBERLAND, in block capitals, letter by letter.

The living room window is at the top of the cottage and from it you can see right across the valley, down to the river, to where the creature, half human, half machine was revving uphill against the grass like the nub of a zip; or a fat fly worrying backwards, for-wards, diagonally for a way out, rubbing his hands on the handlebars, *zzzZZZZzzzZZZZzzzzzZZZZzzz*.

'What on earth . . .?!' It was as if the whole effort of bringing us here, of believing it was the right thing to do, collapsed in the face of that sound.

'I didn't come here for this! Jesus Christ, what's he doing?' Daddy had pushed us out of the way and had the upper casement of the window open, peering out. Mummy was distracted for a minute from her catalogue of unfit-for-human-habitation.

As I fixed the noise to the bike and picked out limbs and the shininess of a jacket, the thrill I felt at the presence of such an unexpected body was like a door opening in the sky and a light shining in. 'It must be one of the boys from the farm,' I said, as matter-of-factly as I could. 'Brian, maybe.'

'Brian!' Amelia turned on me. 'Your boyfriend!'

'I don't even know him!'

'You know his name!'

'We all know his name!'

'Mummy doesn't.'

Mummy didn't ever remember anyone's name, none of my friends, or their mothers and fathers, or my teachers.

'Why are you going red, then?' Amelia danced in front of me gleefully, shaking her fingers in my face, and Biddy looked up at me wide-eyed. 'You are!'

Daddy, who couldn't contain himself any longer, exploded with a stutter of instructions, 'Go and get things from the car! Move!

Out of the way! Help your mother!' He was strangling the top of a chair with both hands and the veins on the backs stuck out like wires. 'Now!'

Mummy took one look at him and I could see her biting her tongue. 'Come on, come and help me,' she said patiently taking Biddy by the hand and leading us all out to the front. 'Daddy's had a long drive. Let's leave him in peace.'

It annoyed me beyond belief how quickly she rallied to him; how she was always in the end fighting on his side. But my irritation as I followed them out was tempered by the vision of the boy on the bike, giving voice to my own longing for escape, and offering the sweet and unexpected consolation of a kindred spirit with whom in my dreams I could abscond.

2

By the second day, Mummy usually gets over the mice droppings, but this time she says she'd rather not come out. She sits in the kitchen with her hands round a mug of tea and says 'you go', she wants to be on her own.

The rest of us have no choice. And where not long ago I would have put up a fight until the only way to walk was yards behind on the threat of no supper, now I relish the possibility of another glimpse of the boys on the farm, and I find myself being helpful, sorting out boots and socks, chivvying the others outside.

We are on our usual loop of the valley, along the road that strings one end to the other, past the row of cottages by the phone box, past the Methodist chapel, where I caught an old man once doing a wee against the wall, up to the letterbox at Sparty Lea, where Daddy posts his article for the paper, and then running hard down the steep hill clumsy in our boots to the empty cottage across the ford and the wild raspberry bushes that sprawl there. Daddy hands us each a plastic bag. Jack is already eating hand over fist.

'Urgh!' Amelia drops a blob of fruit and then the whole bag and hops back from where it lands, wiping her fingers in her skirt. 'They've got maggots!'

'Good protein,' Daddy says as she flounces off. 'No pudding for you lot, then!' as Biddy and I shove our bags on to him and run off after her.

'Girls!' he snorts and Jack is shaking with laughter like Muttley, on and on, filled with the novelty and the delight of being in league with him.

It is weirdly hot and still, with nets of midges in the air and the river glugging over its bed of bottles. As we thread our way back, I concentrate on walking with my head poised, straightening my back, practising what I picture as a *Moon River* elegance. Suddenly up ahead, with a clatter like a pheasant, Biddy is running off side-ways, flapping her hands around her ears. Aready Amelia is hurtling herself after her, plucking invisible creatures from Biddy's arms, batting her hair. Daddy, who has managed to get ahead of us turns, drops the plastic bags which begin to inflate in the warm air, and I watch his white forearms reach forward, his face iron into panic as he begins to run towards her.

In one movement he lifts her off her feet like a hammock and stumbles down the bank slipping in the silt, almost losing his balance, wading into the river, knee-deep, plunging down. I can hear then the low hum as three or four bees continue to swing lazily around them, taking pot shots. I am crouching down, hidden from them. Amelia is in the water, too, still plucking at Biddy's arms, single-handed.

Like an explosion, it is over in a minute, but in the air all around debris seems to be falling and there is a strange suspension of sound that collapses around Biddy, who is now out on the bank, standing bolt upright, dripping wet and shaking with sobs. I force myself forward and make my way down to them as if I've only just caught up. 'What happened?'

Daddy ignores me, stroking Biddy, 'All right. It's all right, Biddy. Come on . . . We must have knocked the lid from a nest. They've all gone now . . . It's all right.'

Biddy is looking straight ahead, her head on a stick, snot streaming from her nose, shoulders curling round to each other.

'Come on, let's go home. Let's get some cake, shall we? Tea time. Let's go and tell Mummy what happened . . .'

'I was the one that rescued her, wasn't I?' Amelia says, pestering him for recognition.

'Have you been stung?'

I blench. Amelia has a way in extremes of doing the worst thing, or the absolutely right thing.

'Biddy, let's see,' I say. 'Show me!'

Biddy peers out of her head as if she is looking over a fence, to each one of her arms, over the sleeves of her smiley purple T-shirt, inspecting the red punctures in their tiny inflated rings.

'Poor you. Did they get in your hair, those horrid bees? What mean and nasty bees they were.' Daddy is hugging her in the direction of the path.

When we get home and count, Daddy has nine stings, Biddy has seven and Amelia three. I, conspicuously, have none. 'I didn't realize what was happening . . . it was all so quick . . .'

No one is listening. Mummy has Biddy on her knee and says we'll get doughnuts tomorrow, when we go shopping. She is bouncing her like she's a baby again, all put back together and Biddy's loving it, being petted, fussing over the raisins in her cake, and I find myself thinking half resentfully, half reassuringly, *see, they will stay together, how can they not?* It is not only Biddy but every one of us, like a different combination between them that they would have to crack in order for either of them to get out.

'Those nasty bees!' Mummy says again and squeezes her, holding on tightly, catching Daddy's eye as if to say, *Look, it can work, it does work, it can be mended . . .*

3

If I hadn't been Ruth, I would have been Bobby. The cottage always reminds me of *The Railway Children*. Partly because of the endless games we used to play in the Railway Children dresses Mummy made us that fitted us for years, in the end, over our jeans as smocks; and partly because in my mind, *The Railway Children* stood for the inevitability of things working out, which is how I used to imagine life did and would. It was a good version of our lives, the version without swearing and rows, the version where, given that everything came right in the end, the daddy had to go only in order for him to come back.

There are the clothes and there are the stories, stories that we remember and retell sometimes for homework, where they've been handed down and embellished each time; sometimes to each other just to make someone sorry, or someone laugh. There's the story of our cat, Clapham who got run over, lived in the cellar for a year without his front teeth, so convincing as a monster that, until he turned up at Mr Spark's as 'Sooty', we had to relocate the bog. Or when I ran away for the fifth time with a duffle bag of Weetabix and marmalade and only got chased because I happened to grab the whisky bottle too. Or the story of how Biddy nearly drowned, and how Amelia nearly drowned trying to save her; how the two of them were rescued by an angel of a man who plunged in with all his clothes on and then disappeared without any thanks.

And then there's the Christmases that Mummy got us to dress up and troop into the stable: Jack as Jesus, us three as shepherds, Mummy: Mary, Daddy: Joseph. We stood in the freezing cold watching our breath smoking in the lantern light and singing, *Away in a manger, no crib for a bed, the little Lord Jesus laid down his sweet head . . . the stars in the bright sky looked down where he lay, the little Lord Jesus, a-a-sleep on the hay,* every one of us, even daddy, right through to the end.

On Christmas Eves we still go down to the farm and Mummy carries back an enormous turkey the size of a baby in her arms, and worries about how she's going to get it into the oven. And Jack and Biddy go with Daddy to find the branch of a tree, which we plant in a bucket of soil and stones and load with ancient heavy papier mâché decorations of aeroplanes, stars and hens.

Once the snow came high as a lorry and we were completely cut off. No electricity. No milk. Daddy read to us, *Just William* and *Treasure Island* until the snow plough dug a tunnel. Someone that year got frozen in the phone box calling for help.

*

But you can grow out of stories like you can grow out of dresses, and this summer, for the first time, I feel the terrible itch to throw them all off. I get up later and later. Today the light is already pouring through the sheet at the window on to the heap of Biddy's nightie, where she has stepped out of it. I bury my head and breathe hot air to my knees, rearranging the spine of the zip and the label that is flapping in my face, *The Last Word in Luxury*.

Right from the beginning, because I was the oldest, it always seemed as if I was beyond holding hands. I was the grown-up. Sometimes now I hold my own hand in secret at the bottom of my sleeping bag, as if one hand were big and one smaller, and dream of what it will be like one day when my small hand is held.

When the latch lifts, there is no warning; it is like a gunshot. Daddy's heavy step levers him into the room. 'Come on you lazy bleeders – up!'

I hear the air rush around him as he bends down and grasps the end of Amelia's sleeping bag, shaking her loose like a pillow from its case and her muffled shriek of protest, 'Gerroff! Leave me alone. It's freezing!'

'Come on, it's the middle of the day!' I can feel the air part towards me.

'I'm up!' I burst out of the bag. 'I'm up, I'm getting up!'

He hovers and then turns on his heel – 'two minutes or I'm back – with the flannel!' – and thuds down the wooden stairs into the kitchen. I prop myself up on my elbows and look around. It is like an air raid shelter. Amelia is whimpering because a button has burst off her best nightie.

When we get to the kitchen, there's already something going on. Biddy is whining, 'But I want to go. I want to go with you.' There's a momentary lull as we come in.

'Why don't you just take her?' Mummy resumes irritably.

Daddy speaks in a controlled and level voice. 'Look, we'll talk about it later . . . It's work. I can't take her . . . Biddy, you'll be bored. It's very, very boring – looking round a gallery.'

'I won't be bored! I want to go!'

The pulse at the side of Daddy's head is twitching. 'You're not going. That's that. Now shut up, eat your breakfast!'

'Why can't I . . .?'

Biddy never knows when to stop and we wait in silence for what will fall, heads down.

It is Mummy eventually who asks, 'Is anyone else going to be there?' blowing it like a bubble that shakes before it pops.

'Like who?'

'. . . that woman, *for instance*?'

'What woman?'

'Oh, come on, you know who I mean.'

'Tell me, then.'

Mummy takes a deep breath and looks around the table as if she can't say what she'd like to. With the heavy and pointed emphasis of explaining to a child, she says, 'The woman who's organizing it.'

'Probably, I should think so . . .'

'Well, what is her name?'

'Does it matter? . . . Dewar. It's Dewar.'

'That's not a name!'

'Her name's Michaela, Michaela Dewar.'

I snort, '*Michaela*!'

Amelia says, 'There's a Michaela in my class – she must be famous!'

I scowl at her witheringly. 'It doesn't mean they're related, you stupid cow . . .'

'Cows eat grass, grass is nature, nature is beautiful, thank you for the compliment!'

I'm consumed with revulsion for Amelia. It's physical. I want to cram my nails into my legs, scratch out my hair. For some reason I think of yellow poppies – their warm softness, that soft sickly smell. Her skin. Touching her skin makes me itch. I can't bear to be near her. Her thick face.

Daddy scrapes back his chair with his plate in his hand. 'Belt up! I'm going. On my own. And that's the end of it!' and he storms out of the room.

'I'm going to the river' I say to Biddy, 'want to come?' It was a week since the bees and I was freezing Amelia out of her triumph, trailing round with Biddy, as if any second, I'd be available to spring to her rescue.

Biddy is sulking, her lip out, looking darkly at the corner of the kitchen table. She shrugs, grunts and turns away out of her chair still not looking up and I follow behind, out into the garden.

'I hate him!' she says.

But as we get around the corner of the house, she begins a hop-scotch and then we race almost on top of each other down the steps that separate the garden from the side of the house, and we break out into the lane, zigzagging down the hill towards the lower field and the river.

We were brought up to be scavengers. We couldn't contain ourselves when Mr Spark told us that the cottage had once been a shop and Daddy suggested to us that the grassy mound next to the stable was in all probability a rubbish dump, and could be bursting with treasures from a hundred years ago. It was quite possible for us to spend the start of every holiday with renewed expectation, excavating – old bottle tops, rusty lids, potted meat jars, the tiny trunks of clay pipes, even the head of a doll. If only we kept going, sooner or later, we thought, we must find real treasure, ancient blue glass bottles, gold coins, rings even. Usually it took us two clear days before we gave up fully, each time, not wanting to be the first to leave the others to the finds. But we never tired of searching the river.

Biddy is singing now and collecting flowers from the ditch along the way, cow parsley and buttercups. When we reach the stile I catch sight of Amelia at the top of the hill coming out into the lane. I scramble over. 'Quick – she's coming!' I have to be the first in the river in case there's a new haul of treasure waiting. Biddy fusses about her flowers and I leave her behind, jumping heavily down the bank which is like a honey comb from all the sand martins. I pull off my boots and socks, roll up my trouser legs and step out stiffly over the pebbles.

The water slices over the tops of my feet. 'Ach! Shit – it's freezing!' Everything in me rises. But already my eyes are skinned, sorting through the runnels and currents. I bend down and scrabble about, the water refocusing around my fingers, methodically making my way towards the bridge. All at once, I catch sight of something white. I prize out from between stones a triangular piece of crazed china and bring it up to view, smoothing it of water.

The best pieces to find have patterns on – willow pattern, particularly, blue and white and worked smooth at the edges. This one is ordinary, a flat piece from a saucer or plate and I skim it dismissively over to the bank.

By now Amelia has her socks off and is making for the mouth of the bridge. I have a radar out for her from the very corner of my eye. 'Copy cat, copy cat. Miaow, miaow!'

Biddy is sitting on a large flat stone with her toes just touching the water, singing to herself, 'Truly scrumptious, you're truly, truly scrumptious, scrumptious as the day that you were born. Tru-ly scrumptious, you're tru-ly scrumptious . . .' Amelia begins to join in.

'Amelia, shut your mouth! You can't sing!' The bile is rising again like tears. Amelia carries on, head down, doggedly and then sails into the moment I dread, hand fishing jubilantly and surfacing with a piece of china, blue faded flowers . . . She *always* finds the best bit!

I can't bear to be touched by her triumph. I stalk out of the water and half dry my feet on the grass, scraping on my socks, my boots and stomp off out of the field on to the bridge. *I fucking hate her!* I have to have something to make it better, to possess something that she'd want and it is only as I lift my head to climb the stile again, that it dawns on me just what that might be.

The graveyard is past the farm, off the path that runs along the river towards Allenheads. Once you get inside and towards the long grass of the oldest graves, dotted around like nests there are small glass domes set in the ground each containing treasures: white alabaster birds, scrolls of letters, delicate flowers. In every one the grass has grown yellow and straggly, pressed to the glass like fingers against windows. Some have been protected with a mesh of rusted wire and it is even more difficult to see what's inside, others have been smashed by a stray marble chipping or a branch and gape splinters and wire.

Amelia and I had been here right at the beginning of the holiday. In one of the broken domes she'd seen a pair of sculptured clasped hands and greedily she'd put her fingers through the jagged hole to reach for them. 'You can't take them!' I said, panicking and horrified at the same time. 'It's a graveyard! Something terrible will happen if you do ...' I was surprised by how easily she gave in, pulling her hand back and reddening as if I'd already told.

When I get to the place, having counted the weeks and the possibilities in between, I'm amazed to see them still there, reaching out at an odd angle like a limb through a hatching egg. I kneel down and poke cautiously between bits of broken glass. A wire holds them in place at the earth end through a corner of the cuff. I twist and tug at them until the hands fall upwards into my grasp. I hold them. They fit perfectly across the length of my hand, cold where they touch, light as bone.

And immediately in my head, there are chords striking *Oh ple-e-ease, say to me-e-e, you'll let me be your man ... Oh please, say to me I wanna hold your hand ... I wanna hold your ha-a-a-a-and ... I wanna hold your hand.*

If only I had been born earlier, so that I was grown-up in the sixties, so that I could have married Ray Davies or Keith Richards, or Bob Dylan. I tape the songs from Daddy's old records: The Beatles, The Kinks, The Rolling Stones, The Who ... He doesn't even like music any more, but he did, when I was little. I was trained to sit by the record player and choose them by their sleeves, for him to write to, one after the other until lunch time or tea time. And now all those words I've known by heart have begun to mean something, to make sense, speaking to me about how a life could be, where there is real love and real feeling. I can sing along in my head, with every nuance in place, every falter, every delayed beat. And those drums, the bass guitar, they strike something right in my spinal chord and the whole sum of my human existence, everything I feel I want, that is missing, is there.

The surface of my skin is tingling as I post the hands into the pouch at the front of my jumper and hold them in place as I go. There's no way I can take them back to the cottage. Instead, when

I get to the steps at the top of the lane, I go on and round to where I can climb the wall into the big triangle of overgrown garden. And then I make for the far corner, along the flattened path to a seat-sized patch hedged in by hawthorn, an outpost from which I spy on the whole of the valley.

Sitting absolutely still, I can hear Biddy and Jack in the front, climbing on to the seat of the swing and beginning to sing as they bend their knees alternately cranking up, *Under the Bam Bush, Under the tree Boom Boom Boom, True love to you my darling, true love to me . . .*

'Bram,' I can't help correcting, under my breath. '*Brram!*' I hate their missing 'r'; it makes me bite my tongue, just as bad as hearing chalk scratching on board, or cardboard across carpet and I have to say it out loud to put the 'r' back in.

And when we marry . . . we raise a fam-i-ly . . . I search as far as I can see, just in case Amelia has been following me. But there's nothing except the swing – *A boy for you, A girl for me, Boom, Boom, Boom, Boom – SEXY!* – and the blur of the river further off. The old toy trowel is still by the wall from where we have been digging and I fetch it over to scrape a hamster's grave in the dry soil, positioning the hands carefully and then scrabbling earth back over to bury them, pulling the long grasses around.

When I climb back out of the garden, I wait for a second at the gate, scratching the midge bites on my elbow distractedly. Biddy and Jack are still jangling on the swing, but otherwise it seems unnaturally quiet. No typing. I step between the cracks of the flag-stone path and in at the back door.

Out of habit I lift my head to listen at the bottom of the stairs, though I hadn't particularly expected to hear the forced, hushed voices coming from the living room. So instead of going on into the kitchen, I stop as if in mid-flight, ready to move only if I am discovered.

'. . . I just can't bear this. Please don't be so cold. Don't be like this.'

'Like what?'

'You know what I mean. As if you're not here. I'd rather you *weren't* here, like this. I can't bear it.'

There's a long pause and then Daddy, even quieter, 'Maybe I should've stayed in London . . .'

'What do you mean?'

'Maybe it was bound not to work.'

'How can you say that?!'

'I just can't seem to give you what you want.'

'You don't know what I want.'

'We're going round in circles – can't you just leave it, let things be for a while?'

'It would be all right if you loved me . . . you say you love me, well prove it . . . you can't, can you?'

'You don't realize how difficult it is for *me*.'

There's silence and then a clutter-thud of an object, a book maybe, landing. 'You fucking bastard! You shit. You fucking shit!'

And then there's a terrible wail that seems to go on and on until it breaks into a soft, low keening. It stops. And then again it comes out, animal and miserable.

Before I have a chance to disappear, Daddy bursts out of the door and down the stairs, almost on top of me. He smells as if he is on fire as he shoves past and off round the corner. We hear him up the steps at the side of the house, two at a time rattling his keys. Then the car door slamming, the engine turning lugubriously, stuttering twice, his foot pumping to a fierce revving and then a screech of tyres and the spitting of stones.

Biddy and Jack are standing face to face hardly moving. The spell is broken by the fidget of the swing and then the renewed sound of sobbing from upstairs, like the sea, mumbling over and over, 'How can he? how can he do it? how could he? how can he be such a bastard?' round and round.

The swing lurches into action again, as if nothing has happened. Biddy is singing, 'You stay in my house, I'll stay in your house, do-de-do-do, do-de-do-do.'

And Jack answers, giggling, 'You sleep in my bed, I'll sleep in your bed.'

'No,' says Biddy, getting louder, 'listen: I'll wee in your bed, you wee in my bed, do-de-do-do.'

Jack is crippled with laughter and can hardly stand up straight.

'Wait . . . I'll pick your nose, you pick my nose . . .' They both collapse.

'Shut up!' I screech at them. 'Everyone can hear! Do you want the police to come? Just shut up!'

David Nwokedi

ABC

Several months before Abraham died a large, blue van with the words *Vernon Opie's Removals and House Clearances* painted in white on its sides, and a beat up old car trundled into Sagacity Square on a chilly Saturday morning. It pulled up outside the Bennetts' house a few doors up from us. There was a woman at the wheel of the car, which was a green Ford Granada Estate car that had seen better days. In the passenger seat was a young girl who I reckoned was a year or two older than me, about Abraham's age. Three other younger children were crowded in the back seat in a heap of suitcases and boxes. All the children were black but the woman was white. She got out of the car, its door hinges creaking badly. She was a round woman about the same age as Mother. She had a cigarette in her mouth and the wisps of smoke obscured what I could make out was an oddly beautiful, pale face with flushed red cheeks. She spoke to Mr Bennett, a tall, thin man with thick-rimmed black glasses and two strands of greying hair that he had swept from one side of his head across to the other. Mr Bennett's strands always looked as if they had been stuck to his head with glue. Whatever the weather, they hardly moved. As the woman spoke, Mr Bennett, keeping one hand in his pocket, used his other hand to point up the road in the direction of Sagacity Terrace, the road that backed on to ours. After he stopped talking he smiled at her and with his free hand he gently caressed his remaining two strands of hair and then patted them down. His other hand remained in his pocket and I could see it move around like he was fiddling with his keys or some loose change perhaps.

'Lovely children,' Mr Bennett said, gesturing towards the green car.

'Thank you,' the woman said and I could hear the trace of an Irish accent in her voice. 'Thank you very much.'

'Coloured children, eh? Not many coloured types around here you know.'

'Not coloured,' the woman said. 'They're brown.'

'Not many brown types around here,' Mr Bennett said. 'Where you from then?'

'Streatham. It's in south London.'

'Oh,' Mr Bennett said. 'And what about the children? Where are they from?'

'Streatham, of course.' The woman looked a little annoyed.

'Are they yours?' Mr Bennett asked.

'Of course they are,' the woman snapped. 'Who else's could they be? Do you think I borrowed them for the day?'

'They could be Barnardo's children. You know. Adopted?'

'Well, they're not.' The woman looked annoyed. 'They're all flamin' mine. They belong to me.'

'And will you be staying here?' Mr Bennett said looking a little uncomfortable. 'I mean living here?'

'Of course we will,' the woman said. 'We left London to get away from all that hustle and bustle and flamin' grime. I want my children to be having some fresh sea air in their lungs.'

'Oh,' Mr Bennett said and I could see his fingers clenching in his pocket. 'Well, I hope they'll be happy here. If you need anything just pop round.'

'Thank you,' the woman said. 'Sure enough I will.'

'It's a pleasure,' Mr Bennett said. 'It'll be nice to have some coloured people around here.'

'*Brown*,' the woman said.

'Brown people,' Mr Bennett corrected himself.

The woman turned on her heels and went over to the van. I couldn't see the driver but I could see puffs of cigarette smoke coming out of the cabin. The woman spoke to him in short, sharp sentences and pointed towards Sagacity Terrace then she walked back to her car and got in. She turned the key in the ignition but it didn't start. 'Bollocks,' she said throwing her cigarette out of the window and then tried again. The second time it started but sounded like it would probably only just make it to Sagacity Grove and no further. Making a three-point turn into a ten-point turn she turned the car around and it slowly crawled on up Sagacity

Square, the van slowly following. When it passed me I caught a fleeting glimpse of the girl in the passenger seat and was sure she looked at me and smiled. She was the most beautiful girl I had ever seen.

Later that afternoon there was a knock at our front door. I ran down the stairs to answer it and looked through the peephole. On the other side was the girl in the passenger seat. Because of the peephole, her head was too big and her eyes leaped out at me as if they were on stalks and her feet appeared to be tiny specks at the bottom of a pair of overly long legs. Her hands had disappeared into her sides too but despite all the deformities created by the peephole I was still taken aback by the vision of beauty before me. Keeping my eye wedged to the peephole I called out.

'Who is it?'

'Angela,' she called back. 'I'm Angela Flood.'

'Do I know you?'

'No,' she said. 'But I saw you earlier when we arrived.'

'Then what do you want?' I said and I noticed that she was becoming more beautiful as we spoke.

'It's the ball,' she said, her eyes looming closer to the peephole. 'Fish's ball.'

'What's fish?' I asked.

'Not "what", "who",' she said.

'Who's Fish then?' I asked.

'My little brother.'

'What about Fish's ball?'

'It's in your garden.'

'Is it?'

'Yes.'

'And how did it get there?'

'Simon kicked it.'

'Who's Simon?'

'My brother; he's older than Fish but not older than me.'

'Oh,' I said, still entranced by her beauty.

'Why don't you open the door so we can talk properly?' she said. 'I feel like I'm in a goldfish bowl.'

'I'm sorry,' I said and I slid the silver chain from the door and eased the door open. Without the distortions of the peephole her beauty took on a life of its own. I inhaled sharply and felt a quivering in my bowels. Her eyes were so deep and so dark I was sure I could see a tawny owl fluttering across her irises. And her eyes were so perfectly placed on either side of the bridge of her nose that I was sure I could almost hear them whispering to each other like two close friends sharing a secret. Her nose was so smooth and round I felt compelled to reach out and touch it but I didn't. Her mouth was delicate, with lips the colour of squashed raspberries. Her hair hung from her head in loose, long dark brown curls like little children hanging off the climbing frame at Geraghty Park, and her skin was a warm brown that reminded me of the colour of Demerara sugar that Mother sometimes put on our porridge in winter. But the most beautiful part of Angela Flood was the line of her face that ran from her chin to her ears; her lower jaw, her mandible. I'd never seen such a perfect jawline. In fact I'd never seen such a perfect person. I knew then that, for the first time in my life, I was in love.

She held out her arm to me, extending her long, delicate fingers. 'Hello,' she said. 'Pleased to meet you.' And I noticed then that she had the tiniest of lisps; hardly there really but there all the same.

'Hello,' I said. 'I'm Thomas, Thomas Wisdom.' And I clutched her hand, not wanting to let it go; it felt soft to the touch and precious. I wished I could keep it.

'We've just moved in,' she said.

'I know,' I said. 'I saw you arriving in the car earlier. The green car.'

'Our garden backs on to yours,' Angela said. 'We're on Sagacity Terrace, number twenty-one.'

'But we don't have a garden,' I said, still holding her precious hand, wanting to examine every detail.

'Oh,' Angela said.

'It belongs to Joshua, Joshua Fountain,' I said. 'He lives downstairs and we're on top.'

'Oh,' she said again and I let go of her hand. I didn't want to but I felt I should. I gazed into the well that was her eyes and the tawny owl gazed back. My heartstrings were pulling inside my chest and it felt as if a ghost train was passing through my bowels.

'It was Simon,' Angela said. 'He kicked the ball over our wall. He was being Rivelino. It was a banana shot; me and Fish were being the wall. Simon's usually good at banana shots.'

'Is he?' I said.

'Yes,' she said and a brown curl fell across her magnificent eyes. I couldn't resist any longer and I leaned forward and flicked the curl away.

'Thank you,' she said. 'Who's Joshua Mountain?'

'What?'

'Joshua Mountain? You said it's his garden.'

'He's our neighbour; he lives on his own downstairs. He's a painter. He paints elderly women with nothing on.'

'Starkers?' she asked and even the way she said *starkers* sounded beautiful.

'Yes, nudes,' I said.

'Wow!' she said and I nodded.

'How long have you lived here?' she asked.

'We've always lived here,' I replied.

'Who do you live with?'

'My mother and my brother, Abraham.'

'Like in the Bible?'

'I'm sorry?' I said.

'Like in the Bible?' Angela repeated. 'Isn't there an Abraham in the Bible?'

'That's right,' I said. 'Mother said he was born in the Ur of the Chaldeans.'

'Oh,' Angela said. 'Where is the Ur of the Chaldeans?'

'I've no idea,' I said. 'A long ways away I guess, somewhere near the Garden of Eden maybe.'

'So will he let me get it back?' Angela said.

'Who?' I was puzzled.

'Joshua Mountain. Fish's ball, will he let me get it back?'

'I'm sure he will but he's not in at the moment. He's probably down at the market,' I said. 'I'll leave a note for him and ask him to throw it over your wall when he gets back.' I knew I would relish writing the note and I would dwell on getting Angela's name just right. 'And it's *Fountain* by the way, not Mountain. Joshua *Fountain*.'

'Oh, right,' Angela said. 'I'll try to remember that . . . Fountain not Mountain.'

'That's right,' I said.

'Well, thank you, Thomath,' Angela said, her tiny lisp turning up at the end of Thomas as if she was trying to say my name backwards. 'It's been lovely meeting you.' She held out her hand to me again and I grabbed it, perhaps a little too quickly. I didn't want to let it go again and I wished she could leave it behind so that I could hold it all day but I kind of figured she would need it. I looked at her perfect mandible again trying to memorize it and her eyes and the tawny owl. I knew that later, after she had gone I'd want to remember everything about her. The curl fell across her eyes again but this time she quickly flicked it away herself with her free hand, the one I wasn't clutching.

'Goodbye then, Thomath,' she said and she pulled her hand free. 'I'll see you again I'm sure and I'd love to meet your brother, Abraham. You can come and meet Simon and Fish too and I've got a sister called Selena. I think you'll like Fish – everyone loves him, he's only little and he can get away with murder.'

And with that she was gone She left me with the ghost train still rumbling chaotically inside my stomach. I rushed to the toilet thinking that I needed to go but nothing happened, I just sat on the toilet for ages thinking of Angela Flood. Within half an hour of Angela's departure I couldn't for the life of me remember what she looked like and I desperately needed to see her again.

In the days after Angela Flood came around I thought about her every day; I dreamed of her and tried to remember her smell and tried to remember her face too when I lay in bed. I tried to conjure up the sound of her lisp in my head but I couldn't find it. From our kitchen window that overlooked her garden, I would stand behind the net curtains and watch her and her sister and brothers whenever they were in the garden. Simon, the brother older than Fish but younger than Angela had the biggest afro I had ever seen, bigger than Michael Jackson's even. So big it almost moved. He had the darkest skin of the four and he had spots too, lots of spots. Sometimes he would stop what he was doing and squeeze one and wipe the pus off on his trouser leg. Selena, the next oldest was beautiful – but not as beautiful as Angela – and she had huge eyes too and I was sure she might well have her own owl fluttering around in them. I noticed that, rather strangely, no matter what they were doing, Selena never smiled. Selena had an afro too, but it was smaller than Simon's and neater. Her curls were much tighter. Then there was Fish. As if to make up for Selena, Fish had a smile so wide you could almost see the sun rise on one side of his face and set on the other. But when he wasn't smiling he was giggling or crying if Simon punched him, which he appeared to do quite a lot. Fish had looser curls, midway between Angela's and Simon's and his afro was uneven and bobbly as if he had been fidgeting when the barber (or his mother) had cut his hair. If Fish wasn't smiling, giggling or crying then he would stand with his mouth wide open as if he was waiting to swallow a fly. Fish's head seemed a little too big for his body and his eyes were big and brown like Selena's and I was sure he would be able to see more of the world than anyone else with eyes like that. Abraham always said that little children are deliberately given big eyes by God so that they can see the world better; see it like He sees it.

They played football in the garden all the time. Simon would line them up into a wall, Fish on one end, Selena in the middle and Angela at the other end and he would get his orange Trophy football and try to curl a banana shot around the wall. 'Rivelino!' he would shout. Sometimes he would hit the ball just right and it would zip around the wall and whiz between the two jumpers that were the goalposts. Most times though the ball would rocket off on to the bushes that surrounded their garden or, even worse, hit Selena or Fish in the face or some other part of their bodies. He never seemed to hit Angela; maybe that was because she was the oldest.

'That'll give you another reason not to smile!' Simon shouted as the ball hit Selena's arm.

'Shut up, you dincy!' Selena scowled and she ran after Simon to try to hit him. He was too quick and he ducked and weaved like I had seen Muhammad Ali do on the telly.

'Dincy!' Selena shouted but she never managed to hit him.

It was pouring with rain the first time I actually went in to Angela's house, the first time I saw where she lived. A few days after our first meeting, after I had fallen in love, Angela came round. I was sitting on my doorstep looking up at the clouds watching the first drops of rain as they started to fall.

'Hello, Thomath,' she said, the lisp making a welcome return through the clouds.

'Hello,' I said getting up.

'Would you like to come over and meet my family?' she asked.

'Simon and Selena?' I said.

'Yes,' she said and she smiled.

'And Fish?' I said. 'The youngest?'

'Yes,' she said and she looked impressed that I had remembered all their names. The corners of her lips turned up and her dark eyes were wide. Her nose twitched a little like a rabbit. 'Fish the baby,' she said and she chuckled to herself and her chuckle seemed to dance in her throat.

'But it's raining,' I said.

'Doesn't matter,' she said. 'I love the rain.' It was raining harder now and her brown curls began to gain weight as the water dropped on her and little droplets hung on the end of her nose and from then on I loved the rain too.

'So do I,' I said.

As we walked around the block from our house to Sagacity Terrace, water squelched under my feet, my hair flattened on my head and little trickles ran into my eyes. I had to keep wiping my face with the sleeve of my coat. Puddles formed in the street like mini lakes and in one someone had dropped a few matches that were swirling around like tiny swimmers in red swimming caps.

As we approached the Flood house, one of my neighbours, Mr Tanker walked past with his hands in his pocket, his side parting that was too far to one side and a smoking Woodbine wedged between his dry lips. 'Tsst,' he grunted not looking up. 'Grrrr,' he said. That was all I'd ever heard Mr Tanker say, *tsst* or *grrrr*, and I don't think I ever saw him look up. He never stopped to talk to me or Abraham or Mother, or anyone come to think of it. He was always on the move, always hurrying by, grunting and groaning to himself.

We reached the Flood house. It was the same size as ours, only not divided into two flats so they had the whole house. There were nets in the windows but no curtains up yet and the door had graffiti sprayed on it – *Up the Reds!* and *Fuk the Systim!* and *Shit on Pigs!*

'Mum's gonna paint over it,' Angela said, noticing where I was looking.

'Oh,' I said. I could hear music coming from within the house . . . *thumpety thump*, *thump*, *thump* overlayed with a tinny rattle. And I could hear what sounded like several dancing feet. We walked up the front path and Angela pushed the door open; the music was louder, I recognized it as the Jackson Five. Angela stepped into the living room and I could see over her shoulder. Selena and Simon were standing next to each other swaying from side to side to the music and Fish was bouncing up and down on a psychedelic sofa as if he was on a trampoline. The Jackson Five were singing as loudly as they could.

'I want to be Michael!' Fish was shouting as he bounced. 'I want to be the Michael!' And because Fish was so little and because he was so small and couldn't speak properly it sounded like he was saying, 'I want to be Bichael! I want to be the Bichael!' I would later learn that Fish would muddle up some of his 'm's and his 'b's and other letters too . . . 'cauliblowler' (cauliflower), 'kwecious' (precious), 'lelloplane' (aeroplane) and so on.

'I want to stand in the biddle! I want to be the biddle one!' And of course he meant 'middle'. Fish wanted to be the middle one. Fish wanted to be Michael Jackson.

Angela sprang into action as if she were an ambulance woman at the scene of an accident. She rushed across the living room and left me standing by the door.

'Come on, get into line,' she said and I marvelled at her leadership skills. I was entranced. 'Fish, get down,' she said. 'Get in line.'

Angela was standing by the fireplace, hands on hips, all motherly. Angela would later tell me that whenever her mother was out she would become the Flood mother. Simon hated it, she said; he was only a year younger than Angela and thought that he should be in charge.

'I wanna be in charge!' he shouted.

'But *I'm* the oldest!' Angela snapped.

'But I'm the man,' Simon said. 'And a man should be in charge.'

'No, Simon, it's the oldest,' Angela persisted. 'And besides you're not a man, you is a boy . . . B-O-Y, boy.'

'If we was in Africa I'd be in charge,' Simon said. 'C-H-A-R-G, charge.'

'But,' Angela said, 'we ain't in Africa, we's in blimmin' Sagacity.'

'Trinidad and Tobago then,' Simon said. 'If we was in Dad's country then I'd be in charge.'

'It's just Trinidad, Simon. Dad only came from Trinidad not both of them. You dincy.'

'Shut up, Selena,' Simon said.

'But we ain't, Simon,' Angela said, hands still on hips. 'We ain't in Trinidad or even Tobago and even if we were you still wouldn't be in charge cos you is too dincy.'

'Dincy, Simon!' Fish shouted he was now off the sofa and standing next to Selena.

'Shut up, Fish!' Simon shouted.

'You missed out your "e", Simon,' Selena said.

'What, Selena?' Simon was annoyed. 'What the fuck are you talking about?'

'Your "e", Simon. You missed out your "e" on "charge".'

'What?' He was sweating a little now on his brow.

'Dincy, bincy, Simon.' Fish started rolling on the floor.

'Shut up, Fish,' Simon said. 'What "e", Selena? What fucking "e" are you talking about?'

'On the end of "charge".' Selena folded her arms looking like a matriarch. 'C-H-A-R-G-E, there's an "e" on the end of "charge", everyone knows that.'

'C-H-A-R-B-E,' Fish giggled.

'See, Simon,' Angela said. 'You is too dincy. How can you be in charge if you don't even know how to spell it?'

'And besides, Simon,' Selena said scowling, 'Angela and me is fenminists and the fenminists say that the women should be in charge.' She scowled some more.

'Bollocks to that,' Simon said and he scowled too.

'Dincy, wincy, bincy, Simon,' Fish giggled and rolled over again.

'Shut the fuck up, Fish.' Simon kicked out at Fish catching him on the top of the thigh.

'Owww!' Fish wailed and the tears were quick to come.

'Leave him alone, SI-MON!' Selena shouted and she knelt down to rub Fish's thigh and stop him from crying.

'Dincy ... (sob) ... wincy ... (sob) ... bincy ... (sob) ... lincy ... (gurgle) ... flucking Simon,' Fish sobbed. Selena dabbed at his tears with a tissue with rose petal markings on it.

'Don't swear, Fish,' Angela said still motherly. 'You know it's not nice.'

'Flucking Simon,' Fish gurgled again, a bubble of snot forming in his nose.

'Yeah, Fish,' Simon grimaced. 'Don't fucking swear.'

'And you too, Simon,' Selena looked up. 'Stop it now.'

It was only then that the others noticed me standing by the door. They looked up at me. Simon was still grimacing and his huge afro appeared to be swaying a little, Selena wasn't smiling, and Fish's mouth hung open like he was catching flies and the snot bubble had now burst and was dribbling over his top lip. He licked at it with his tongue.

'This is Thomath,' Angela said and the way she said my name, backwards, caused the ghost train to return to my stomach and I could feel the passengers holding on for dear life. 'He's my new friend, he lives round the corner in Sagacity Square.'

'Hello, Thomas,' they all said in unison and Fish said it through his tears and none of them had a lisp like Angela's.

'We were going to be the Jackson Five,' Selena said folding her rose petal tissue and stuffing it up her cardigan sleeve.

'And I wanted to be the Bichael one.' Fish's sobbing had almost stopped completely now.

'But I think I should be Michael,' Simon said. 'I've got the biggest 'fro.'

'But you can't sing, Simon,' Selena said.

'And *you* can?' Simon almost spat the words out.

'But *I* can, actually,' Angela said and I figured that Angela probably could. Her speaking voice was as sweet as the honey that Mother bought from the Co-Op on Grammar Street, only sweeter and not as cheap, and I was sure that if Angela's singing voice was anywhere near as sweet it would be sold in jars but it wouldn't have *Economy honey* written on the side, no, it would have *Angela's Honey voice – Sweeter than the Angels*.

'It's good that you're here, Thomath,' Angela said and she grabbed my hand and pulled me into the front room. Selena helped

Fish get to his feet and Fish blew a raspberry at Simon. Simon scowled again. Angela's hand felt warm and delightful to touch. I could feel each delicate finger pressing into my hand and I wished there and then that a strange disease would afflict us both and the result would mean that our hands would weld together and remain forever entwined.

'They've got TFD,' I imagined Dr Barnabas our doctor having to tell Mother and Mrs Flood in his sombre and morose surgery.

'What's TFD?' Mrs Flood would be bound to ask.

'Together Forever disease,' Dr Barnabas would reply, scribbling something on his notepad and then licking the tip of his pen.

'Can anything be done?' Mother would ask.

'No,' Dr Barnabas would say. 'Nothing at all, I'm afraid. It's incurable. They'll be together forever. It's very rare but it happens.'

'Oh,' Mother would say. 'Does that mean Thomas won't be able to do the washing up any more?'

'They'll have to do it together,' Dr Barnabas would say. 'But look on the bright side Mrs Wisdom, whenever it's their turn the washing up will take only half the time. Many hands make light work and all that.'

And I wouldn't mind at all, I would love to do the washing up with Angela. In fact I would love to do anything; put the bins out, empty the washing machine, bring in the post . . .

'Thomath!' It was Angela; I had drifted off. 'Did you hear what I said?'

'I'm sorry, Angela,' I said. 'I was thinking about washing up.'

Angela looked puzzled. 'I said you can be Tito,' she said.

'Who?' I said.

'Tito.'

'In *The Wizard of Oz*?' I frowned. 'The dog?'

'No, you dincy,' Selena said. 'In the Jackson Five.'

'There was a dog in the Jackson Five?' Now I was confused.

'Fuckwit,' Simon said.

'Fluckwit,' Fish said.

'Shut up,' Selena said.

'The Jackson Five,' Angela explained, 'Tito not Toto. Tito Jackson. We're going to be the Jackson Five. I'm going to be Michael, Selena is Jermaine, Simon can be Jackie . . . (Simon frowned) . . . Fish, Marlon, and now that you're here Thomas, you can be Tito.'

'Me?' I said. 'But I can't sing or dance.'

'Doesn't matter,' Angela said. She'd let go of my hand but she was still standing close enough for me to smell her honey fragrance. I watched her raspberry lips as she spoke and her perfect white teeth behind them like a group of tidy school children in their new white shirts lining up for a school photo. 'Tito played the guitar. You just have to move around a little and pretend to be playing a guitar.'

'And besides,' Selena said. 'Dancing's easy.'

'As simple as 1-2-3,' Angela said.

'Do-ray-me,' Simon said.

'A-B-C,' Selena said, just as Michael Jackson began to *bah, bah, boom* as their song 'ABC' started to spin on the turntable. Michael Jackson's brother's fell into line behind him with their harmonies and do-wops and the Flood family's dancing feet began to move. It was to be the first of many times I would watch the Flood family dancing. Angela began to sing along with Michael Jackson and I marvelled at how smoothly and sweetly they danced as if they had rehearsed the moves over and over every day; even little Fish moved as if he was born to dance. 'Gloove it!' he kept shouting. 'Gloove it, baby!'

'Come on, Thomas,' Selena said moving her hips, 'just join in. Move your body from side to side and pretend to play the guitar.'

Self consciously I trudged over and stood in line behind Angela. My feet felt heavy and my fingers felt clumsy like uncooked sausages. I moved from side to side and twiddled my fingers as if I was playing Tito's guitar. Fish looked up at me, his big eyes dancing as much as his feet. 'Gloove it!' he shouted and I tried to groove as best as I could.

When Angela got to the line '. . . I think I love ya!' I knew it was worth it. I hoped it was me she was singing to, it was unlikely I knew but I hoped all the same and therefore I was happy to shake it, shake it baby and gloove it with Fish. I was happy to pretend to be Tito playing a pretend guitar. It was as simple as that, simple as A-B-C.

Charles Fernyhough

The Thought Show

from *A Box of Birds*

They turn up in fancy dress, expecting a party. They can arrive at my lab done up like naughty French maids, jolly pirates still drunk from the sea, or maybe a pair of gorillas with realistic flaring nostrils. Once they broke into someone's amateur dramatics costume cupboard and came straight here with the spoils, and I spent an hour teaching the essentials of nerve physiology to both ends of a moth-eaten pantomime horse. I tell them that neuroscience is a serious business, but it's hard to be serious about anything when you've chosen your second-year options and there's no coursework due this side of Christmas. Gareth shows up first, glancing around at the framed photos of professors on the corridor walls, wondering which door is my lab and what he would have to do to get in there. James swaggers on behind, carrying his public-school confidence like a bulky parcel on a busy street, expecting people to get out of his way. They're not meant to be up here on the research floors at all, given the security situation, but this is the only part of the Institute where I can hide their threadbare costume dramas from fellow scientists' eyes. Besides, I have to get some facts down them if they're going to have a chance of passing anything this year. At least if they come up here to my office, they can't attract any attention. Persuade them to keep the noise down, and no one will have to know they're here.

'I'm going to need a volunteer,' I tell them.

Gareth dumps his file onto the comfy chair and offers himself nervously. Today he's turned up as a Franciscan nun, complete with black veil, polyester tunic and clunky plastic neck-cross. His eyes are anxious and shadowy, and can't stand anything for long.

You get the constant impression that someone's shooting at him.

'I'm going to need you to sign a consent form. What we're doing involves pretty harmless magnetic fields, but we need to get the paperwork right.'

James finally gives up on trying to read the secrets of my desktop and settles down in the other comfy chair. 'She's going to experiment on your brain, Gaz. She's going to wire you up to her machines and find out what makes you tick.'

'Am I wearing *that*?' Gareth says.

I grapple with the box. I come up holding a twelve-kilo titanium helmet padded thickly with foam. A spaceman visor slots over integrated goggles. A spinal column of processors and cables hangs down from the back.

'For a little while,' I say. 'Just long enough for us to find out what you're thinking.'

'Better take your wimple off, sister,' James says.

I've turned the lights down in the office. The one-way glass of the observation window looks out onto the black emptiness of the lab. Outside it's dusk, a November afternoon in the heart of the Forest Campus. It's quiet without the tube-lights buzzing. James and I are perched on the workbench by the door, separated by a pile of research papers. Gareth is sitting in the comfy chair with his head inside the helmet, which is feeding real-time outputs to a desktop machine linked to a distant mainframe. The output of the software is going to a series of floor-mounted projectors planted in a fairy ring on the carpet. The space between us is filled with a huge 3-D hologram of Gareth's brain.

'What does it look like?' Gareth says.

'Colourful,' James replies. 'I'd say the rude thoughts are the pink ones.'

Gareth makes a snorting sound behind the visor, and a blob of brilliant yellow shoots out from the centre of the light-show and dissolves into the rose-threaded haze of his frontal cortex.

'Can you actually tell what I'm thinking?'

I laugh, and realise I shouldn't. 'This isn't the movies, Gareth. You can't read someone's thoughts like you read a computer file. Anyway, the resolution wouldn't be up to it. You can see which brain lobes are active, but that's pretty much all. It's a toy, really. A demonstration for interested students.'

'Think of something pleasant, Gaz,' James says.

His friend's lips move behind the visor. Blue streaks of neural activity loop from front to back of the brilliant ghost-brain, and a warm red glow swells in his limbic system, that blurred loop of nuclei lodged between the two hemispheres.

'Not *that* pleasant, perv-features . . .'

I'm starting to wonder how far back this friendship goes. The fancy-dress thing, this nerdy jargon, the shared certainty about what's funny and not funny: it suggests a schoolboy closeness. A history.

'Have a look,' I say.

Gareth lifts the visor. As soon as the light sparks on his retinas you can see a smudge of activity way over in his visual cortex, on the far right from where we're looking.

'That's you seeing. The bit at the back is where you process visual information.'

'So you could download this stuff . . . you could put my thoughts onto some massive hard drive and have a virtual Gareth Buckle sitting there on your computer?'

'Like I say, this isn't Hollywood.' I click on the remote and zoom in on an amethyst flashpoint in his frontal lobe. 'Even if you had the best resolution in the world, you would only be able to see which neurones were working. You wouldn't be able to see *inside* that neural activity – what it means to the person who's having it.'

James is trying to look unimpressed. 'OK, so where's the bit where he does his thinking? Where's the bit that makes him *him*?'

'It's all him, and none of it is him. It's the way all the different bits work together. Consciousness is probably just a lucky by-product of the brain's enormous complexity.'

'You don't get out much, do you, Miss?'

I pretend not to hear.

'So, if we hang around long enough,' Gareth says, flipping the visor shut again, 'we might see consciousness emerging?'

'No,' I say, thumbing the remote and quitting the software. 'We're only allowed to zap you for a couple of minutes at a time. Sorry.'

I reach behind me and undim the lights.

'Wow . . .'

'So this is what you do in your top-secret research centre? You experiment on people's brains?'

'You can't experiment on people's brains,' Gareth says. 'It's unethical.'

He's keeping the helmet on, like a kid who won't get out of a fairground ride, thinking he'll spot the silent secret of its magic.

'Why's that?' Now the lights are up, James' passion looks a little over-staged. 'Because they're people? Because they're supposedly intelligent enough to get together and show moral outrage?'

'They use other sorts of brains. The non-human kind. That's why she'll be in such trouble if anyone finds us up here.'

'What, like mice and rats and shit?'

'Affirmative.' The nun in the MEG helmet is getting excited. 'The mammalian nervous system is pretty uniform. You can study a mouse's brain and learn all you need to know.'

'No wonder they've been round here breaking your windows.'

I think of the circular email that went round after the latest attacks on the East Wing. Professor Gillian Sleet, the lithe and permatanned Director of the Institute, reminding us of the need to maintain vigilance in light of the new security situation. No one knows if those Conscience activists were students or not. The trouble is, we don't know who's a danger and who isn't. Just be careful, they tell us, and trust nobody. Which is precisely why these two are not supposed to be here.

'The research teams in this building are studying why nerves die, and under what conditions they can regenerate. We use animal models to work out what goes wrong in certain neurodegenerative diseases.'

'Alzheimer's. That's what she works on. I saw it on your website, Miss.'

James gestures at the box on the floor at Gareth's feet. 'So what's that got to do with Dr Churcher's magic helmet?'

'Nothing, directly. The concept is that she can model what goes wrong in the human brain on a much simpler system. You're dealing with an incredibly complex machine. You have to start somewhere.'

'What, so you make a load of mice go doolally?'

I hesitate, wondering how much to tell them. All the answers are there in the holding-room across the corridor, locked away in the terabytes of data that is my experiment on amyloid plaque formation. I feel a sudden pang for my ninety-nine mice, born by mail-order, raised under artificial light, just so I can find out whether an overdose of protein in their brains sends them drooling into dementia. It's the same guilty dread I feel at the thought that it might not work, that they will have lived and run their mazes and died for nothing. But you don't let yourself have that thought. Wherever you go, as a scientist, you don't go there.

'We manipulate the gene which controls the formation of a certain protein. We think it's the build-up of this protein in the brain that causes Alzheimer's.'

Gareth finally extracts himself from the helmet and holds it out to me.

'*You* put it on, Miss. We want to see what makes *you* tick.'

My skin prickles. I light up with a vicar's-daughter blush. All my life I've been dodging this, hiding my secret behind determined smiles, hoping the question would never come. But then something happens that throws you wide open, and you sense people looking in on the shattered illusion of you, marvelling at the workings. I tell myself it's just the hangover of another late night at the computer, lost in my online gaming zone, but it's more than that: it's the woozy, broken-up feeling of being in a million places at once, watching automatic routines from the inside, of *being* those routines, all the trillions of mindless reflexes that make up me. They're watching me, interested. Seeing someone doubting her own existence: it must be a curious sight.

'Nothing ticking,' I tell them, as casually as I can. 'There's nothing ticking in here.'

James gets up from the bench and goes over to the one-way mirror. He stands there looking into the blackness of my closed-down lab, one hand shading his eyes.

'So what exactly do your demented mice do in there? What's the big paddling-pool thing?'

'Flotation tank,' Gareth quips. 'It's very stressful being a scientist.'

'Water maze,' I say, calmly searching my desk for their essays.

'The big paddling-pool thing is basically a big paddling-pool. You add milk to the water so it becomes opaque. You put a mouse in somewhere around the edge and see if it can find its way to a submerged platform. That way you can test the animal's spatial memory.'

James is looking at the big paddling-pool thing, trying to decide if it's cruel to make a humanely-reared mouse swim through milky water.

'You mean you're still using live animals for research? When these days you can do it all on computers?'

'Sorry, James, you've listened to too much Conscience propaganda. *In silico* experiments can give you a few pieces of the jigsaw, but at a certain point you need to look at real living organisms and see how they behave.'

He takes his essay without even glancing at the mark. I catch Gareth staring at the stack of gaming notes I've left out on the desk by my computer. There are webcam printouts, directions for navigating between obscure virtual locations, lists of items traded, usernames of a few hundred obsessive role-players. My own *in silico* experiment: a game called Des*re.

'Gareth? Did I get an essay from you?'

He's trying to jog my mouse, the computer one, to see what lies behind the branching-neurone screensaver. My late night comes back to me in yawning colour. He wants to find out what room I'm in, who I've been trading with – where, in this glittering nexus of linked webcams, I'm headed next. He's an addict of this game too, I realise with a buzz of reluctant solidarity. One of Des*re's million-strong worldwide club.

'Is it true you live in a treehouse, Miss?' he asks.

'Yes. Is it true you haven't handed in an essay all term?'

He picks up his lever-arch file and hides his face behind it. The label says GAZ'S RANDOM NOTES ON NEUROSCIENCE.

'Gaz has been working on something else.' James taps his nose confidentially. 'A research project. It's going to make him rich.'

'What sort of research project?'

'He can't tell you. Not until he's sold it to Jed Mulcahy.'

Jed Mulcahy is the chair of PowerServe, and about the ninth richest man on the planet. PowerServe sponsors a few of our students. In fact, I've a feeling Gareth is one of the betas they support.

'Tell him he hasn't handed in a single bit of work, in any of his subjects, all term. I've had a message from his college about his inappropriate behaviour. They're worried about him.'

Gareth lowers the file and regards me curiously.

'Can I see it?'

'Of course not.'

'I'll have to hack into your account, then.'

'You could try. After recent events, they've gone a bit tight on security.'

'He can handle security,' James says. 'You know he hacked into the Pentagon? He was, like, *twelve*.'

I think of the new bank of firewalls they put in after the latest attacks on the East Wing. You now have to enter a daily-changing security code just to get on to the networked computers. The structural genomics data they're working on downstairs need special protection, apparently. I remember the Bishop's press release after the latest anti-vivisection outrages, about the importance of scientific work being allowed to continue while we strive to find alternatives to experimental research with animals. That doesn't help this feeling of dread. They look harmless enough, with their big smiles and prankish undergraduate humour, but I'm still going to find myself in desperate amounts of trouble if anyone catches them up here. I want them out of here, I want my house in the trees, a large Jack Daniels and my own company until bedtime. Not the thought of some uniformed thug walking past at any moment, pushing the door open on this flagrant breach of security guidelines.

'Friday. I want your essay by Friday.'

Gareth writes that down.

'So,' James is saying, 'do any of your dotty mice actually get chopped?'

I watch him slouch back into the comfy chair and push off his trainers. He's wearing a Fred Flintstone hairpiece and a tee-shirt that says BIG IN NORWICH. His lips are dry, and there's an irritated roughness, like eczema, spreading around his eyes. I've heard this tone of voice before, of course: the incipient whine, the wince in his cheeks as he hurts himself on the words. No doubt the people who firebombed an empty storage room in the East Wing had it, took it with them to their Conscience meetings to argue for a better world without cruelty to animals. But James is no Conscience activist. He's just testing me, pushing on the edifice to see if it'll break. He wants the easy kick at the cruelty of animal research, but he hasn't the heart, or the arguments, to see it through.

'It's sometimes necessary to lesion our animals to establish which brain mechanisms are going wrong. But, like I say, in this lab we're mostly using transgenics. We don't have to tamper with their brains at all: we let their genes do it for us.'

'But you have to "lesion" them sometimes.'

He stares at me, sensing a weakness I didn't know about.

'Sometimes,' I say.

'So are they conscious when you're chopping them up?'

'That depends on what you mean by conscious.'

I wish he'd look away now. You think you can hide it, by speaking when you're spoken to, smiling back when people smile at you, and maybe giving a little obligatory blush when it's a man. But then, out of nowhere, someone sees right through you, notices how you stumble over a response to a question, or leave a glance out of a window hanging a half-second too long. That feeling of being centred, that *X* that's supposed to mark the spot of the soul: it gets shown up as the nothing it is. James has scented it, the doubt that's at the heart of me. It's like I've thrown a door open onto a party you can hear from the street, only to show that there's nothing there.

'I mean what *you* mean, Dr Churcher. I mean what it feels like to be alive. To experience the amazing qualities of existence. I'm not talking about neural pathways or pretty colours in the brain. I mean what it feels like to be *you*, Dr Yvonne Churcher. Age thirty-something. Possibly single. To be that person, in this room, right now.'

I redden, and hate myself for it.

'Here, in this room, is not really the place to discuss this, James.'

He holds the gaze. It's too determined; its need to embarrass me is too much on show. I want to laugh, but Gareth gets in first.

'Yeah, save it for the debate. I might let James ask a question if he's lucky. Are you coming, Miss?'

I glance at the invitation card pinned to my corkboard. Gareth has invited me to something, a college debate on issues arising from the East Wing attacks. Motion: a species that wants cures for its own diseases should not test them out on its inferior cousins. Just what you need, when thousands of euros' worth of damage has been done to your world-class research centre: a bunch of students talking about it. But Gareth is scheduled to be speaking. I'm his tutor; I'm supposed to be supportive about this kind of thing.

'I don't know. I might be busy.'

He looks disappointed. I try to read the card from a distance.

'Just to jog your memory, Miss, it's this Tuesday eventide. The medieval burgh of Fulling. Ye Bishops' Hall, Market Square.'

'Yeah, come along,' James says. 'Come and listen to a bunch of bed-wetting freshers spouting on about how humankind is basically evil and fluffy little animals are the only things worth loving in this world.'

'You're one,' Gareth says. 'You're one of those bunny-lovers.'

'I'm *nothing*. I'm not anything.'

He yawns extravagantly, dismissing the argument as easily as he started it. He doesn't really care what happens in that lab next door. He just wants to win something, some game of his own making, beat someone, it doesn't matter who.

'Have you ever been targeted, Miss?' Gareth is asking me.

I shake my head. Paint on my car once, when I was a doctoral student at Warwick: I don't call that being targeted.

'So you must really believe in all this animal research stuff. If you're prepared to risk the attacks and everything.'

I make a doctorly nod. I do believe in it, I'm trying to say; I'm just not very good at arguing my case, explaining where the conviction comes from, why I can spend my waking life working with animals that will never see daylight, then go home and brush my teeth and sleep soundly. In this business, you keep your reasons to yourself. Instead I'll have to convince them by other means, find a way into their curiosity, looking for that moment when you just start to sense that they're interested, and you feel the dizzy tilt of understanding on the move, shifting, breaking away, starting to slide. I tell them that the brain is a box of miracles, a collection of exquisite mechanisms that can outperform any machine on earth, and that the only way we'll find out how it works is by breaking it down and trying to understand the pieces. I flap my hands around too much and I notice James noticing this. At the end I stop talking and bathe in the reflux, all that silence flowing back at me, a tide of spent words looping around my feet and lifting me into weightlessness, a weird kind of peace. He has me in his gaze, that cool fascinating fixedness: not fighting me now, more like what comes after fighting.

A quiet tide. Then he speaks.

'You take it to pieces, Dr Churcher, and then you can't put the pieces back together again.'

I laugh. You shouldn't laugh at men, it's fatal. But I can't help it: this is a mid-brain reflex, some neural cluster buzzing some other neural cluster, and going nowhere near that mythical centre, whatever it is that's supposed to be *me*. He's blushing now, scorched by an older woman's mockery, and I can feel the tingling dread that tells me I've gone too far. He's hauling up the smile, hardening it, putting a bit of menace in it, a squeeze of anger. It's too hot in here. All the doors and windows sealed, and electronic locks on all the doors, and just the two of us trapped in this moment, fighting for air.

It's true: I do have a secret. It's not about what I do for a living, or whether those ninety-nine mice suffer when I drop them into milky water and see if they can swim their way out of trouble. My secret is about me. I use this word, this feathery personal pronoun, like you might say the name of a foreign town you're headed for but have never actually seen, hoping the act of utterance might bring it closer. But I don't believe in that town. I never did. That feeling of centredness, of me-ness, that keeps other people rooted in their lives: well, it passed me by. I have this fantasy that I'll do what Gareth wants me to do, I'll take the thought-helmet and put it on, dim the lights and let everyone see what's going on inside. To start with, no one will notice any difference. There'll be the low-level buzz of life-or-death routines, the reflexes that keep the machine working. As I turn around to see James sitting there, there'll be the swirl in the back of my brain corresponding to the sight of him.

But then he'll ask me again, 'How does it feel to be *you*, *here*, *now*?' And there'll be nothing. No shape, no centre, nothing you could call a thought. Just one neural cluster buzzing another neural cluster, one lot of bio-electrical traffic taking the ring-road around the soul; one deluded meat puppet sizing up another deluded meat puppet and wanting to fight it or fuck it or whatever. 'What about how it *feels*?' James will ask me. 'There must be Something That It Feels Like To Be Yvonne.' I'll shrug and say it feels like this. You sitting there with your fading blushes and your day-old stubble, wanting to fight me or fuck me, both, I don't know. Knocking at the door, trying to work out why there's no answer.

Calling my name.

Wondering why there's no one at home.

David Harsent

from *The Wormhole*

Dexter possesses certain odd powers. He has drawn to himself a boy named Daniel and a young woman named Selina. They have the run of a city where the dead are not at rest.

Selina liked to ride the subway so, more often than not, the subway was their method for getting around town. Daniel thought she was looking to rub up against the dead. Dexter thought so too, but he had reasons of his own for taking the train. Somewhere between midtown and Bank Street he brought things to a halt for a moment, like switching the city off, waiting a beat, then switching it back on.

They were no longer on the train, but they weren't on the platform either. Selina heard a rumble fading down the track, then there was silence. Dexter started off like a man all set for a hike.

There was a spur off the main tunnel, then a second spur, then a third where things opened out: enough room for a little plank and rag shack or a tar paper lean-to. A string of them had been built either side of the tracks: a subterranean shanty town. There were lights high in the tunnel, each shedding a dim yellow disc on to the upper curve of the ceiling; these were supplemented by occasional light bulbs that had been jacked in to underground lines that fed the city grid. The TV sets shedding a silver-blue glow of their own on to the walls of each and every shack were powered in the same way. Further down the tunnel, oil drum fires flickered and flared.

Daniel could see, in the half light, figures going to and fro. 'Who are they?'

Dexter told him. 'The homeless, the hopeless; rejects and romantics. Bad dreams have pushed them out of doors.'

'They live down here?'

'That's right.'

'Why?'

'Safer, drier, they have a power supply, they've cracked a few waterpipes and fitted them with stopcocks, they can build these little houses; they're a community. Mostly, though, because it's trouble free. When the "Clean Streets" law came in, these people moved down a level.' He spread a hand to take them in. 'The lowest of the low; the city's untouchables.'

'How do they get by?'

'The same way they did when they lived above ground. They panhandle, they forage, they steal.'

A couple of the dead went by, shadows passing through darkness. Selina picked them up like smudges on radar.

She wondered if the dead had a language.

The nonstop rustle-and-slither was rats. They were a constant. You always heard them, but sometimes you saw them; a slick brown river flowing over the carpet of garbage or heaving up from the underside.

Dexter, Daniel and Selina walked ankle-deep through trash. Finally, they came across a circle of people sitting round a fire that was hemmed in by a square of house bricks. Good things were going from hand to hand.

Dexter sat down with them. Selina and Daniel did the same. Dexter helped himself to what was going round.

They sat and talked for a while and everyone had a story to tell.

From time to time, a train went through, bringing a hot wind with it. The carriage lights of the train were a single blurred line under which lay a blur of faces. The noise banged back off the walls like giant jackhammers.

A man said, 'My name is Jarek. I came to the city on the lookout. I came in the hope . . . They picked me up at the train station and told me about the good times to be had. For a while, it was just like that; couldn't have been better. Then I became aware of things starting to fall away. I'd wake up in a different room; or if not that, there would be items I couldn't account for. Sometimes I would notice an unpredicted change in the weather. Little things that made my eyeballs itch. Pretty soon I realized that stuff I'd brought with me – you know, a snap or two, a memento, the usual safeguards – were no longer mine. I had to move; there was nothing else for it. Outside was a different issue: seeking warmth, eating what I could find, sleeping *en plein air*. You can walk all night, you can roam, you can crisscross, you can find a place and get in, or get down between, and it's OK on a balmy night, I mean, not A-OK, and you can't see the stars, but just so long as you don't have plans . . .'

He took a sip of what was going round and held his hands out to the fire. Daniel thought he'd caught a whiff of the smell Dexter spoke of: deep and fruity and mortal.

Jarek said, 'You know the stuff folk throw out? I got a TV, a lo-fat grill, loafers, Old Navy sweats, three pictures in frames, some cups, a whole box of Vioxx, a Schaeffer pen, Best of Soul, a wind-up clock – school clock, Roman numbers – three folding chairs in sea-green canvas, a bag of books that I read and sold on but I kept one or two, I kept the one . . . I can't remember . . . the animal story, a stove, a rug with yellow flowers and a fringe, storage cartons, a butane lighter, a box made of sandalwood with a silk lining for cufflinks or whatever, a long-necked vase, this was just two days of sifting, two days or three, this coat, a fire iron, and I brought it all down here, then some wood from a site and a window that came entire, plus a roll of tarpaulin, plus cans and pans I also found, that was in a kitchen alley, and I built my house. I've got a dog keeps the rats down and an all-metal knife, fork and spoon unit I took out of McDonald's.'

Jarek had a trim beard and a little woollen hat; his eyes were half closed as if he were struggling to remember all this. A train went through and the fire flattened in the slipstream.

He said, 'They picked me up at the train station and they painted a pretty picture. I just had to do this and do that. For a while, it was pure heaven. Life eating out of your hand. But then . . . I wouldn't characterize it as a downfall or a slippery slope, it doesn't work like that. Just, one day, you realize that it's all a bit nondescript; then it's shades of grey for a while; then the thing steals up on you. After that, you have to live a certain way. You have to find a means . . . Up above, there's the weather to contend with. In addition, there's authority. Authority doesn't make things any easier. Down here, we're much of a muchness. Down here, I'm one of a kind.'

Jarek left them, when his story was done, and wandered into the darkness. Dexter, Daniel and Selina stayed to hear more from others, after which Dexter got up and led the way deeper into the labyrinth. People were scuttling to and fro between the sheds and shanties, sometimes calling to one another, a shrillness that echoed through the web of tunnels, and fires were being lit.

'Fires against the night,' Dexter said. 'It's an old instinct.'

Daniel said, 'But it's always night down here.'

'It is. But each evening, they seem to sense the failing of the light in the world above them.'

The flames flickered on the walls, illuminating tunnel graffiti: imprints of splayed hands done in red or blue, TV characters, product logos, trains drawn in a hundred different ways. Someone had written HALFWAY TO HELL in bandit display-face; lime-and-pink with a heavy black outline.

A train went through and they were on it. When Selina looked out, the tunnel fires were a streaky line, yellow and orange, her own face imposed on top; and then, seeming to lie beyond both, the reflection of a room full of people, the whole thing out of focus at first, then coming clear.

It was a concert hall, the orchestra already on stage, a grand piano in position, the audience fallen to silence. The conductor appeared, followed by the soloist. They bowed; they took their places; the pianist adjusted his stool very slightly, bowed his head, closed his eyes briefly, then looked up at the conductor to say, 'Yes.'

Selina put a hand to her mouth. A sensation went through her like someone drawing a wet thread in her spine. The pianist was Jarek.

The conductor made his move and Selina heard the first notes of the Emperor Concerto. She stared: the flowing line of fire; her own face; the concert hall; Jarek's first attack, his mouth a tight line, that little crease of a frown.

She could feel Dexter at her side and said, 'What is this?'

'His other life. The way things could have gone.'

'Why didn't they?'

'You heard him.'

'That was the life he lived; the life he's living. What prevented this one?'

'Love,' Dexter said. 'Love got in the way. It turned things around. It's why he left and came to the city.'

'Did you make that happen?'

'I don't make things happen.'

'What does?' She watched Jarek as he played, fingers rolling through the trills. 'What did?'

'A chain of events,' Dexter said. 'A chain.'

Selina was locked on the image in the window. 'Where is he?'

Dexter peered over her shoulder. 'Paris, is it? Rome?'

The train ride was all the way uptown, then back down. Selina stayed for several return journeys to watch the concert. Daniel dozed. Dexter took an interest in the passengers, their secret lives buzzing round their heads like flies round a midden.

Jarek stood up to take his bow. The audience was on its feet. Outside, fires bloomed in the darkness.

Esther Freud

untitled

'I don't know if I've ever mentioned my friend Caroline?' Lambert
said as a thick white plate of kedgeree arrived at the table, sweeping past the square of silver cutlery, sliding soundlessly on to the
linen cloth in front of Lara. 'But I had a letter this morning,
and . . .' he paused to acknowledge the arrival of his chops, 'it
seems she's not at all well.'

'Oh. I mean, no. I don't think you have.' Lara stared down at the
slivers of browned fish, the gold yolk of the egg, the parsley sticking to the rice. She wanted to start but it seemed rude. 'Is she . . .'
She never knew if you were allowed to mention age to people who
were old. 'Is she . . .?' She said it brightly. 'Is she very old?'

'Well . . .' Her father took up a sharp knife and cut into the
meat. 'Not terribly. A few years more than me. Sixtyish maybe?'
He sighed. 'Quite young.'

Lara nodded as she scooped up her first mouthful, the soft
grains, cinnamon and clove scented, the tiny seeds of caraway
cracking between her teeth, and wondered when, if ever, she would
think of sixtyish as young.

'It made me wonder . . .' her father continued while the waiter
poured tea, 'if I shouldn't visit. She's taken a house in Italy for the
summer. She takes one every year, and every year she invites me,
but this time . . . this time I thought I actually might go.' He looked
down then, frowning, giving Lara a chance to observe him, see
how this declaration was affecting him, a man who made it a point
never to leave London, had not left it, as far as she knew, since
before she was born. Why, she'd asked him once, do you never
travel? And he'd shrugged and said, why travel when you're
already in the best place there is?

For a while they ate in silence and then, still chewing, he fixed
Lara with a look.

'Have you ever been?'

'Where?'

'To Italy.'

Lara shook her head. She'd been to Paris once, and to an island off Ibitha, and one year she and her mother had thought they might go to America, but the woman they were hoping to stay with had never written back to say they could.

He was still looking at her. 'I thought maybe you'd like to come?'

'With you?'

His eyes widened. 'Yes.'

'Really? I mean yes. I would.' They smiled at each other – a seal on their pact, and then spirals of alarm, of dread, of delirious excitement shot through her body with such force that her appetite disappeared and finishing her breakfast seemed suddenly as arduous a task as being asked to plough a field.

Lara's father, Lambert Gold, lived in a dark and thickly padded flat halfway up a wide, carpeted stairway. There was a small kitchen, a small sitting room, a large study, and a bedroom into which she'd only ever glanced, but which had a pale green plant of such beauty growing up against one wall that it always surprised her, it seemed so out of keeping with the dark interior of the rest of the flat. Through the half open door the heart shaped leaves and twining stems seemed to actually be breathing, stretching towards the light, shivering very slightly in a breeze, the leaves always in spring colour, whatever time of year. This plant was the one thing that reminded her that Lambert had ever known her mother. She had a lemon scented geranium on a low table beside her bed, but unlike her father's plant for which she didn't have a name, the geranium was forever changing, ageing, growing new shoots, darkening and lightening with the time of year. The stalk was gnarled and brown, the dead leaves dropped in a little curling pile on to the plate below, but when you rubbed against it a scent so rich and airy filled the room that it made you stop whatever you were doing and breathe in.

Ever since she'd known her father, and it bothered Lara sometimes that she couldn't remember the day they'd met, he'd been writing a history of Britain in the twentieth century. Some sections of it had already been published, a fact he railed against, because each time this happened it meant his work schedule was disrupted by requests for articles, interviews, letters to which he must reply. There was a sense about him that he was forever warding off interruption, must really, ideally never be disturbed, so that it meant the few people who did see him felt themselves to be the chosen, and every second spent in his time was a gift bestowed.

Lambert's real name was Wolfgang Gold. As a child he'd been known as Wolf, but he'd renamed himself three months after arriving in London, seeing his new name in print for the first time the day after his eighteenth birthday when he'd written an angry letter to *The Times*. Why did you choose Lambert? Lara asked him, wondering what she would call herself if her own name ever became more of a burden than it was worth, and he said he chose Lambert because it was less threatening than Wolfgang but still related, a sort of private joke to himself. He'd come across it in the obituary pages of the newspaper, William Lambert 'Bertie' Percival, a colonel in the army who'd died, peacefully, in his sleep. What had he been angry about? She always forgot to ask him that, and when she did remember it was never the right time.

They were travelling to Italy by train. The train, Lambert decided, would be more civilized, more comfortable than a plane – they could dine in style in the restaurant car, but they both knew the thirty-six hours of the journey would give him more time to adjust to the idea of leaving Britain. 'We've got a very early start, so it may be easier if you stay the night with me,' he suggested. 'Then we'll be sure we don't lose each other at the station.'

'Right,' Lara agreed, as if this were all quite normal, and so, on a warm evening in July, three months after her seventeenth birthday, and one week before the Royal Wedding for which the whole of London was waiting in anticipation, she heaved her bag up the steps of his Kensington block, rang the bell, and prepared to spend the first night of her life under her father's roof.

'Welcome, please, come in,' Lambert nodded formally, his accent, for some reason, unusually pronounced, and for a moment they stood self consciously together in the hall. 'I've eaten,' he said, as if this may be a worry, had better be made clear, and even though she assured him she'd eaten too, he backed into the kitchen where he opened up the fridge. The fridge was tall and white, much larger than the one she and her mother owned, but much emptier too. There was half a lemon, a bottle of old milk and something flat wrapped in white paper. 'I have some tongue?' he offered tentatively. But she told him she'd had macaroni cheese. 'I ate with Mum,' and she patted her stomach as if she really had.

There was no spare room at Lambert's so instead he made up a bed for Lara on the sofa in his study with a sheet and a tartan rug he used to drape over himself when he was cold. But hard as they searched they could not find a pillow. Eventually they discovered that the leather seat of his armchair came away if you tugged at it hard enough and so they wrapped it in a towel and propped it up on the end of her make shift bed.

Goodnight, they said, once Lara was in her nightie, having brushed her teeth and washed her face, and she tried not to listen as he took his turn in the bathroom. She read her book, shutting off her ears to the arc of his pissing, the clunk and roar of the flush, and then some minutes later, the choking humorous gargle as he rinsed his mouth. She slept lightly, the ridges of the buttoned leather sofa making her dream she was at sea, shifting between one smooth wave and the next, and then too soon, but also after an endless buffeting, she heard the pull of the sitting room curtains and felt bright sunlight stream in against her face.

'Morning,' Lambert greeted her, and seeing she was awake he moved off to the kitchen to fill the kettle. It was wordless, their arrangement, seamless, as if they'd lived together all their lives. Lambert stayed in the kitchen while she pulled on her clothes. Then he, still in his dressing gown, shut the door into his bedroom, while Lara slipped into the bathroom, washed her face, examining it with microscopic scrutiny in the harsh morning light, grimacing at the dark round of a pimple lurking below the surface of her cheek. She brushed her hair, arranging it so that a strand fell over the spot and then, dissatisfied, she fluffed it up so that it didn't fall so flatly on her head. Don't look, she told herself, still looking, knowing her attempts were hopeless, and despair settling like a black umbrella, collapsing, she arranged her features into one of optimism, and forced herself away.

Lambert already had the tickets. How did he get them? It seemed inconceivable that he'd gone out and bought them – made his way to the station, stood patiently in a queue. Or maybe someone had done it for him? Someone practical, who knew about these things. Lara looked them over in the taxi. Two return tickets for the boat train, from Victoria station right through to Pisa. All they had to do was find the platform, the train for Dover, their seats. Lara followed him, sticking close as they hurried through the mass of people, straining her eyes for a clue to the right platform. It was early, but the station was crowded, backpackers sitting like flocked seagulls on the ground. Families dressed for a day out, on their way south to Eastbourne or Brighton, and businessmen with matching briefcases, trousers pressed to a fine point above their shoes. And then, with a jolt Lara realized she'd lost him. She looked around, saw only a sea of summer heads, and as she searched more wildly, clutching the handle of her bag too tight, she was gripped by the desolation of someone who has given all responsibility up. Christ, she thought, I have no ticket, no idea where I'm going – and then she caught sight of him again, taking his change, stowing a swathe of newspapers under his arm. 'Dad!' she yelled, and it shocked her to feel how quickly she'd become a child.

There were only five minutes now before the train was due to leave. Lara felt the imagined whistle blowing right under her skin. But Lambert moved towards another kiosk, where, taking his time, he bought a box of matches and a packet of Gitanes. You can buy them at duty free, she would have told anyone else, but she stood obedient while he chose and handed over change. 'Three minutes,' she hissed just under her breath, and then, turning, he began to run, his bag flying, his shoulders jostling between backpackers and tourists, day trippers, people with all the time in the world. 'Excuse me, so sorry,' his apologies floated back to Lara, running behind, and then they were at their platform, hurtling along its length, pushing the bags ahead of them, leaping aboard their train.

'It is very important,' he panted, 'how you leave your destination.' A whistle blew and the sound of doors slamming rattled every carriage.

'More important than how you arrive?' Lara sank gratefully down into a seat.

'I'll tell you tomorrow,' he smiled, and he opened up a paper and with convincing nonchalance, began to read.

Jane Rogers

from *The Experiment*

Conrad locks the door of his hotel room and leans against it, trying to calm his breathing. The bedclothes are still thrown back, his washbag tilts against the bedside lamp, yesterday's shirt and underclothes are on the floor by the bathroom door. It doesn't look as if anyone has been in. The small man's face looms in his mind's eye; the flat confident appraising stare, waiting for Con to react. Is the plan to scare him, then jump when he runs? Moving cautiously, he sits on the edge of the bed. If he doesn't run, he's a sitting duck; either way, they've got him.

He runs his fingers over his face, as if the softness of his eyelids, the slight friction of the morning's growth of stubble, are new. His face, his head, his whole body feels fragile as an egg. He is dizzy with lack of sleep. He tries to remember if the small man was at the conference yesterday, if he might be a delegate after all. With his pale eyes, his contained way of moving; no, if he had been there before Con would have noticed him.

Fear jerks him to his feet. He makes himself sit down again, but his bowels have turned to water. After he's flushed the toilet he pulls down the lid and sits on it. There's no point in rushing out of the place like a madman; nothing could be more of a giveaway. They cannot definitely know it was Con. The small man's approach may have simply been a calculated guess. The most important thing is to behave naturally. Pack up, check out, catch the bus to the airport. The calm behaviour of a blameless man. Catch the bus to the airport and . . . His thinking falters, a dark blip. *Catch the bus to the airport. Just do it.*

As he approaches the hotel desk, holdall in hand, he realizes he will be one of the first to leave. People are staying to lunch. He can see a knot of them clustered around the entrance to the dining hall, waiting to be led to tables. The thought of lunch is intolerable; the creakingly slow service, the jockeying conversations about grants and publications, the continued presence of the small man – no, not lunch. It can't be so strange, to leave straight after the morning session. He could plausibly have an early flight.

Outside he draws the cold air deep into his lungs, forces himself to cross the street and use the ATM, to show he is in no hurry, and walks with measured steps to the bus stop. No one obviously watching. He studies the Sunday timetable with growing disbelief. Thirty-five minutes till the next bus. Taxi? No, he'd be alone; there's safety in public transport. *Think. Think.* But he can't. He's walking along the pavement, the way the bus would go. Walking towards the airport, but it's ten kilometres from the city centre – walking is clearly mad. Walk to the next bus stop? Not running, not hurrying, just walking. His feet are blurs, his breathing short and fast, there's someone coming towards him. *Don't look up.* A woman's legs, no hesitation, she's past. *Keep moving, don't run.* Up ahead there's another bus stop, with a different set of numbers. Drawing level he realizes these are city centre buses. In a bus he'd blend in with other people, instead of being exposed out here on the street. He scans numbers, destinations, times, but before he has made sense of it there's already a bus and he's clambering into its hot stale interior. There's a machine for stamping your ticket but he has no ticket; the driver seems oblivious. Con ducks his head and sits, glancing quickly around the other passengers; elderly people mostly, a couple of young mothers with children. He allows himself a deep breath of their comforting used air, cushions his scarf against the window and leans his head on it. The rattling vibration of the bus's motion is a long, snoring breath.

He is in the monkey house. He recognizes the nightmare before it even materializes, recognizes the lurch in consciousness, the fall. He knows what is coming. It should be possible to turn, to wake, but he is powerless, limbs weak as trailing underwater weeds. The first cage swims up at him, the small grey inert body, the pool of yellow vomit, the stench of the place penetrating him through every orifice and pore.

With a massive wrenching force like dragging a tree from the earth by its roots he heaves himself free of it and opens his eyes. The bus is in a queue of traffic, inching forwards in slow juddering jerks. Up ahead he sees a *Bahnhofs* sign. He could get off, a railway station is a good place to be.

Walking on to the concourse he is pleased by this serendipity. Here he can escape the decisions he would have had to face at the airport. Looking up at the departures board he feels a kind of elation. Destinations across Europe are on offer: Vienna, Rome, Paris, Berlin, Bologna, Munchen, Amsterdam. He can indeed escape. With relief comes hunger. He buys sandwiches in the buffet and sits on a high stool by the window cramming food into his mouth. Once he's on a train he can try to catch up on his sleep. Staring out across the platforms he finds his eyes drawn to an unpleasantly familiar figure. Surely the small man isn't here? Surely he hasn't followed Con's arbitrary progress from the hotel to the station? It must be someone else. A train slides in on platform 2 and Con's view of 3 is blocked. He dumps the half eaten sandwich and grasps his bag. *Get away from here, now. Get right away.*

Glancing at the departures screen above the counter he sees the next train out is for Bologna, Bahnsteig 8 at 13.50. If the small man is on 3 (is looking for him on 3? Or knows exactly where he is, and has simply chosen that as a vantage point?) then to go up and over the Bahnuber to platform 8 is a good option; the man can scan passengers at ground level but not those passing above his head.

Con reaches 8 at the same time as the train. He dodges through the crowd on the platform, then forces himself to slow down, straining his ears for sound of pursuit. He'd be more noticeable, running – a tall man people step aside for, clearing a swathe. He walks the length of the train, stumbling once as his legs break into an involuntary run, glancing into the faces of the newly disembarked passengers. They barely look at him, absorbed in their luggage, their children, the buttons of their coats which must be done up against the freezing air. When they look beyond him towards the exit they do not register surprise, they see nothing unusual at his back. He passes another carriage, notes it is empty and dodges back into it, slamming the door behind him. Stands for a moment trying to steady his breathing. He should stay here near the door till the train moves – if they come down the platform looking for him they'll think this carriage is empty. It would make sense to hide in the toilet but he can't bear the idea of them finding him there, trapped, nowhere to run.

Once the train jerks into motion he takes a corner seat, muffling himself in his scarf and fixing his gaze on the door at the opposite end of the carriage. But he knows they could come at him as easily from the door behind as the door ahead, and anyway even if he saw them coming, what could he do? Gain an extra thirty seconds' panic? If the small man is on the train . . . It doesn't have to be the small man. It could be other people, his accomplices, people Con has never seen before. It could be anyone; he'll have no way of knowing, there is nothing he can do to protect himself.

The train picks up speed. No one else has come into the carriage. After a while Con lets himself be soothed by the flat winter landscape rolling past his window. No one could have guessed he would go to Bologna. Even if the small man was on platform 3, he is not to know which train Con got. He is not necessarily chasing him anyway. And Con is speeding towards Italy, where he can employ his schoolboy Italian. Speeding in the opposite direction to home, away from Eleanor, the chief source of his distress. Eleanor, whom he once thought he was so very lucky to have married.

Conrad and Eleanor had been seeing each other for eleven months when Eleanor became pregnant. It was 1975. She was twenty-five and he was twenty-three.

'Annie says the people at the university clinic are good,' Eleanor told him. It was sunny and they were sitting on the wall outside the pub looking down into the canal. Conrad watched a mother duck shepherding her brood in and out of the weeds at the water's edge.

'Good at what?'

'Advice. Fixing it.'

'Fixing what?' he asked stubbornly, knowing perfectly well that his slowness would only make her more impatient.

'Abortion, what do you think?' Eleanor looked across at the gangs of other students sprawled around the tables. 'Why are you being so dense?'

'I don't agree with abortion. I mean –' quickly, as she turned to face him, squaring up for the argument, 'yes, a woman's right to choose and all that, but unless it's a rape or something – I mean, within a relationship, shouldn't it be discussed?' His voice sounded craven in his own ears.

'What will we discuss?' she said in a reasonable tone. 'How I'm going to look after it while I do my house job? Or how you are, working eight hours a day in the lab? Or what we're going to use for money?'

'We can discuss it.'

'Keep your voice down. There's no need to tell the world.'

'OK. Let's walk along the canal.' If this was the only time it would be discussed, then they would discuss it now, for good or ill. But Eleanor was objecting.

'I've got to be back for a histology lecture at two.'

'Fine. There's an hour.'

'You've got to inject your mice.'

'The mice can wait.' He stood aside to let her go down the steps to the towpath. It was too narrow to walk side by side.

'So what d'you think I should do? Give birth and have it adopted?'

'Of course not.'

'What then?'

He felt a sudden spacey unbalancedness, as if he were starting across a tightrope. Head up, one foot in front of the other; don't think of the drop. 'We could get married.'

'*Married*?'

'Yes.'

She kept on walking in front of him; he couldn't see her face. The silence extended.

'Why not? People do. They . . . they get married and have children.'

'What for?'

He pretended to laugh. 'Because they want to.'

'Do you want to?'

'Yes.'

She turned. 'You really want to get married?'

The spark of anger he felt was a relief. 'Yes. Is that so strange? We're going out together, you're expecting my child, I want us to get married.'

'But it never entered my head.' She began to walk on. After a while she said, 'I don't think it's a very good idea.'

'Why?'

'We're too young. I mean we'll both probably meet other people we like.'

He knew she would.

'And in terms of our careers the timing's terrible. If we *were* going to get married and have kids, in five years time might be about right.'

'But this has happened now.'

'OK. But I could have an abortion now and we could still choose to get married and have a family in five years time, if we really wanted.' Her tone showed him how unlikely she thought that was.

'In five years time one of us could be dead. The abortion might lead to sterility, you might never conceive again –'

'You're being ridiculous. The whole point is, women can have control of their fertility.' El was on the pill.

'So what went wrong here then?'

'I don't know.'

'I rest my case.' He could see what was going to happen as clearly as he could see the rubbish clogging the canal up ahead. If she had an abortion it would lie between them. A mucky connection. She would use it to move herself on. But the more he cared, the easier it was for her not to. He had a vision of two kids on a seesaw, one clinging on fearfully, and the other, at the extreme end, gleefully bumping and jolting up and down. He forced himself to speak lightly. 'You just had a proposal of marriage.'

'My third.' She turned and smiled at him, then leaned in and touched her lips to his. 'I'm honoured. I'm going to histology, but I'll think about it.'

He wondered who the other two were. Paul Johnson would be one. But he didn't know the other.

'Four actually,' she said, 'if you count Timothy Evans at primary school.'

'Fine. I'll see you tonight.'

When they met after dinner Eleanor had already called at the counselling centre. 'I was cycling past at five and they were still open.'

'And?'

'If I said I didn't know who the father was, it would be simple.'

He couldn't think of a reply.

'You would never have considered marrying if this hadn't happened.'

She was right. Why was he thinking of it now? He hated her. 'Yes I would.'

She sighed theatrically and folded her arms. 'Oh yeah.'

'Look –' His mind was blank.

'I'm looking.'

'Look, it's simple. You're pregnant, let's get married.' He felt his hot blush rising.

'Is it some antiquated notion of honour? You've ruined my reputation so now you must do the decent thing? Is it that?'

'No. The reverse.' At last, lucidity. 'Exactly the reverse. I want us to make a commitment. I want to live with you. I want it to be permanent. It's not cool, it's not what any one else is doing. But you being pregnant – gives us the excuse.'

The tiny silence before her reply was encouraging. 'You were waiting for this to happen.'

'No. Of course not, you're on the pill. But now it *has* happened, I can see it's what I want.'

'What about me?'

'I don't know.' There was a relief in having said it. Whatever happened. In having stated his position.

'Neither do I.'

Gathering out of his relief, swelling with the force of it, came a magnanimity which astonished him: he could pity her. She didn't know what she wanted. He did. He loved her and that had made him vulnerable, she could damage him with her not caring. But now in a swoop the positions were reversed: he was fortunate, knowing what he wanted. She was the lost one. In the safety of his secure footing he could wait, and whatever happened would not be all loss. 'OK. When you know, you can tell me.'

After a moment she burst out laughing. 'Thanks. What if I never know?'

Her laughter broke their immobility – it was possible to reach for her and pull her into a hug. Their bodies were warm together.

'You haven't got that luxury. You've got – what's the cut-off point? Fourteen weeks?'

She shook her head. 'If I go in the next week they can do suction. I'd be in and out within the hour.'

'Like cleaning a car.'

'What?' She was laughing.

'Suction. One of those vacuums they have at garages.'

'That's disgusting.'

'Yes. Don't do it.' He kissed her. He could feel the power. It had transferred from her to him, most amazingly. He could kiss her, he could pin her arms to her sides, he could walk her slowly backwards and lower her to the bed; peeling his face from hers he could tell her, 'Don't move', and undress her garment by garment while she let him raise first arms then legs in his hands, watching him, her eyes almost blank with surprise and lust. For the first time, Con had the power.

Knowing it makes it happen. He used to believe that. She said yes; he knew she would. You can't make happen what you want to happen. But when you shift from wanting it to knowing it, it happens. It comes to you, whatever you desire, it comes and offers itself up.

Maura Dooley

from *Malachite and Verdigris*

Now that I know this speak I can tell him what the old tongue was like. Just telling makes for a feeling inside down deep. Like drawing water from a well. I'm the well. The pail shudders as it goes down and brings up something you can only look through.

I can't remember a word of the old tongue, see. Nevermind, says he, you'd know it if you heard it. Would I though? Know it? Will I though? Hear it? If feel it atimes. It's the kind of happiness as makes you cry. A long remembering kind of happiness. He says there are words for that in other speaks. Heimat, is one such. Hiraeth, is another. I never heard those speaks spoke though.

When I was very young we lived on a farm away from all the trouble. I knew nothing. There would be silences and looks. When I'd gone to bed I'd hear neighbours arrive. I guessed who it was from the noise of a car engine or the exact combination of shuffle and knock that picked out Sam from Kamal or Sophie from Bip. Somehow I knew not to ask. Say nothing. Maybe that kind of not-saying made its mark on me. Because when I found them – the green children – it never occurred to me to tell anyone at all.

School stopped, after the Scattering, and I noticed then for the first time that I was an only. *Are you a Lonelyonly?* Aunt Em had used to say, laughing, knowing that I wasn't. The house was always stuffed with friends and there was my cat Smiler, the farm dogs and Kamal's stable down the road. Life was full. But all that changed.

If Dad hadn't been so busy with the meetings and those silences on top of the farm and everything, he might have noticed more when I slipped off. When, now and then, he'd ask what I'd been doing, I'd get a talking-to all of a sudden about the Disappearings, how I should stay in the farm, study, be safe. But he'd forget again. To tell the truth, I think he knew we were the back of beyond. Who would come snooping here? The flat fields, the big sky, the water stretching and stretching. So I pretty much did as I liked. Most days I went out to look.

The Committee had early on sorted out food and fuel, so although my findings of berries or kindling were useful they were only trimmings. I knew that. I was looking for something altogether different. And I didn't know what it was at all until the day I found it.

Dad needs the dogs for the sheep. They never leave the farm much. So it's Smiler that comes with me now. Imagine that. Aunt Em used to joke about the way he stuck by me. 'Here comes Dick Whittington!' or 'The Cat and His Boy' or 'My Nephew and Other Animals'. I'd smile. Though it wasn't very funny, even the first time. I like Aunt Em. Liked I should say. Smiler, he'll come miles but stop suddenly, in the middle of a field, halfway along a length of wall, as if he'd seen a ghost and he'll mew like mad. You never heard such a racket. It took me the first few times to know that this was the end for Smiler. His territory must be marked out with invisible lines and nothing will move him into the next kingdom. So I have to go on alone and you wouldn't think it would make much difference. He's only a cat. But the first time it happened it did make me feel the *Lonelyonly*. It did really.

It's all behind us now, Dad says, and we have to 'move on'. I know that's right but it's not just memories get in the way of that. It's other things. Out walking I keep to the Government paths. You don't know what you're going to find, if you don't. So when Smiler ran off through the sedge that day I didn't want to follow. Cats have their own rules but we were far from home and I know how he hates water. So in the end, where's the harm, I thought. In all my walks I've never yet met trouble . . . and I followed.

You can see a long way in our neck of the woods. It's flat and clear and that spring day the fields were drying out and the rhines were sparkling. I soon found Smiler. He'd followed a vole and was just finishing it off as I arrived. He turned his back on me, crunching. Cats like privacy. I stood waiting. Only then did I begin to wonder why the path was so clear. The grass smooth, the reeds bent back. Purposeful. No animal could have done this but a human one. And as I thought it I heard the smallest noise. Smiler heard it too and I followed the line of his earpricked gaze.

There was nothing to see but reeds. I edged closer and realized that what I had taken to be sedge, with the first purple of some early flowering flags threaded through, wasn't a natural thing at all but something made. The reeds were twisted together through lengths of willow, what my dad calls salley wands. The wands had been cut and bent and standing in the marshy banks had sprung new leaves so that the whole was a living, growing screen, a kind of green fence. Moving towards it, suddenly I was terrified of what I'd find but I could not stop myself from plunging my hands into the leaves.

Beneath my fingers the fence moved easily. It was hinged. Reeds and grasses had been plaited and laced in and out of the willow frame, so that it swung open towards me like a well made door. I found myself peering into something resembling a low green cave. Before I could stop to think who could have made such a thing and for what reason, I heard a snatch of breath. Here were two creatures like nothing I had ever seen before, huddled together, their faces full of fear and as alike as two peas in a pod.

I had hoped and hoped as somethin' might happen. The winter long, well, him and me as used to that, not having much, but this as worse. He as very bad. It was the chill I think and saddeness. We had not seen another being for so long that when the boy's face came in through the leaves I felt as I'd die of frightenedness. But I know now that there was gladness there too. It was the beginning and the end of everything.

Dad had made lamb stew and Kamal was due any minute.

    – *We'll need to talk Joe, so you push off and busy yourself after, would you?*

One day, I was going to ask what they needed to talk about, so late and so often, but that night I had other things on my mind.

    – *What makes things go green Dad?*

    – *Chlorophyll. You know, it's when plants . . .*

    – *And what about humans Dad? Are they, like, green, ever?*

Dad laughed. Once, that was a sound I thought I'd never hear again. Now though, he's better, busier.

– *Only if they're seasick. Or from Mars maybe.*

I said nothing and he looked up sharp.

– *We've still got those science books if you want, Joe?*

His voice was almost hopeful. Then, seeing my face, he said quickly,

– *If it's plant life you're interested in, you could go and pick some kale.*

– *We need something to go with this.*

Cutting off the curly leaves and filling a bag with them I thought to myself that I should try harder for him but those books were all Mum's and I can't go near them. Now though, it seems different, I need information. I need knowledge. I took the second bag I'd brought and began to fill it. Fewer leaves this time. This one was for us.

Kamal wiped his plate with a chunk of bread and raised the gravy soaked crust at me.

– *You've got better and better at this,* he said, *cheers!*

I nodded but I didn't want to discuss dough recipes.

– *Kamal, you were nearly a doctor, what makes someone turn green? No jokes.*

But he wasn't about to make any. Mention Kamal's real love and he's away.

– *Depends on your pigmentation, for one thing. Hard for me to turn green exactly, but if you're light-skinned, well, sickness, exhaustion, starvation. Yeah, hunger mostly. Unless it's Islam you're after? We had a green man once, a kind of saint. Al-Chadir. He led his people through the darkness and the desert to seek the source of life. Immortality. So, when they got there and he stood on this special bright rock and drank this special water, he got everlasting life.*

– *And turned green?*

– *Well, no, his cloak did. Anyhow, I don't suppose we're meant to take it literally exactly.*

He looked uncomfortable for a moment.

– *But, say you only ate green things all the time? I mean from birth, right through.*

There was a long pause. Dad said carefully,
– *You mean, like your mum? A vegetarian?*
I hadn't even made the connection. There was no connection. I shook my head, angry all of a sudden.
– *Never mind. I've got to go.*
Dad turned back to the stove. His voice was muffled.
– *You've always got to go these days. Time we talked.*
But I was a scuffle of dust and the slam of a door.

Maik Nwosu

In the Shadow of His Excellency

from *A Gecko's Farewell*

One wind-swept night, he announced at the village square that he would levitate homeward at six o'clock in the morning. The announcement did not really cause a stir. Everyone in the village had become used to the school principal's eccentricities. He was the only one we knew with a doctorate, in physics, from Oxford – and an abiding love for what he called 'practical science'. On one occasion, he had announced that he would walk barefoot across the village stream. He had managed a few steps before his magic, as the villagers saw it, failed him. Another time, he had attempted rainmaking in a bid to save the village from drought. He had shut himself in the school laboratory for seven days and nights, and had remained incommunicado until a belated rain season set in. He claimed the credit, but not a few of the villagers saw providence in the occurrence.

'After the rain comes the argument,' he had responded to such comments.

To me, he had given a long lecture on the correlation between his 'meteorological adjustments' and the subsequent rainfall. We got along well, and I could be said to be one of his followers. When he had tried to light up the village via a complex solar project, there had been those who had derided his failure. I had appreciated instead his efforts to improve the quality of life in our doubly doomed village. Thereafter, he seemed to abandon his utility projects and returned once more to his romance with the spectacular. He had first toyed with the idea of engineering a flying dog before he finally settled on levitation.

'What is this all about?' I wondered.

'Space conversion,' he said, with a new light in his eyes. 'If man can master space on his own wings, there's no limiting how far he himself can travel. Think about it: a roofless universe.'

The very cynical among the villagers remarked that, well, only a man such as Dr Lookout who was not fortunate enough in his vertical dimension would be so taken with the idea of levitation. If he heard such comments, which was very likely in such a small village, they did not bother him. He was not originally from the village, but he had lived there for so long that the villagers had accepted him as one of them. His talk about levitation unsettled that aspect of their certainty. Nevertheless, on the appointed day – at six o'clock, his 'solemn hour' – we all gathered faithfully to witness the promised spectacle. To everyone's disappointment, he declared 'an unexpected technical hitch' and postponed the demonstration. The villagers reluctantly dispersed to await his reinvitation, which we all believed would only be a matter of days. But there were other forces at work, being marshalled by no less a figure than the head of the federal government . . .

He was called His Excellency, the Son of Heaven. His divine aspects were not evident to me, or to many other people, but the name had more to do with might than genealogy. His legend, stripped of its foliage, was simple: he had shot himself to power in a bloodtingling *coup d'état* and had vanished into the silence of the night. Virtually no one ever saw him. And no one heard him. But we were in no doubt that he remained the locus of power in the government of the day. His agents walked our earth like terminal sentences, as if to remind everyone – including themselves perhaps – that although His Excellency chose to live in seclusion, the omens of his power were footloose and ubiquitous.

We were therefore amazed when the news went abroad that he was to pay a visit to our village to commission a rural electricity project. If the Son of Heaven had declined to commission a number of grandiose projects in key urban centres, why would he make a sudden appearance in the middle of nowhere to unveil a rural project? It was an enlarging puzzle. Was it a publicity stunt by the local administration, or was there something about the project or the village that His Excellency knew ahead of us? Or was there something about our enigmatic ruler that made him favour what the government press termed 'grassroots appearances'?

The electricity project, although it did eventually produce epileptic fits of light, was generally regarded as a fraud. It showed us that, yes, the village was not irreconcilable with the principle of electricity but, no, the local administration would rather continue the custom of looting the public treasury. The village itself was typical: a loose congregation of hamlets lost on the road to the future. Once upon a time, it had been a major trade route. His Excellency's ancestors, the news filtered out, had crossed that route on their way from the Arabian Peninsula, laden with trinkets and frankincense. It was difficult though to look upon the visit as a personal tribute to a crossing that had happened, if indeed it had, hundreds of years ago. In those years, it was said, the village was called Sahara; it had been considered important enough to be named after the largest desert in the world. These days, however, it is simply called Sa'ra.

But His Excellency did make the visit, and he opened a new chapter in his legend. The week after he came calling, all the dogs in the village went berserk. There are several explanations of the linkage between him and that epidemic, both the improbable and the malicious. This much is certain: in the course of the commissioning ceremony, he had stroked a dog that had somehow broken through his much-dreaded security cordon. Although he had made a show of being a dog lover at the time of the incident, his security guards were court-martialled upon his safe return to the presidential villa. Their sentences ranged from dismissal from the army for dereliction of duty to death by firing squad for treason. Everything else is speculation.

Sa'ra was already famous for dogs, because our people knew several bewitching ways of turning dog meat into delicacies: dog goulash, dog forget-me-not, dog stew, dog *suya*, dog heart special. Now, it became notorious. Mad dogs ran around like wolves, howling at invisible presences but biting at everything that moved. The initial panic became an exodus. Many fled to neighbouring villages and even faraway cities, preferring a refugee status to the dunghill of memory. Some of us remained behind, and quite a number – especially women and children – became victims of the ghouls His Excellency's visit had unleashed on us. There was a general quest for comprehension. In that season, an opposition newspaper ran the headline, *Their Excellencies, the Dogs of Sa'ra*. The editor disappeared without a trace, as if he had been swallowed by the yawn of his own sarcasm.

It was a horrible time for me. Binta, my fiancée, was among the dead. Dr Lookout, the school principal, was among the wounded. He had been so named by students because of his manner of prefacing almost every statement with his favourite admonition: 'Look out, you!' He had been fortunate enough to be attacked in front of the dispensary, and on a day the medical attendant was inclined and able to be useful. He survived, but he suddenly discovered that dog meat was not good for digestion. Binta was not so fortunate. She was set upon by a pack, and they scissored her to death before anyone could get to her.

She had been my colleague at Sa'ra Grammar School. We both taught English; she to the senior students, I to the junior ones. It was Dr Lookout's style to have the newest graduates teach the senior classes. Unlike me, Binta was not from Sa'ra, but our fondness for each other bridged every distance. For me, it had been affection at first sight. For her, it had taken longer. Together, we had made the drab staff room and village sufficient for each other. After she died, and after she had remained unburied for so long in my heart, I knew the story of my life had become neatly divisible: Before Binta and After Binta. Between the two periods of emotional want was the time of grace that had sufficed. I was helpless with sorrow. And so, in a general sense, was the village.

Help came via His Excellency's Salvation Squad, a band of loyal soldiers specially trained to kill in his name. They arrived in the village at dawn, flying a kite for what later became known as the Sa'ra Termination. By noon, there was not a single dog alive in Sa'ra. A village without a dog. Like a dog without a village. Before the coming of His Excellency, no one would have believed that it could be so. Ever since people could remember, it was said, Sa'ra had been known for dogs. It was said the original settlers, weary from crossing the desert, had chosen to stop there because its large population of dogs had promised an enriching sort of nutrition.

Then, Sa'ra had been a village of wild dogs that the settlers had had to tame with superior intelligence and to curry with spices. His Excellency's thirty-minute visit changed all that and interrupted centuries of history.

I began to see a pattern in these events. The last time His Excellency had ventured out of his fortress – to commission an ultra-modern abattoir or something like that, in a village as lost as Sa'ra – his presence had been linked to a guinea-worm epidemic. The place was called Feather Junction. There was nothing feather-like about its geography, but it had the largest feather market for miles around. No one knew exactly how it had come about that while other people feasted on the flesh of birds, the people of Feather Junction gloried in the feathers. A popular explanation was that the early settlers had been preyed on by a rapid procession of accidents and diseases until they struck on the idea of sacrificing feathers to their gods. Soon afterwards, the preservation – and embellishment – of feathers became an important local industry, beckoning to both kings and clowns.

During his visit, His Excellency was presented with a bouquet of ostrich feathers, the traditional gift to royal visitors. As part of that royal custom, he was also presented with a basket of water for the blessing or cleansing of the air and the earth. All those on whom the drops of water from the ostrich feathers fell eventually became human vectors of a guinea-worm epidemic. There were several insinuations, but no one openly linked His Excellency to the epidemic. Meanwhile, death roamed Feather Junction with an oversized basket. Whispers learned to tunnel – and to skip.

One week passed before His Excellency's Salvation Squad arrived, leading hurriedly recruited doctors and nurses. While the medical team attended to those still within the realm of easy salvation, those whose cases were considered severe were taken away by the Salvation Squad. None of them ever returned. The epidemic abated, and the people gradually learned to live with their grief. The half built abattoir was never completed.

For Tamia, the affliction provoked by His Excellency's visit was sleeping sickness. Although a small settlement, Tamia was fairly well known because of its fabulous White Mountains, which once every decade or so spewed forth raw rage from their volcanic depths. The government had, in its strange wisdom, chosen the settlement as the site for a model housing estate. His Excellency had accepted to lay the foundation stone. He made the journey aboard a military aircraft, spent less than thirty minutes or so at Tamia, and returned to his fortress in Abuja, the capital city.

The next morning, no resident of Tamia stirred until it was almost noon. That was the beginning. From that day, sleep pitched its tent in Tamia and possessed its residents, so much so that in a matter of days almost no one could be relied on to keep awake for more than a few hours in one cycle of day and night. While some were lucky to fall asleep in their beds, many others succumbed in the farm or on the road or in the marketplace. The consequence was that the interior geography of Tamia was soon dotted with hoary-eyed and sleep-disabled residents. The settlement shut down, exchanging its own sort of somnambulism for a state of being that later became known as His Excellency's Nightmare.

The Salvation Squad arrived with a microphone, needles and horsewhips. First, it summoned the entire settlement to the village square. Only a few people were awake enough to hear the summons; even fewer people managed to stagger to the venue. Those who answered the summons were injected with a substance capable of banishing sleep. Some of them would later die from insomnia; some others would readjust unevenly to the pattern of day and night. Those who could not answer the summons were set upon and whipped awake. Some of them would end up in hospital with broken heads; some others would have self inflating nightmares of horsewhips for the rest of their lives. Tamia became the Village of Whips.

In the intervening period between his infrequent travels, His Excellency merged with his own shadow. And we lived in that shadow – of fear, pain and death. He was said to sleep through the day and stir at night. And because he devoted only a few hours to his official duties, the capital city soon began to teem with diplomats and entrepreneurs queuing up for days and weeks and months to be granted audience – perhaps – at the Presidential Villa. While indices of growth dipped, His Excellency's schedule remained inflexible – a few hours given to the business of government and twice more devoted to the orgies he was reportedly fond of. He was said to wake up at dusk lusting for virgins and to go to bed at dawn dreaming of spices.

This climate bred a species of anarchy in which local administrators and military governors massaged their egos ominously. Despairing of queuing interminably to see him, government loyalists overzealously interpreted the mind of His Excellency, often with disastrous consequences. A gathering of new-age feminists was violently broken up because it was thought His Excellency would not approve of such an assembly. A circus was disbanded because of a suspected parody of His Excellency. A protest by university lecturers led to the closure of the universities. A strike by nurses prompted the detention of some unionists. These were some of the milder instances.

Thinking for His Excellency was in itself a hazardous undertaking, because he would occasionally rouse himself during the day to enforce the correct interpretation of his will. His harvest season was the most dreaded time of all. Some soldiers and politicians who had fallen out of favour were rounded up and tried for coup plotting. Only one sentence was possible: death. A military governor was stripped of his citizenship and 'deported' to a neighbouring country. The opposition reported that he had had an affair with one of His Excellency's mistresses. An outspoken cleric was invited to the presidential villa for consultations. He was never seen again. His Excellency's aides insisted the cleric had not been seen in or around the villa at all. A government minister was tried for misappropriation of funds and sentenced by a tribunal to 'a jail term as His Excellency may decide'. He had tried to defraud His Excellency in their plot to loot our common wealth. Silence became his sentence.

I believe many of us preferred His Excellency safely locked away in the villa, even if his many lieutenants ran amok in his name. It was a better state of affairs than to have him importing inexplicable terrors into our already dreary lives. Were the outbreaks of diseases coincidences, or were they – as the opposition claimed – ample evidence that His Excellency was so insidiously evil that he transmitted it everywhere he went? On the contrary, thundered the government newspaper, the 'disease missiles' were acts of terror perpetrated by dissidents and anarchists out to discredit the government. Amidst the clamour of voices, it looked as if, having already been condemned to the present, our present would become our future.

The clamour spoke to me with a deeper voice. His Excellency had always been associated with death. In primary school, he had been suspended for wrestling a goat to the ground and slitting its throat. He was that strong even as a little boy. In high school, he had narrowly escaped rustication when a boy he went out to swim with drowned under suspicious circumstances. After high school, he had been considered too much of a dullard to be admitted to the officers' course at the defence academy. He had therefore had to rise through the ranks. And he had done so, with unusual speed, by being associated with almost every military coup, in which he preferred the bloodiest roles. When he had finally decided to sit at the head of the table, he had ambushed his former colleagues at a military command meeting and thereafter wrote his name on the portals of the Presidential Villa with their blood.

Foreign power brokers, who had grown disenchanted with his predecessor's attraction to Marxist rhetoric, aided his ascension. It was difficult to believe that his predecessor had had the heart or head for Marxism, but his speeches had been increasingly sprinkled with such phrases as 'Western imperialism', 'bourgeois conspiracy' and 'the maturing of Africa'. It had seemed to me like a man trying to hide behind his posturing. The fact that he had overthrown a popularly elected government had created severe image problems for him both at home and in many foreign capitals. When his sort of 'Marxism' translated into the mass expulsion of aliens, he unwittingly authored his own execution. His Excellency had come to power promising 'restoration'. He had been hosted in countless Western capitals and described as 'a friend of the free world' and 'the hope of a beleaguered continent'. The romance lasted until his government became entrenched, then he reannounced himself – with unusual verbosity – as 'an independent independence'. A bit of shocked silence followed before some of his former friends began to recall their ambassadors in protest at his 'regressive' policies, or to describe him as 'a barking dog trying to create an axis of evil'. Silence became their answer.

Now that he was at the helm, was he experimenting with forms of genocide, or were we witnessing the physical effects of his spiritual decomposition? Whichever, the diseases that trailed him, more often than not spread without discrimination, seizing both local administrators and ordinary residents. Soon, local administrators who had been eager to impress His Excellency by inviting him to unveil one ill conceived project or the other began to conduct clandestine commissioning ceremonies, where they still did so at all, or to freeze their projects into a perpetual conception stage. In public, they still sang 'His Excellency forever' – louder than ever – but there were no longer any ecstatic invitations. The rhythm of fear became the ruler of the times.

Coiled in his shadow, His Excellency appeared to take no notice; itself a very ominous sign, as Dr Lookout carefully remarked. As for his levitation project, it remained frozen in its horizontal status.

Vicky Grut

from *The Understudy*

As soon as he stepped off the plane, Marek could feel himself starting to sweat. It was only April, but here it was already far hotter than London. It did his hangover no favours. As soon as he reached the terminal building he found a drinking fountain, then sat down and waited until the crush around the luggage carousel had died down. He was one of the last to collect his bag and head out through the glass doors towards the buses and taxis. His brain felt dry and swollen. Idiot, he said to himself.

Some of the younger people in the office had insisted on taking him out for a farewell drink the night before. At the time he'd been touched, but now he was cursing them. If only he'd said no to the double whisky at the end, drunk more water, gone home a little earlier – if only *everything* had been different. If he'd caught his charter flight this morning he'd have been taken care of from now on. There'd have been a tour guide to meet him at the airport, a coach to deliver him to the hotel, and nothing to do for the next two weeks but stumble from his room to the pool or the sea. As it was, it had taken all his powers of persuasion and ingenuity to get them to put him on a plane at all. He was very lucky, the girl at Gatwick kept telling him. She was by no means OBLIGED . . . Yes, yes, yes. (Idiot.)

Marek looked around for a taxi, trying to remember where he'd packed the letter with the hotel details. The thought of stopping to open his luggage was more than he could bear. If he could just remember the general sound of the resort name perhaps he might be able to explain things to one of these taxi drivers. How did you say 'hotel' in Greek? Surely they'd know the names of all the local hotels. He racked his brain. Something with an M, perhaps. Marianne? Marietta?

245

He watched a group of ramblers in their stout and sensible shoes assembling at one end of the bus shelter outside. In the distance, scores of more unhealthy looking men were piling on to several coaches; mathematicians arriving for an international conference someone had said. His eye skipped on. Then saw her.

She was standing off to one side, away from the main crowd: a tallish, slightly angular young woman with pale brown hair hooked back behind rather prominent ears. It was the peculiar quality of her stillness that drew his eye, that and the way she was dressed – grey shirt and black jeans – incongruously sombre in the middle of all the brightly coloured holiday costumes around her. She was holding a handwritten sign, which had slipped to one side as if she'd been standing like this for some time. *M Pearce*, it said – misspelled, of course, but he had learned very early in life to be flexible on that score: Mark, Marcus, Marek, Pierce, Pearce, Piesniewicz – he answered to anything vaguely along these lines. His mood switched from despair to elation. He hurried towards her.

'Hi. Hullo, there. Hey! Hi! Miss!'

She looked at him in confusion.

'Pierce.' He pointed to her sign, grinning. 'Marek Pierce. That's me.'

'Oh,' she coloured up a bit. 'Sorry. I . . . I've seen so many people coming out I'd practically given up hope . . .'

'It's too hot to rush. I let them all go ahead of me.'

Her hand was cool and dry skinned, pleasant to the touch; he almost didn't want to let it go. His rescuer.

'Sorry to have kept you waiting,' he said. 'I didn't expect . . . In fact I was just looking around for a taxi . . .'

'A taxi?' She frowned. 'That was never the plan. It should have said on your schedule that I'd be meeting you . . . Didn't Belinda give you a schedule . . .?'

Belinda? That must be the censorious young woman at Gatwick? ('I'm not OBLIGED . . .') He shook his head. 'Never mind. I'm here. You're here. That's all that matters, eh?'

Still she didn't move.

'Are we waiting for anyone else?'

Another of those awkward smiles. 'I'm sorry. The car's just over there.'

It was a neat blue Fiat, the kind of car that hire companies favour. Only now, as he slid into the passenger's seat, did he understand quite how bad he was feeling. Exhaustion and nausea washed over him in alternate waves. If I could just close my eyes for ten minutes, he thought. Somewhere on the edges of his attention he was aware that his companion was talking about the weather. '. . . very pleasant . . . Later on, of course, it gets incredibly . . .'

His brain began to distort her words into a song of exhaustion, forcing them into a maddeningly repetitive rhythm. If she'd only stop talking for five minutes so that he could rest.

'. . . any earlier, of course, and it's quite . . .' Five minutes was all he needed. Five minutes of silence. The sleep lust was becoming almost unbearable.

'Look . . .' He sat up a bit and shook himself. 'I really appreciate your being here and everything but to be honest I've got the mother of all hangovers right now . . .'

She looked startled. 'Hangover?'

'Hangover, yes. You must have heard of the condition in your line of work.'

There was a considerable pause. 'There are some painkillers in the glove compartment. But there's nothing to drink them with.'

'If I can just close my eyes . . .'

'Oh,' she said.

He leaned back in his seat.

The road was bleak and straight. Through the blur of his lashes he saw a man in a pointed hat standing under a tree beside a lake with an evil looking herd of goats. I must be dreaming already, he said to himself. Come away, come away, said the sleep rhythm in his head. Let go of that last rope. Float. Vaporize. Let oblivion suckle you and clean the inside of your skull. Give in to the sweet blackness. Black sweetness. Give. In.

αβχ

As she drove, Frances stole curious little glances at her companion. He was not at all what she'd been expecting. She'd imagined someone altogether taller and smarter, older, more authoritative. When she saw him walking towards her at the airport – a compact young man in black jeans, a very crumpled lightweight jacket and the kind of black-rimmed glasses Arthur Miller used to wear in the early 1960s – she'd been sure he was walking towards someone else.

He was direct, that much was clear – the way he announced his hangover, no messing about, no pretending it was something he'd eaten on the plane, just straight to the bald and unforgiving facts. And now the way he fell asleep: quickly, unselfconsciously, head tipped against the side of the car, his small mouth slightly open, his neat, well made nose and chin pointing skywards. The more she saw of him the more Frances was beginning to be grudgingly impressed. Only a very confident man would behave like this at the beginning of a job. Someone less self assured would have struggled to stay awake and make conversation with her in the car. Most people who had any dealings with Harry tried pretty hard to ingratiate themselves with her. Keep in with Frances if you want anything from Harry, they said to each other behind her back. And it was true: in the last few years she'd become Harry's right-hand woman, the holder of the keys, the voice in his ear. But this man didn't seem to care. He just went right ahead and made himself comfortable. Harry would like that about him, she thought. Harry responded well to confidence.

She glanced at her watch as she turned down to the quayside: 11 am. On the other island they would have finished breakfast by now. She wondered whether Harry had remembered to take his tablets.

αβχ

After what seemed to him like a very short time, Marek became aware of a change in the noises around him. Instead of the steady rhythm of the car engine there were thuds and bumps and muffled yells. He wanted very much to carry on sleeping, but the noises were pulling him up like a little fish, up, up, up to the surface of consciousness. Now he was fully awake and very much afraid. Something was wrong. Everything was dark and very loud. All around him was a kind of roaring. I have died and gone to hell, he thought. And then, even worse: Not dead yet. Still time to panic. Can't breathe. Can't see. Must get away. Must defend myself.

He swung around blindly, throwing all his weight into the move. She was there to meet him. Even before he fully understood what he was doing, she was ready. Her forearm came up to block his swing. She caught his wrist with her other hand and held him, and like this they stopped. He was staring at the woman with big ears and she stared back, silent, unblinking. It was a moment of peculiar harmony, as if they were meeting in a faraway place, stripped down and perfectly matched. He felt he saw right to the centre of her. He saw her essence, and he was sure that it was the same for her.

Then the shutters came down again. She let him go and he sagged back against his side of the car. His back was slippery with sweat.

'What's going on? Where are we? What is this place?'

'The ferry, of course,' she said coldly.

'Ferry? What . . .?'

'The ferry to the other island, of course.'

'The OTHER island? What the hell are you talking about?'

Around them the car deck was filling up. The air rang with the slam of doors and the shouts of the crew at the mouth of the boat, directing the last of the vehicles on to the ship.

She frowned. 'Did Belinda not explain?'

'Belinda? Who is this Belinda? What's going on? I didn't book anything with a ferry. *What's going on*!?'

Something lurched and shifted in him. Paranoia burst into flower: rich and complex, pulsing with colour. Oh Bolt, Bolt! So merciless and righteous! Just because I wouldn't admit to the disciplinary charges! Always have to be the one hundred per cent winner, don't you Mr Bolt? Lure me away from home, far from English soil, away from family and friends, get me drunk and on to the wrong plane and then . . . . What? Then he saw that the woman had gone a kind of bloodless colour, the colour stationery catalogues describe as 'ivory'. Her breathing was quick and shallow. She was just as startled.

'Let's start again, shall we?' she said. 'Where do you think you're going?'

Marek wiped one hand across his face. 'To the hotel, of course.

The Marionette or the Mariner or whatever the place is called . . . I can't remember the damned name. I thought you knew it. Where do *you* think we're going?'

'Robyn's house,' she said firmly, making one last desperate attempt to drag him into her version of reality. 'Robyn's holiday place.'

At the far end of the car deck they were winching up the gate now. The noise went through him like a band saw.

'Robyn, Belinda. I've never heard of any of these people. What's going on? I thought you were the Sunsplash rep . . .'

Her face went a shade paler, if that were possible. 'Who are *you*?'

'Marek Pierce, of course. I told you that, back at the airport.'

'MAREK? Didn't you say . . .? I'm sure I heard . . . Didn't you say MATHEW . . .?' She stopped. Everything went very flat. For a moment he had the impression she might attack him. Then she turned away, towards the still-opened mouth of the ferry. 'Oh Christ!' She began to scrabble with the car door. 'That means he's still back there at the airport. He'll be . . . He'll be . . . They're going to have to let me off . . .'

Marek watched her stumbling back towards the entrance of the ferry, squeezing herself through the gaps between the cars and the streams of people flowing in the opposite direction. She reached the crew just as they had completed the closing of the gate. Her hand waved at the bright scrap of sky. He heard fragments of her voice, high, fluting, meaningless, above the roar of the engines. The men shook their heads. No, no. Impossible. He saw her body twist and return, trying to control the panic, trying to wheedle and plead but she was too wired to be really charming. And what was the point? Couldn't she see it was beyond these men to do what she wanted? She might as well be asking them to stop the globe or reverse the tides. The gate was up now.

The men seemed to be shouting back at her. He could imagine it. Stupid woman! Leave us to get on with our work. Stop making us feel bad. Why did you get on the boat if you didn't want to cross?

She turned and began to make her way back to the car, slack and defeated.

Marek opened the glove compartment and peered inside. It was impersonally clean: a couple of maps, the folder of hire documents and, as she'd said, a packet of painkillers. He snapped off four of them and slipped them into his pocket for later.

On the way to the upper decks she maintained a frosty silence, as if the whole thing were his fault. 'I just don't believe this is happening to me,' she muttered at one point.

'Happening to *you*? What about me? How long is the crossing?'

'Two and a half hours.'

Marek swore softly. Two and a half hours, plus another two and a half to return, and after all that he'd just be right back at the beginning again: no closer to his hotel and none the wiser about how to get there, and today of all days when his skin felt like paper and his head was running a drumming workshop. 'Bang goes the first day of my holiday,' he muttered.

But there was no point in getting angry. His priorities now were to get a glass of water to wash down the painkillers, then perhaps a coffee and something to eat. He looked around for signs of a bar or cafeteria.

'Would you like . . .?' he began.

She'd gone.

αβχ

She elbowed her way through the crowd looking for a quiet place to call from. If she was really quick and really lucky she might just be able to save the situation. It wasn't too late yet. She found a vacant toilet and locked herself in, trying not to touch anything, nor breathe too deeply, nor to think too much about why the floor was wet.

She dialled Pearce's mobile number. Her hands were shaking. If she could just manage to get hold of him before he called the house and got Robyn into a panic. If she could just persuade him to wait until she could get back to the other island. They could get the very first ferry of the morning and still be there in time for tomorrow's opening meeting. But without Mathew Pearce, she knew Robyn wouldn't go ahead with the planning meetings, and if these were cancelled she knew in her heart that it would be the end of the project. Adrian would go off to shoot his next commercial. Guy would return to the dull mysteries of his City law firm. Before they knew it, it would be winter and Harry would start drinking again in earnest. This was their only chance.

Almost as soon as she finished dialling the message clicked on: 'It has not been possible to connect you at this time. Please try again later.' Shit! Shit! Shit! She tried Belinda's mobile: the same. She repeated the sequence of two numbers several times, hoping, hoping, but it was always the same. She was almost in tears. So much work had gone into getting them to this point. How could it fail now? It MUSTN'T.

Harry wouldn't care, of course. If he could see her now he'd be laughing out loud. 'Serves you right, Frances,' he'd say. 'Serves you right for trying to be so bloody PRUDENT and Girl Scoutish . . .' But she had long ago learned to distinguish between what Harry *wanted* and thought important, and what Harry *needed*.

At last, in desperation, she tried the main office number. This time someone answered: 'AMO Consulting. How can I help?'

αβχ

Once he'd taken two painkillers and downed a bottle of mineral water Marek started to feel a lot better. The knots and bands about his head and neck were loosening. He ordered himself a mint tea at the bar, found himself an empty table, and the world began to settle down in a very acceptable way. The sunlight stopped hurting his eyes and became pleasantly mood enhancing. He'd brought an English paper with him from the plane. He shook it out now and began to read.

When he saw the woman coming towards him through the crowd he experienced a pleasurable kick of recognition, as if she were already an old friend, inextricably woven into the fabric of his life. He realized, though, when he came to hail her that he didn't know her name.

'Hullo!' he called. 'Hullo! Hi! I'm over here!'

She slid into the seat opposite him.

'Want to have a look at today's paper?'

'God no!' Her mouth twisted with distaste. 'It'll just be about the bloody war.'

It was true. The paper was full of the war – which seemed to be lurching along at a chaotic and alarming rate, like a horrible stain spreading over that corner of the map. 'You're right,' he smiled at his companion. She was pale, he noticed. The two scratch-like lines around her mouth showed up more sharply than before. 'Are you OK?'

'I've had some bad news. The person I came to meet, Mathew Pearce, the real one – I thought I'd missed him back at the airport, but it's much worse than that. He didn't even make it to the plane. He's not coming.'

'They said at the airport that a lot of people are cancelling their flights right now, worried about terrorism and all that.'

She looked impatient. 'It's nothing like that. He's had an accident.'

'Oh.'

'I kept trying their mobiles and getting no answer, so finally I called the main office back in London and they told me. He was on his way here. Belinda was taking him to the airport. And then a truck just drove them off the road. Belinda's not too badly hurt. They're keeping her in overnight but people seemed to think she'll be OK. But Mathew Pearce . . . Mathew Pearce . . .' The woman seemed close to tears. 'Mathew Pearce is in intensive care.' She ducked her head and began hunting around in her bag. 'I'm sorry. I've been under a lot of pressure recently.'

Marek had the impulse to reach out and touch her arm, but he remembered how quickly she could turn from repose to battle readiness.

'Have you known him long?'

'No.'

'Is he someone you met over the internet?'

She stopped halfway through unwrapping a packet of tissues. 'What are you talking about?'

He began to feel irritable again. 'I'm just trying to understand the situation. You're waiting to meet a man. You've no idea what he looks like. You find out he's in hospital and you're in bits. The only thing I can think is . . .'

Her frown tightened, then dissolved. 'An internet lover?' For the first time he thought there was a hint of amusement somewhere in her expression. 'Good try, but no.'

'Well, who then?'

She took a breath and then she stopped, and tugged a bit at the collar of her shirt. 'Would you mind if we go out on deck? I'm finding it hard to breathe in here.'

They left the cafeteria, falling into step together. Already. He was smiling.

Stop looking at me like that, she wanted to say – so frankly full of interest. I have no room for looks like that. I am too old for you, maybe not in years but in every other way. Why don't you try that German girl by the window, or the laughing dark-haired creature by the door? They are young and on holiday like you. I am not.

And yet it was not unpleasant to be looked at like that again, she had to admit it.

Natasha Soobramanien

Another London

A week after Paul's fifteenth birthday he stopped wearing his present, a leatherette bomber jacket from Chapel market. Years later, at the age of twenty-five and thinner than he'd been at fifteen, Paul took to wearing that jacket again. He wore it so often that in the end the leatherette flaked away when you rubbed it, like dead skin.

Genie remembered this as she watched Paul being loaded into the back of the hearse. He was zipped up in some kind of cool-bag, its rubberized black fabric reminding her of the jacket. She imagined unzipping it, then stopped herself, wondering if he would be naked. When she had gone to identify him he was covered from the neck down by a white sheet.

'Yes, that's him,' she'd said, though she knew it wasn't true. What did this waxy, bloated mess have to do with her honey-coloured brother? But if she claimed that the body was his – had been his – at least now they'd leave him alone; Mam, the police, everyone. She'd let them think this was him, she thought, even as she checked for and found the *Eloise* tattoo fluttering across his bicep, even as she remembered how the bruise-blue of that tattoo ink had always made her think of dead bodies.

Now, standing here with Tante Hilde and Alphonse, she no longer felt in control of this fiction. They had come out to the plane to meet her. As Alphonse hugged her, she breathed in his dusty cumin smell and looked down at Tante Hilde, the wind lifting her thin dyed hair, exposing her freckled scalp. Genie thought how much smaller she looked now, weighed down by the guilt that all elderly people must feel at the death of a much younger person.

Tante Hilde was squeezing her hand so tightly it was hard to squeeze back.

'How terrible,' said Tante Hilde, almost to herself, 'that you did not find him in time.'

But I did find him, thought Genie. And then I left him.

Sliding into her seat she glanced behind to see if they had secured him. There had been turbulence on the flight over. He must have been bumped around down there in the hold. Was his body bruised? Could corpses still get bruises? It was odd to think they had travelled over from Rodrigues on the same plane. It was odd to think of him as a corpse.

Of course Paul had not taken out travel insurance and Mam did not have the funds to repatriate the body. Genie had offered to dip into her deposit but Mam had refused.

'You don't want to live with me all your life, do you? Anyway, he's dead now. What difference does it make where he is?'

It was Mam she felt for. Mam who had never planned to return here, and certainly not to bury her son. To leave her son on an island she had long stopped thinking of as home.

As they drove out of the airport, along a road bordered with coconut trees that suddenly looked faded and tired to Genie, she thought how the grief she felt was not so much for Paul's death as his life. This waste was not the waste of the life he had yet to live. She couldn't even think of him as having died young. Something about the way he'd been these last few years suggested he'd hung around long enough waiting for something which wasn't going to happen. And then she thought, *I'm so cruel*.

It was physically that she felt it – that pain in her throat as though she were choking on something, something stuck in her throat like the Jawbreakers he used to give her in secret because Mam had banned her from eating them, terrified she'd choke. She found it hard to breathe or speak.

I'm so cruel, she thought, almost laughing, when she remembered forcing a heavily stoned Paul to watch some footage she'd found on a website: a Chinese cobra had swallowed a calf too large to digest and was now, to its apparent shock, slowly starting to regurgitate it, its jaws unhinged in a terrible grin; the calf, limp, a raw pink, slick with the snake's gastric juices which had dissolved its skin. Paul had remarked, fascinated, that it looked as if the snake were giving birth to the calf.

She'd followed Paul from London to Mauritius, and then on to Rodrigues, where she'd found him. Now, back in Mauritius, driving through narrow roads shuttered by dense walls of cane, she wondered again at her strange familiarity with this landscape. Nothing here seemed foreign to her: not the cane-fields, the red earth, the book-shaped eruptions of rock. This had surprised her when she'd first arrived; Genie's Mauritius had always been so much further away than Paul's. After all, she had not been back since they'd lived there for a time as children. She had only been five then.

She remembered being met at the airport by a man who had picked her up and swung her around. Mam had said, 'This is your dad.' It was clear he was not Paul's papa: he was dark, blue-black dark like a prune, her papa. Genie laughed when she saw his hair because it looked like hers, standing out from his head in wild curls. He was a gravitational force, he made the world spin for her, the way he would pick her up and swing her around, hoist her on to his shoulders or tip her upside down until she was screaming and red-faced, with excitement or fear she didn't know, and he would haul her up again and set her upright on her feet, the world still turning and churning with the pull of water being sucked down a plughole, and she would fall down and Mam would get cross.

And she wondered now where Paul was in this memory: standing apart from them, hanging from the railings which separated new arrivals from the waiting, by just one foot, by the tips of his fingers, swinging wide on one hand, away from them, as though he didn't really care how he fitted into this new family, this new country.

They had a new brother too, Jean-Marie. He was Papa's son. But he was much older than she and Paul. He was a teenager. Jean-Marie let Paul help when he worked on his motorcycle, teaching him the names of all the parts and tools. Paul told her later how he'd loved the way Jean-Marie spoke to him when they were working together, asking him to pass this or that in a business-like manner, speaking to him as though he were an adult, an equal, as though he really were of use, not like Jean-Marie's friend Maja, who called him *caca ti baba*, or *babyshit*. Genie too was wary of Maja: she had never before encountered a grown-up who did not smile back. And not like Papa, who always treated Paul as though he were in the way. But Paul always spoke fondly of the time Genie's papa had taken him to the races, heaving him up on to his shoulders so Paul could see the horses better. He'd screamed and screamed for their horses to win but none of them did, though one had been the subject of a drawn-out steward's enquiry. After the races were over, when everyone drifted away, they had picked through all the thousands of betting slips which littered the floor, looking for winners which might have been dropped by mistake.

The funeral home was in Port Louis, where she had come the week before with Alphonse to distribute her *Missing* posters. They had parked in the new waterfront development and walked across to the old part of the city, to the central bus depot at Immigration. Paul might not be in Port Louis, but if he ever came here, Alphonse had told her, he would most likely come by bus and the bus would bring him here. So she had gone inside shops nearby which were dark inside and full of strange products – tinned long-life cheese from Australia, skin-lightening creams from India – and left leaflets.

The hearse turned down Queen Elizabeth, the central reservation lined with leggy palms, taller than the surrounding buildings, the ridges of their trunks uniform and metallic. Not like the squat palms she knew from their garden, with trunks which looked as though they had been knitted from some thick yarn. She had spent a lot of time in that garden and still remembered the textures of the trees, the citrus colours of the hibiscus flowers, the steaming, early morning grass. There were chickens there, and a cockerel that would wake them with his crowing. He was fiercely territorial. Whenever they had to pass him in his patch of yard, he would run for them, his sharp beak pecking at the air, hoping to strike an ankle. Once he caught Paul, though Papa dismissed the injury saying that Paul should leave the poor bird alone. Paul was very angry then, saying that the cock had attacked him and that night, Paul had a nightmare about Evil Cock. He and Genie slept in a bed together in a curtained-off area of the front room, and as he thrashed and screamed, Mam and Papa came rushing to their bed and shook him out of it. Paul mumbled, turned over, and fell into a deep sleep. The next day when Genie woke up, Mam burst out crying. Genie's face was covered in bruises. Paul looked shocked and impressed that he had caused her so much damage. 'It's all Evil Cock's fault,' he muttered, but Papa did not agree and gave Paul a thrashing.

Jean-Marie did not intervene, but later that day, when they went out into the yard, Evil Cock was gone. For dinner that night they ate *carri poule*. Paul refused to eat it. Papa made him stay at the table until his plate was cleared but Paul ignored him, tears rolling down his face. Mam got angry then and had a row with Papa which only ended when he slapped her. And after that, Paul bent his head to his plate, gagging slightly as he ate, the tears rolling quickly, plopping from his chin into his food.

Jean-Marie had a talent for disappearing at times like these. You only knew he was gone when you heard the sound of his motor-cycle starting up, then it faded away and that always sounded sad to Genie, like someone saying goodbye. Sometimes Paul would run down the road after him.

Mam would not let Genie go out until the bruises had faded. So she played in the garden. There was a hole in the garden wall. She put her eye to it. She saw the street dogs and the street children, she saw goats being herded past. She saw Paul with his new friends. One of them, an older boy, ran towards the wall, poking what she thought was a fat hairy finger through the crack.

'Touch it!' he ordered.

Genie put her finger out and touched him. Then he laughed and they all ran away.

And once she saw a funeral procession, the mourners in black, wailing, eyes rolled into their heads.

The women in the neighbourhood would not talk to Mam but they were very nice to Paul and Genie. The woman next door who made and sold cakes gave Genie a bag of Neapolitans – little jam-sandwiched cakes with pink icing she made for weddings or christenings. When Genie took the bag home and showed Mam,

Mam got angry and took it from her. And then Papa got angry with her and asked why she had done that and in the end he slapped her and left the house, slamming the door in an echo of that slap and leaving Mam to slide down the wall, the way shadows did, weeping bitterly, the cakes rolling about her on the floor.

Papa had not stopped talking on their way to the airport. Jean-Marie drove them there in his friend's car, while Papa sat in the back with them keeping up a constant stream of jokes, tweaking Genie's cheek, hauling her on to his lap and hugging her so tightly it hurt and she struggled to be released. So he loosened his grip and let her climb off.

When they walked through the departures gate, Paul and Genie were almost walking backwards, waving and waving until they turned the corner, out of sight, Mam striding on in front, only turning back to scold them, telling them to hurry up.

'That's London.' Paul had said, leaning across her with all his weight, pointing down at the sticky patches of light below. 'It looks like God's been gobbing.'

Mam would normally have snapped at him for that *malpropté*, but she seemed not to be aware of anything around her. When the plane began to buck and shudder in anticipation of its landing, Mam seemed equally apprehensive, leaning further back into her seat, hands gripping the armrest, as though trying to resist the inevitable descent.

They had flown for hours over an empty grey desert. When Genie had pointed it out to Paul, he grabbed her head – still annoyed that she had been given the window seat, still angry that they were leaving Mauritius – and pushed her face up to the glass.

'You idiot,' he said, 'that's the wing of the plane.'

By the time they left Mauritius, Paul was speaking Creole. But back in London, Mam insisted that he spoke only English. So he wouldn't get confused, Mam said. But he told Genie that he still dreamed in Creole.

Paul had gone to Mauritius for six months as a teenager. When he came back to London he could speak Creole again. But sometimes, Genie felt, it was as though he had never come back at all.

*

As they pulled up outside the funeral home and Genie got out, she found that it was raining, a rain so fine she thought at first it was smoke or mist and then the mist dissolved into individual drops and she realized.

As the director and his assistants opened the back door of the hearse and pulled out Paul's body, Genie felt a rush of relief: this feeling she'd had the last few years of somehow outliving Paul, as though she had overtaken her older brother in age, was suddenly gone.

There was nothing left to do now except wait for the funeral and return home with Mam. There was nothing more she could do for him now except go back home and make another London for herself.

Benjamin Markovits

Setting Forth

from *Imposture*

When Lord Byron (three years, almost a lifetime ago) had first engaged John Polidori as a travelling physician, the poet had palmed his cheek gently and said, 'I like to admire myself . . . in a youthful mirror.' No wonder the poor girl was taken in; and Polidori, after she had gone, repeated the line to himself. It offered him surprising comfort, suggesting as it did larger connotations to a life that had become cramped with insignificance. It was a strange phrase, though, that seemed, like a smoothing hand, to rub away his own features and replace them with a reflective sheen. All that it left of himself was the impressionability of glass, the rosiness of youth.

They met for the first time a few months after Polidori came down to London from Edinburgh, the youngest medical student ever to take his degree there. He was hardly nineteen years old; and, in spite of his conviction of the great, the inevitable good fortune that awaited him, he had been kicking his heels at home, looking for a position. And then he received his summons from Dr Taylor – his friend and mentor, well connected in Norwich's radical societies. Polidori jumped at any excuse for a diversion, and returned from Norwich as late as he could, only a week before Frances's wedding: his favourite sister was leaving home, an event which, as he knew at the time, played its part in persuading him to follow. He was almost bursting with his 'news'; and sweaty with sleeplessness from his coach ride, as he was, he sought out his father, Gaetano, straight away. The house, as Mother put it, 'had been thrown up and down' by the confusion of 'last minutes'; and the old man used to escape by taking a cold bath on waking, before breakfasting *en famille*.

Dr Taylor had passed on to his protégé a remarkable offer. Lord Byron, it seemed, wanted a physician; and a mutual friend had asked Taylor for a recommendation. Polidori, who was not without literary aspirations, had followed the story in the papers; his mentor also indulged his sweet tooth for more private scandal. The poet's wife, in bidding for a separation, had hoped to prove him mad. There was gossip, of course; though so far the name of Byron's sister had escaped the smear of press ink. And stories of his lordship's Harrow and Cambridge days ('when friendships were formed too romantic to last') had been successfully hushed up. Then there were the more distant rumours of what Byron himself reportedly dismissed as his 'genial gift for adaptation' – a necessary facility for any traveller – the spirit to take a place and its people *as they come*, which he had indulged freely, particularly in Turkey. In any case, he was looking to go abroad again and wanted a young man, a doctor, to accompany him.

Some of this Polidori communicated while averting his eyes from his naked father; he was faintly dispirited already by the contrast in their cleanliness. The old man's skin took on a blue shadow under the shock of the cold, and his hair lay in sleek lines down his neck. His temples were fair and bald, and his jowls hung silkily with the smooth additions of age. When he rose out of the water at last, a steady drip depended from his shrunken member; the wet percussion of it was a constant reminder of where not to look. 'I have been blessed by many sisters,' Polidori thought, involuntarily. A habitual complaint, a part of the family idiom: *poor, put-upon, cossetted Polly,* and all his girls.

There was Frances, his nearest companion in age, with a dirty Italian complexion, her brother's cleft chin, a hooked, boyish nose, and tremulous thin lips, the only outward evidence of her soft heart. She was about to marry a man named Rossetti, another émigré; handsome enough and well connected, though somewhat flighty perhaps. Or rather, gifted with a grace that suggested if not inconstancy then the lightness of touch that produces it. He was the wrong husband for her. What she wanted – well, the prospect of her marriage had astonished Polly (as the family called him) into a sense of his own loneliness, which, in spite of his visit to Norwich, he had found impossible to shake off.

But there were others too, three sisters more. The youngest of these, Esmé, with a fat blunt face like the palm of a hand, had followed Polidori into the bathhouse next to the kitchens. Red curls fell to her shoulder; freckles thick as clover surrounded her eyes. She had greeted him clamorously on his return from Norwich, and now trailed him downstairs. She was greedy for him and wanted always to know what he thought, what he carried in his hand, what pleased him, how he planned to fill the time. Her satisfaction, his restlessness – stuck at home, at his age! – played curiously, fitfully off each other. If only he found such comfort in himself as Esmé did. What did he offer the little girl that he denied himself?

She slapped her naked soles on the broad wet stones crying, 'tell me, tell *me*' from time to time, and splashing whenever she could. Polidori felt the burden of his age. As the oldest child, great things were expected of him. But his recent idleness had disappointed his father and consequently perhaps, Polly still trusted too thoroughly in him; he wanted to please.

Gaetano looked squarely at his son. 'I am not sure,' he began, not in the tone of uncertainty but rather with the false hesitation of someone softening bad news. His accent had retained something of the sourness, the refinement of his native Tuscany, the musty thinness of cognac. 'I am not sure . . . his lordship would prove a . . . beneficial example to you. You are' – and here he looked down himself, ashamed either of his doubts or the intensity of the sentiment – 'a wonderful boy, of great natural talents, but easily led astray. Easily seduced . . . by enthusiasm. Lord Byron has not impressed in me' – the arrogance of this plain old man! – 'a confidence in the stability of his character. His influence would be pernicious.'

Somehow Polly had been expecting this; in spite of his father's love, and such indisputable good luck, somehow . . . He began to make his case, but Esmé was tired of being ignored. 'Ding dong bell,' she cried out, 'ding dong bell', touching her father's little piece this way and that with her pink hand. Her laughter was like the sudden stopping of a horse on loose stones. Polly picked his sister up in his arms, where she wriggled abominably; his father gave him a look over her wild head. As if to say, better she were yours, at your age, than mine, at mine. His thin lips flattened to a line. Polly said only, 'But you must see – you must see – the great honour' – and stopped short. The organ of his father's fertility vaguely oppressed him.

The wonder of it was that Gaetano, of all people, *should* have understood the allure of Lord Byron's companionship. He had served, in his own youth, as a secretary to the great Italian dramatist Conte Vittorio Alfieri, whose mistress was the Countess of Albany, herself the widow of Charles Stuart, the Young Pretender. On the strength of these connections, Gaetano had retired to London and set up a profitable business as a translator and Italian instructor. Alfieri's *influence* had been the making of him.

And, in fact, Polly's news did put Gaetano in mind of 'those youthful associations', and he recounted over breakfast 'for its instructional value', the story of his eventual dismissal. Polly had heard it before and Frances shot her brother an amused look, which Gaetano saw and pointedly ignored. He was the kind of father unembarrassed by repetition; repetition, in fact was the gavel of his authority. 'The Count,' he said, filling his mouth with a slippery forkful of fried onions, 'recovering from an illness and consequently low-spirited, begged me to keep them company in the evenings. At one point, the Countess (from what private quarrel who can guess?) asked Alfieri why my youthful thighs were rounded while his own were flat. "Stuff and nonsense," Alfieri replied, wrinkling his nose, resentful of that illness, age, from which none recover. They passed on to some indifferent talk. But from that time I no more had the honour of being one of the exalted party.' Gaetano declared this portentously; with only a trace of self mockery, he persisted through the sombre echoings of his children, who had heard the line before. Though he added more sharply now, to press home his point: 'neither could I complain of this. I myself felt that the question had been unseemly, more in character for a drab than for a discreet and modest lady.'

Gaetano wore his prudishness, in the broadest sense, as a kind of honour: the world was better left untouched, it stained one so, and he had, for the most part, refused to handle it. Apart from his tireless fertility, from the dirty business of making and raising eight children. He hadn't entirely renounced the world, only that part of it lying outside his own powers to chastise and create. Nor could he suppress the pleasure he took in this little triumph over the great man: though it was only the inevitable, and ordinary triumph of youth over age; of plump legs over bony. Lord Byron's offer to his oldest boy had reminded the father of the company he had forfeited in his own youth; and Polly, in fact, read in Gaetano's disapproval only the ordinary, and inevitable envy of a father for his son.

After all, his father had always *wanted* him to write, to preserve the name of Polidori in the aspic of literature; to go, as he said, one better than himself, an honourable translator. In fact, Gaetano had pushed him to take up medicine precisely because it was a useful career for a man of letters, on several counts. And Polidori had consented. Yet here was a chance to further both ambitions: the greatest poet of his age wanted a physician. But Gaetano still urged him to decline the offer.

In the weeks to come, their argument persisted; a quiet war, consisting of isolated shots, occasional skirmishes. And Polly, for once, stood up to his father. He accepted the poet's invitation to tea and arrived at Piccadilly Terrace as nervous as a schoolgirl. It was Lord Byron's sister, Augusta (familiarly known as Goose), who greeted him first; a plump, lively woman. Her mobility of expression largely concealed the dullness of her sleeping face. There was something about her nose, flattened at the tip, that suggested the bullying hand of stupidity pressed against her. She immediately remarked on the resemblance between the young men. Stroking the hair off Polidori's forehead, she examined them, side by side – teasing both her brother and his 'friend' with the sisterly, sensual touch of her warm palms. They smelled of cloves. Byron's stomach had been upset by nerves, and Goose had been brewing a concoction to quiet them. His apartments at Piccadilly Terrace were cluttered already with the imminence of departure. Polly, in fact, sat down on a box of animal feed, as he guessed by the stable odours rising from it. The couches were covered suggestively in his lordship's clothes. Byron said, 'What do you think of him, Goose?' lying back amidst his own tangled accoutrements. And she looked at Polidori with a look not so much cunning as having the joy of cunning in it. 'I think he'll do, at a pinch.' She seemed happier, easier, than either of the men. The duns like crows clamouring at dusk. His lordship's manner, as always in the shadow of farewells, almost painfully sweet. This was when he said, 'I like to admire myself . . . in a youthful mirror,' taking Polly's cheek in his hand, as the young man stooped to kiss his fingers. It was a kind of parting gift, an act of persuasion. Who could resist him?

Polidori turned home that night in high spirits. He left the brother and sister entwined upon a low couch. The image of them, of their quiet freedoms, stuck in his thoughts and acquired over time the slow, bright heat of contained fire. His father was waiting for him in the study. He attempted, in the strongest terms, to dissuade his son from going. The tenderness of his paternal concern had soured into anger, almost into indifference. 'Lord Byron will be the end of you,' he predicted coldly. 'A fresh pot fired too quickly cracks at once. You will not survive the heat of his *amour propre*.'

Polidori, still standing, refused to be abashed. 'His lordship has treated me,' he said to Gaetano, 'more than generously, as his equal, his friend.' He mentioned Augusta's flattering remark, not without qualification, hoping to appeal to his father's family pride. 'Of course,' Polidori added, 'my youth lends more colour to my countenance. To my hair, curls and lustre. And besides all that, I am perhaps as much as a tiptoe taller.' He blushed as he spoke but managed to keep back the tears; it cost him a great deal to defy his father. Rebellion made him childish again.

And then, on the eve of Frances's wedding, Polly almost relented. (Afterwards, he never forgot this chance, not taken, to yield to an ordinary life.) Father and son decided to leave the house to the women. They sauntered arm in arm through the streets of Piccadilly, both somewhat chastened by the thought of losing Frances to that smooth-skinned man. Polly recounted one of the games the two of them played as children. He would offer Frances his hand, and she would pretend to bite it: just closing her lips and teeth across his knuckles, until he abruptly withdrew, his fingers wet from the touch of her mouth. Then they repeated the act. And each time, looking up at him black-eyed, she bit down harder and harder on his flesh, until her teeth reached bone and he cried out and spent on her the fruits of his bad temper. 'This, too,' he said, 'was a part of the game: my anger afterwards.'

Gaetano, as they made the rounds of St James's Square, elaborated on the true reason for his reluctance, which he had been partly keeping back. He said that he understood something of the burden great men thrust upon their companions; something of the patience, the simplicity of character, the easy confidence necessary to carry the weight of another man's arrogance. That he himself had suffered, terribly, in his youth at Alfieri's hands, at the unanswerable claims of the poet's self love. Those evenings he spent with the Count and Contessa offered, of course, wonderful compensations, but he felt, in their presence, the blood drain from him, his life blood thinning away. 'Fui terzo tra cotanto senno,' he declared, quoting Dante. 'I was third, amid such company.'

And he feared his son possessed something of his own sensitivities; indeed, to a still more painful degree. That he might not survive the contact of so fiery a comet as Lord Byron. That just those qualities for which a proud father entertained such hopes – Polly's honour, his fine feeling, his appetite for life – would expose him to the full force of impossible comparisons. This was his phrase: 'impossible comparisons'. 'Fui terzo tra cotanto senno,' he repeated; even at his most vulnerable, a pompous bully.

Polly promised him, as they crossed the traffic of Piccadilly on a mild night just muffled in the light cotton of a spring haze, that he would write to Lord Byron at once and decline the offer. His father embraced him quaintly. His full-sailed belly pressed against his son, as he held one hand against his own heart, while the other reached to touch the young man's shoulder. But by the next evening, Polly had changed his mind. He had watched Rossetti stretch his pale hand towards his sister for a ring; and had wondered, addressing Frances in his thoughts, and smiling a little, 'Why do you not bite him? Why do you not bite him?' – rather unhappily, too.

On Monday morning he set off for Lord Byron's apartment, hoping to intercept the post. He found his lordship at home, writing letters. 'You've changed your mind again, I suppose?' the poet said looking up, not unkindly. Polly rather enjoyed the feeling that his lordship had taken the measure of him, already. He nodded, smiling too, to save his voice.

Within a week, he had made his preparations. Byron was leaving in the morning for Dover. They were taking two carriages: a rather grand contrivance, fashioned after Napoleon's model, for Byron and his friend Scrope Davies, a small, thin-faced man, dressed in unhappy perfection. Polidori and Hobhouse – another friend, fatter and more serious and sillier at once – would set off first, in Scrope's calèche, to fool the bailiffs. His lordship asked the young doctor to appear at dawn; he wanted to make a good start.

It was a fine thin April morning. Polly arrived while the poet was in bed. His sister answered the door in her negligée. She said that Byron complained of a headache, he had only just come in from dancing. There were biscuits and soda water in the drawing room, in case Mr Polidori had not yet breakfasted. Goose returned to Byron's room. He heard his laughter, a low, sweet sound; a melancholic's kindness, in feigning good spirits. Somewhere Frances lay in that young man's arms.

Polly broke a biscuit and tried to eat it. It was too dry, it would not go down. He was all dust and nerves. The room lay in the disrepair of departure. A Harrison clock ticked audibly, like a throat that will not swallow. There were several cases, of clothes, of books. A broken vase lay shivered on the marble hearthstone, yellow tulips scattered confusedly, rumpled here and there by the weight of the shards. The slick of wet had spread already to the floor and stained it. French doors gave on to a balcony and he stepped out; the watery blue of sky was just deepening with day. A fine sheet of sunshine, like cotton drying on a line, lay fluttering on the paving stones. The world was all before him. He turned to look up the street, but took little in. Only a girl, her back to a wall, shivering in the young dawn. Her cheeks hollowed by shadows; her aspect pinched. The greed or hunger in her glance made him turn away. His prospects seemed too wide for the view at hand: the narrow corridor of buildings, the growing rumours of traffic from Piccadilly. The wind blew unevenly, of sweet and sour mixed, the stench of sewage just rising from the gutter, and the fresher tonic of the spring. He held his hair out of his eyes then turned inside again, to contemplate his new life on a grander, imagined scale.

Ogaga Ifowodo

Word Games in Prison

The Monday of our promised liberty having come and gone, we commenced to reconcile ourselves to our new lodgings. We knew we had to take our minds off any thoughts of getting out soon. When Yellow brought our dinner later in the evening, we worked our way, as tactfully as we could, to the point of asking him to take a message outside for us. To our surprise, he readily agreed to do so. He advised that we wait till everybody had gone home and he was left alone with us. We couldn't object to that and the hope of finally making contact with the outside was already too good to be true. Not wishing to let the moment go without making the most of it, I asked him for pen and paper.

'What for,' he asked.

'To write the message we want to send.'

And fearing that he might then bring just one sheet of paper, I added, 'Also, I need to write a poem.'

'So you are a writer too? Another writer who works for the CLO. Do you know Nnimmo Bassey?'

'Of course, I do.'

'When he was here, I did my best to look after him. In fact, he was here the night you were brought in, on a post-release visit. I told him that a member of the CLO was here and I'm sure that by now they know you are with us. So don't worry too much. As for paper, we don't have any but I'll look. If I find any, then you're lucky.'

As he left the room, he said, 'Later in the night, I'll tell you something.'

He wasn't as furtive as he had always been each time he stayed a while to talk to us. Maybe none of his bosses were around. Summoned, perhaps, to Abuja to explain why so and so were still walking free. True or not, his readiness to be our courier, not to mention his confidence today, was unusual.

At his appointed time 'later in the night', he came into the room. He brought in two sheets of paper that were once white but now ochre. There were grey and brown spots on them, blotches left by roach and lizard droppings which he had brushed off. One of the sheets had two rough edges and three small holes where termites, perhaps, had nibbled at it. He also brought in a transparent Bic ballpoint, a full inch of it from the tip blackened from an overflow of ink that had dried inside. I tried the pen; there was still some ink in the tube and it wrote well. And – oh bless you Yellow! – two rolls of toilet paper. I took them into the pantry, taking care to place them where they could not be seen from our room. Yellow cautioned me not to attempt writing in the daytime.

Then he picked up the dinner plates and standing with them in his hands, said, 'I am an Ijaw man. Working for the SSS since the execution of Ken Saro-Wiwa and the Ogoni 8 has been torture for me. You will say, "Why don't you resign?" Unfortunately, you cannot simply resign from this job. And even when you do, you remain under watch. I can't say much, and it won't make sense to you anyway. But I want you to know that I sympathize with you. By the grace of God, nothing will happen to you. Don't worry.'

What could we say to him? He was breaching strict orders to establish human contact with us; he had poured his heart out to us and allowed his emotions to interfere with the performance of his duties. He was human after all; as one of our guards, the fellow was probably as vulnerable as any of the victims over whom he kept watch. Our duty was to act in a way that did not betray his confidence, even if that did not change the fact that he worked for his and our oppressors. Our eyes followed him out of the room. Then we looked at each other.

'Do you think he is really Ijaw? This could be a tale he tells every captive here,' Akin said.

'Maybe so. But if he delivers our message, then I'll be prepared to grant him the benefit of the doubt,' I said. And added, 'In any case, being Ijaw is not in itself enough to make him the silent sufferer or undercover agent of the Niger Delta cause that he would have us believe he is.'

We were prisoners, political or not, and so a social species condemned to be acted upon. What could we do with this sort of information that we were not in any position to verify? What use could we make of it anyway except to hope that whatever moved him to bare his heart would also move him to help us in some way? The rest would have to lie in the womb of time, to be unveiled at its own choosing, when, perhaps, it would be irrelevant to us. What we could not, under any circumstance, do was to lower our guard for even a moment. If we never forgot that he worked for the SSS, and so was one of our jailers, we would steer clear of any booby-trap.

Akin turned to his book. And still not ready for the effort of tackling mine, I began rewriting 'The Shorter Road to Lagos' in my head. But Akin would not allow me a moment of quiet. Every now and then, he would crack the silence of the room with laughter. He was having such an awesomely good time with *Angela's Ashes* it seemed he couldn't have restrained his mirth for a second even if he tried. I had first seen the paperback copy of the book on top of Harry Garuba's desk during his brief spell as a member of the editorial board of *The Post Express*, the same newspaper Akin worked for. I still hadn't read a page of the novel and the best I could do to understand Akin's ungovernable mirth was to recall Harry enthusing over the book in that wonted way of his: jerky expressions held together by a lingering smile, saying this time, 'You know, it's a really funny book . . . and I love the way it ends . . . you know, nobody's done it like that before . . . the entire chapter ending the book . . . just one word. It has to take an Irish man to do that kind of book . . . they are mad enough,' the gaps getting so much longer by the end that the smile needed the help of distracted page turns and a drag on the ever present cigarette to clinch his point.

None of us in his office that day had read the book, so we had only Harry's enthusiasm to recommend it. Which was more than enough, for it was a given among us up-and-coming Nigerian writers all born in the sixties – especially the poets, most of whom knew him closely – that you could tell a book you had to read by the way Harry held and smiled at it. His office in the English department of the University of Ibadan as well as his campus flat were the younger writers' Café and Road House in

Ibadan the same way Odia Ofeimun's in Lagos were for both the younger and the older. The duo, though older than the oldest of the 'weeping willow poets', as one uncharitable Ibadan scholar ill-humouredly called them, had been informally inducted into our generation.

And here in prison, Akin was breaking every one of his ribs reading this 'really funny book'. When he had been rendered completely helpless with laughter, Akin would apologize for disturbing me, but after a minute or two of muffled quakes he would bellow ever louder than before, unable to contain the pleasure sure to kill him otherwise. At a point, I stopped my mental rewriting of the poem to watch him and share as vicariously as possible in his merriment. Inevitably, I asked him to let me in on this rib-cracking tale that threatened to undo him with laughter. He tried his best to give the funniest snippets, the ones that had rendered him powerless on the floor. And as poorly ejaculated as they were due to his inability to stop laughing as soon as he got started, I found myself wanting to snatch the book from him. There was no chance of that happening anyway, unless of course I could and was ready to break off his arm. So Akin read with jolly cheer while I continued to write silently in my head.

In degrees, he calmed down and was able somehow to discipline his laughing glands. It was all in consideration for me, but guffaws still escaped every so often. Without any writing aid of any kind, I was stumped in the middle of my effort to sustain the rhyme scheme with which I had begun the poem. I had had to break it just to forge ahead for the time being and was now having even more trouble returning to it. I decided to take a break. I pulled out my *Criticism and Ideology* and could only envy Akin as he gaily turned the pages while I braced up to the serious intellectual task ahead of me.

Towards evening, Akin declared he would clinically die of laughter if he did not take a break. By then I needed jollier diversion almost as much as air itself. Ever since our first night in the room, the big roster board had not ceased to draw my attention. And often, I would stare at it, as if assured that some secret lay in its scanty entries that would bare itself if I gazed hard and long enough. I returned to it now. Then I saw not the secret unveiled, but a game – making as many words as possible out of those on the board. I had started with the word 'state' from the State Security Service header. And had made the following anagrams – *at, ate, eat, east, tea, sat, sate, seat, set, test, teat, taste.* And that was just one word. The possibilities seemed endless with the names of all the states still to go, not to mention the longest word on offer, *headquarters.* In a moment, it became a game of coming up with an anagram within one minute from any word we chose. We timed by counting sixty heartbeats. But there was no prize, and the fun soon overtook any need for competition and timing. Whoever found a word-within-the-word announced it.

Without discussing it, we found we had been playing with every word except *headquarters.* It offered the greatest thrill and challenge. With its many vowels and consonants, just how many anagrams could we make out of it? *State* alone had produced twelve words, no thirteen; Akin had added *tat,* evidently the fruit of scrabble games. So absorbed were we playing with words that we had forgotten to eat our dinner. We had been startled when we heard the barricades as Yellow came for the plates, and to take the message we wished to send. We asked him to come back for it; he would be taking it with him in the morning when he was relieved by the day guard.

We quickly wrote a one-page note explaining briefly how we had been arrested, what had happened to us since then and, most important, our current location. About one hour after, Yellow returned for it. We had folded the note in four and now with a bit of amusement watched him further fold it until it looked like a candy cube. Then he tucked it in his underpants over which he wore green khaki shorts and the outer trousers of what, but for its informality, would qualify as his regulation green-yellow *adire* attire. (Just how many copies of the same outfit, made to exact specifications, did he have?) It was to be delivered at the CLO, or if Yellow thought that too risky – he didn't think so – to Toyin Akinohso in Festac Town. I feared that with the note now so tiny, he might lose it. He assured us that it would be delivered, bade us goodnight, and left.

Although it was now very late, about midnight, we returned to our game. Only *Sokoto, FCT, Abuja,* and *headquarters* now remained. We couldn't coin more than *to, too, took, so, soot* out of *Sokoto*. FCT being mere initials without a single vowel promised very little. *Abuja* yielded only, *baa* and *jab*. Finally, *headquarters*! We began. And it seemed there was an infinite mine of anagrams there. At first, we were finding new words almost every second and could hardly wait for each other to finish announcing his find. Then, naturally, the pace slowed as we exhausted the more obvious ones. But with a little thinking and careful searching, we would hit another. And another. And still another. Until we swore there could not possibly be any other word to be extracted. But no, there was! In anticipation of the fun ahead, I had decided to sacrifice half of the remaining sheet of paper. It was dead in the night now, so we could write. We listed the number of words we had milked out of *headquarters*. Two hundred and twenty-three! Here they are, but not necessarily in the order that we called them that night:

Head, heads, header, headers, hear, hears, hearer, hearers, heard, herd, herds, ha, had, has, hare, hares, hat, hats, hate, hates, hater, haters, hatred, haste, hard, he, heed, heeds, here, heat, heats, heater, heaters, hearse, heart, hearts, hearted, her, hers, hue, hues, hued, hut, huts, ear, ears, earth, eat, eats, eater, eaters, ease, eased, east, equate, equates, equated, era, ere, err, eras, erase, erased, eraser, adequate, ah, ahs, ahead, at, as, ash, ashes, arse, ass, asset, are, area, areas, art, arts, dare, dares, dart, darts, dash, dasher, date, dates, dear, dearer, deer, deers, death, deaths, dearth, deter, deters, due, dues, duel, duet, duets, dust, duster, quart, quarts, quarter, quarters, quad, quash, quashed, queer, queers, quest, quests, us, use, used, user, usher, rat, rats, rate, rates, rated, rash, rather, red, reds, reed, reeds, read, reads, reader, readers, rest, rear, rears, reared, rude, ruder, rudest, rue, rues, rued, rust, rusts, rusted, rut, ruts, tar, tars, tea, teas, tease, teased, teaser, tee, tees, tree, trees, tear, tears, tread, treads, the, there, these, thread, threads, tare, tares, terse, terser, trade, trades, trader, traders, trash, true, truer, sad, sat, sate, sated, sea, see, seer, seed, sera, set, seat, seated, sear, seared, sere, shade, she, shea, shed, shear, sheer, sheet, share, shared, shat, shred, stud, squad, squat, square, squared, star, starred, stare, stared, stead, steed, steer, sue, sued, sure, surer.

The barricades startled us. It was dawn! We looked out the window. Although it wasn't daylight yet, it was already light enough to see. Smiley had come to take a head count and be sure we were still there. Satisfied that we hadn't escaped, he shut and locked the door.

Two hundred and twenty-three words! Even when we had left out doubtful ones, denied the help of a dictionary as we were. We had, for instance, left out such obvious words as *Easter*, *sutra* and *tsar*, being proper nouns and/or foreign words. And such old forms as *hast*, *hadst*, *thee*. I realized much later, after my release, when I checked in the dictionary that *tsar* and *sutra*, not to mention the old forms of verbs, could have passed. After my release, our word game was one of the first anecdotes of prison I recounted to the friends who came to welcome me back home at my apartment in Surulere. An Oxford dictionary, sporting the dust of six months of neglect, lay within reach (as if waiting for this moment!). Dying to see how well Akin and I had done without its help, I had grabbed it with no particular goal in mind. But my friends had doubted that so many words could be coined from one word, however rich in vowels and consonants it may be. They had insisted we play the game anew, four of us at first, until E.C. Osondu (EeCee for short) who had recently declared short fiction his preferred genre after confessing – wrongly in my view – that he was no poet, joined us. Of course, I had an advantage, and I regret that I did not insist that we play for stakes! It was during this replay by five of us that the words *ether*, *etude*, *rasher*, *suede* (how did I forget that word after all the trouble Raibean gave me at Sèmè over my suede shoes and Samsonite suitcase!), *suet*, *urea* and *ureter* came out of *headquarters'* protean womb. The play – or replay, as I suppose we must call it – had also produced such words hitherto unfamiliar to me as *aster*, *darter*, *shad* and *quasar*. Even now, I have no doubt that over a dozen more words might still be milked from that one word.

We had spent almost the entire night minting words out of a word, but far from feeling worn out, were only disappointed that we seemed finally to have exhausted the seam. If any of us had announced another word, the other would have immediately felt obliged to find just one more. Towards the end, we had spent upwards of ten minutes working the by now weak veins of *headquarters*, yet each time the sense of competition we had begun with and abandoned at the peak of our fun had returned. But if not physically, we were, at least mentally fatigued. We took to our beds, now so familiar that the atrocious dirt and smell no longer bothered us. Yet, we felt there had to be some words we didn't know, or which, if we knew, had so carefully concealed themselves in the detritus of our rigorous mining that we could not retrieve them. Maybe tomorrow. Or any of the days ahead. As it happened, however, we seemed really to have surpassed ourselves that night. Try as we may as the days went by, we could not find another word. I had fallen asleep still looking for just one more word. And promptly fell into a dream in which I made calls of words that Akin kept pointing out could only be from my native Isoko language and definitely not from *headquarters*!

Hermione Lee

Manhattan Days

1 September 2004–27 June 2005

I am here for ten months, away from home, family and academic job, on a fellowship at the Cullman Center for Scholars and Writers at the New York Public Library. I am on unpaid leave from Oxford University, here to work on a biography of Edith Wharton, whose city this was for many years. I have sublet (with much protocol involved) a small apartment from a Columbia academic, on West 94th Street, between Broadway and West End. My ''hood' is in an ordinary unfashionable part of town, where Duane Reade pharmacies, Radio Shacks, Payless Shoe-shops, Starbucks and McDonalds, small friendly diners and little Thai, Peruvian, Italian and French restaurants all rub shoulders. There isn't a tourist or a postcard in sight. Within two minutes from the door, on Broadway, there's the Gotham Wine Mart, a local theatre that shows old films, a 'Europan [sic] café' with every type of cake, pizza and coffee, open till very late, opticians, a bookstore that buys second-hand copies, newspaper kiosks, men selling fruit on the streets, a visiting knife grinder's van, 24-hour corner groceries doubling as flower shops, the Gourmet Garage for all possible food needs, a health store turning out lethal-looking organic drinks from gigantic vegetables, a gym, a church, a bus stop and the 96th Street subway. Five minutes down the road is Riverside Park, and the river.

The bright, light apartment is on the fourteenth floor. Up two flights of stairs there is an enchanting roof garden, landscaped with trees and shrubs in big tubs and groups of wooden chairs and herbs for everyone's use, where I will spend a great deal of time, reading and drinking wine late into the evening, watching the sun set over the Hudson river and the coloured lights flashing on the

Empire State Building, the air traffic and the birds and the 'rear window' views of other people's lives in the apartments all around. I am very glad that I didn't accept the offer of a much larger apartment on Roosevelt Island, in the middle of the East River. ('How do you *get* there? By cable car?' one of my most New Yorkerish New York friends asked, aghast.)

I arrive on 1 September 2004, while the Republican conference is going on far downtown. I switch on and watch at once – Reagan's funeral rites being replayed (the great American hero), attacks on Kerry's 'flip flops', protestors outside (who, it transpires, get carted off and kept without amenities or contacts for many hours) – and then go out across the road in what seems like another country, in the warm September heat, to have a meal at Alouette's, where the manageress is French, the waitress is half-Italian and half-Finnish, and the couple next to me are Spanish.

Bush's speech to the convention plays on 9/11 throughout, unquestioningly links Osama Bin Laden and Saddam Hussein (a 'madman'), keeps referring to the Second World War (the Normandy beaches, Churchill), idealizes Reagan, quotes Ecclesiastes ('a time for hope') and yokes the concept of 'freedom' and the justification of war in phrases which I hear now for the first time, like 'Freedom is on the march' and 'A calling from beyond the stars to stand for freedom'. His jokes go down extremely well: 'I have a certain swagger – what in Texas is called walking.' (Much waving of Texan hats.) 'I knew I was in trouble [with my English] when Arnold Schwarzenegger corrected me.' (Schwarzenegger's phrase for Bush's opponents as 'girlie men' is one of the main conference headlines.) Governor Pataki of New York – I thought he was supposed to be a moderate – describes Saddam Hussein as 'a walking, talking weapon of mass destruction'.

The gap between the Republicans at the convention and most New Yorkers seems gigantic. This is the first thing that strikes me and will do over and over again; the sense of two nations, utterly split. Someone says to me, 'When you leave New York, you go to America, and that's scary.' The people I meet first, friends of Jean [Strouse, the biographer who directs the Cullman Center], say that they can't bring themselves even to watch the convention. (As soon as I hear this at dinner, I read a piece in the *New York Times* about 'media-avoidance' during the convention. Everyone is recycling the same newspapers and radio programmes.) The New Yorkers I talk to say that Bush makes them physically sick. Or they make fun of him, his pronunciation, his stupidities. I remember the physical distaste which so many people like me had in England during the Thatcher years, for the sound of her voice, her physical mannerisms, quite apart from her policies. It's like that here: people who hate him, hate him personally, viscerally.

After my first evening out, in a beautiful nineteenth-century brownstone house in the Village, where we sit in the back garden by candlelight talking about politics to the sound of crickets, I share a taxi uptown. Everyone is dropped off except me, and I have my New York taxi-driver baptism, which goes like this:

He (white, middle-aged, spectacles done up with Sellotape, irritable manner, fast driver): Where are you from? What do you do?

I tell him I am a British academic, here to work on a book.

He: Well, there's an important literary event coming up this year, the publication of the third volume of Norman Sherry's life of Graham Greene.

Me (amazed): So there is!

He: I have a question for you. When Norman Sherry quotes Graham Greene saying, about Arthur Hugh Clough, he's the only grown-up poet of the nineteenth century, what does he mean?

I try to make a comparative analysis of Clough, Tennyson, Arnold, citing 'Amours de Voyage' and 'Dipsychus', as we tear up the West Side.

His parting shot, as I pay him: Also, doesn't Sherry use 'Amours de Voyage' as a quotation in one volume of the biography?

This is a very different kind of taxi encounter from the one I have some months later, on my way to the ballet at the Lincoln Center, in the rain. (I never really 'get' the ballet, but this is the place to learn about it: I am beginning to understand what a powerful hold Balanchine had on the cultural life of this city.) The driver asks me what I am going to see. A little bit later he asks me hesitantly: 'At the ballet – what language do they speak?'

*

The first day of the fellowship is like being back at school. We are on our best behaviour and eye each other warily for signs of potential neurosis and aggression. The most nerve-racking moment is when we are allocated our office space by picking a number out of a hard hat, since only five out of the fifteen offices have windows. I take a deep breath and draw my lucky number, 13, a room with a view on to the lions standing guard outside the library, the trees on the library terrace, and Fifth Avenue. This, for ten months, will be the place where I read and think, collect an unmatchable archive of research books, write a large chunk of Edith's life, send long emails home, and look out of the window at the changing New York seasons. In this paradise for writers, the fellows (an interesting mixture of historians, biographers and novelists, academics and journalists) are allowed in before and after public opening hours. It's a strange feeling to walk down the marble halls and the back staircase of the library late on a Sunday evening, to the all-night exit on 40th Street, knowing that no one but you is in this vast and wonderful building.

And to be at the heart of Edith Wharton's city is a moving experience for me. At the Metropolitan Museum of Art, on a Friday evening in April, I tear myself away from my usual haunts – the Rembrandts and Vermeers, the Sargents, the eighteenth-century Indian miniatures, the tiny, breathtaking Duccio (recently acquired for a rumoured $45 million), the post-Impressionists – and go looking for the Cesnola Collection, the lonely rooms where Ellen Olenska and Newland Archer had their farewell scene in *The Age of Innocence*. This was a fictional licence on Wharton's part, since the novel is set in the early 1870s, and the thwarted lovers meet at the 'new' Met, which didn't move to the Park until 1880, when the Cesnola rooms – in what is now the Medieval sculpture hall – were, in fact, a great draw. But Wharton wanted to invoke a sense of sadness and of a long-past time: Ellen looks at the little objects, labelled 'Use Unknown', and thinks that once they mattered to people; and in a future still distant to him, Newland will poignantly remember this scene. No one at the information desk has heard of Cesnola (the Museum's first director) but a request for 'antiquities from Cyprus' gets me there. Though it's in a different room now, some of the tiny artefacts from the waves of overlapping civilizations do still have baffled, hopeful labels like 'small boxes, may have been used for holding needles'. Like Ellen Olenska and Newland Archer, I am alone in the rooms; in the distance, I can hear the Friday evening string quartet playing in the gallery above the main entrance hall. I am so Whartonized that I feel a peculiar, imaginary sense of contact with the characters of her great novel. When I go to the old-fashioned splendours of the Century Club and see the regulars sitting under the eloquent portrait of the young Henry James by LaFarge, I feel as if I'm witnessing the very last traces of Wharton's 'old New York'. (Indeed some of the members look as if they might have grown up with her.) On a grand first night at the Met, when the donors are dressed to the nines and having their dinner in public state on the Dress Circle landing, gawped at by the rest of us, I hear two society journalists, scribbling furiously in their programmes, commenting on the outfits: 'Look, that's the *second* time Mrs V has worn that black Chanel suit this season!' It could be a scene out of *The House of Mirth* or *The Custom of the Country.*

Outside, in the real world, I learn what it feels like to be a New Yorker. I start trying to preserve a little zone of space around me, to see if I can make a whole journey without being pushed or shoved. I learn to ask for what I want fast, loud and firmly, with no English diffidence. I know exactly how fast to swipe my Metrocard so as not to have to swipe it again with people swearing at my back. I know the eyes-lowered routine everyone adopts when they hear the door clang in between the carriages and a homeless person comes through with yet another heartbreaking pitch to make. I start to recognize them: the big woman with no shoes who spends warm days in Bryant Park and cold days in Grand Central Station, the man who holds the door open at the McDonald's with a little bow, the man who sleeps standing up against a smart Italian clothes shop window, a one-man image of the city's bizarre contrasts between excess and deprivation, the youngish woman who lies on the ground outside the Gap and howls with sorrow. I get over my shock at being talked to everywhere by strangers, like the old lady turning round on to a conversation on the bus about eating out, and saying, 'What restaurant are you talking about? I have to know!' or the one who watched me run up just in time to catch a 104, and blessed me: 'May the rest of your day be so lucky.'

Like everyone who spends any time here, I come to think of Manhattan as a public theatre. Spaces on the subway and in the newspapers are regularly given up to 'only in New York' anecdotes, and there's one to be had on every corner: the down-at-heel guy I pass on Fifth Avenue with a plastic cup and a cardboard sign reading 'Bad Advice: $2'; the convention of seven hundred Santas running to have their photograph taken on the library steps outside my window; the man yelling into his phone, 'So now I've got to support *two* women?'; the lady with a little dog I see in Riverside Park, both wearing sunglasses; the angry woman I half fall on to, jolted by a sudden stop on the subway, who glares at me and moves to another seat, snarling, 'You know what!' (the first time I've heard this ubiquitous phrase used as a curse); the little boy saying joyfully on 96th Street, 'Look, look, Daddy, there's a whole moon!' Out at dinner with Jean in our favourite restaurant in the whole of the city, the Café Luxembourg, our gossip is broken into by the woman at the next table trying to persuade her elderly companion to marry her. Loudly she warns him: 'You're like that poem by Emily Dickinson! Because I had no time for Love, Love had no time for me!' I think she was thinking of 'Because I could not stop for Death' – but I didn't like to say so.

There seems to be less division between indoor and outdoor life here, and no embarrassment about bellowing out personal griefs, secrets and joys in the street. You hear children being educated, lovers quarrelling, evenings being planned ('Yes, I think I'll have a tuna sandwich tonight') and, above all, deals being made. There are days when everyone you pass seems to be shouting about money, while the trucks and cabs and helicopters and sirens and roadworks and building sites and the subterranean roar of trains and revving up of gigantic SUVs just keep on and on going. Julian [Barnes], in New York for a week in the spring, says that when he goes out he wants to say: 'Shut up, City.'

I come to relish the quiet corners: the secret circle up a flight of steps at the west end of 93rd Street, where Anna Huntington's eloquent statue of St Joan overlooks Riverside Park; the little flower garden further down the park, tended by serious, devoted volunteers; the Josephine fountain in Bryant Park, which on a sunny day glints in front of a view of the trees and the library and the very top of the Chrysler Building; the triangle of Verdi Square, with Verdi and his characters on the stone plinth, outside the entrance to the cottage-like 72nd Street subway entrance; the dear little London-ish park round the Natural History Museum on 79th Street, with the names of all the American Nobel Prize winners to date carved on a bronze shaft (plenty of space for future names) and a time capsule containing artefacts 'intended to offer insight into daily life today', with a notice which politely 'asks that it remains sealed' until 1 January 3000.

The city shows off extravagantly wherever you look; it can be marvellous and it can be foul. I walk towards it across Brooklyn Bridge on a hot blue sunny Sunday with about a thousand other people, and tears jump to my eyes with the sensational beauty of it, the construction and romance of the bridge, the traffic of the waters, the south end of the city with its tragic gaps. Then I make the mistake of going to Ground Zero, now such a poisoned battleground of vested commercial interests, and it's a horrible tourist attraction, with people taking pictures of – nothing. On the third anniversary of 9/11, I walk, by chance, past the 6th Avenue Fire Station in the Village, a shrine to the dead: photographs, wreaths, the flag at half-mast, an old man bringing flowers, a 'Support Our Troops' sign, and on the wall a line from Whitman: 'They have cleared the beams away/They tenderly lift him forth.'

New Yorkers love spectacle; they get so much of it that sometimes they don't even notice it. Four acrobats are abseiling one evening in red jumpsuits up and down the front of a building on 6th Avenue, for no apparent reason, and everybody walks on by with hardly a glance. One morning a gigantic yellow chicken, about eight foot high, skipping from foot to foot, is handing out flyers for a restaurant chain on the corner of Broadway, and the rush hour just ignores him. But the evening before the New York Marathon (which, to my great and patriotic excitement, I see Paula Radcliffe go right past me on her way to winning), there is a big firework display which does get an audience. I am going to the opera, as I do compulsively and expensively throughout my stay, and everyone is standing on the Lincoln Center piazza, around the fountain, watching the sky. Just before the operas are due to start in both houses, the Met and the New York City Opera, the fireworks stop, everyone claps, and we all go in, well pleased, to see another big show. At the opera I hear some magnificent things, including Handel's *Orlando* with the divine counter-tenor Bejun Mehta, Elizabeth Futral in Strauss's *Daphne*, Ben Heppner and Barbara Fritolli in *Otello*, a beautiful *Rodelinda* with the mighty Stephanie Blythe – for which the set is a slowly revolving eighteenth-century Italian villa – the effectively stomach-tucked Deborah Voigt in *Un Ballo*, a moving *Rosenkavalier* with Susan Graham and Angela Denoke, and the great José Van Dam in *Pelleas et Melisande*. And I see some ludicrous, gargantuan spectacles. There is more cherry blossom on the Met's stage for *Butterfly* than I've seen since I went to Washington in springtime. At *Valkyrie,* the Wagner-lover next to me said, gazing at the gigantic horns Wotan was sporting on his helmet: 'After three *hours* you do *ask* yourself, what *is* he wearing on his *head?*' At *Aida*, not satisfied by the horses, the temples, the dancing girls, and the huge armies of priests, the woman behind me says to her friend, 'I thought there would be elephants.' Many performances are half empty (one caustic non-opera-loving friend tells me, 'Everyone who goes to the opera is *dead.*') But everything I see is wildly applauded.

There's always a lot of noise at concerts and the theatre. People keep coughing and dropping things and repeating the lines of plays to each other and making loud comments, like the lady behind me at a concert at Carnegie Hall, who says to her husband, looking at the programme: 'He used to have such a big nose, Pollini, he must have had it fixed. He looks a lot better now.' I go to the Takacz Quartet's memorable Beethoven cycle at the Alice Tully Hall (which for once is attended to in absolute silence); for one of these I am sitting with Philip [Roth] and his friends. During the first movement of the first Razumovsky quartet, some very loud bells go off, clearly a malfunction in the hall's alarm system. The musicians play on heroically. After the second movement, Philip says sadly: 'I miss the bells.'

An altogether different kind of musical evening is the Bob Dylan concert at the Beacon Theater. There's an amazing array of old hippies and young rockers, the nostalgic smell of marijuana comes drifting up from the musty seats, and (after an endearingly easygoing set by the old trooper Merle Haggard, who says, 'We don't have roadies, we have nurses'), the performance is so shatteringly loud and aggressive that 60s-era fans like me, still hankering for *their* long lost Dylan, are holding their ears, while trying to make out the horribly distorted versions of 'All Along the Watchtower' or 'I'll Be Your Baby Tonight'. The sinister, ravaged old master in his long black coat and winklepicker shoes shuffles sideways on to his electronic piano, and never once picks up his guitar. But a small child, probably not more than two, is dancing in ecstasy all evening on his mother's knees.

And there is a kind of childish enthusiasm to this worldly, hustling, competitive, rich-and-poor polyglot city. On the morning in February that Christo's 'The Gates' are due to be revealed in Central Park, I wrap up very warm and go and stand on the mound at 106th Street and Central Park West. A small excited group of families with children, dogs, and cameras, are waiting to see the rolled-up 'saffron' drapes, made of pleated nylon sail-material, released to hang down and wave in the wind from their horizontal bars, about ten feet above the ground, supported by two verticals, and so repeated and repeated all over the park at two- or three-feet intervals. Each Christo volunteer has to get hold with a long pole of the hook at the end of the Velcro strip, and pull on it so that the drape unfurls and the cardboard roll inside it drops down, to be disposed of, no doubt ecologically. At first they have difficulties latching on to the hooks, and we all clap enthusiastically each time they succeed and bring another drape down. One unfortunate volunteer gets hit on the nose by the falling cardboard roll, and starts bleeding copiously. This is treated by the spectators more as part of the show than as an emergency. Christo and his Yoko Ono-ish partner Jeanne-Claude, whose hair matches the drapes, make many speeches to the media about the inconsequence of art and the need for pure, ephemeral pleasure – perhaps a good thing in a city so much given up to consumption and the cost of space, and certainly good for its winter tourism. For weeks, vast throngs of people wander up and down, smiling and taking shots and often wearing orange, at first beatific and after a while a little bored. (I overhear one tourist on Fifth Avenue looking at one of the city's orange construction signs and saying, 'Oh, look, they've made the signs the same colour!') There is a sharp division between those who find the event consoling, joyous, and a liberating escape from the horrible politics of 2005, and those who despise it as 'bread and circuses', mindless and pretentious. I wanted to like it, but don't, because I find the individual objects themselves so ugly and their repetition so dull. And they aren't 'saffron'; they are terribly orange. All the same, when the event is supposed to be over, but the Gates haven't been taken down yet, I see them at night from high up, from a window of an apartment on Central Park West, with no one there, ghostly shapes in the snowy park, and for a moment I like them.

The Gates had to be constructed in winter, when the trees were bare, so they could be seen. I am very conscious of the elements in this, the most built-up city imaginable, and I keep being told that this year they are extreme. In early December, the little grocery stores put out their Christmas trees all down the pavements, and a warm, dark smell of pine brushes past you on the city streets. But the winter gets shockingly cold, and I learn a new weather term, 'frigid'. I like seeing sledgers and skiers in the middle of the town after the big snowfalls, and I love walking in the white and black park, but when an arctic wind is slicing through Times Square, great lumps of grey snow are blocking every step, people are slipping and falling, vast skeins of white are blowing into my face, and my tongue starts to feel frozen as soon as I open my mouth to breathe, it all seems a bit much. Some days are so dark in the caverns of the mid-town streets that it's hard to remember what sunshine might be like. Everybody, including me, gets the flu, even the obsessives who rub their hands with stuff from little bottles of anti-germ lotion before every meal out, and never touch the handle of taxis or restroom doors. Then there is a short and magically beautiful spring, when the cherry and plum blossoms glow with radiance, right down the middle of Broadway; and in May, Central Park turns a deep, lovely green. When Jenny [Uglow] comes to visit, we brave the northbound subway and go up to the Cloisters.

We see the Unicorn captured inside his wooden fence in his magic tapestry garden, and then we sit outside in pale sunlight, in just as immaculate a garden, overlooking the Hudson. In the park, we nervously set out into the Ramble, expecting to be mugged at every corner: all we meet is a benevolent little group of birdwatchers.

But for all these small pleasures, the times are dark. The war, the deaths of many working-class young American soldiers and many more Iraqis, the torturing of prisoners at the Abu Ghraib jails, and the insistent playing on terrorist fears to justify American military presence and to get Bush re-elected, dominate the whole year. The only subject of the autumn is the election: for about two months the fellows talk about nothing else. Every detail of the debates between Bush and Kerry is gone over and over. Bush is mocked for his grotesque diction (pronouncing 'mullahs' as 'moolah', talking about 'my good friend Vlad'mir'); there are rumours that he had a little 'feed' hidden in the back of his jacket and that his batteries ran out halfway, and there is much analysis of his facial expressions, which are like a rat sucking a lemon, while Kerry makes everyone anxious by his wordiness and stiffness. But the level of the debates seems so low, the lying so palpable, the limits to what can be talked about (not Israel or the ecology, for instance) so drastic, the political coverage on TV so coarse and biased, the anti-Kerry ads, turning him into a dangerous, cowardly liberal (wolves coming out of the forest etc.) so vicious, that these minute, careful analyses seem almost beside the point. Everyone I talk to in this city is trying to believe that Kerry can win: the exit polls confirm it; and hopefulness continues right up to the point, at 11.30 pm, when Bush gets Florida. At once everyone gives up and goes wretchedly home. In the morning, New York feels half empty; on the steps of the library there are people crying. The explanations come rolling in: a Civil War repetition of the divide between the coastal and north-eastern voters, and those in the mid-West and the South; the failure of the youth vote (as one cynical friend has it, the 'youth vote' went: 'Oh, I though it was today! Oh, I missed it, Dude!'); the playing on the terrorist fears of 'Security Moms'; the 'evil genius' Karl Rove attaching referendums on gay marriage to the ballot papers; the power of the religious right and the 'moral issues' obliterating tax, welfare or health care issues. Chad, the young doorman in my building, who is a philosophy student at Columbia when he isn't opening doors or running errands, says to me, with tears in his eyes: 'I can't do much in my station in life, but this makes me want to commit myself to a life in politics.' But the main feeling of the people I know or read (mainly like-minded metropolitan academics and writers) is that they don't feel they belong to the country they live in.

Whenever the British government's allegiance to Bush's foreign policy is discussed, I am asked the same question: How could your leader, who is clearly intelligent, support our leader, who is so dangerously stupid? (I don't know the answer to this question.) I must admit I will be asked much more often about Charles and Camilla's marriage, an event which leaves me cold, but about which even the most hard-hearted New Yorkers wax rather sentimental. On the day of the British election, I don't hear anyone discussing it. In the evening, at dinner with about eight people, the BBC World Service is switched on, to indulge me. Admittedly it's British election night at its most absurd: Peter Snow jumping about in front of his graphs, Michael Howard giving his constituency acceptance speech next to a member of the Monster Raving Loony Party who keeps making loud burping noises, bumbling local electoral officials, and so on. But when everyone starts to roar with laughter and say it's like Monty Python, I begin to feel resentful. After all, I say feebly, this is a rather significant election! But it's no use – while we treat American politics as tragedy, in America, British politics play as comedy.

The year's most terrible and shocking event is the tsunami, but this is a silencing catastrophe, not as much talked about as matters which lend themselves to outrage, analysis, satire, or cynicism. There is the Terry Sciavo case, with all its gruesome parade of special interests and hysteria, but which interestingly marks the first downturn in Bush's popularity, with the moral majority propaganda trumped by the 'process' Conservatives who hate federal intervention in state law. There are the squalid bizarreries of the Michael Jackson trial ('now in its seventh year', comments Jon Stewart in his very funny spoof news programme, *The Daily Show*). There is Martha Stewart coming out of prison (Question: What is Martha Stewart's post-prison fashion statement? Answer:

A wool poncho.) There is the wall-to-wall, day-in-day-out papal mourning (during which I hear one hushed-voice CNN reporter saying, of the scene outside the Vatican, 'Quiet has fallen on St Patrick's Square.') The millions of mourners going to Rome are unfortunately described as 'a tidal wave'. There are the local, but bitter outrages about the President of Harvard saying that women are no good at science and students at Columbia accusing staff of pro-Israeli bias. And ever present, the anguished debate about the war, largely unacknowledged by the government, and summed up, two days before I leave on 27 June to go back to an England shortly to be rocked by terrorist attacks, by an editorial in the *New York Times* which makes three statements: 'The war has nothing to do with September 11th. The war has not made the world, or this nation, safer from terrorism. If the war is going according to plan, someone needs to rethink the plan.'

These world events seem to buffet violently around the tiny, protected space of quiet work I am in. And there are individual deaths this year which have a powerful impact. Three American writers die while I am living in New York: Susan Sontag, Arthur Miller and Saul Bellow. The reactions to their deaths are very different. Sontag's arouses a good deal of malicious commentary about her burial in a cemetery in Paris (white roses, Debussy flute music, weeping Kosovans) and the on-going feuds between those who loved her; not much attempt is made to revalue the work. In the popular media, her name still serves as a shorthand for beyond-the-pale liberalism. Pat Buchanan, talking about terrorism on NBC and saying 'The reason they came over here and attacked us is because of what we're doing over there' is derided by the host: 'You sound like Susan Sontag!', and everyone laughs. Her memorial concert, held at the very beautiful Zankel Hall, is full of writers, and has a heartfelt speech and performance by Mitsiko Uchida, dressed in flowing black and white, who plays Beethoven Opus 111 and Schoenberg. The Brentano quartet play Beethoven 132. It is all so solemn, cultured and reverential that I half want to see Chico and Harpo Marx coming through the auditorium selling popcorn and oranges. Miller's death in February is much more widely covered, though it has to compete with The Gates, and only three items are noted: *The Death of a Salesman*, his stand against McCarthy, and Marilyn Monroe. He is immediately sainted as 'the' American writer of the twentieth century. When Saul Bellow dies – by far the greatest writer of these three – there is deep anguish and mourning among his old friends, and some fine literary tributes are paid. But the general media pays much less attention than to Miller: the announcement of his death on Channel 13 on 4 April comes low down on the news. In about three seconds, his age (89), his Nobel Prize, and his death 'surrounded by family . . . of natural causes', are announced: and then he is gone, swallowed up by the world. I expect to see bookshop windows celebrating his life and work, but there is nothing. In Barnes & Noble on Union Square, going in a week after his death to find copies of his work (stepping over a large, absorbed group of Japanese youth all avidly reading their graphic novels), I can't find anything at all of his under 'B'. His death brings into sharp focus the sense I have that the world of 'high culture' is much more embattled and vanishing than it's felt to be in Britain, surrounded, literary Americans often say, by a vast waste land of mindless trash and junk. There is a feeling of great loss, of the end of an age: Philip says that he used to call those old men 'the generals'.

Towards the end of the fellowship we are all working longer and longer hours, putting off the day of packing till the last moment. Some have finished their books, some are going back to university duties, some are staying on in the city. We all know a little of each others' histories now, and we treat each other courteously, tenderly and humorously, wondering if we will ever see each other again. The quietest and most observant of all the fellows, a Spanish and Russian-speaking novelist, says to me wryly in my last week: 'Time is running.'

Joan Michelson

A Piece of Paving

from *The Story Behind the Poems*

My husband died on his way to work as his train was pulling into our local station. The thought that it was a ten-minute walk from home offered some solace by keeping the ending within reach. It was a place where we had stood together, a platform I too used regularly for my commute to work.

In his poem, 'Intersection' or 'The Pedestrian Crossing', left in various drafts in his computer, as if he could see ahead and already had the ground covered, he wrote that sooner or later we circle back to the same encounter with our former selves. At our local crossing, we are at our most numerous 'a family . . . a full-size tribe, perhaps even a whole nation'. The irony he offered is that we need go no further for our experience of the world. In a 'typical North London cluster of retail businesses – fruit shop and chemist, news-agent, gift shop, pizza bar – you can complete the list yourself', Crouch End Broadway is his 'Great Silk Road' and 'Golden Gate Bridge'. It is here he shall 'retire to', 'exit from' and 'reappear' to linger in a ghost self, a latter day Walt Whitman, his shirt collar open, his face with an unearthly light, tall and bearded, leaning 'against the BT switchbox . . . watching the crowds . . . and commuters come through in the morning and flow back on the evening tide'.

This image which he offers flies up to look down the length of the Broadway and along Tottenham Lane, the half mile or so to Hornsey rail station, opened in 1850 – on the suburban line from Moorgate and Kings Cross heading north to Hitchin. As if given the extra vision of a seer, with one self he can see through cars and buildings to another, himself, standing on the station platform. In his poem he invites past and future into a continuous present. He moves himself beyond his time as if he will continue to watch himself crossing the Broadway and turning left to continue on to the enduring rail station.

As he imagined numerous selves, so I, after he was gone, felt accompanied. Another way to say it is that I was besieged by the presence of his absence. Wherever I went, he went. The absolute of death – and dead he was, boxed, buried, gone into the earth – was mocked by dips of memory that kept repeating imagined returns. The struggle to rescue myself found an outlet in the shaping of poems. Detail, like an outer physical self, was a limb to hold on to. As if learning a lesson or mantra for salvation I recited the facts. He fell on to a piece of paving on Hornsey Station platform. He was on our commuter route. Like a felled tree, he crashed.

From these particulars, the poems 'Commuters' and 'Crash' emerged, first as one, then separated. Although my husband didn't die in a crash, either public or private, he crashed on to the stained, cracked concrete of the inbound platform. This happened before the attack on the twin towers in New York or the terrorist bombing of commuter trains in Madrid but after Clapham Junction when, on December 12, 1988, commuter trains carrying 1300 passengers collided just after 8 am. So this is how it happens, I told myself: in the middle of life, without warning, on the way to work, lives are ended. A commuter, he became one of many watching himself go. And I went on helplessly looking out for him.

As his ghost self continued to see, so I saw him in his footsteps. Wearing the backpack he had been wearing when he fell, I set off to catch my train to work and found myself following him; or walking beside him and falling back. And, as we experience over and over, in our waking visions and our dreams, the presence was almost palpable, then suddenly absent.

For months I carried scraps of the poems in my head unable to see a shape for them. Then one morning in February, about a year after the death, I had a long wait at Hornsey station because the trains were backed up. A crowd began to form. Still feeling unshelled, I shrunk into myself and, avoiding the thickening mass, looked down at the hard surface beneath my feet. The sun came out and cast an extra light showing dark spots which in my mind's eye turned to black blood. My heart missed a beat. What if I were standing where he had stood and fallen?

About this time, the train pulled into the station. Looking up, I saw bodies standing pressed together and faces pressed to the windows. The train stopped but briefly and the doors were kept shut, allowing no one to exit or enter. The trapped commuters were the living dead become the dead.

According to the dictates in my husband's poem 'Letter from Satan', as one of a team of poets, it was my work to record in accurate detail what I had seen. Then the bloodstains on the platform turned to ink leaked from an old-fashioned fountain pen, the kind of pen I imagined in the hands of Satan's scribes.

This waking dream of trapped commuters and encoding in the platform as in a cemetery stone, worked its way into the poem 'Crash'. Meanwhile, from television footage of overturned commuter trains with close-ups of lost phones and bags, came his flung backpack. This became the resolving image in 'Commuters'.

In the poems I sought to keep hold of death both as an event fixed in a particular time and place and as an unending presence. We merge to separate. I wear his backpack and yet he wears it. And it follows its own trajectory, coming to rest in the bed of Hornsey station rail tracks.

Commuters

Your day pack heavy on my shoulders
I leave the house with you and walk
quickly towards the train. Always
it is Friday, a bright winter
afternoon, the day you missed
the meeting and the phone took
its full load, leaving us
wondering where you'd gone.

From the start, you always walked
a little faster. I push my pace.
I don't want to miss the meeting
either. But when we reach the steps
I'm out. The hare is you,
taking them in leaps by twos
as if you're born again and Life
is calling. I'm the tortoise.

Step-by-step I crawl through litter
counting up the forty-seven
to cross the bridge and catch the train.
By now your waving is a shadow.
Our parting calls are echoes. *See you
later*. I see you later. Your pack
hits the siding and collapses,
flattening on the track.

Crash

In the dream everything made sense:
the crash at Ladbroke Grove, Clapham Junction,
Hatfield, Potters Bar, more ahead.
We all get up, get dressed, pick up our bags,
get out there on our way to work. We work

or die. This is work, recording details
in the after-echo where things stare.
Years away I see a spot like blood
turn inky-black and gleam as if fresh-leaked
into the early light from an old pen.

Dead on time the London train pulls in.
It stops. But there's no room for us. The dead
in stained commuter clothes stand tightly-packed
against the doors. The ink I use turns red.
It floods the platform and the railway bed.

Marina Warner

from the Prologue to *Phantasmagoria:*
Spirit Visions, Metaphors, and Media

July 18, 2005

Nobody in the street knew where the mummified saint was, and I had left my guidebook in the hotel room. Bologna is a city famed for free thinking in science and politics, so my request for directions to the body of Santa Caterina de' Vigri, preserved entire in a reliquary chapel since the fifteenth century, met with embarrassment and, sometimes, incredulous laughter. It was a very hot day, quite unseasonably hot for June, and only a holy fool – or an Englishwoman – would pursue such a quest down one side street after another. But I had seen a photograph of the effigy, and female saints and Catholic magic have always held a spell over me, so I persevered.

Eventually, past the barrier on a side street in the process of excavation, there stood the church of Corpus Domini. Inside, through a bare antechamber, and in the very depths of the convent buildings beyond, I found la Santa, in a reliquary chamber of her own, oval in shape, musty, shadowy, glinting with silver and gold ornament, crystal and velvet; there are no windows, and the walls are all richly encrusted with dusty ex-votos in the shape of flaming hearts and other body parts. The whole room is her reliquary. Caterina died in 1463 at the age of fifty, and is sitting up in the middle of the shrine quite straight in a glass box, looking younger than her age. She is wearing the white wimple, black veil and brown habit of her order, the Poor Clares, with the knotted cord of her vows. Her eyes are shut as if in concentration; her face has developed a brick-red complexion while the rest of the flesh that is visible has blackened till her thin fingers and bare toes look like a small monkey's, with touches of rouge on the toenails. She is wearing a narrow ring on her wedding finger (as a bride of Christ) and all around her, on the circular walls of the reliquary shrine where she keeps vigil, there are bones among the offerings, resting on faded silk cushions in crystal caskets.

She liked to pay the viol, and her instrument lies in one cabinet to her left, very small and looking very mute as well. On her right, in another cabinet, the manuscript of the book of meditations she wrote is on display. Called *Le sette armi spirituali* – the seven weapons of the spirit, it belongs to the late medieval movement for private prayer, which was radical for its time.[1] Her script is very fine, regular and shapely, and I took the language at first to be Byzantine Greek, though she in fact wrote in her own Italian dialect – again a rather modern gesture, presaging the Reformation. These personal things are full of her, more so than her effigy. Her musical instrument echoes one that has come unstrung, held by the statue of the angel that kneels by the body. Caterina also spent her time in the convent painting in a rather old-fashioned iconic style, and examples of her work are mixed in with the ex-votos.

She is sitting surrounded by these memorials to her earthly existence, preserved in her embalmed body, because she appeared to her sisters in the convent in a vision soon after her death, and told them she wanted to keep them company.

As happens with special saints, her body was miraculously still pliant (and fragrant) when her tomb was opened fifteen days after her death, but as soon as the Abbess ordered her 'to sit down under obedience' she 'sat down submissively'. Only then did rigor mortis set in. [2]

According to Catholic belief, a holy person, especially a virgin, will remain incorrupt in death while awaiting the reunification of body and soul on the Last Day. In Catholic cult, the belief – the hope – inspires effigies of the body of the deceased saint, displayed in their miraculous entire and imperishable state. Such corpses testify to their owners' spiritual wholeness – 'immaculate' meaning unmarked, literally and metaphorically – and any visitor to Italy or Spain will have seen such figures, lying under an altar in their 'urna' or casket. They are almost always recumbent, sleeping as they wait for the last day and the resurrection of the flesh. Sometimes the visible parts of the body are crinkled and blackened with age (Santa Chiara in Assisi) but mostly, they have been embalmed, using wax as the most visible element: Santa Fina, who died in San Gimignano in 1253 at the age of fifteen, is brought out twice a year in procession; also in Bologna, in the University Church of San Sigismondo, a wax effigy of Imelda Lambertini, who died at the age of twelve in 1338 and was beatified in 1862, lies in her glass coffin beside her bones. She is crowned with a chaplet of white flowers, her face's lifelikeness has been enhanced by real eyelashes, and on her feet she wears a modern schoolgirl's cotton socks. Santa Vittoria, a virgin martyr, is preserved in her glass coffin in full view in S Maria della Vittoria, Rome – in the same church as Bernini's *Ecstasy of St Teresa*. In her case, the wax sculpture sheathing her skeleton has cracked and the bones of her fingers poke through.[3]

Any travels in Catholic territory will lead to more discoveries of such effigies, many of them of more recent date, lying on cushions in glass cases under altars, sleeping the sleep of the just before the last trump. But Santa Caterina de' Vigri is sitting up, a wise virgin.

Her shrine was later all frilled and furbelowed by the team of baroque stuccoists, painters and carvers who worked on the church interior, and it survived the bombing raids of 1943 which smashed the rest of the decorations. La Santa's living likeness, this life-in-death effigy of her kippered corpse is much too grisly for most of us now, even those of us who have been brought up Catholic and who, like me, are curious about the religion's magic rites, its play with the flesh and the spirit. When I came into the side chapel, my eyes were fastened on Santa Caterina sitting there so still, and the presence of a woman kneeling at a prie-dieu behind me barely registered – or rather, I took her still form to be another statue so, when she moved, it was so unexpected in that charnel chamber that, all of a sudden coming to life, she made me jump out of my skin. I had entered the shrine and thought nobody else was there and I was awed and not a little scared of the mummy enthroned in front of me. But like the twitching eyelids of a corpse in a horror film, the woman getting up from the prie-dieu gave me a shock, for she introduced life into the frozen atmosphere. I had expected death to hold everything in that chamber in its grip.

Then, with a harsh scraping on its metal grooves, a small shutter slid across an invisible aperture, and the face of a nun appeared. She shushed, and wagged a finger at my camera. 'Vietato' (forbidden), she whispered. Later, I followed this sister into her vestibule, where she sold rosaries and souvenirs, votive masses and candles, and some literature about la Santa; she was young and round, and bundled up in an old-fashioned habit, the kind you no longer see nuns wearing. I had to pass my euros tightly rolled up to get them through the lattice of the grille behind which she officiated, which went from the counter up to the ceiling.

In Santa Caterina's presence, I felt I had entered the ambiguous, terrible and enthralling borderland between animation and lifelessness. The effigy of Santa Caterina gave me a vivid experience of the uncanny, the mixed-up feeling famously discussed by Freud in his essay of 1919.[4] A lifelike effigy like Santa Caterina's throws the question of spirit into sharp relief; it excites inquisitiveness, to plumb the mystery of its lack.

When I came out of the shrine into the main body of the church, I found a trace of the search for that principle. In an open side chapel across the nave, an inscription on a large marble monument read simply *Galvani*: it was the tomb of the great physiologist who was a Professor of Medicine at the University of Bologna, where he died.

Luigi Galvani (1737–98) probed the effects of electricity on dead matter, and in 1786 wrote up the famous experiments he made when he caused the corpse of a frog to twitch and kick.[5] His experiments recast divine relations to life itself, and Galvanist theories implied such foundations to animate being that I was surprised to find him buried inside a church, in a side chapel of his own with such a fine, proud monument. For after his work, a different metaphor was needed to convey God's activity, that divine effect on human clay that Michelangelo had conceived, for example, in the much overused image of the Creation of Adam. There, God the Father touches his creation with his finger as if running a current through him. Electricity and vitality were indeed mysteriously interwoven, and far beyond anything Galvani analysed: in cloning experiments today, a spark kick-starts the process of cell division and thus development of the embryo. In some senses, Dolly the sheep and first clone to live was 'galvanized' into life.[6]

Galvani's surmises about the nervous system and electrical charges were soon to be challenged and eventually overtaken by closer understanding of electricity,[7] and his experiments were enthusiastically taken up as a form of pseudo-scientific entertainment. Giovanni Aldini, Galvani's nephew and assistant, pressed the implications farther, and performed with corpses of animals much larger and more sympathetic than frogs, from species with whom audiences could identify. He even administered electric shocks to parts of human cadavers and to severed heads to make their facial expressions alter as if they were moving and responding. It was Aldini who inaugurated shock therapy for mental illness, a method still in use in some parts of the world today, though it remains incompletely understood. After him, Franz Mesmer deduced from his own theories about electricity and its relation to vitality, another form of spiritual cure which in the late eighteenth century gained an even more enthusiastic society following than Galvanism.

These apparent trespasses across the border of life/death contributed to Mary Shelley's nightmare vision of her scientist, Dr Frankenstein. After an evening discussing Galvanism in the Villa Diodati on that famous stormy night in the summer of 1816, Mary Shelley produced, from her own dream of reason, the most mythic monster of modern times. As she wrote in the preface, 'The event on which this fiction is founded has been supposed . . . as not of impossible occurrence.'[8] Her cursed protagonist Frankenstein acquires 'the capacity of bestowing animation'. From exhumed body parts gathered from charnel houses and burial grounds, he prepares 'a frame for the reception of it, with all its intricacies of fibres, muscles, and veins . . .' In his excitement he believes, 'Life and death appeared to me ideal bounds, which I should first break through, and pour a torrent of light into our dark world . . . if I could bestow animation upon lifeless matter, I might in process of time . . . renew life where death had apparently devoted the body to corruption.'[9] At last, Frankenstein, progenitor of a thousand mad scientists in fiction and cinema, 'infuse[s] a spark of being into the lifeless thing that lay at my feet', and the creature he has made opens one 'dull yellow eye'.[10]

As I say, it surprised me to emerge from the hushed and fervid atmosphere in Santa Caterina's shrine and find Galvani memorialized there as well. But somehow the two great citizens of the place balance each other in the business of understanding the relation of body to spirit, embodied identity and remembered individuality. Caterina de' Vigri, a hallowed figure of the Catholic faith, remains present in her body, incorrupt on account of her virtue, because divine privilege has prevented mortality claiming her. Such a marvel proves that sanctity thwarts nature and time and miraculously overturns their laws. Meanwhile, Galvani showed that a frog which had been killed could kick its legs and respond to stimuli as if it were still alive.

In her glass box, Santa Caterina looks like the embalmed effigy of Jeremy Bentham, who left his body to University College, London, to be displayed as an 'auto-icon'. Like her, he is also sitting, displayed in the main corridor of the college, in a wooden box with folding doors which are opened for viewing the figure. But Bentham's mummy preserves his identity for posterity precisely because according to his principles, the body is the seat of the person and there is nothing beyond it. He also desired, he said, to keep his friends company at dinner on the anniversary of his death and he is still – it is said – brought out to take his place at the table at the annual gathering of the Bentham Society. But he was a sceptic, and he was bidding posterity to accept his mortal remains as vacant matter, no different from any other inanimate thing.[11] While la Santa is sacred, a hallowed recipient of suppliants and adorers, the rationalist philosopher Bentham was claiming the freedom to be profane and let his corpse remain in the world. He has not quite succeeded: his preserved and clothed body does not settle into the invisibility of the other statues in the College corridors; he still spooks me, however often I see him sitting there, alert and kind of smiling.

Caterina's prolonged presence refuses time, as measured by mortality and physical decay: she is waiting for the day of judgement in the body she will reassume in a perfected and radiant form at the promised resurrection of the flesh. As for Luigi Galvani and his fantasy shadow, Dr Frankenstein, they threaten to quicken the dead. Jeremy Bentham also communicates his continuing presence through his preserved and seated body, looking for all the world the very thing, and in his case, he maintained that this is all there is. His fleshly envelope is him and yet not him. In some elusive way, Santa Caterina and Jeremy Bentham in death both manifest the people they were, across time.

By a profound paradox, the Christian, religious effigy and the sceptical philosopher's auto-icon are solid, present, corporeal and material, whereas the force that the scientist Galvani detected and applied is immaterial – or more precisely, it inheres in the material world but is mysterious, elusive, and ethereal. The proximity of these different figures of the dead, and the inversion of religious and scientific approaches they communicate, describe an arc in a story I wanted to tell.

1 Santa Caterina da Bologna, *Le sette armi spirituali* ed. Sr M Giovanna Lo Bianco (Bologna, 1998).

2 Votive picture with prayer given to MW at the shrine.

3 In Montefiascone, in central Italy, for example, the shrine of S Lucia Filippini (1672–1732) centres on her incorrupt body, displayed in the centre of the church in a glass casket: she has been embalmed, and her white face appears cast in pale wax. Its girlish smoothness contrasts the characterful portrait of her hanging in the nearby convent of the order of Maestre Pie, which she founded to teach girls in free schools.

4 Sigmund Freud, 'The Uncanny' in *The Uncanny*, translated by David McClintock, introduction by Hugh Haughton (London: Penguin, 2003), pp123–163.

5 Luigi Galvani, *De viribus electricitatis in motu musculari* (Bologna, 1791). It was part of the advanced, enlightened character of Bolognese learning that he was assisted by Lucia Galeazzi, his wife, as he described in his account of the experiment. Galvani wrote a eulogy to her when she died, and was buried in the side chapel beside her. Luigi Galvani, *Elogio della Moglie Lucia Galeazzi Galvani* (reprint, Bologna, 1937).

6 Galvanise has at least two meanings: applied to treating metals, it means coating iron or steel with zinc through an electrolytic process in order to protect it from corrosion; figuratively, it means something closer to Galvani's work, the revitalisation of a moribund or torpid organism: 'I was galvanised into action.'

7 He was interested in the nervous system and its invisible transmission of signals throughout the body, and proposed that the effect arose from the

electrical charge of the external muscle (positive) and the internal nerve (negative); he had in point of fact introduced an electrical current through the body, but this was thought at the time to be a kind of animal electricity, and was called 'galvanism'. Alessandro Volta (1745–1827) in Pavia, showed that galvanism has no connection to animals, and realized that in Galvani's experiments, the body merely acted as conductor.

8 Mary Shelley, *Frankenstein* [1817], Chapter 4, of Bantam Classic ed. (1981).

9 Shelley, *Frankenstein*, Preface.

10 Shelley, *Frankenstein*, Chapter 5.

11 Henry Wellcome, the voracious Victorian collector of all things pertaining to the history of medicine, acquired a section of Bentham's skin, which was included in the exhibition, 'Medicine Man', British Museum, 2003.

Michel Faber

Me and Dave and Mount Olympus

I lived through the 1980s, but was not touched by them. They might as well have been the 1880s, for all the notice I took of the defining characteristics of the decade. I didn't own a wide-shouldered jacket with rolled-up sleeves, a double-breasted suit, or indeed any item of clothing that cost more than a pot plant. I dressed myself from charity shops, right down to the socks and underpants. I didn't own a watch or a television, got around by bicycle, cut my own hair, and was not acquainted with any person who owned albums by Billy Joel, Bruce Springsteen, Sade or Spandau Ballet. (Maybe it was because the few friends I had were lesbians.) The prospect of buying that newfangled invention, a CD player, was as remote as investing in a Picasso. A high-flying career in the corporate sphere, or a steady job of any kind, held no attraction for me. Who needs money when so much of the food in supermarkets is exactly the right shape to fit down the front of one's trousers, hidden by a loose jumper? Who needs status when one is an Artist, already living on Mount Olympus?

At the dawn of the 1980s, my first wife and I were in fact living in Fitzroy, a shabby inner suburb of Melbourne, Australia. Both of us were writers, misfits, snobs. In the grand intellectual tradition of Wyndham Lewis, Sylvia Plath, TS Eliot *et al*, we detested the common horde – lowbrow Philistines, the lot of them! We lurked in our tiny student flat, reading *Four Quartets* and *In Memoriam*, admiring shoplifted art books, discussing each other's poems, and avoiding contact with the polluted sea of humanity around us.

Eventually, my wife found herself hankering for Winchester, her childhood home, and we decided to emigrate. England, after all, was the epicentre of high culture. It was where Tennyson and Virginia Woolf were from. Sylvia Plath would surely have been from there too, if she hadn't had the misfortune to be born

American. And Winchester, although I knew zero about it, had a grand ring to it. Yes, we must go.

Our lifestyle was so monastically frugal that we were able to save money *on the dole* – enough money for two airfares and for an advance payment of our cat's quarantine, and some more besides. We boxed up all our books, entrusted our cat to our lesbian friends, promised to send word as soon as we had a cosy new address to which books and cat could be forwarded. We flew to London, caught the train to Winchester, spent one demoralizing afternoon wandering around searching for my wife's lost childhood, then caught the train back to London. Everything in Britain cost five times more than we thought it should, and everyone we met was five times more unfriendly, unsympathetic and suspicious than we hoped they might be. We had collided with the eighties without knowing it.

In our Aussie *naïveté*, we fancied we'd pick up a few part-time jobs in the metropolis, get a cheap flat, and resume our shabby-genteel existence. Before emigrating, we had researched which art galleries contained our favourite paintings, but we hadn't looked into job opportunities. The economic and political landscape of 1980s Britain was *terra incognita*. Thatcher, to us, meant an olde-worlde artisan who mends cottage roofs with straw. It was a shock to be informed, by the hassled-looking people in the job centre, that the British state expected us to work full time at 'proper' jobs. Waitressing or sweeping stairs for a few hours on a Tuesday morning didn't count. My memory is hazy, but I think someone may even have mentioned the word mortgage.

Within six weeks, some of which were spent paying extortionate rent for an unfurnished room in a condemned slum in Queen's Park, my wife and I understood we weren't going to manage. So we arranged to return to Melbourne, back into the arms of easy work, warm weather and a lax social security system. We caught the train to Heathrow, having spent the last of our English currency. Unfortunately, I was confronted with some bad news at the airport: I wasn't allowed on the plane. My documentation wasn't in order. I'd been so confident of spending the rest of my life in the UK that I'd neglected to get a re-entry stamp for my passport. My wife was allowed to get on the plane – which I persuaded her to do – but I, with my unstamped Dutch passport, was no longer classified an Australian resident. I had to travel back into London, go to the Australian consulate, and answer tricky questions about Aussie Rules football and trams, in order to prove that I wasn't a spy; then I would be given permission to return.

And so it came to pass that I was stuck alone in London, with no home and less than a pound in my pocket. I had a cheque refunding the quarantine for our cat who'd never joined us, but I was determined not to cash this – it was all we'd have for a new start back in Melbourne. The next flight that would take me without demanding a fresh fare was exactly a week away. In the meantime, I would have to survive. A kindly receptionist at the Australian consulate got me off to a good start by giving me a cup of instant soup, and a biscuit 'for dessert'.

The full story of that week in London would take many pages to tell. I kept a diary – the only time in my life when I've done so. Days are long when you have nowhere to go and nothing to do; homelessness is amazingly boring, especially after sunset. My diary gave me something to do while London passed me by. Some of the incidents described in those crumpled looseleaf pages come straight from the script of a Hollywood B-movie, like the time I slept in a park and a warden's sniffer dog sensed me hidden under a bush, only to be yanked away by his owner with a gruff, 'Come on, there's nothing there!' Other incidents have the sad flavour of life on the streets. Checking phone booths for forgotten coins, being fumblingly molested by a lonely man offering me a place to stay, walking miles to places where there's rumoured to be work only to find a sign saying No casuals required, being caught washing my hair in the McDonald's toilets, foraging food from bins and bus shelters. Some of the things that happened were quite sweet, like the time I showed up at the office of the feminist publishers Virago to blag a poster of gay icon Radclyffe Hall to give to my lesbian friends back home. (Virago gave me the poster, and a catalogue as well, despite the fact that I was a sour-smelling young male with mud on my parka.)

But what I want to talk about here is an encounter that actually changed me. The sleeping-in-the-park/foraging-for-food stuff didn't change me. I was young; I was having an adventure. I was a denizen of Mount Olympus, slumming it down on earth, experiencing cold and hunger the way Zeus experienced being a swan. My mind was immune to the filth that accumulated on my outward form.

As the week wore on, I discovered Counterpoint Night Shelter for Homeless Youth in Soho. It was in Shaftesbury Avenue then; it's since moved. In 1982, twenty years before Shaftesbury Avenue became a place where I go to autograph my books, it was a place where a policeman told me I might find shelter from the cold. I spent two nights in Counterpoint, dossing down among the capital's other undesirables – glue-addicted lads, foul-mouthed elfin girls with scabby hands, cockney chancers, pimply schizo-phrenics, baby-lipped punks, doe-eyed teenagers whose memories of family life were already growing dim. Despite my homelessness being partly my own choice, the staff let me in, gave me a bunk bed, fed me toast and tea. Frontline charity, I discovered, is pro-vided not by governments but by volunteers, weary-looking ex-hippies and housewives who are used to being attacked by the people they're trying to help.

I first met Dave the Welsh skinhead in front of the high, wrought iron gates of the shelter. We were both waiting for 8 pm, when the volunteers would emerge and decide who was in and who was out. We were the only ones waiting; most applicants showed up much later at night, when other ways of making time pass had been exhausted. Dave offered me a fag; I said I didn't smoke. He seemed unable to believe this extraordinary fact, and kept forgetting it. Despite some facial scars and wrinkled hands, he looked to me about fourteen years old, with a mild, puzzled expression in his blue eyes. He was dressed in bovver boots, army fatigues, a hideous woolly jumper that seemed to have been knitted from old road kill.

A van passed by on the street; he pointed it out to me. 'Nice,' he said. 'Nice van.' We stood next to each other in silence, and I felt what I always felt when enduring the company of people very unlike me – stoical disdain. In a week from now, I would be back inside my ivory tower and this lamebrained lout would have van-ished from my world like a discarded bus ticket.

By nine, Counterpoint's happy family was all signed in. We sat in a dingy kitchen papered with advice and info for the homeless, alcoholic, pregnant, drug addicted. The windows were cracked, dirty stained-glass – this building must once have been part of a church. Kim Wilde and Shakin' Stevens blared from the radio, interspersed with news of war brewing in a place I'd never heard of, the Falklands.

After a while big plastic canisters of food were brought in, donated by a nearby shop. All thrown together, these remains of uneaten meals looked unappetising, but we ate every scrap. A tousle-haired boy complained over and over that the cops had taken away a full container of his glue, even though he wasn't sniffing it at the time. The others mocked him or aired their own grievances. Aloof, I prepared myself for sleep.

Dave and a tiny skinhead girl spent ages play-fighting over their respective pairs of bovver boots, concealing them, throwing them, pulling each other to the floor. The girl's face was so wrinkled it was as if she'd never used it for laughing before.

A volunteer came in and told everyone to settle down; it was almost 10.30. 'Also, finish your fags and don't light any more. Anyone smoking in bed will get thrown out.'

'What else can we get thrown out for?' enquired Dave as he pulled his woolly jumper over his pale, spotty torso.

'Sniffing glue, making a racket, causing damage, going into the girls' dorm . . .'

Dave snorted. 'Christ, can we breathe?'

The volunteer smirked back. 'I don't know why you keep coming back here, if you don't like the service.'

Just before bedtime, the tousle-haired boy announced that he was ready for a new way of life: he'd decided to become a skin-head. Delighted, Dave offered to shave his head for him, and asked if anyone had a pair of scissors. Nobody did, except me. I hesitated momentarily, in case I never got them back or ended up being stabbed with them. Then I handed them over.

Dave and the new recruit rushed to the toilet. Within seconds greasy hair was dropping, snippet by snippet, into the sink. I watched over their shoulders.

'Good scissors, these,' commented Dave, almost in awe, as if he'd never had the opportunity to handle high-quality tools before.

In no time the boy's scalp was ready for the soap-and-razorblade phase of his transformation. There was quite a lot of blood then, with the willing victim hissing, 'You're cuttin' me 'ead to fuck!'

When the job was finished, Dave handed me my scissors back. 'I cut 'is 'ead to fuck,' he conceded, with a big grin. 'First few minutes, you're real careful, then you just get bored.' In case I should misunderstand my role in the drama, he added, 'It wasn't your scissors, like. They're good scissors. Good scissors.' And he nodded meaningfully, sincerely, to emphasize how helpful I'd been.

In that moment, as we stared into each other's eyes, I realized a number of things simultaneously. First, I realized that he was stupider than I'd imagined, that he had the intellect of a small child, and that this puny intellect was all he would ever possess to see him through what remained of his life. Second, I understood that he was a human being, and that I was a human being, and that we were equal in the eyes of the universe. We were each man-shaped parcels of flesh and bone, standing face-to-face on planet Earth, making noises with our vocal cords, digesting the same food, sweating the same sweat, preparing to lie down next to one another.

I'd lived among the poor for years. I'd stood in dole queues with them, sat in dingy laundromats with them, done the same dead-end jobs, waited my turn next to them in charity shops to try on cast-off shoes. Yet they had always existed in a separate reality from me. In my colossal arrogance, I'd seen the world as an artists' playground, a hive of creative industry, in which all the billions of non-artists were mere parasites, to be tolerated or ignored. There was no possibility of real contact between me and them; it would be like trying to discuss Shakespeare with a dog. The stupid are content with their stupidity, I'd thought; only the intelligent are capable of existential angst.

Now I understood that human beings are *all* alienated from each other, that nobody feels truly understood or appreciated, that we are all misfits. Rich and poor, stupid and clever, black and white, gay and straight, we're thrown together like a miscellany of poodles, Labradors, huskies, chihuahuas and Dobermans dumped in the same kennel. We need shelter, food, the hope of finding a mate, reassurance that we won't kill each other.

OK, so this Welsh skinhead could never read *Four Quartets*, could barely read the *Beano*. As for me, I was unable to grasp the vital difference between one haircut and another. This gulf between us was unimportant. What was important was that we were both homeless, both humans in trouble, both dependent on the hospitality of do-gooders. We could trust each other just far enough to sleep in the same room for one night. That's the bare minimum our species requires a precious bare minimum that is lacking whenever there is war, rape, racial hatred. I'd always thought that the world's evils were caused by lack of intelligence, by people behaving like animals. Now I understood that what's lacking when people treat each other cruelly is not intelligence, it's animal recognition. It's the awareness of being the same species.

Dave had asked me for my scissors – a weapon with which he could easily have killed me – and I'd handed them over. In that exchange, we understood as much as we needed to. He and I had sniffed each other and we didn't bite. Humans need that. To sniff each other and not bite. Art and culture are extras. We are animals first.

A week later, I returned to Australia. Years passed. My wife and I moved to Sydney, our marriage disintegrated, I finished some novels and was none the happier for it. It became increasingly difficult to get part-time jobs mopping stairs and doing people's ironing. A well-off woman whose house I offered to clean told me she had a policy of never employing servants who were as intelligent as her; it led to problems, she said. I finally gave in and got a proper job: I trained as a nurse. I learned to take care of people's bodies, their animal needs. Nurses may have diplomas, but they're really animals, licking their fellow creatures' wounds, bringing them food, watching over them while they get better or die. The volunteers who staff homeless shelters understand this.

Nowadays, I make my living writing books, a benign pursuit that hurts no one and gives many people pleasure. I'm not going to claim I write for the semi-literate Welsh skinhead I called Dave in this memoir (but whose name, in truth, I can't recall). But in some hard-to-define way, perhaps everything I write is touched by what he taught me.

Biographical Notes

Nick Barlay is the author of three acclaimed novels, *Curvy Lovebox*, *Crumple Zone* and *Hooky Gear*, which map out the underbelly of contemporary London. He was mentioned in Granta's 'Best of Young British Novelists' in 2003. He has also written award-winning radio plays, short stories and wide-ranging journalism. He was born in London to Hungarian refugee parents. www.nickbarlay.com

Douglas Cowie was born in Elmhurst, Illinois and lives in North London. He is the author of a novel, *Owen Noone and the Marauder* (Canongate).

paulo da costa lives on the West Coast of Canada. His first book of fiction *The Scent of a Lie* received the 2003 Commonwealth First Book Prize – Canada-Caribbean Region and the W. O Mitchell City of Calgary Book Prize. His poetry and fiction have been published widely in literary magazines around the world and translated into Italian, Spanish, Serbian, Slovenian and Portuguese.

Maura Dooley has published several collections of poetry, most recently *Sound Barrier: Selected Poems* (Bloodaxe Books, 2002) and edited anthologies of verse and essays, amongst them *The Honey Gatherers: Love Poems* (Bloodaxe Books, 2003) and *How Novelists Work* (Seren Books, 2000). She teaches at Goldsmiths College, London.

Originally from Normal, Illinois, **Carrie Etter** moved to England in 2001 and teaches as an Associate Lecturer in Creative Writing at Bath Spa University. Her poems have appeared in *The Forward*

Book of Poetry 2005, The Liberal, The New Republic, Poetry Review, the *Times Literary Supplement* and other journals and anthologies in the UK and US.

Michel Faber was born in Holland, raised in Australia and now lives in the Scottish Highlands. His short story collections are *Some Rain Must Fall* and *The Fahrenheit Twins.* His novels include *Under The Skin* and *The Crimson Petal and the White.* He loves Krautrock and doesn't own a television.

Jane Feaver was born in Durham in 1964. After reading English at university, she worked at the Pitt Rivers Museum and then, for over a decade, in the poetry department of Faber and Faber. Five years ago she moved to Devon with her daughter and now runs the charity Farms for City Children.

Charles Fernyhough is the author of *The Auctioneer* (Fourth Estate). He works as a psychology lecturer and creative writing tutor, and has recently contributed to the books pages of the *Guardian, Scotland on Sunday* and the *Sydney Morning Herald.*

Esther Freud was born in London in 1963. She trained as an actress before writing her first novel *Hideous Kinky,* published in 1991. *Hideous Kinky* was shortlisted for the John Llewellyn Rhys Prize and was made into a film starring Kate Winslet. In 1993 she was chosen by Granta as one of the Best of Young British Novelists. She has since written four more novels, *Peerless Flats, Gaglow, The Wild* and most recently *The Sea House.*

Iain Galbraith's poems have appeared in anthologies and journals, including *Best Scottish Poems 2005* (Scottish Poetry Library), *PN Review,* and the *Times Literary Supplement.* A small selection will appear in *The Allotment: New Lyric Poets* (Stride, 2006). A translator of contemporary poetry and drama, he was recently awarded the John Dryden Prize for Literary Translation.

Vicky Grut's stories have appeared in literary magazines and anthologies, including *Valentine's Day: Stories of Revenge*

(Duckworth, 2000), *Reshape Whilst Damp* (Serpent's Tail, 2000), *Resist* (www.pulp.net, 2004) and *New Writing 13* (Picador, 2005). In 1999 she was a winner of an Asham and an Ian St James award for short fiction. The extract in this volume is from her novel, *The Understudy*.

Romesh Gunesekera was born in Sri Lanka. His new novel, *The Match*, is published by Bloomsbury (March 2006). His first novel, *Reef*, was published by Granta and was shortlisted for the Booker Prize. It was also awarded a Premio Mondello in Italy. His other books are: *Heaven's Edge* (New York Times Notable Book 2003), *The Sandglass* (BBC Asia Award) and a collection of stories, *Monkfish Moon*. He lives in London. www.romeshgunesekera.com

Kirsty Gunn is the author of four novels: *Rain*, *The Keepsake*, *Featherstone* and *The Boy and the Sea* (published by Faber and Faber, May 2006) as well as a collection of short stories, *This Place You Return to is Home*. In 2004 she was awarded the Scottish Arts Council Bursary for Literature. She is married with two daughters and lives in London and Edinburgh.

Abdulrazak Gurnah was born in 1948 in Zanzibar, Tanzania. He is the author of the highly acclaimed novels *Memory of Departure* (1987), *Pilgrims Way* (1988), *Dottie* (1990), *Paradise* (1994) which was shortlisted for the 1994 Booker Prize, *Admiring Silence* (1996), *By the Sea* (2001) and most recently *Desertion* (2005). Abdulrazak Gurnah teaches English literature at the University of Kent at Canterbury, England.

David Harsent has published nine collections of poetry. The most recent, *Legion*, won the Forward Prize for best collection, 2005. His work in music theatre has involved collaborations with a number of composers, but most often with Harrison Birtwistle, and has been performed at the Royal Opera House, the South Bank Centre, the Proms, Carnegie Hall and on Channel 4 TV. A new opera with Birtwistle – *Minotaur* – is scheduled to open at the Royal Opera House in 2008. Work in progress includes *The Wormhole* and a new collection of poems. He is a Fellow of the

Royal Society of Literature and Distinguished Writing Fellow at Sheffield Hallam University.

Desmond Hogan is the author of two books of stories and five novels. He won the John Llewelyn Rhys Prize in 1980 and the DAAD Fellowship Berlin in 1991. His book of short stories, *Larks' Eggs: New and Selected Stories* (Lilliput Press, 2005) has just appeared.

Chenjerai Hove was born near the mining town of Zvishavane, south of Zimbabwe, in 1956. He trained and worked as a high school teacher while studying privately with the University of South Africa. Later he studied literature and linguistics at the University of Zimbabwe. Hove's publications include five poetry collections, four novels, and two journalistic books of essays. His novel, *Bones*, won the 1988 Zimbabwe Literary Award and the 1989 Noma Award for Publishing in Africa. He is currently the Resident Writer for the city of Stavanger, Norway.

Ogaga Ifowodo, lawyer and activist, has published three volumes of poetry: *Homeland & Other Poems*, *Madiba* and *The Oil Lamp*. He is a fellow of the Iowa Writing Programme and recipient of the PEN USA Barbara Goldsmith Freedom-to-Write Award. He holds an MFA from Cornell University where he is currently pursuing a PhD.

Stephen Knight was born in Swansea in 1960. He has published a novel, *Mr Schnitzel*, and four collections of poetry: *Flowering Limbs*, *The Sandfields Baudelaire*, *Dream City Cinema*, and, for younger readers, *Sardines and Other Poems*. He reviews poetry and fiction for the *Independent on Sunday* and the *TLS*.

James Lasdun was born in London and now lives in Woodstock, New York. He has published several books of poetry and fiction, including *Besieged* (selected stories), of which the title story was made into a film by Bernardo Bertolucci. His latest book is *Seven Lies*, a novel.

Hermione Lee, who grew up in London, is a teacher, biographer, critic and broadcaster. She has written books on Elizabeth Bowen, Willa Cather, Philip Roth, and Virginia Woolf, a major biography of Woolf, and a collection of essays on life-writing called *Body Parts*. She is currently completing a new life of Edith Wharton. She is the Goldsmiths' Professor of English Literature at New College, Oxford, a Fellow of the British Academy and of the Royal Society of Literature, and in 2003 was made a CBE for services to literature.

Frances Leviston was born in Edinburgh in 1982. She read English at St Hilda's College, Oxford, and has a Writing MA from Sheffield Hallam University. Her first collection of poems will be published by Picador.

Carola Luther grew up in South Africa and moved to England in 1981. Her first book *Walking the Animals* (Carcanet) was short-listed for the Forward Prize for best first collection in 2004.

Benjamin Markovits was born in California and grew up in Texas, London, and Berlin. He has worked, variously, as a teacher, an editor, and a basketball player. His reviews and essays have been published in the *Observer*, the *New York Times* and the *London Review of Books*. He has written two novels, *The Syme Papers* (2004) and *Either Side of Winter* (2005). Setting Forth is an extract from his forthcoming novel, *Imposture*, to be published by Faber in spring 2007. He lives with his wife in London.

Jamie McKendrick's last book of poems was *Ink Stone* (Faber, 2003). He edited the *Faber Book of 20th-Century Italian Poems* (2004) and is currently working on a translation of Giorgio Bassani's *The Garden of the Finzi-Contini*.

Joan Michelson teaches Creative Writing at Birkbeck College, University of London. Her poems, essays and fiction have been published in magazines and book anthologies including previous volumes of *New Writing*. Her poetry chapbook, *Letting in the Light*, was Editor's Choice publication, Poeticmatrix Press, USA in 2002. She won first prize in Londonarts International poetry competition, 2005.

David Morley originally studied and worked within science. He develops and teaches new practices in scientific as well as creative writing at the University of Warwick, where he is Director of the Warwick Writing Programme. His next collection of poems *The Invisible Kings* is the second section of a cycle that began with *Scientific Papers*, both from Carcanet. He reviews poetry for the *Guardian*.

Paul Muldoon was born in 1951 in County Armagh, Northern Ireland, and educated in Armagh and at the Queen's University of Belfast. From 1973 to 1986 he worked in Belfast as a radio and television producer for the BBC. Since 1987 he has lived in the United States, where he is now Howard G.B. Clark '21 Professor in the Humanities at Princeton University. Between 1999 and 2004 he was Professor of Poetry at the University of Oxford. Paul Muldoon's main collections of poetry are *New Weather* (1973), *Mules* (1977), *Why Brownlee Left* (1980), *Quoof* (1983), *Meeting The British* (1987), *Madoc: A Mystery* (1990), *The Annals of Chile* (1994), *Hay* (1998), *Poems 1968–1998* (2001), and *Moy Sand and Gravel* (2002). A Fellow of the Royal Society of Literature and the American Academy of Arts and Sciences, Paul Muldoon has won the 1994 T.S. Eliot Prize, a 1996 American Academy of Arts and Letters Award in Literature, the 1997 *Irish Times* Poetry Prize, the 2003 Pulitzer Prize for Poetry and the 2004 Shakespeare Prize. He has been described by the *Times Literary Supplement* as 'the most significant English-language poet born since the Second World War'.

Blessing Musariri qualified as a barrister as a member of the Middle Temple UK in 1997. She also holds a Masters in Diplomatic Studies, neither of which qualifications indicates that she would ever choose to be a full-time writer and sometime English teacher. She writes poetry, short film screenplays and adult fiction but often feels more inspired to write for children and has had two titles published.

David Nwokedi was born in Nigeria in 1965 to a Nigerian father and a British mother. He grew up in Newhaven and Brighton. He is a qualified social worker and has worked in Brighton and

London. His first novel, *Fitzgerald's Wood*, was published in 2005 and he is currently working on his second novel.

Maik Nwosu is an assistant professor of English at Kennesaw State University, Georgia, USA. A fellow of the Akademie Schloss Solitude in Stuttgart, Germany, he has written two published novels, *Invisible Chapters* and *Alpha Song*; a collection of short stories, *Return to Algadez*; and a poetry collection, *Suns of Kush*. Nwosu has received literary, journalism, and academic awards – including three literary prizes from the Association of Nigerian Authors.

Sean O'Brien is a British poet, critic, playwright and editor. Five award-winning collections were followed by *Cousin Coat: Selected Poems 1976–2001* (Picador, 2002). His essays, *The Deregulated Muse* (Bloodaxe), and an anthology *The Firebox: Poetry in Britain and Ireland after 1945* (Picador) appeared in 1998. He is Professor of Poetry at Sheffield Hallam University. His version of Dante's *Inferno* is published by Picador (2006).

Shereen Pandit has been writing fiction since 1996, before which she was a lawyer and law lecturer, as well as a trade unionist and political activist in South Africa and the UK. Her short stories have been published in numerous magazines, journals and anthologies. Several of them have won competitions in the UK and Ireland, most recently the Booktrust London competition. She also teaches writing in schools and colleges and to refugee and immigrant community groups.

Don Paterson works as an editor and musician, and teaches at the University of St Andrews. He lives in Kirriemuir, Angus. His most recent collection of poetry is *Landing Light* (Faber), which won the T. S. Eliot and Whitbread poetry prizes. *The Book of Shadows* (Picador), a collection of aphorisms, was published in 2004.

Paul Perry is the author of two critically acclaimed collections of poetry, *The Drowning of the Saints* (2003) and *Wintering* (Dedalus Press, 2006). He was a James Michener Fellow of Creative Writing at the University of Miami, and a C Glenn Cambor Fellow of

Poetry at the University of Houston and his work has appeared in numerous publications, including *Poetry Ireland Review, Cyphers, TLS* and *The Best American Poetry 2000*. Currently, he is Writer in Residence for the University of Ulster.

After working overseas for a few years, **M. Pinchuk** has spent the past nine years in London. In an ideal world, she would have lots more time to write and would divide her time between northern California, Turkey, Finland and the United Kingdom. 'Memories Like Photographs' is her first published story.

Roy Robins read English Literature at the University of Cape Town, receiving a masters degree in 2004, and is a part-time lecturer in its English and history department. One of twelve African writers selected to participate in the 2003 Caine Prize African Writers' Workshop, his short stories and poetry have appeared in anthologies and he is currently completing a novel. He has reviewed books for the *New Statesman* and the *Observer*.

Jane Rogers has written seven novels, including *Mr Wroe's Virgins, Island* and *The Voyage Home* (Abacus, 2005). She also writes for radio and TV, and has edited OUP's *Good Fiction Guide*. She lives near Manchester and is Professor of Writing at Sheffield Hallam University. www.janerogers.org

C. D. Rose gets seasick.

Natasha Soobramanien was born in London in 1971. She was brought up in London, Hastings and Hong Kong. She co-organizes the live fiction night, Plum (www.plumlive.co.uk). 'Another London' is the first chapter from her novel of the same name.

Greta Stoddart was born in 1966. She works as a poetry tutor at Goldsmiths College, London and for the Poetry School. She is also Writer-in-Residence at Exeter University. Her debut volume *At Home in the Dark* (Anvil, 2001) won the Geoffrey Faber Memorial Prize 2002.

Anuradha Vijayakrishnan was born in Cochin, India in 1974 and has a Bachelor's degree in Chemical Engineering and an MBA from XLRI, Jamshedpur, India. She now lives in Chennai and works with Citibank. She has had poetry and fiction published in magazines and anthologies. She has received training in Carnatic music. Writing is a passion she pursues after midnight mostly and sometimes by daylight if the urge is unstoppable.

Eoghan Walls, born and raised in Derry, was educated in University College, Dublin, and is undertaking a PhD in the Seamus Heaney Centre for Poetry in Belfast. He has spent the last years teaching in Rwanda, Germany and Northern Ireland, and was shortlisted for a 2004 Eric Gregory Award.

Marina Warner's award-winning studies of mythology and fairy tales include *Alone of All Her Sex: The Myth and the Cult of the Virgin Mary* (1976), *Monuments & Maidens: The Allegory of the Female Form* (1985), *From the Beast to the Blonde* (1994), and *No Go the Bogeyman: Scaring, Lulling and Making Mock* (1998). Her novel *The Lost Father* (1988) was shortlisted for the Booker Prize; she has since published *Indigo* (1992), *The Leto Bundle* (2000) and two collections of short stories including *Murderers I Have Known* (2002). Her Reith Lectures, 'Managing Monsters: Six Myths of Our Time', appeared in 1994, and 'Fantastic Metamorphoses; Other Worlds' (Clarendon Lectures) in 2002. *Phantasmagoria*, her study of spirits, will be published in the autumn of 2006 by Oxford University Press.

Chris Womersley was born in Melbourne, Australia where he currently lives and works as a journalist for *The Age* newspaper. He has had short stories and poetry published in numerous journals and is finishing his first novel, titled *Among the Dead*.

Copyright Information